IN A
FIELD
of
BLUE

IN A FIELD of BLUE

a novel

GEMMA LIVIERO

LAKE UNION
PUBLISHING

Published by Lake Union Publishing, Seattle

www.apub.com

Amazon, the Amazon logo, and Lake Union are trademarks of Amazon.com, Inc., or its affiliates.

ISBN-13: 9781542009447
ISBN-10: 1542009448

Cover design by Faceout Studio, Derek Thornton

Printed in the United States of America

I would have poured my spirit without stint
But not through wounds; not on the cess of war.
Foreheads of men have bled where no wounds were.
I am the enemy you killed, my friend.

Wilfred Owen (1893–1918)

RUDY

1922

CHAPTER 1

You must come home immediately were the words typed on a shade of disaster, since the Royal Mail's oatmeal notepaper was too often a prelude to bad news in previous years: a death, an accident, an unpaid debt, or an incident that might shame the family. The words on the telegram I imagined my mother speaking seemed to suggest this was highly personal and must only be discussed within the family home.

On the train, I scanned the passengers devouring the articles in their morning copies of the *Manchester News*—where I was in fact employed—about unpaid wages and cuts to public housing and spending. And in between these were continuing stories of war, of rebuilding efforts in France and Belgium, of commemorations, and stories of bravery still emerging.

My heart had grown weary of seeing headlines about another soldier found buried in the erstwhile mud seas of northern France. For four years I had steeled myself to read the articles written by my cohorts about the discovery of a man, hoping and yet not hoping that it was my brother Edgar. We prayed for even the smallest piece of evidence to suggest a fate that would immortalize him at a particular point in the battlefield. But mostly we sought news of an improbable kind: that he was still alive somewhere in Europe, incapacitated or incarcerated, without a way of contacting us. It is a terrible thing when the mind plays games with the missing.

Bert, our property overseer, met me at the station in the open, leather-seated Talbot purchased with borrowings by my father shortly before he died, and the debt carried grudgingly long after that.

Bert was one of two staff left in our household, which, during my early childhood years, had serviced three children, two parents, an aunt, a tutor, a grandmother and her personal maid, and half a dozen house and maintenance staff. The household's permanent residents as it stood at this time consisted of Abigail (my mother), Bert, Peggy (our housekeeper), and me also, if you included my regular weekend visits. My brother Laurence would only make the odd show, whenever he was short of money in London and needed some other place to entertain friends on Mother's credit.

"How is she?"

"She is as fit as some, Master Rudy," said Bert in his strong northern lilt that embedded me instantly, and with comfortable familiarity, into the place I called home for twenty-two years. "And still better than many." Bert had always been an optimist.

"Then what is it? The message sounded urgent."

"We've come upon a strange situation that your mother cannot deal with."

"Is it my brother?"

"We've heard naught from him in weeks."

That was good news at least.

"I'll try as best I can, though there's scant detail," he said as I climbed into the passenger seat.

He did try, but I was left with more questions than answers. Apparently, a woman accompanied by a small child had arrived speaking French, and she sought only to converse with me. Though my mother spoke some French and attempted conversation, the woman was reluctant as yet to tell of her purpose.

We joggled along the well-worn, narrow Lancastrian tracks, through thick woodlands and pastures my brothers and I had explored as children, until finally descending a short rise toward Lakeland Manor, nestled between fir trees and leafy gardens at the southern end of Windermere lake. With most of its shutters closed that day, the normally imposing structure appeared sullen, perhaps growing weary of the current occupants, who did not offer any of the extravagant festivities it had been used to in its former days of excess. After a sharp turn off the lane, a pillared gateway opened onto a gravel drive bordered by formal gardens, stone vases, and fading blooms that bowed us through to the front terrace and the building's entrance enwreathed with red and green ivy.

Bert was edging toward seventy then, and the maintenance of the house and gardens was becoming a larger task for him with each passing season. In recent years he had also been spending much of his time helping several of our tenanted farmers cultivate their land. Our family had come to rely heavily on the income from the rents. Despite that he was not paid as well as some on more affluent northern estates, he was extremely loyal, and this made it difficult to question him on the odd patch of weeds and several cracked pavers I spied along the garden paths. I knew that he would be aware of the disrepair.

Lakeland Manor was symmetrically Georgian in style, though some classical influences such as the Corinthian columns at the entrance and the large arched Palladian windows down the center were applied during the construction at the whims of my great-grandmother.

Our gray stone home was three stories high in the main building, flanked by additional two-story wings, as well as an extra structure that was once used as servants' quarters on the far side. From the large foyer, stairways on either side led to the upper levels, and much of the rear ground floor was dedicated to a grand hall for entertaining, surrounded by a viewing platform above on the first story, where most of the bedrooms and some guest suites were also situated. Part of the top floor had served as Edgar's rooms in his final years at home. The wing on the right housed my parents' very spacious and private suites, or "the villa" as my mother liked to refer to it. Along with the addition of some modern conveniences, the manor was just as impressive in its historical finishes as it was in structural design, with Italian marble fireplaces, turned mahogany balusters, ornate gilded wall lights, and polished oak floors throughout.

Peggy rushed to meet me in the foyer. She had entered our employ in her early twenties and had been our family housekeeper for over thirty years, and more recently my mother's personal carer also. Peggy's role was much more than that of housekeeper; rather she had been the glue that held us together and a stabilizing influence in our lives, who helped care for us through infancy, who groomed my brothers and me to a standard that Mother would approve of, and who saw our faults and loved us regardless.

When the greetings were quickly over, Peggy revealed that she was just as perplexed as Bert about our guest. Though she wore a more knowing look, and perhaps bore an instinct for the major chain of events to come.

"The guest is in the drawing room. She's been there waiting several hours. Your mother is back there now also. And she's in a mood."

"The woman has not given any clue as to her arrival?"

"Only that it is of much importance she speak to you as soon as possible."

"Is she inquiring about purchasing the property, do you think?"

Peggy cleared her throat. "I do not feel that she is of that persuasion in her current circumstance."

I breathed out heavily. Though the work and travel should have tired me, the expectancy and urgency had kept my mind sharp and anxious.

"I will bring you some tea," said Peggy, taking my hat and coat.

The drawing room doors to the right of the foyer were large and heavy and checkered with glass. I could see before opening them that Mother was in a window chair looking toward the gardens and a low autumn sun. Sitting on the floor several feet away from her was a small child, who held a soft toy bear. As I entered, Mother viewed me uneasily, and I followed her shifting gaze toward the other side of the room.

With her back to us, the visitor stood examining a painting above the mantelpiece. She wore a fitted white dress over a narrow waist, and her dark-auburn hair was pinned high to display her long neck. A travel bag, which had seen better years, sat near her feet. I went straight to Mother, whose expression spoke her feelings. She sighed, relieved to see me, her shoulders slackening with exaggerated drama. I kissed her cheek, and in her usual way, she accepted it with a nod.

"I wondered if you would get here," she said seemingly politely, though I recognized the not-so-subtle complaint that she had waited too long.

I glanced at the woman who was yet to turn.

"I took the first train," I told her in a failed attempt to lessen her disapproval.

I nodded a greeting toward the male child, who upon consideration I thought to be somewhere around the age of four and whose face gave nothing away, blank and waiting for someone to draw some kind of feeling on it.

"Rudy," said my mother, "this is Mariette."

The woman turned, standing partly in shadow, but even from a distance, I was able to take account of her remarkable features. She wore no powders, her complexion golden-brown and clear, but with a hint of sleeplessness below her large ebony eyes. She had a face not unlike those I'd admired in galleries of ancient Egyptian art, with dark, arched brows and a long, fine nose that stretched almost to her Cupid's bow lips above a small, pointed chin. She was so striking and rare I found it hard to look away.

She stepped toward me into a broader patch of late-afternoon light from the window, perhaps even aware of the effect that illumination would have on her, displaying the glorious, rich colors of her skin, hair, and youth.

"Bonjour!" she said.

"Bonjour!" I said. "It is nice to meet you."

"She speaks no English," my mother said, side-viewing me to reveal her skepticism as to the reasons for the stranger's arrival.

"To what do we owe the pleasure?" I translated in my school-taught French, grateful to have retained the skill. "Madame . . ."

"My name is Mariette," she replied in French. "There is no need to address me by any other."

"Fine," I said, and wondered briefly if she was perhaps mad or lost. She straightened the skirt of her white muslin dress, which hung to the floor. She was clearly not a slave to the shorter fashions of the day.

"Have you moved close by?"

"No. I have come to meet you." She glanced cautiously at my mother. Perhaps she was hoping Mother's prying eyes would not be there to watch. My mother's somewhat disdainful look put most people ill at ease much of the time. "I have traveled far."

The bottom of the stranger's skirt was muddied, the leather of her shoes worn in places. I was intrigued and asked her to sit down. She did not do so but moved at least toward the chair I had indicated. Closer then I saw there were more cracks in the façade: fingernails bitten low, tiny lines beneath the eyes.

She looked across at my mother, who seemed a little annoyed, though I guessed she was also in some pain. Mother suffered badly from migraines in recent times, along with melancholia and other ailments that had stopped her enjoying her middle years.

The child had become restless and put his face against his mother's skirts.

"Would you like to sit down?" I asked again.

She looked at the chair that I pointed to but remained where she stood.

I waited while she seemed to brace herself to face me once more.

"I have brought you your brother's son," she said, surprising me in English.

"Laurence's?"

"No."

There was a period of silence while I sought to make sense of what she was telling me.

"Edgar's?" I said.

She nodded.

My eldest brother, Edgar, was presumed dead, missing since the final year of the war, four years earlier.

I did not have the will to look at Mother.

There was more, of course, to come that I would learn in the days to follow. But in order to progress this story, it is necessary to go back briefly.

CHAPTER 2

1900

Peggy brought in the finely woven cream angora-wool blanket, stored with dried rose petals in a blue-dyed linen bag while awaiting my arrival, along with several woolen and linen dresses stitched with pastel-colored animal motifs, to be worn for the third time.

"It's a boy," said the midwife after another long and arduous labor, and my mother did not turn her head to verify and marvel as I was placed in a basket, apparently "yowling like a cat in heat." This was described to me by my second-oldest brother, Laurence, who had likely exaggerated such description from elsewhere and took great delight in reminding me that I was the last male in the pack and therefore without any rights at all. A third child, my brother also relished telling me, had been a nuisance to everyone, especially Mother. Though experience with my mother has told me that there was some truth to his words, I believe that any indifference at the time wasn't because my mother didn't love me on sight, but it was that she was simply tired of difficult births.

For our earliest years of education, Mother hired a tutor from London to ensure we spoke as close to the same King's English as she did. At the age of ten, we were sent to complete our education at the boarding school my father had attended at Bedford. At school, my academic skills were ordinary. I was ordinary. But of course, teachers didn't tell me that. Not at first. They only told me I was ordinary when my father was late to pay the bills. Then they could tell me I was ordinary as much as they wanted. But by that stage I had already numbed myself into my own sense of mediocrity, where I could dwell undisturbed.

There was one thing that made me stand out, and not by an act of bravery or by an award for excellence. But by one small defect that would partly explain my preference for solitude. And it was Laurence who highlighted it to me.

I did not become aware of my stuttering until I was six. When I saw a fox one day, I proceeded to alert my brothers, who were outside with me. The word would not eventuate, though I thought it was normal that others often filled in the remaining syllables for me. Laurence began mimicking me, running around calling out words that I had previously had trouble with. "Kitchen," "pillar," "octopus," "rabbit" . . . and on they went, and on I went trying to say them, unaware of his intent, the first letters becoming one long, insidious snake until Laurence could not contain himself anymore and rolled around laughing on the lawn. Time and exercises healed the worst of it by the time I reached thirteen, and occurrences were now rare, but in stressful situations the "snake," as I simply named this beast that lived within me, would still slither around my tongue to take its strangling hold when I least wanted it to.

My brother Edgar, the oldest, was my favorite brother and, I had always suspected, my mother's favorite son. I had looked up to Edgar, who was five years my senior. He had taken me under his wing from an early age, and I felt much loss when he left for boarding school. And though I preferred a solitary life, for the times that I wished to discuss a species of birdlife, a sense of the weather for sailing, and many other things we had in common, I dearly missed him.

Edgar was someone who knew what to say, how to say it, someone who excelled at most things. When we were small, it was always Edgar who fixed the problem, and always Edgar I went to if there was something I needed explained: medical curiosities, astrological wonders, or sums. He almost always had the answers, and if not, he would find the book that did. I didn't begrudge that he was special, that he was everyone's favorite. Rather, I felt every achievement he did, as if we shared the same heart at times. During each of his long absences, I missed hearing the soft tones of his voice and the light laughter it brought from Mother. Our world seemed less complicated when he breezed through the door during school leave.

It was Edgar who, during my second-to-last year at school, came to tell me that our father had died and to collect me for the funeral. It was a shock of course that our father was gone from a heart attack so quickly, but it was perhaps then we realized how little we knew about him; how absent he'd been from our lives, spending most of his time at his wine import business in London; how little he'd known about finances; and how the situation had been cleverly covered up by extemporary loans over several years. Stuart, our father, had overcapitalized, over-purchased, and over-assumed his own business sense. We discovered that he had put all his money into French grape production to create his own wine to sell, which had set about the decline, never once considering that such an enterprise would not thrive. Mother, suspicious about some of the dealings but unaware of the whole situation, had passed on Father's accounting books to Edgar, who was forced to sort out the mess: selling Father's London apartment and some lands to pay off debts and reducing other expenses. If it weren't for Mother's personal funds and assets, our circumstances would have been much worse.

I returned to finish my school years, and Laurence to his law studies. But Edgar abandoned his university education, deciding he needed an immediate income, and war had been convenient. I was sixteen when Edgar left for officers' training, and not quite eighteen when we received the telegram advising that he had gone missing in action somewhere south of Armentières in France, during a ferocious German offensive that took near one hundred thousand of our British men in less than a month. "A frightful mess," said the reporter in the newspaper. Peggy wept, Bert buried his sadness in his tasks, Mother became ill, Laurence thought it morbid to remain in mourning, and I numbed myself with memories and disbelief. I took the news badly, to say the least, my sorrow relentless for those first weeks: dreaming nightly of our times as children and Edgar's return and waking each day to the same empty rooms that reminded me he was gone.

As our estate finances were dwindling, it was necessary I join the workforce. I moved to a cheaply rented unit in Manchester. Mother's connections saw me employed at the newspaper to sell advertising door to door, before I advanced to the position of writing copy for department stores and shop owners and my aptitude for illustrating was discovered. The work, which was writing such phrases as "delight the senses" for ladies and "for the professional man" alongside such drawings as suits, soap products, and smiling women, was something I had accepted as my future. And while sketching the wildlife and scenery around the Lakelands had been a favorite childhood pastime, I did not hanker for an illustrative advertising career. I simply yearned to be home to run the house and manage the tenanted farms as my grandfather had done, to plough the earth myself, to build a stable full of horses that would perhaps be shown or sold.

However, I had already accepted that under the terms of inheritance, which saw Laurence next in line to inherit Lakeland Manor, as well as the state of our labor shortages and unprofitable farming lands, I might not have that option.

After Edgar's disappearance, I tried to comfort Mother, but she preferred the confines of her rooms and the company of tea and medication, attempting to return as she had been, which she never did. Her headaches worsened, and her nerves weakened as time wore on, which often left her unwilling to leave her villa.

The family was badly broken. But it would take retrospect to realize that it was barely together in the first instance.

CHAPTER 3

1922

It was unlike Mother not to attempt an immediate inquisition, but the mention of Edgar by the Frenchwoman had severely affected her. She had grown smaller and paler before my eyes. When she clutched at her chest, I rushed to her side. Mariette had picked up her child and made for the foyer. I glanced in her direction as she left, her head held high and lips pressed together, seemingly without regret at her own words, but she was acute to have seen the effects of them at least.

I rang the service bell for Peggy. Mother stood up unsteadily, and as I made to help her, she shook her head in the direction of Mariette, who had by that time exited the front door. Mother leaned so heavily on me I half carried her back to her room. She turned to me as we walked and gripped my arm hard. "She's lying."

As wary as I was also, I would need to hear out the rest of the woman's story. I could understand why Mother had made her assumption. It did not make sense that someone would wait four years before coming forth with such a claim as this. Without knowing any facts, I speculated that it might simply come down to money and that perhaps Mariette had been unaware of our declining financial situation. Admittedly, our house made us seem more affluent than we were. Our name alone, my mother's name at least, had been known and respected

in Manchester and London for years; she had avoided any scandal surrounding my father's disastrous business dealings, and no doubt was
keen to avoid any other.

So why would the Frenchwoman lie? To bring a child so far from
home did not seem frivolous. Edgar's regiment had confirmed that he
had gone missing in battle. There seemed little hope. He had been
somewhat prominent in London society prior to signing himself up for
war, and many knew and respected him. He had been well connected,
and sometimes his appearance in the paper at a social event seemed
to suggest he was of considerable wealth. There had been a newspaper
article about him some months after he went missing, a picture of a
dashing captain on the front cover and the headline "What a Waste"
above it. I imagined that such news might spread abroad, or if the
French stranger was a frequent visitor to London, she might then have
read the article herself.

After Mariette's revelation, Peggy had bustled after us, accompanying Mother to her private wing.

"Get rid of *her*," my mother hissed, climbing into bed, with Peggy
promising to return with her medicines to help her sleep and a facecloth
cooled with lavender water, the scent of which always clung to the air
inside her room. Though the aches and her fatigue were the physical
side of her maladies, I believe the illness that breaks the will to live was
the worst of them. She had lost all interest in life and was far different
from her youthful photographs on the walls of the library: bright, lively,
placing her lips against my father's cheek just before the photographer
pressed the flash; and another astride a horse in tight riding pants, well
before the suffrage movement helped abandon women's etiquette of
sidesaddle.

Lovely and slender, with light-brown hair and hazel eyes, she was
well known for her intelligence and quick wit, all qualities that had
been whittled away with age to reveal a shrunken version of herself. And
there, amongst the images also, was my father: strong, commanding,

dark hair, and crinkling eyes that sparkled under certain lights. He loved a laugh and a drink, spending more and more time away in London as the years went on. And my mother, somewhere between the last birth and my father's new business venture, had stopped showing him any affection, had stopped inviting people to tea, and had stopped loving life.

After much fussing by Peggy, my mother lay with the small cloth across her forehead, her hair now blended with strands of aging white, her skin pasty, her mouth lined from years of discontent. I felt for her then. The life she had dreamed of gone too quickly and replaced with nothing but bad news. Her favorite son gone, her middle son foppish and only concerned about himself, and her younger son reserved and unlikely to achieve anything that might inspire her to see more light between her dark moments. I wanted to sit by her, hold her hand, and tell her that everything would be all right, doing what Edgar might have done, but her eyes were closed, and that meant all in the room were closed from her also.

Peggy followed me down the hall and whispered in my ear: "You had best see if the woman and the little one need a place to stay tonight. Bert said they walked here from whencesoever they came. It may well have been all the way from the station." I thanked her for her concern. She gave me some instructions concerning a room and then returned to stay with Mother while I attended to our guests.

I found Mariette once more in the drawing room, perched on the edge of the chair, the child lying restlessly on the floor at her feet. I curiously examined the boy for some connection with Edgar, but found none, and, admittedly, shared much of Mother's skepticism at that moment.

"She seems a little upset," said Mariette. It was not said haughtily or spitefully but rather as if she had expected Mother's reaction.

There were obviously questions I should have posed right then and there, but the timing seemed wrong somehow with the darkness closing

jacket sleeves. He had olive-green eyes, dark-brown hair, and a golden-brown complexion, much like Mariette's, and wore a newly tailored shirt and short trousers that I imagined were purchased for the benefit of our meeting.

"It is very nice," she said, her softly sensual voice suddenly infiltrating the small space beside me at the window.

"I think you should have everything you need here," I said, finding it hard to meet her steady gaze.

She seemed very familiar, unaware there were certain proprieties about space between men and women who did not know one another. The women I had socialized with liked to glance away frequently when they talked and had an air of vulnerability and entitlement at the same time. But Mariette stood close, her eyes not leaving me. I found it difficult to know where to look, so I chose the view from the window again. She read me perhaps and my awkwardness and thus admired the view also.

"I knew this would be very beautiful," she said, the last word elongated and syrupy in her accent. "But it is even grander than I imagined."

"You speak English well," I said.

It appeared that the French she had chosen to speak on her arrival had simply been a guard against my mother's interrogation until I came. I wanted to ask her what exactly she was expecting as a result of her visit and what she knew about our family. I could not yet formulate an opinion of her, nor pose cleverly designed questions to ascertain a reasonable truth, until I had performed some preliminary investigation. I moved toward the door.

"Peggy will check on you shortly. Make sure you have everything you need. I expect I will see you later, and we can discuss things then."

She looked back at me from the window, and I could see her expression change slightly, a sudden darkness at the mention of a conversation that none of us were looking forward to but one that would require some painful detail. The boy looked her way anxiously then, perhaps willing his mother to see me gone quickly.

"I know this is a lot to take in," she said. "I know that you must be shocked. I am sorry about your mother."

I nodded. "I'm not sure what to think just yet."

I left her then with these guarded words, and without guarantees, to head toward the library on the top floor to search through the letters from my brother, to uncover anything that could link her to him, that could prove the boy was Edgar's. Part of me wanted it to be true and part of me wanted them both gone so I did not have to deal with the matter that I suspected would lead to further complications.

Edgar's letters were bound and kept in a desk drawer. I wondered how many times Mother had opened them. I read each letter, attempting to find something that would give Mariette away. Only one line gave me something. He had said that while on a day's leave, he and a friend had gone into town and he found the girls there very pretty. But that was all he said. My brother had no serious girlfriends prior to his departure. If any visited the country estate as his guest in the summers, there was never a second visit. Edgar was methodical in everything he did, with any outcomes carefully engineered. The plan for Edgar had always been school, a degree, a partnership in a respectable accountancy firm, and, only then, after careful consideration, a wife.

I went to my room, tidied myself up, washed, and changed my shirt. I was intrigued if not keen to meet Mariette at dinnertime and wondered about Peggy busy in the kitchen, contemplating the dietary requirements of the child. I checked my reflection in the mirror. It was the same freckled face I had seen that morning: no great, wondrous change. Many said my father was handsome, and since I had inherited some of his physical characteristics, I supposed, though without his grand stature, there were some redeeming features about me.

I checked on Mother, who was in the dark now, lying motionless beneath the duvet, before returning back along the hallway to the dining room. Two places had been set, and I wondered where the child would take his meal. In the early days, as small children we ate in the kitchen, while our parents took their meals in the dining room. It wasn't until we started school, and each showed some signs of adulthood, that we were allowed to join them at their table.

I waited for ten minutes with some anxiety about the meeting, but it quickly disappeared when Peggy came in with only one plate of food. Mariette, having journeyed long by sea, by train, and on foot, and with the child now asleep, had requested to take her meal in her room. But she told Peggy to tell me that she was very appreciative of my generosity as a host.

"She also asked me to give you this," said Peggy. "She thought you might like it. She said it's yours to keep."

As soon as Peggy left the room, I eagerly opened the envelope, which contained a photograph of Edgar. He was not in uniform but in civilian shirt and trousers, standing amongst a group of people: three other men, and Mariette. In the background was a field of fruit trees, in careful lines, and a small low-set house. The paper was cracked and ragged, as if it, too, had experienced combat, and part of the image had been torn away at one end. Edgar looked relaxed, hands in pockets, smiling downward at something, away from the glare of the light, too bright perhaps, behind the photographer. The secretive smile hinted at restrained joy. I knew it well. On the back there was only the date: the year before we received word of him missing.

On the way to bed, I stopped by the kitchen to thank Peggy for organizing several meals, then returned to my room, which overlooked Bert's square hedges and tinted gardens along the front entranceway toward oak trees and distant meadows that rose and dipped over sheep-grazing knolls. I spent most of the night wrestling with the sheets and pillow, with many thoughts running through my mind. Once I turned on a bedside lamp to look again at the photo; another time I tried hard to eliminate the image of Mariette's tawny skin and black diamond eyes. Why would she give a photograph of Edgar away? Why would she not keep it to treasure? Unless she planned never to go, expecting always to be close to it. Or perhaps the image, the memory, meant little. As small as her gesture might seem, her parting with it bothered me, and neither of my own suppositions satisfied me. I eventually fell asleep, waking when the sun was balanced high above the distant fells.

I scolded myself for sleeping late and quickly changed. Halfway down the stairs, I followed the sounds of voices to find Peggy at the small table on the rear terrace with Mariette and the child. Stretching between the house and the lake was a green lawn, patched in places with many more of Bert's favorite flowers embracing the surprisingly fine autumn weather, then wide stone stairs that stepped down toward the lake. A small boathouse near the water had been erected in my boyhood years, and my sailing boat was stored there.

Between the women were a pot of tea and several thin slices of toast spread with butter and marmalade. I could hear the discussion as I approached. Mariette was asking a question in well-versed English about the fish in the lake and the wildlife. The fact that she had pretended to understand only French before my arrival meant that she knew something of me already, that perhaps I had a more receptive temperament than my mother.

Mariette seemed to carefully measure my expression as I approached her.

"Good morning," I said.

"Good morning," they both replied.

"I see that you have begun with English today."

"I must apologize for that," she said, immediately aware of my meaning. "I was very nervous. Your mother . . . I probably seemed very rude."

Not as rude as my mother can be, I wanted to say.

Mariette wore the same dress, her hair partly pinned, with thick curling strands over her shoulders. Her expression looked wearier than before, though it did not in any way lessen her beauty.

Peggy poured me some tea as I sat down, then asked if she could show Samuel the gardens. Mariette looked longingly at the boy before speaking to him in French. He nodded and keenly jumped off the chair to take Peggy's outstretched hand. Mariette watched the pair leave us, then turned her attention on me.

I took a sip of tea, my throat becoming suddenly dry in her presence. In the same white dress that she had arrived in and under the glow of the morning sun, she looked ethereal, and I found myself staring, like a young boy, at her lips, marveling at their naturally dark plum color. I cleared my throat and focused on my shoes briefly to empty the image from my head and fill it once more with the words I'd rehearsed.

"Mariette, I'm afraid your arrival has been a bit of a shock for my mother, as you can imagine. She lost her son, and then to learn four years later that she has . . . that she is told she has a grandson."

"I know how it looks, Rudy," she said, my name spoken with her hand to her throat. "But I can assure you that I knew your brother intimately and that I loved him for a period. And as a result of our love, of your brother's love for me, we had a child. A child that he never got to see."

The force with which she expelled these words took me aback. I felt that she was sterner than she needed to be, as if she expected an adverse response.

"I have come a long way to tell you this at an expense I can scarcely afford. I am here because I felt you needed to know. Edgar would have wanted you and your mother and brother to know."

As alluring and confident as she was, there was still much doubt at my end.

"It may have been prudent to write perhaps. Mother loathes the element of surprise."

"Writing is not my strong point. Besides, I thought a letter would not have given as much substance as to present the boy in person."

"Where do you come from?"

"Just outside of a town called Bailleul."

It was a name that I had read in Edgar's letters, amongst a handful of other places.

"Do you have family there still?"

"No. The town was reduced to rubble. Our orchard has a crater the size of your drawing room, and many of our animals were taken by Germans."

I felt a pang in my chest at her loss, but I still could not rely on this as truth.

"Why did you wait so long to come here?"

"I did not plan to at first. Samuel was ours: Edgar's and mine. I did not wish to share him with strangers. Then as my son grew, I wondered what Edgar would want me to do." She paused briefly, appearing pensive and wary of the words that would follow. The mention of Edgar's name, I felt she knew, was painful for me. "It was not a decision I made lightly. I must admit I was fearful about meeting you. As time wore on I realized that by bringing Samuel here I was also returning Edgar in a way, to the place he loved. I began planning it two years ago, saved up the money to come when I felt that Samuel was old enough to travel."

She looked at me directly then, willing me to challenge this.

"Then I must ask the obvious question. Do you have Samuel's birth certificate?"

"You have to understand that there were times when the urgency of the situation did not allow for the orderly rules found in a place free from war."

I wondered if it was her intent to show that I knew little of the hardship she spoke about. Regardless, I felt some guilt.

"But I have a certificate of marriage." She pulled a piece of paper from her carry bag and placed it on the table in front of me. I stared at their names, if indeed it was she, Mariette Lavier and Edgar Stuart Watts, sealed in script. "I also have this, which was given by a dear friend of ours as a gift." She handed me a small silver spoon engraved with the name *Samuel Edgar Watts*.

For several seconds I was torn between mistrust and longing before the first feeling momentarily fell away. The names on the certificate could have been cleverly forged if not for the signature of my brother. It looked rushed, but it was undoubtedly his. My heart felt crushed with emotions. If she weren't there, I would have run my fingers over the writing, touched perhaps one of the last pieces of paper Edgar held, the last words he might have written.

"How did he die?" I asked.

Her voice softened then. She could see that I was having difficulty looking at her.

"I suspect I know only as much as you and your mother. He was fighting at the front, and then . . . there were so many dead. Some were unrecognizable. That is all I know. I tried to learn more, of course, since."

She reached then across the table and put her hand over mine. I would have leaped across the table and cried into her shoulder, but she was a stranger and I was a man groomed with rules about such intimacies.

"Will you tell me about him and as much as you can?" I asked, trying hard to strengthen the sudden frailty of my speech and fearful that my stutter might return.

She told me then how she had met him on his leave, in the town near where she lived. She was instantly taken with his unforced charm and decency above all.

"He was a true gentleman but even more so a soldier. I know the men loved him, and he loved them also. He would do anything for them."

Edgar had been sent to the town of Bailleul to recuperate from a minor injury. They met when she was delivering fruit from her father's orchard to Edgar's place of convalescence. He was later billeted at her house. They were friends first, she said. After he returned from his next campaign, they were married. It was wild and impetuous, she said, and her father was not happy about it at first, but Edgar completely won him over. They were married; then Edgar went missing shortly after.

"He was very different from other men," she said.

"How so?"

"He was silent, sometimes distant, but yet incredibly present also. That probably makes no sense to you."

It did. Edgar could express deep caring without the use of words, and he noticed everything even when you thought he didn't.

"Do you have any letters he might have sent you?"

She shook her head.

It was difficult to fault her story, but there were still many holes to fill. If he had married, why didn't he write home about it? He had written frequently in the early days. Why not about this? Was he carried away with their relationship with no time to write? Or was he ashamed of something?

The situation I found myself in was certainly unusual, and one I thought I could somehow free myself from with perhaps a small sum of money and a promise of written correspondence. But I was yet to understand that I was already trapped by Mariette, and shortly with no want for release.

"He used to talk about your holidays at the beach. He had a collection of shells in his room."

Peggy and the child were crossing the lawn toward us, the boy pointing toward his mother.

"It was Edgar who told me that his mother might have difficultly liking me but that you perhaps would better deal with the situation. Which was why I chose not to talk to your mother yesterday. I know it was impolite, but I thought that she would throw me out, and I had no other address or knowledge of your employment that I gained upon my arrival. Perhaps it would have been easier there. I am sorry I caused such a spectacle."

"You were right to have me summoned," I said, wondering whether Mother might have been as charitable concerning accommodation.

"Edgar was a good man, and he would have been a good husband and father, too. I cannot tell you how his death broke my heart."

Something struck me suddenly.

"Did anyone else from his regiment know you?"

She reached for the certificate, quickly returning it to her bag.

"There was a man, but I don't remember his name. He came and told me that Edgar was killed, and then he was gone. I should have asked more questions. I should perhaps have sought him out."

So there really was nothing that she could tell me. *Was it all too convenient?* I had to ask myself. Yet there was detail that she had said about Edgar. No one would have known about the trips to Blackpool when we were small and the collection of shells that Edgar kept in a box in his room. I could not have imagined Edgar discussing such things with other men. But even as I thought this, I doubted it also. Who knows what people discuss when they lie for hours in wait for the enemy, and with no guarantees for the morrow.

Peggy was now carrying the child, who had begun to cry.

"He never found out he was a father," Mariette said, rising from the table, as Samuel's cries brought an end to this turn of conversation. "I know my arrival must come as a shock to you. There is much to absorb."

Mariette stepped gracefully down the stairs toward Peggy and the child.

"He was suddenly upset by something," said Peggy. "The poor mite heard a noise and thought there were wild animals lurking behind the oak trees. I tried to show him there was nothing there to hurt him."

"He is too young to understand much . . . not yet four, and he scares easily," said Mariette, the boy climbing between the women, across to his mother. "If you will excuse me."

"Of course," I said, standing, as she passed me briskly to enter the manor. I sat down again numbly, the information overloading my brain, as the child's wails faded behind me.

"Are you all right?" Peggy asked at my side.

"I'm not sure," I said, watching the wind disturbing the surface of the water, my own thoughts scattered.

"You should have a rest today. I will get you some water."

"No, thank you, Peggy. It is probably you who needs the rest. Thank you for looking after the child."

She started to walk away and then stopped.

"There is something there," said Peggy.

"What are you talking about?"

"The boy. There is something there of Edgar. Not that it is any of my business."

"Peggy, it is every bit your business also."

She graciously nodded, then left to see my mother.

Mariette's story was believable, from her description of Edgar's character to the things he said about me. But there was still something about her visit that did not sit well. *Why now?* Saving the money to come here sounded feasible, but the excuse that she grew to suddenly realize what Edgar might want her to do seemed rehearsed. Was she here only to present the child, or was she biding her time to tell us more?

CHAPTER 4

Mariette didn't come out of her room for several hours, and there was no noise from the child. I went to the library to inspect the photographs on the wall. I was curious at what Peggy had said. But I couldn't see the resemblance. The child, if he was Edgar's, did not look like any of us as children. He was olive skinned and narrow shouldered, and his eyes weren't as deeply set. But such distinctions proved nothing. The look of the child sometimes counted little toward birthright. We did all carry features of our parents, but we were all very different as well. Edgar with Mother's walnut-colored hair but Father's bright-blue eyes, Laurence very much like Mother with her hazel eyes, and I dark-haired and blue-eyed like Father. Though Peggy was only ever looking out for our interests, I presumed that she could also be feeling sympathy for the child.

I was dreading lunch. When Mother took a dislike to someone or something, one could rarely turn her around. I knew she would have woken up thinking this problem had gone away, that I would have made that happen; Mother was habituated to her various instructions being followed without question.

First to arrive at lunch, I found that the table was set for only two; Peggy advised me that Mariette had excused herself from joining us for reasons unknown, but one, I imagined, had something to do with my mother. Mother came in with a little more color to her cheeks. She wore a lavender dress to the floor, pearl earrings, and her hair in a chignon. She was still very handsome, and the resemblance between my mother and Laurence was striking. I stood up to pull out the chair for her.

"Are you feeling better?"

"You know how I'm feeling," she said.

"The weather is beautiful today," I said. I wanted the lunch to be light and not subject to my mother's fluctuating and often despondent mood.

"Don't try to distract me from what is happening. Peggy told me that she is still here. And the *child*." The last word was spoken with a resentful undertone.

The change in my mother was significant when she learned of Edgar missing. She never fully recovered from the news and had found very little joy in anything. Father had perhaps taken a little of the joy out of her life toward the end of his. But it was Edgar's death that caused a permanent melancholy, which had further aggrieved her physically. I had felt her grief, and understood, though looking at her today, I had to wonder why she didn't concentrate on her two living sons. Laurence, a bit of a fop, may have been that way in part because he'd had the least attention of us all. And I, well I certainly didn't have the charisma of Edgar, but I was here at least to look after her welfare.

"Mother, she has a child and is still very tired from travel. I must allow her the benefit of the doubt. She has said some things that do indeed tell me she knew him. Loved him even."

She *tut-tutted* and looked away, and I was concerned that she would have another episode.

"Mother, please, if you will. Just keep an open mind. If for nothing else but to indulge me."

I passed her the photograph and told her that I had seen the marriage certificate and about the things that Mariette had revealed, in particular what she knew about us. Mother stared for many seconds at the granular image of Edgar as she swallowed back her emotion, her feelings carefully checked. My news had clearly affected her; her hands trembled as she passed back the picture.

"So she knew him!" she said. "That doesn't necessarily relate to paternity, does it? Forgery is not hard to come by. She could have heard about him or overheard a conversation he'd had with someone else. She could have planned this visit the moment she learned of his death."

She was steely despite her ailing health. I wondered if she felt somewhat bitter about this other life of Edgar's, the years in France we'd been excluded from.

"I'll admit," I said. "There are many avenues to be explored."

"Do you believe her? Please tell me you aren't just enamored with her. She is very pretty, Rudy, but sometimes women are most cunning, and they use many devices to get what they want."

I wondered then if Mother had used some herself.

"Mother, I can only go by what I've heard. On that basis the case she presents seems plausible. I can't just send her away. We would have to live with that if it turned out to be true . . ."

"The Flemish have had it hard. I feel sorry for them. They have lost homes, they have lost much. But there are also some who exploit that sort of hardship and use it to full advantage."

I could not discount what Mother said, even though the undertone was a shade more discriminatory than speculative. She was suspicious of every foreigner.

"I think we should go to the police," she said. "They will sort it out. She needs at least to be taken somewhere else while we examine any documentation."

"Mother, I don't think that's necessary. I will question her further and get to the heart of it. I will seek help from Roland, and if I feel that she is not telling the truth, I will indeed send her away." Roland Alderman, our family lawyer, had been in my parents' employ since before I was born.

My mother sat there sadly, staring at her plate of food. She was very thin, and I did worry so about her health.

"I can't deal with this just yet," she said.

I nodded and patted Mother's hand. "I will take care of everything. I will take some leave to help Bert with some of the house maintenance and sort out the business of Mariette and her son while I'm here. And where possible I will keep them out of your way for the time being."

It wouldn't be hard. My mother spent a great deal of time in the villa.

"Then promise me that you will be guided by your head, Rudy. You have had it in the clouds for much of your life."

"Yes, Mother," I said to humor her. It was not unusual for Mother to bring up my personality at these times, and in doing so highlight her preferences. But I was used to it. "You must eat something."

I watched her sip soup and eat a roll with butter, satisfied at least she would not leave the table without something. Our conversation turned to matters relating to the estate. She had been scrupulous about every penny since my father's death, and part of the property management, in Edgar's absence, had been passed on to me. She asked me to inspect her accounting for the farming leaseholds, several of which were becoming more uncertain.

As was our custom I let Mother be, to sit in peace with a sherry. I kissed her on the cheek, my hand on her shoulder. She grabbed my hand and held it a few seconds, encasing it greedily in her own, as if she should lose me, too. And it was one of the rare moments that she showed how much she loved me. Perhaps it was only need, but I felt her reaching for a connection. I wanted to tell her that everything would be all right. But I couldn't of course. Edgar was not coming home, Laurence was still being an ass, and our financial situation was worsening with each passing year. I loved my mother, and I would tell her if she'd let me. But I had never really understood her expectations of me. She was complex.

I read through the mail—several bills and an invitation to a meeting to discuss the future of the county's conservation—before stepping out into the foyer. Peggy met me on the way through to the kitchen and advised me that she had taken a tray of food to Mariette and left it there beside them, both asleep.

I took the opportunity to find Bert bundling hay on the grazing pasture close by, to learn that the maintenance budget was fully spent for that month. He said he was wondering if he could sell one of the younger horses since I was now so often in Manchester and there was no one to ride them, whether the money for the sale could go toward several repairs.

It made sense, but I went into the stable and stroked the nose of Sheriff. He seemed happy to see me, rubbing his face against my shoulder and then tapping his feet. It had been a while since I had paid him attention, and he needed a run, he was telling me. I saddled him and rode far across the meadows and glens, up the rocky hills in the north and down the winding tracks to the woods where we had all ridden as boys, each with our own horse. I walked Sheriff then until I found the circle of trees we used to sit against to talk.

Through the tree trunks I spied a fox, and it brought back memories of my brothers and me hunting with sticks instead of guns. Though one time, Laurence had surreptitiously taken our uncle's Boer War rifle and, believing it was not loaded, had pulled the trigger, only to learn that it was when a bullet clipped my ear. There is a tiny piece missing from it now. The force of the rifle had thrown Laurence backward hard onto the ground, winded and screeching with indignation. Edgar had grabbed the rifle, lifted him up by the shirt, and punched him on the jaw to add to the misery of his fall, and Laurence had run off wailing. I didn't feel the wound on my ear, but I saw the blood and began crying also. Edgar had checked my ear, told me it was still there but the small nick hadn't improved my looks any, and I had laughed through the tears. He had been there for all my early follies. And I found the memory of my brother's bright-blue eyes, crinkling all the way to his wide-mouthed smile, so clear at that moment that I found the tops of my cheeks were suddenly wet with tears.

I hadn't grieved for long at the initial news of Edgar. There had been too many other things to deal with in the early stages: Mother's declining health, losing many of our farmers to the war effort, and the ongoing and exacting management of our finances. By the time the war was over and Laurence—who had also joined the fighting toward the end of it—arrived home uninjured, the news of Edgar missing had grown old. Though Mother still felt it acutely, and I fought to believe and make sense of it.

Now Mariette was here verifying his death, and these words of finality reignited the grief.

Edgar had died for a cause. A necessary death, we were told. The Germans had not got their way. In some sense that sounded right, but what was right about war?

I wiped away the tears and thought that I must get to the truth of Mariette and her news. I must spend time with her. I must learn everything she had to tell me. I would do it for Mother, but I would do it for the child also. A small child, if he were indeed Edgar's, deserved the truth as well.

I rode my gray gelding back to the stables and turned at the last moment to see Peggy at the front door, waving to draw my attention before walking hurriedly toward me. By the time I dismounted, she had drawn close, appearing very anxious.

"It's the woman. She is in the hall. She is leaving with the child."

Peggy took the reins from me to walk the horse back into the stable as I moved quickly to enter the house. Mariette was just inside the door and wearing a different dress, a black one with lace at the hem, and the boy was in a corduroy coat, ready for travel.

"I'm sorry," she said, "that I have bothered you with all this. I will leave. I know it has been hard on your mother, and I don't expect anything from you."

I noticed that there were beads of sweat on her forehead and her skin was a paler shade today so that the shadows beneath her dark eyes stood out in a frightening way. Her breaths were also shallow, and she had trouble focusing on me.

"Mrs. . . . . Mariette," I stumbled. By the marriage it suggested her name was now my own, which was most difficult yet to say. "You must stay. I don't doubt your story, but there are things I would still like to know."

It was hard to explain or tell her that I was dubious of her story without offending her. It was a delicate balance between what she told me and what I felt in my heart was missing.

"I can't stay. I really can't," she said, and leaned down to pick up the child. "In some way it feels wrong that I have come."

She walked out the front door and down the steps, and I felt a sense of helplessness, almost loss. I did not want her gone. I did not want the child gone. In a most unusual sense, it felt as if Edgar were leaving a second time.

I followed her outside.

"You must let me drive you to the train or wherever it is you wish to go. It is too long by the walking trails to get there, especially with the child."

"We will be fine, Monsieur Watts," she said, looking beyond at the road. "We walked yesterday and made it here all right."

She appeared confident in her speech, but I felt also a sense of hesitancy and needfulness when she turned to view me, her eyes glassy and liquid black. I was speechless and transfixed, unsure of what to say.

Suddenly, those eyes flickered several times, breaking the spell, and she began to sink to the ground. I had just enough time to catch both her and the child before they hit the stone.

CHAPTER 5

I called out to Peggy, who by that time was already returning from the stable. She had seen what had happened and hitched her skirts to walk swiftly toward me.

Clutching the child's hand, Peggy followed me as I carried Mariette up the stairs and down the hallway to the guest room. I laid Mariette down on the bed and felt her forehead, which was hot to touch, and Peggy picked up the child, who had begun to wail.

"I will fetch the doctor," I said. "I fear she is very ill."

"Come now, Samuel," said Peggy to the little boy. "We must go and find something for you in the kitchen. Maybe some sweet biscuits." The child wouldn't hear of it and was unlikely to have understood her English, his wails getting louder with every step she took away from his mother. I attempted to repeat in French above the cries to no avail.

"Hush now," said Peggy in the firm but soothing tone she used for all us boys. This seemed to have some effect, and she carried him away.

I put a light cover over Mariette then left for the doctor. It was quicker to ride Sheriff across to his residence than take the roads by car.

The doctor arrived a short time after my return. He was in the room with Mariette for some time while I paced the lower ground rooms like an anxious father-to-be. The child in the meantime had been placed in the old nursery, with a wooden rocking horse that Peggy had pulled out from storage. Samuel had been briefly amused and distracted before the doctor stopped in to examine him also, a task that was quite distressing, according to Dr. Macklin, who met me in the drawing room afterward. He seemed to believe that Samuel had never been seen medically before.

"I examined the child to make sure there were no similar signs of contagion . . . I must say he was rather difficult, and Peggy had to hold him. He made quite a fuss. He is fine," said the doctor, "but I'm afraid the woman has an infection. A rather serious one that has affected the respiratory system. She must rest and drink plenty." He gave me a small bottle of tonic to ease her chest to be administered morning and night. It was also his assumption that she would have felt terribly unwell during her travels.

"How serious is it?" I asked.

"Does she have family?"

"None we know of."

"Then I suggest that she be watched closely for any change. Contact me immediately if there is."

He was elderly and had been with us for years to check our early heartbeats and sicknesses. He was always a curious man, perhaps because he was a man of medicine and this came to him naturally, and he asked about Mariette's appearance here. I explained the situation, to which he looked both quizzical and alarmed. I also told him about my mother's concerns, and he sympathized with her also, suggesting it would be challenging to learn such news.

"If I can be of further assistance," he said.

Under such circumstances, and given the urgency of contacting anyone who might know her, I justified my reasons for invading Mariette's privacy. Her bag was still at the front of the house, and I opened it guiltily, looking for the marriage certificate. Inside her bag there was very little clothing, a small book that looked oddly familiar and so badly beaten it was tied with string, and the piece of paper in question, which I passed to the doctor on my return to the drawing room.

"Does this look legitimate to you?"

The doctor took it closer to the light by the window to examine it carefully.

"I do not quite know what they do in the French provinces, but it appears legitimate to me on the surface. See the type . . . Certain equipment would be needed to produce the quality, so she would have had to know someone with such a machine or steal such ready-printed papers from the clergy. Which is not improbable, I suppose. And of course I can't be certain if the signatures are those of the actual persons. If you like, I can contact the registry over there and have the ceremony verified at least. Presuming of course that any such paperwork was registered."

Given what Mariette had said earlier about the town being destroyed, I realized it could be difficult to prove.

"You say you believe the signature is your brother's?"

"It certainly looks like his handwriting. Yes."

"How old did she say was the child?"

"Under four. She didn't say exactly."

The doctor looked back at the paper in his hand.

"Hmm. I think that perhaps there is another question you might want to ask her. Such as exactly what was the relationship between them?"

His query seemed a little impertinent and not the least obvious, and his meaning for such was vague.

"The child is clearly not used to adult supervision and instruction, and I see some evidence that he may have gone untreated for prior illnesses. But perhaps he didn't have access to the right medical facilities. A wildling almost . . . but I'm drifting off course here . . . I've examined enough children in my years to know the boy, though certainly small for his age, shows an extraordinary amount of awareness, and I would suggest at the very least he is closer to the age of five in his development. Of course one would have to do a complete examination to be more accurate. But I think the question here to be posed, though I should leave it to your discretion as to when and if you do, is at what point was the relationship productive?"

"I'm not sure I follow you, sir."

"I've seen various informalities surrounding the births of children, but this marriage certificate is dated around the time the child was likely born. It may well be valid, but she might not be telling you everything."

I looked at the paper, confused, running my eyes over the names again.

"Do the mathematics, dear boy. If I'm correct, the age of the child doesn't quite fit legitimately with the date on the certificate. There are indeed more questions you need to consider."

The discrepancy the doctor had put forward was suddenly obvious. A child born before a marriage was not only potentially detrimental to the issue of parentage and therefore the legitimacy of endowment, it opened up a line of inquiry of a more delicate matter, and I had no idea how one would pose such a query to a woman, or at the very least question her word.

"I'm not saying that this ascertains she is of dubious character, or that there might not be other reasons to account for perhaps a lack of physical development; however, sometimes in these cases, especially in the chaotic state of the land at the time, we are left with many moral curiosities. I can tell you that the French and British unions during that time certainly rose, and not all resulted with a certificate."

"I see," I said a little awkwardly. "Thank you, Doctor."

Before he left, he wrote down in his notebook the details from the certificate, and I also made a handwritten copy of it before returning the piece of paper to Mariette's bag as I had found it.

Inch by inch perhaps all the clues were leading to the truth. It was of some comfort that the doctor's intuition told him the marriage certificate was likely valid, but his other words left me wary; a child born outside of marriage was not something Mother was yet ready for.

Without definite proof of anything, I decided against mentioning the doctor's considerations.

I sent Bert to the postmaster to send a second message to my employer, saying there was a family matter that must be attended to and that I would need to spend further time here to sort it out. I could not afford to lose the work, but matters at Lakeland Manor had left me no choice but to stay.

Peggy was a godsend over the next few days. She cared for Mariette like she would any of us, helping her bathe, checking her temperature, taking her broths, and applying cold compresses. I would check in from time to time, though I was more a spectator while respecting her modesty, as I imagined she would not like to be seen in this state. Though on the third day, Peggy asked me to attend to Mariette's comforts, as she was busy with the child.

Mariette found it hard to lift her head off the pillow. I helped her sit up with cushions to feed her some soup, but she pushed my hand away and sank back down beneath the sheets. The child was kept away, miserable for much of the time. Bert took on more duties for Peggy during this period, purchasing meat and vegetables from the village. We all pitched in, and I regularly reported to Mother, who was looking more wan, I think because of the amount of attention paid to the stranger. Though there was something a little softer about her. She was not totally hard or without feeling. She did indeed look sympathetic as to the seriousness of Mariette's condition, having suffered herself for so many years. And as for me, seeing the frailty of Mariette at this time and feeling somewhat remorseful for her predicament, I developed a sense of protectiveness toward both our visitors.

During Mariette's convalescence I helped repair broken palings and pavers and attended to the gardening. Bert was quite stiff in the joints, and in the previous two years, I had seen a rapid degeneration of his movement. With his decline, diminishing wheat yields, dwindling sheep numbers, and limited funds to service all of it, I saw Bert's future at the manor shrinking, his departure imminent.

Having had much farm experience, Bert lent his hand where he could. The farmers had become our friends, and we tried as best we could to get them through the downturn. The difficult decision ahead was the likely sale of land to developers. However, as the beneficiary, it would ultimately be Laurence's decision. And since he'd had little interest in the place, selling most of the estate was the likely scenario. With Edgar's death still officially inconclusive, Mother's responsibility for the estate, as Edgar's designated interim trustee during his war absence, had continued in the meantime, and much of the management had then been passed on to me. However, I suspected that Laurence's patience would run its course, and he might soon present his claims to the estate.

One evening after dinner I knocked on Mariette's door to check on her improvement. She called out for me to enter, and I found her propped up on the pillows in a plain white nightdress. She turned her head as I approached, her eyes clearer, the lamplight beside her bed allowing her a more radiant than sallow complexion at this time, and her brilliant red-brown hair fanned across the pillow. "Will you sit with me?" she said with a frail voice and heavy-lidded gaze.

I sat on a chair beside her on the bed. Her expression was open and trusting, her life seemingly in my hands. She was a mystery to me, a stranger from a foreign country, and with a past that I knew very little about. But I felt close to her then, in an unexplained way, and by the time I would leave the room, even closer still.

It was clear she was feeling better, but she still appeared very weak. Even lifting herself to a more seated position seemed to be an effort.

"Thank you, all of you, for taking care of me," she said.

I shook my head to steer her away from any compliment.

"How is Samuel?"

I reassured her that he was in good hands.

"You could have sent me away, but you didn't," she said.

"We wouldn't do that."

"Your brother said that should something happen to him, it was not in your nature to turn me away."

I wondered if she knew what she was saying or whether she was just rambling in a haze of illness.

"What else did he say?"

"He said that when you were very small, you were fearful of the waves. He would always have to carry you when you had not yet grown your sea legs. One day he let go of you in the water, and a wave swallowed you under and dragged you away. He called and called your name, thought you had gone. And then he saw you. You had not been dragged as far as he thought, and he pulled you in, and you were shaking and wailing with fear, and he said that he was laughing because it was the happiest sound he had ever heard."

I remembered that day, sort of. I remember him calling my name.

"He also told me that he didn't like that he got all the attention. That perhaps if he were to go, you would be taken more seriously."

She stopped talking suddenly and closed her eyes. The only movement was the faint flickering of soft light beside her and then her breathing grew steady and even. I crept from the room, closed the door, then sat against it and put my head in my hands as tears escaped for the second time. Two things I thought about. The first was that Edgar had thought about me enough to talk about this, and the second was that everything seemed to be pointing to the fact that she was telling the truth. I did not imagine him to be so open about such feelings with someone he wasn't close to.

The next morning, I had a message from the doctor to say that he could not reach the church where the marriage was officiated, because the building was destroyed in the war, but he did learn that the priest who presided in the parish had survived and was living elsewhere.

It would seem, young Rudy, that she may be telling the truth. But I can't, of course, confirm with only this. I would suggest you seek your family

lawyer and take the details to him also. He would best know about search-
ing for birth records if they exist and if the union is legitimate in the eyes
of the law.

I did indeed intend on seeking more information, and I thus took
the copy by car, this time to our lawyer.

Roland greeted me affectionately.

"How is your mother?".

"She is well enough," I said, the meaning behind the words perfectly clear to someone who knew much about our situation.

"And Laurence . . . still taking full advantage of London life?"

"I rarely see him, but I imagine so."

The mention of his name seemed to bring out a certain fear in me,
as if he might appear at any moment to complicate further the already
sensitive and perplexing situation unfolding at Lakeland Manor.

"I need to advise you that just recently Edgar's name has been
added to His Majesty's officially published war records; his name was
inadvertently left out of the publication initially as you know, and for
reasons no one can actually tell me," said Roland. "This confirmation of
the death as killed in action means of course that Laurence is one step
closer to his claim for the estate."

I knew this change was coming and dreaded it. Mother had delayed
it long enough with her grief. Laurence's control was not what anyone
else wanted, but it was according to the law and my father's will, which
made it binding that everything would succeed down the line. There
were others who executed differently, but I was still part of a rigid
beneficiary system that my father had not had a lateral mind to alter.

I handed him the copy of the certificate, about which he asked a
number of questions and, with such a sharp mind, was able to needle
most of the information from me, even the parts I did not wish to
reveal. Roland assured me that he had "opened many a closet" during his profession and would not be shocked by anything. Upon our

parting, he advised he would pursue more details on my behalf with a sense of urgency, given the matter was delicate.

After another three days of rest, Mariette was sitting up without any difficulty, and the child, who had been sleeping in the room next to Peggy's, rushed in excitedly and climbed the bed to reach his mother. The night sweats had disappeared, and her appetite was slowly returning. She hugged Samuel, though she placed some distance between them, with the fear she might still pass on the infection.

She looked flushed, perhaps embarrassed to be in night attire with hair unkempt.

"I hope you don't mind me being here again."

She did not respond to this and thought hard about something else.

"You were here one night. I remember. I hope I didn't say anything strange. I was quite weary."

"No," I said, deciding against reminding her. "There is more color about you today."

"Thank you again for letting me stay. I think I was quite delirious the day I attempted to leave. But I will attempt it again as soon as I am able. In the meantime, I will dress for the day. I'm feeling ready to face the world again."

I wasn't sure if I should say anything else at that point, in particular about her talk of departure. I stood up and spied the silvery lake and, above that, miles of powder-blue sky. It was paradise here, and I longed to share it then with someone who might appreciate it as much as I did. I reached for the door and felt a sense of lost opportunities if I did not say something. I turned back to see she was watching me curiously.

"If I may be so bold as to suggest that there is no need to leave in s-such a hurry," I said, stammering, perhaps too eager to speak the words. "You are welcome as a guest here until we can come to some arrangement. I would like you at least to stay here until your strength is returned."

She smiled coyly down at her hands.

"Thank you. I would like that. *We* would like that."

I nodded and turned to leave again.

"Do you doubt me?" she asked.

Her question took me by surprise. Despite my growing feelings for her, I still did not have an answer that would satisfy her.

"There is one thing that would help me win over my mother."

"It is the marriage certificate, *non*?"

I smiled then. Was I so transparent, or was she especially canny? I suspected both.

"Yes," I said.

"Could you please pass me my bag?"

I retrieved her leather travel bag, and she reached toward the papers at the bottom. She paused suddenly, and I thought briefly that she had seen that its contents had been disturbed. I was about to own up to it when she pulled out the paper and handed it to me.

"Thank you," I said, replacing the bag she passed to me and tucking the folded document into my shirt pocket, hoping that Mother would accept what appeared the likely truth: Samuel was Edgar's son, but at the very least, Mariette was Edgar's widow.

"Was there anyone else in attendance?"

"Yes, my father, Jerome Lavier, several months before he died."

I felt it wrong to question any further at that point. What she had told me was of little help to any investigation concerning the marriage, but as I left the room with the image of her sitting nestled amongst the cushions on the bed, her being here felt right, as if the transition of her arrival had never occurred. Everything about that moment felt as it should. I walked with lighter steps along the hallway to find Peggy and the child in the kitchen, Samuel swinging his short legs carelessly from a chair. He had grown used to us, his eyes not darting toward anyone who entered a room, but his thoughts comfortably elsewhere.

"Samuel, how would you like to see the horses?"

He nodded, but as we stepped toward the stable, he looked around him furtively: "Are there bears?" he asked in French.

I admit I was yet to understand the fears of a child, of images they might have seen and perceived as real.

"No," I said. "We have sent them all away for good."

He was not convinced and stood still.

"Samuel," I said, "what's the matter? Who's telling you these things to scare you?"

He shook his head. He perhaps did not wish to say.

"Well, you truly don't have to worry about anything that might harm you here. I grew up here, and in all my time never once encountered a wild animal that would hurt me."

He took another look around him, satisfied, and continued more sure-footed than before. I had not engaged with the boy, had rarely spoken to him, and he had been reserved, perhaps even a little frightened of me. And more so of Mother, I daresay; even more so than of bears.

He smiled and said that he had been with Bert to watch him brush the horses in the stable, and he had even seen me riding one. And it was as if a person had suddenly emerged before my eyes. Now relaxed, he chatted to me about his time with Bert as I walked him first to the chicken coop, to spy for eggs, and then toward the stable.

I asked him then if he missed his home, but his expression became solemn, and he chose not to answer. I asked also if he knew of his father, to which he said nothing. I guessed perhaps it had been difficult for Mariette to talk about a man he had never met, and especially since he was so young. I thought, daydreamed even, that it might be something I could discuss with him later on. I had so much to tell him about Edgar.

He told me in young speak—lots of words but few details—about the train ride and the boat ride to get here. Though he spoke in French, he knew the English word for horse and many others, and I was very impressed with the intelligence of the boy.

"Can you tell me a little bit about your home?"

He shrugged, then looked at me shyly.

"Do you miss it?"

He shook his head, rubbing his foot back and forth on the ground like a horse eager to gallop away. He seemed reluctant to talk further or maybe just bored. Inexperienced as I was with children, I distracted him with other things. I explained how my brothers and I used to ride and race and that I have a scar where I fell from a horse and tore my thigh. He seemed intrigued by such stories, and I regretted telling him, quickly reassuring him that I was on a very fast horse and the horses we had now were gentle.

He was at first fearful and would not step near the horses, but finally I coaxed him. I lifted him to place him on Sheriff, whom I trusted with my life, and I walked them both around the paddock.

I couldn't help but compare the features of the boy and Edgar. He had a very pointed chin, unlike Edgar, a darker complexion, and a narrow frame, but there was also an uncannily haunted expression that Edgar carried, where one never knew whether he was listening to them or not, but in fact he was carefully dissecting every word. I thought about what my brother might have done with Samuel; he most certainly would have taught him to row, sail, and ride.

It was quite dark by the time we left to return to the house for dinner, and the child was whisked away by Peggy to be taken to visit his mother again. Though Peggy didn't speak French, she spoke the universal languages of arm movements and voice tone, which a child always understands. I could see that a close relationship was quickly forming.

Finding Mother in her rooms with a headache and the curtains closed, I advised her very briefly of the steps I had taken with Roland to examine Mariette's claims. In the dim light, she squinted at the certificate I presented her and paid particular attention to Edgar's signature, before waving it away. She was feeling too poorly to study the document at length, but examined it long enough to have gleaned its potential for validity. I also suggested to Mother that Mariette and the boy stay at

Lakeland until the conclusion of the investigation. "A presumption of innocence until proven otherwise," I said, to which my mother, quick-witted as she was, said, "Or the reverse." She did express feelings of concern that Mariette had been so ill. She could at least find common ground there. Peggy had filled her in, I believe, on everything else, and perhaps it was Peggy who had softened her the most.

The following day, much revived, Mother sought out the boy and asked if he would join her for lemonade on the terrace. Was this a trick, I wondered, to get him to reveal something? Only a week ago she had wanted him gone. But she seemed brighter, perhaps due to better health. She had powdered her face, applied some color to her cheeks, and Peggy had pinned up her hair into a style that she loved. She engaged Samuel in conversation and asked Peggy to bring her several children's books we had read as boys, and Mother sat and pointed to English words and asked him to repeat them. I spied the pair from inside and found Mother to be quite delightful when she was in this mood. She was a good teacher, something I had not realized until that moment. Both patient and careful, she kept the boy enthralled with her explanation of the pictures.

When I returned an hour later, she had paper and pen, and Samuel was writing words.

"You can keep it," she told him about the picture book he favored most, and I caught Samuel walking around the gardens with it and reading the words out loud. He was so taken with the book, and fearful it might disappear for good, that from that moment it was rarely out of sight, and in the afternoon when I took him to see the horses again, the book was tucked safely under his arm.

The next day Mariette felt well enough to eat a full meal and met with my mother and me for breakfast in the dining room. Mariette dressed, arranged her hair, and put on a beige belted dress that had belonged to my mother. Mariette's well-worn clothes needed cleaning, and Peggy in the meantime had provided her with dresses that Mother had grown tired of.

The gathering was a little uncomfortable at first, our meal eaten mostly in silence interspersed with my explanations to Mariette about farming methods and her queries about the history of the property and comments about the kindness of Peggy and Bert and Samuel's new-found love of horses, before running out of things to say.

"You speak English very well," Mother said to Mariette, but made no further reference to the first day when Mariette pretended otherwise. With Mariette's embarrassed bow of the head, my mother's point had produced the effect she sought.

"Mariette," my mother said after an awkward silence hovered above our partly-eaten boiled eggs and toast. "I am led to believe by my son and my housekeeper that there is merit in what you say, and you should be aware that we are attempting to validate your claim by various methods. The marriage certificate appears legitimate enough. But do you have any family left . . . anywhere, who can prove that you were in a relationship with Edgar? That the child is his?"

It was blunt, and I would have stepped in to answer for her; however, Mariette seemed unruffled.

"As I told Rudy, I have no family remaining. The war left little evidence of anything."

"Quite," said Mother, also unperturbed. "If I am to give you the benefit of the doubt that you are indeed my son's wife and the child is my grandson, I have to ask, what is it that you want from us? Did you plan on living here? I have to be very honest with you. We don't have money to spend on extravagances anymore, and I'm not even sure that we can afford to house and serve you in the manner that Edgar would have wanted."

I saw Mariette swallow anxiously. My mother was imposing, and I felt a little of Mariette's anxiety myself, desperate that she would give a winning answer. I might add that my mother always got to the point of things. She never shied away from hard questions or difficult decisions. I had to admire her assertiveness and will at times in this world of ruling men.

Mariette put down her knife and fork and looked directly at my mother.

"Madame," she said softly. "I loved your son. He was good to me, and I felt it a duty and an honor to present you with his own son. I could not go through life denying you of ever meeting him, and trust me . . . to come here was not an easy decision. As for your concern, I am not here to take your money, nor press upon you for hospitality, especially as I have no need for extravagances. But I do hope that you will recognize Samuel, who is an innocent thrust into an uncertain environment from birth and who will never truly know his father as I had the fortune of knowing him. I can tell you that your son was devoted to you, and I do remember him being unsure about writing to you, whether the truth about war would upset you. What to tell you of the damage that was done to his body then barely recovered by the time he was sent back to fight again. I can only tell you that the last time I saw him, he was battered and eager to be done with it all to return to you. He said that when he thought that he must be strong, he would think of you and remember the unwavering faith you had in all that he did."

I had been so focused on Mariette that by the time I had turned to Mother, I was alarmed to find that her watery eyes and quivering lips had betrayed a lack of composure. I refrained from asking if she was all right, as I could see that she was attempting to maintain her self-control and would have objected to any fuss. She put down her fork, which had been in her hand, a now useless implement, and picked up her serviette to dab first at her mouth. She blinked several times.

"Thank you for your candor," she said, and commenced to stand. I, too, began to rise to help her, but she waved me away.

"Tell Peggy to bring the tea to my room, please, Rudy."

I nodded.

She walked from the room, and Mariette looked dismayed. "I'm so sorry," she said. "It seems I've upset her a second time."

"No, Mariette, you have reached my mother's heart," I said, smiling, for the words had reached me, too.

We finished the rest of our meal quickly in silence, and I escorted Mariette to the kitchen to collect Samuel; then we sat on the front terrace near the entrance gardens to watch Bert feed the ravens that bobbed across the lawn. His "friends," he called them. Samuel ran toward Bert while Mariette called out to him to walk slowly. The birds fluttered skyward as the boy approached, but once at Bert's side, the ravens flew back down to peck at the seed he had scattered on the ground.

I took a sneaking glance at Mariette, at her profile, at the shape of her long nose that extended from just beneath her brow to just above her small, perfect lips. She was breathtaking, and I wanted to hold her then, to tell her how I was glad she had come, how the words of my brother had given us some kind of closure.

She turned, sun on her face, and shielded her eyes, as if she knew I was about to say something.

"Mariette, thank you so much for coming."

She smiled serenely, and I saw that her cheeks were flushed.

Peggy arrived with a note to give to Mariette.

Mariette opened the note, looked at it briefly, then closed it again. She seemed suddenly uncomfortable, and the pleasant feelings I had just experienced dissipated, for I feared bad news.

"What does it say?" I asked.

"I think it is from your mother, and she is asking me to leave."

I was stunned. Mother seemed very different at breakfast. Could I have misjudged the tears in her eyes for something else: offense perhaps?

"Do you mind if I read it?"

Mariette looked at the note and my hand outstretched as if there were a chasm there that was too large to cross, before finally releasing the note, and it was then that I discovered something else about Mariette. She spoke English, but she had not learned to read it.

I smiled and looked at her, and she could see instantly that I had become aware of her secret. Mother was taking a chance, as we were yet to hear from Roland, but I must admit the contents greatly pleased me.

"Mother has kindly asked you to stay. She said the guest room can be yours and Samuel's indefinitely, until we come to another arrangement."

I handed it back to her, and she looked at the letter. A mixture of happiness and amazement spread in equal measures across her face.

"Is that all she says?"

"Yes," I said. That was my mother. Clear and to the point, and I don't remember loving my mother any more than I did that day.

But despite my feelings, there were still things that weighed on me as I slipped uneasily into sleep that night. Like shapes in a fog I could not yet discern.

CHAPTER 6

I had received a reply from my employer to say they had covered for me with existing staff but that I had only till the following Monday before they would advertise for a replacement. My days at Lakeland were quickly coming to an end, and I dreaded leaving.

Bert was in the work shed by the stable, repairing some broken furniture, and I found Samuel beside him. Mariette had at first been reluctant to allow Samuel too far out of her sight, especially on the lake-side, so we tended to group on the terrace and gardens off the kitchen at the front of the property. But it was difficult to stop the boy from running and finding garden tools and other potentially harmful objects to amuse himself with, and he would sometimes disappear out of sight, much to his mother's worry. I watched Mariette try to herd him back to the house without luck.

It was Bert who came to the rescue and offered to take him to the work shed to distract him for a while. Mother had asked me to check the condition of our bayside property at Bardsea, which we were planning to sell. As well, to bring back a wall clock and a painting, and any other objects of value that she feared might be taken. The house had been rented out fully furnished after Father died, to help with financing, but it had sat unoccupied for a long period, and with people spilling into the cities for work, finding replacement tenants seemed unlikely.

Mariette hadn't talked much more about Edgar because, she told me, there was not much more to tell. I had relayed these exact words to Mother, and she had simply said the truth would come out at some point, but from the casual way she spoke, I felt she had already made up her mind. Something about the boy had struck a chord. Something about the child perhaps had reminded her of Edgar, a mother's sense maybe.

Mother had viewed the child as one would at a zoo or exhibition in the initial stages, but this quickly developed from curiosity. I believe she had seen something familiar there also, though hadn't yet admitted such. Mother seemed to find reasons to leave her room, returning a plate to the kitchen that she would not have otherwise done, gravitating to the rooms where the child was, perhaps just to judge for herself and watch him for signs of Edgar. It was hard to not be enchanted by his elfin-sweet face and thick straight fringe that draped his eyebrows.

I excused myself from Mariette to go to the car, and she followed me. She asked what I was planning for the day and curiously asked if she and her son could accompany me on the journey. I must admit, I didn't really want to leave her.

Mother had not interrogated her any further about Edgar. I could tell she was restrained around Mariette. She did not ask questions, and I believe that Mother was in turmoil over her feelings toward her. I did not feel it wise yet to share the possible age discrepancy of Samuel, as proposed by the doctor, versus the marriage certificate. I liked that Mother was warming to Mariette and did not want anything to mar the burgeoning relationship.

We sought out Samuel in the shed. At Mariette's suggestion of a drive to the sea, Samuel appeared not to hear, preferring to stay watching Bert's hands at work.

"Don't you want to come?" Mariette asked him in French and then again in English, to teach him. The boy then strangely looked to Bert for counsel, which I found most amusing.

"What? No words?" Mariette asked.

"Maman!" he said, and shook his head.

Bert kept busy filing a piece of wood to varnish, ever the diplomat and not inclined to interfere.

"Bert," I asked, "is it all right if he stays with you?"

"Yes," he said in his softly gruff voice, without raising an eye or pausing from his task.

Mariette furrowed her brow, then bit her lip.

"I suppose it is fine." She turned to me. "I imagine from all the travel, he is not keen for any more at present. It is just me, if that's all right with you?"

"Of course," I said, though quite what else could I have said?

I was not as good at driving as my brothers, and the car stalled a couple of times. We drove the winding country roads that took us south past woodlands. The air that breezed through the windows was cold, but this didn't deter Mariette, who was perched close to the door to catch the wind. We could smell the salt air before catching sight of the bay and the village houses beyond the hills.

The two-story white brick house, with sweeping coastal views and a large and overgrown back garden, sat high at the top of a road that meandered down through the village toward Morecambe Bay. The front door, exposed to the elements, looked in need of oiling, and paint was peeling from the windowsills. But these were things to me that didn't lessen the house's value, only heightened its appeal. Here it didn't matter that the house was neglected. The house did not have the majesty of the manor, but it was more attractive by its quaint simplicity.

I unlocked the door and was met with an earthy closed-up smell that disappeared quickly with the gust of sea wind that followed us in. Mariette breezed through the rooms, typical of someone who does not have the patience to put on airs. She rubbed her hand over dusty banisters not to test for cleanliness but to feel the smoothness of wood, and she curiously looked in cupboards and canisters.

I first checked the rooms for broken windows and signs of vagrancy, and everything appeared in order, then placed in the back seat several items that I thought Mother would want returned. Mariette followed me into each room during my final task, taking stock of minor repairs in a notebook. Once my appraisal was completed, she joined me at a top front window to view the village. We were both silent before she eyed me studiously, as if there was something she wanted to say and couldn't. I felt awkward being this close and alone with her, and when I spoke, my shaky voice revealed this.

"Do you want to walk to the sea?"

She smiled brightly.

"Yes, I do."

She reminded me of a very young girl as she bounced ahead of me down the stairs, holding up her skirt. She wore another of my mother's dresses, this time in sheer peach organza over the top of a cream shift with a wide cream sash tightly bowed at the waist, accentuating her slender frame, the hemline stopping only inches above the ankles. She wore a little hat to match that was flat on the top, which tied under her chin, and with a flower made in the same organza. It had been Mother's favorite outfit for a time. And as she reached the door, she turned to wait for me. I wondered whether I had been transferred to someone else's life. I felt strange and wonderful around her. She was linked to a tragedy, the fact that my brother had been killed after meeting her, had died perhaps only miles from where she lived, and yet her presence seemed to outweigh any sadness at that moment.

Though the sky had pulled across its cover of gray, we weaved our way through the village and toward the shore. When we reached the sand, Mariette wasted no time in taking off her shoes and hoisting her skirts upward slightly, revealing her lower legs. I took my shoes off, too, trying to assume composure and avoid staring at her in fascination.

Leaving our shoes behind, we walked along the sand flats, and when the first spots of rain appeared, I asked her if she wanted to turn back.

"Of course not!"

She walked toward the bay across the stretch of sand. Beyond that the water was not the usually brilliant, glistening blue today but a deeper, duller, menacing color.

She'd never been in the sea, she told me, yet she boldly and eagerly entered the shallow water. I cautiously followed her, keeping close. Unlike during our holidays in Blackpool, we rarely swam here as children, since the tides compromised the rigidity of the shorelines, and we were only allowed to wade a short way from any solid ground to search for cockles and inspect the shore crabs. There were gullies, and the flat sand shifted with the change in tides to become like quicksand.

"Don't go too far out!" I warned.

"Don't worry! I will go as far as I think I can."

She did not see until the last second that she was in danger of stepping into deeper seas where the shelf of sand deceptively dropped many yards. As she moved to step into the watery void, she realized her misjudgment and lost her balance, then attempted to correct herself. I lunged to catch her, and she turned to cling to me, peering down into the water behind her. When she turned back around, our faces were so close, and during the brief interlude that we were fused, I pondered irrationally whether to kiss her. She laughed fearlessly to break the moment, and I released her gently so she could carry on with her exploration unperturbed.

We proceeded to wander carelessly along the more solid shoreline, our clothes blown tightly against our bodies as we attempted to talk above the whistling winds. Viewing the sky that was filling with rain clouds, I knew that our time here was limited and suggested we make our way back. There was silence for a period as we walked, almost loitered, back toward the grassy sandbank.

It dawned on me suddenly that she had told us little about the people she had lived with in France. She had given us glimpses, but much of her stories were filled with descriptions of geography and just occasionally the turmoil of war. And much of her talk had also been about us, Edgar's memory of family.

"Do you have any family anywhere that may be alive, do you think?"

"No," she said firmly. "No one."

Some children had run over the hill toward the sand with colored buckets, and it distracted her briefly. She turned toward them, catching the loose strands of hair that flicked her face.

"If you weren't here, where would you go?"

The smile she had on her face waned slightly, and a frown appeared briefly, fighting the urge to remain in the middle of her forehead.

She turned back to me, eyes darker than before.

"I would go home, of course, to what's left. Pick up from where I was before. Work perhaps at an orchard somewhere. We grew apples and pears in our orchard. Did I tell you that?"

"No."

"Yes, the war took it all away."

"I'm sorry."

And I confined the walk with a period of silence, not knowing how any words could compensate.

"It was madness most times," she said. "Being near the front line. The crackling of rifle fire at night, the shelling that was intense for days. One day we narrowly missed out on being bombed, a mortar shell taking out part of our property. But I only experienced a small piece of it, compared with others. It was much worse for Edgar, for soldiers. It was dreadful for everyone."

"That sounds frightening. It must have been very unnerving to live like that from day to day."

She bent down, picked up a seashell, and examined it, then showed it to me.

She smiled, and I smiled back, unsure of what it all meant, what we were to each other. I had feelings for her, strong ones. Were they the thoughts of a naive, hopeful boy or something deeper? Talk of Edgar should have driven away any physical feelings toward her, but I felt close to her, and a bond had easily formed. I had to know her better, as I believed there was so much more to know.

We put on our shoes, and she corrected her skirt. Then we proceeded slowly in the direction of the house again: reluctant to leave or reluctant to fight what I felt perhaps we shared. But a final burst of heavy rain sent us closing the remaining distance quickly. I opened the door to let her through, and we shook the heavy drops from our clothes and watched the rain briefly through the doorway. I half thought to close the door, imagining us alone. She suddenly stepped forward and kissed me on the cheek. As I reached toward her, she stepped away just as suddenly and ran for the car.

I felt young then, and silly, and I locked up the house and followed her, sliding into the driver's seat and winding up the window against the wet.

"Thank you," she said as the car hummed and bounced once again past farmers' fields and through tunnels of overhanging tree canopies along the road northward.

"I have often wondered what it was like to have sand between my toes," she said. "Only once did I step on sand, though it was too brief to remember."

I wanted to ask where and when, but the silence within the car felt strangely warming and no longer awkward, and the window washers that moved rhythmically back and forth lulled us dreamily into other thoughts. The kiss had broken down some of my guardedness.

We returned, and Peggy, rolling dough in the kitchen now with Samuel, saw the state of our damp clothes. Mariette slipped quietly back to her room, and I stood to explain, but Peggy put up her hand, gave her famous raised eyebrow when she saw something she didn't wish to hear, and handed me a piece of paper.

The note was from Roland, asking me to come and see him when I had a chance. *There is much to discuss.*

The rain had eased, so I rode Sheriff to Ulverston, back in the direction we had just come from, and tied him outside Roland's office. I was still floating from the time I spent with Mariette, from the kiss that had sped my heartbeat, and the excitement and trepidation at what I was about to learn.

Roland sat in the office behind his big desk, a stately place, though not as tidy as many: books opened and notes attached and papers scattered into somewhat organized chaos.

"I'm terribly sorry for the current state," he said. "I have a rather large case on. It is a matter of the future of the Lakeland. Developers . . . they are hanging around and buying up lands here from those who can't afford to keep them, or without children to hand them down to. But now . . . let me see." He took out some papers from beneath a pile on the desk and examined them quietly for several seconds.

"Firstly, I have requested a copy of the revised listing of service personnel missing in action, which is for your mother. I will forward it to you as soon as it arrives."

I nodded my thanks.

"As for the other matter, I attempted first to find a birth certificate, but there was no registration recorded for a Samuel Edgar Watts. I tried several variations from that, but the date you have given me and the vicinity does not show up anything. I did, however, retrieve a list of addresses of those with the same name of Lavier . . . the maiden name of the woman in question here, I daresay. There were none with the name 'Mariette Lavier' from the region, though several with that surname in various places in and around the area. You could write to those addresses if you wish. But if what she says is true about her family, then I expect it will likely turn up nothing."

He passed me a neatly handwritten list of names and addresses.

"As for the marriage, this is probably the most interesting. The certificate was signed by a priest from a village that had been destroyed, and I was pleased to learn he was still alive and living in another parish further south. I did manage to contact him by way of telegram, and he responded immediately by letter. There were several he married hastily without the use of banns, since the war had no tolerance for them. The register in the church was destroyed, and he has since been trying to put together a list of names himself. He does vaguely remember a wedding just before his village was bombed, but he said that after the war, he was very busy with foreign soldiers marrying Frenchwomen. He does, however, remember a girl named Mariette with auburn hair."

"Did he mention any witnesses?" I asked while scanning the letter he had passed to me.

"Only that he has a vague recollection of the father of the girl being present, but that's all unfortunately. Meanwhile I checked the name you gave me, and there is a registration of death for a Jerome Pierre Lavier from Bailleul in 1918 . . . But I think there are more queries you need to pose to the young lady, such as if there were any other witnesses, documents, and specific dates. To help learn more you would need to be aware of someone perhaps there at the birth. And I daresay that legally, as well as convincing your mother, these are items that are most certainly important."

I said it seemed strange that we are such a suspicious lot that we no longer simply rely on the word of someone. And he agreed.

"It is exactly that suspicion that keeps me in business," he said.

I wondered what Mariette would think about the depth of our investigation, most of which she was unaware of. She seemed unconcerned that we were checking the validity of the certificate. She had to be telling the truth, I told myself. It seemed absurd to think otherwise. There was too much now: a wedding, a photo, and not least a child. And of course, which I still held to be in her favor, her word.

"And then there is one last thing and possibly something that could set back some hopes for the child should a claim be made for the inheritance. There is no birth record of Mariette, either."

Feelings of hopefulness faded slightly. "Perhaps she was born with a different name."

"Perhaps. It is probably the most important issue. Here in summary is a woman without a record of her birth, a child without a record, a missing husband in war. It is a most difficult and sensitive situation. Are you aware of all the terms of your father's binding will?"

"Yes, I am."

"Because if Samuel is somehow proven to be Edgar's son, everything changes. I believe that the evidence as it stands is unlikely to result in a successful claim, and I also have to assume that Laurence would likely challenge it if it were presented."

"That's an understatement," I said, and he chuckled, shrewd to have recognized my undertone, and all too aware of our traits.

"As you know, under the terms of inheritance," he continued, "if such a claim is proven to be true, Samuel would replace Laurence as the heir to the estate, in which case Abigail would be his legal guardian until he comes of age. And during this time she can still make all decisions concerning the estate. But it seems that without more evidence your brother may well have a strong case against such a claim if it were to be raised. I'm not sure if it's your intent to pursue the avenue that Samuel is Edgar's son, but if it is, then you would undoubtedly require additional proof. And without records and witnesses, I'm not sure this can go much further."

I could not see Laurence giving up any part of the estate without a fight. He would most certainly make a challenge of his own. But if Mariette was telling the truth, then it would also do Edgar a great injustice to not fight for her.

My head had been filled with ideas on the ride back to the manor. There was no denying the fact that my feelings were racing ahead of facts, but I still believed there were further truths from Mariette that had yet to emerge. I felt there was something she was keeping from me that would be the solid proof I needed. Could it be it was something to be ashamed of? Perhaps the evidence she provided would make the timing of the birth and the marriage more visible. Could she be protecting us from certain knowledge, protecting our name?

Mother was waiting in the dining room as I arrived. I had decided that I would not discuss this privately with her first, that I would open the discussion up with all of us together. It would at least require Mother to continue speaking directly with Mariette rather than through me. Mariette had already said she was not here for the money, and though I believed it for the most part, there was a niggle there, from the wryness and the look of the lawyer who was used to many and varied devious states of play, and something else, my own instinct, telling me that pieces of the story were missing.

Mother made polite talk, and the two women avoided much eye contact, though they sat directly across from each other during dinner. Mariette wore her freshly laundered white dress, and I had to presume she was relieved at not having to wear Mother's dresses in front of her.

After dinner I spoke about the meeting with Roland as they watched me expectantly. Though for some reason, perhaps because of the way I felt for Mariette—I can say with more clarity that love was beginning to cloud my judgment—I did not mention that "Mariette Lavier" did not actually exist as such. This was an issue I would raise with her privately.

"And there is no birth certificate for the child. Could it be in some registry somewhere, never being lodged?" Mother was looking at me when she asked this, reminding me that I was yet to reveal to her a possible discrepancy surrounding Samuel's date of birth, but the question was for Mariette.

"We did not have time," said Mariette. "He came early, with fighting still around us. It was mayhem to the end. That is all I can tell you. The sister who delivered my baby died, and the hospital is now gone."

"It seems there are a lot of dead people in the story and the war is convenient for missing information."

I was a little ashamed of Mother since Mariette had already described to me how bad it had been there.

"Madame, it was not my intention to dupe you as you are suggesting. I would never once think to take anything personally from you. I feel very proud that I have been able to bring you your grandson."

Mariette had not known Mother long enough to know that her barbs were customary. That if she said nothing cynical at all, we would be worried about her.

"Mariette, is there any way we can get in contact with anyone you know of who could verify the birth or the marriage?" I interjected.

"There are people who knew us briefly at the time, but I do not know their surnames or how to contact them."

Mother threw up her hands.

I stopped the conversation there and asked if Mariette could leave while I spoke to Mother alone.

"You should have spoken to me in private," she said, annoyed, once Mariette had left the room.

"Mother, it is now something we have to decide on."

"I can tell, Rudy, that you are for the girl and the child, and I do pity both of them. But I cannot include them on a permanent basis without proof. It is obvious she had a connection with Edgar somewhere, somehow, but this is a temporary arrangement only, while we verify the child is indeed Edgar's. I'm not saying she is . . . that way, deceitful, of course, but legalities we must pursue. I have been very generous, and though, sincerely, I like them I'll admit, must I be the only one who is thinking clearly and without any bias? We must tread carefully if we are to make informed decisions."

She had a point of course. Even though I'd convinced myself that the feelings I was developing toward Mariette were separate from my beliefs concerning the legitimacy of her claim, such feelings would not be considered helpful to ongoing investigations.

"And you know very well what this means for Laurence."

I could also see Mother's dilemma. It was her duty to protect all parties, Laurence included. And she knew as well as I did that any change would not sit well with him.

She stood up. "I need the war record that has Edgar's name. Tell me the moment it arrives. I need proof of that as well. And even then I am not sure I will believe he's gone."

We parted, and upon nearing my bedroom, the faint sound of sobbing led me back down the hallway toward the guest room and Mariette.

"I'm so sorry," she uttered quietly from behind her shut door.

I knocked softly, and the crying stopped. She opened the door, eyes puffy and red, then turned to sit down at the edge of the bed.

She put her finger to her lips. With Mariette's improved health, Samuel had been moved back to the annex attached to her bedroom, where he was sleeping.

Mariette was holding a piece of paper.

"Your mother will never trust me," she said softly.

I moved to sit next to her.

"If it's any consolation, I believe you, Mariette."

"I did not want to do this because it would seem there is something sinister in the reasons I am here. This is only for you to see and not your mother."

I recognized Edgar's handwriting on the small note she handed me. It stated that should anything happen to Edgar, Lakeland Manor and the estate were to be passed to any child resulting from his union with Mariette Lavier, appointing her also as the trustee for the estate until the child came of age. It also mentioned several personal items that were to be passed to me. It was signed by Edgar but not dated.

Some might say that forgers are clever, and information about a person shrewdly obtained, but I believed the note was in Edgar's hand, in the way his *t*'s trailed so finely, and his signature so much of his personality in the large but delicate strokes. It wasn't only that I recognized the script, but that I felt him in the words also.

"Why didn't you show me this before?"

"You know why."

I had in fact seen the glaring change that would affect Mother. Edgar had removed all Mother's rights, and she would be at the mercy of Mariette if she were to stay on at the manor.

"He wrote this when we parted for the last time," she said.

If she knew I suspected a different age of Samuel, she did not show it. Perhaps it was only that which I felt was missing from the things she had told me earlier, and something she felt might affect Samuel's chances of acceptance or inheritance. I was tempted to question her about the date of his birth, then wondered what benefit it would serve. As a matter of course, more details would surface, and I would delay it till then. Regardless of timing, Edgar and Mariette had sealed their union perhaps not only for love, but to protect the child.

"I thought that just bringing the boy, who I believe is so like his father, would be enough," she said. "I thought the certificate would be enough. But this letter especially affects Abigail."

She was right. Mother would be hurt. Edgar couldn't change the terms of Father's will, but he could appoint a temporary estate manager and trustee in the event of his absence, or for a child not yet of age. Only in the event that something happened to Mariette would the estate management fall back again to Mother, along with any guardian-ship of beneficiaries.

It must have meant that Edgar trusted Mariette, after knowing her for such a short time. Some might think such precautions about any future children extraordinary; yet knowing Edgar's attention to detail, I did not believe this was out of character. But what I was most curious about was why he would replace Mother with someone who did not understand the business. Unless of course Mariette knew much more than she was letting on.

"But please say nothing of this yet!" she implored, and held out her hand to receive back the notepaper. "This bequest will make Abigail suspicious of me once more. I have to allow more time for her to see that my intentions are good, and to accept Samuel as her own blood. And, Rudy, even when the will does eventually come to the attention of your mother, I promise that Lakeland Manor will always be your home and hers."

She was in fact simply buying time, and with every intention of presenting the will at some point.

She closed her eyes and rubbed her temples. "I'm afraid the day has caught up with me and I am very tired. Samuel will no doubt be up early."

A will, a photo, a marriage certificate, and the priest who could perhaps identify her should it come to that. But even that would not be enough for Laurence. I knew him too well. Mother was relying on the typed record from the registry of deaths in service to come to give her closure on her son's death. As if this would somehow signify a change. But I wasn't so sure she would ever find closure, and she would perhaps never fully trust Mariette even if she accepted this as Edgar's true and final wishes.

And if Mariette was not here for the boy, why was she here? She knew well enough about the estate and the effects of the will: a fact that would haunt me in times to come. Despite her verbal declaration of intent, the idea that she might be here for the money that the estate could bring her crossed my mind. But I vowed not to allow myself to think such things that might dent my feelings of goodwill. The child, I believed, was Edgar's, and Mariette was innocent of any kind of subterfuge. She was strong and independent, yet I felt she was vulnerable as well. I would still, given there was yet some information unknown, do everything I could to protect her and her son.

CHAPTER 7

Mariette had taken hold of my thoughts; the kiss replayed over and over in my mind. I was not looking forward to returning to work in Manchester or wallowing in my small flat the following week with images of her at the manor without me.

If I could work the land and the house like Bert and plough a field and groom the horses for the rest of my days, I would be a happy man. I could not bear the idea of losing access to the estate, though I felt it was simply a matter of time and money, regardless of whose hands it fell to. I had no high-paying career ahead, or grandiose ideas like my father. I was not like Edgar, who was born for success, or Laurence, who was born for London society. I was perhaps part like my grandfather, who enjoyed the country life, and part a new breed in the Watts clan also: someone who craved ordinary. I had not even contemplated a wife, not like Edgar, who said he would marry one day as if there was no doubt that this had to happen, or Laurence, who loved the attention of women. In the absence of any serious relationships, I had already prepared myself for a life of bachelorhood.

After breakfast on the terrace the following day, Samuel was keen to find Bert again to collect the eggs from the chicken coop at the back of the stables. I asked Samuel if he liked it here, and he nodded politely. He had grown more confident in the time since he had arrived, and without the dolefulness and trepidation he had first displayed. He ran off in the direction of the stable after Mariette excused him early from the terrace table.

We talked of Samuel and her desire for him to ride a horse, and I learned of her love of horses also. She told me she had ridden many times during her childhood. I was pleased we had that in common and wondered whether she might own riding clothes.

"You have brought such a small bag of items," I commented. "Did you want to send for the rest of your things?" I hoped that I didn't sound too expectant.

"No," she said distantly, watching Samuel disappear from view. "It is all I have." She excused herself quickly, perhaps to avoid any further talk of Edgar's will. However, I had made the decision not to say more about it unless she first raised it.

Peggy had continued to raid Mother's treasure trove of clothes that she was planning to give away to the poor, but she found the fashions, though as fine as any other, were from the previous century. I sought out my mother to learn how accepting she was of Mariette wearing more of the clothes Mother no longer wore.

"I think she has enough of my castoffs now. I insist that we use a portion of finances to buy her some clothes. Take her to Kendals." Mother's favorite fashion emporium in Manchester since her dress-maker retired. "I suspect Mariette will be here for some time yet, and while she is here, she must at least represent us at her best. I suggest you take her to the city as soon as you can."

Despite everything going on, Mother was still about propriety. The fact that on the odd occasion we had a visitor, we must at least appear with means. And in a rare show of spontaneity and appreciation, I leaned down to kiss her on the cheek.

"What was that for?" she said, a little red-faced.

"It is for all the things you are trying to do and will do again."

Since it was not yet midmorning, we had time to catch the train and be in Manchester before noon. Peggy said that she would keep an

eye on Samuel. Mariette had seemed a little embarrassed by the suggestion at first but agreed to go. She told Samuel that she would bring
him back something.

"Would you like him to come, too?" I asked.

"As you have already witnessed earlier, he is tired of travel, and he
travels even worse than me."

Bert drove us to the station, somewhat fast I might add, fearing
we'd miss the last morning train, and Samuel stayed with Peggy with
promises of sweet treats. I sat beside Mariette on the train and saw some
people view her curiously. She displayed a youthful curiosity peering out
from the train windows to wave at strangers on the platform, to search
for the stationmaster who whistled the departure, and then to point
to objects along the way, speaking without fear of someone hearing or
judging her in some way.

We disembarked onto the exchange station in Manchester, filled
with the sounds of human commerce. The streets were busy with shop-
pers, noisy with trams and cars and horses and carts. Mariette absorbed
everyone and everything, as if afraid she would miss out on something.
In Kendals emporium, she viewed the women's fashions as she walked
along, and I could tell that others were intrigued that someone so young
could be dressed in the restrictive fashions women had freed themselves
from a decade ago.

The sales assistant was at first curious and awkward perhaps because
she was unsure of Mariette, who was not shy in rushing to the dresses
and pulling them off the rack. The assistant was slightly vexed, as if
being faced with a boisterous child, but she soon fell under Mariette's
charms also and seemed eager to find dresses to suit her.

Two dresses were chosen for her, but I think Mariette would have
loved anything. The first was pale yellow-gold with a large sash on the
hips, short sleeves, and a cropped coat to match for the cooler months
just ahead, with fur around the collar. The second was in a dusky pink
with a dropped waist, chiffon overskirt, and flowers embroidered over

one shoulder. The back was cut low, exposing much of her smooth skin. As well, I bought her a black shawl, a pair of shoes, stockings, a velvet wrist purse, and hats to match both dresses. She purchased with her own money—even though I pressed upon her that I would pay—a silk handkerchief from the men's section and butterscotch sweets from the confectionary department for Samuel. I watched her count out the money carefully, calculating every cent that would remain.

I still had enough in the allowance to take her to lunch at Lyons Tea Rooms and return by nightfall on the train. She kept the yellow dress on, and I watched the men pass us on the streets. She was unusual to look at, a certain exotic foreignness about her that made her also mysterious, and I felt proud to have her on my arm. I do not know if she was aware of the interest she caused, but I am certain that she did indeed feel beautiful, and I caught her spying herself in the glass windows as we passed.

Mariette was thrilled that there were French-sounding meals on the menu. I ordered the sole, and she ordered a cocotte of game, and we chose profiteroles to follow. With two glasses of wine, it was then my time to talk, to tell her more about my life, about my stutter, about my love for my brother, though I tried very hard not to sound too deep and turn the situation into another wake. I wanted to feel better about the past, and in some way I thought that Mariette and Samuel had been sent here for that very reason. As if my brother had willed it so.

By the restaurant window, she watched the people in the streets and chatted about the differences between Britain and France. How the people in France liked to stare back, but the people here pretended they weren't looking. I laughed at her assessment. She appeared young at heart and unafraid. I assumed she would barely have turned eighteen when she fell pregnant, according to Dr. Macklin's assessment. And this was another thing that surprised me about Edgar: that he would take to someone so young. The women he had courted in the past had been his own age or several years older.

On the way to the train, I had the sudden urge to take her somewhere else. I had heard of a club, recently opened, that played jazz music, and I was keen to listen. Mariette and I took a table, and I ordered glasses of champagne. She had never been to a club or a dance hall, she said, but she was excited to try one. Perhaps in some way I was trying to copy what Edgar would have done, and I could see clearly how he had fallen in love. However, our time there was brief. I suggested we leave so as not to miss the last train. I was also looking forward to spending some time alone with her.

On the return train Mariette was still talkative at the start, but the travel and the excitement caught up with her, and she fell sideways onto my shoulder. She smelled fragrantly sweet, and I yearned to wrap my arms around her and breathe her in for the entire journey. Her company, I had begun to crave, and from this point forward, my addiction worsened.

Bert was not there at the station to meet us, and I realized that I had given him an earlier time for our arrival. I wondered guiltily how long he had sat there before he had given up.

I insisted on carrying the bags of shopping, and Mariette took off her new shoes to walk barefoot, to feel the dewy soft grass beneath her feet as we cut across fields to reach home. The half-formed moon shone down on the end of our very pleasant day, and Mariette had made me feel happier than I had for some time. I wanted her then like I had never wanted anyone else. I stopped her on the track that followed the descent into the blue, star-filled valley close to home, put down the bags, gently grabbed both her shoulders, and kissed her. I can't say what came over me, only that I am human after all.

She responded with ardor at first, and then pulled away abruptly. I felt uncertain then as to whether I had crossed a line, followed suddenly by shame that she was my brother's wife.

"I'm so sorry, Mariette," I said humbly. "That was careless of me and in no way your fault."

"Of course it is not my fault! You are a man, and that is what men do."

I thought she was being serious at first, and I felt worse, that I was some kind of animal also. But she followed this quickly with a small laugh and then ran ahead of me toward the moon that hung nearly to the ground.

"And I would be a hypocrite," she called behind her, "if I blamed you in any way. If you are guilty, then so am I."

She was intriguing and beguiling, and I watched the yellow shimmer in front of me, daring me to run my hands over it. But I daren't of course. There was a certain order to such things, and I was determined, in that moment anyway, to not lose control of my head.

We reached the house, and she went into her room but not before she put her hand to my cheek, then kissed the spot where her hand had lain.

She left down the hallway, and I was filled with such excitement and wonder that all I could do was lie down on top of my bed, unchanged, and think of her for hours until I was showered in sunlight through the window and finally fell asleep.

Peggy woke me a short time later and said that Mother wanted to speak with me.

I dreaded it. Her summons usually meant she had found complaint. I sought out Bert first in the work shed to give him my apologies.

"No need," he said. "I had a nice sleep in the car while I waited. When it got too late, I supposed you had decided to sleep at your apartment."

This didn't make me feel any better. I sought to make it up to him by helping him with more maintenance that day and perhaps giving him an afternoon off if he would accept it. I had behaved like Laurence, I thought, uncaring of the inconvenience caused to others. I dragged myself to Mother's villa, and she was still in bed. On her side table, there was a photograph of the three of us as boys, taken at the rear of the property: Edgar with his eyes averted, perhaps at a more interesting happening on the lake; Laurence daring the lens to find only him; and me looking curiously unsure at the both of them and attempting to understand where I fit in, if indeed I did.

"Are you well?" I asked her.

"I've had better days," she said. "And tomorrow I daresay will be one of them. But that is not why I have called you in." She paused. "Mariette visited me this morning."

I waited silently and withheld my surprise that Mariette would be so bold as to visit Mother in her private rooms, and at what could have been so important. Could Mariette have been displeased with me? Could she have said something about what had happened between us? Could she have presented Edgar's will?

"You have done a wonderful job. She has shown me the two lovely dresses, and she told me how well you looked after her."

"Yes, it was a good day!" I said, relieved, but the relief was only brief.

"Rudy, I will only say this once. Mariette is a bright girl, and I can see why any man might fall for her. But don't make a fool of yourself. You have a duty as her chaperone and only that."

I realized later that I must have carried every thought on my face, that perhaps I was as naive as Mother had always thought.

"And if I *should* make a fool of myself?" I dared.

She looked away. She did not intend on saying anything else.

I walked from the room, wondering what Mariette might have said. Pride told me not to query Mother's full meaning and what else was on her mind. I did not want the cold message in my ears, but I assumed she was saying that if Mariette was indeed Edgar's wife, then she must remain so. And it reminded me again that Edgar was Mother's favorite, though she would never admit it of course.

What would it take for Mother to love me like she did Edgar? And was it so wrong for a man to fall for his dead brother's wife?

Feelings of doubt were now creeping in, backed by the fact that I hardly knew the woman. Most of her stay had been spent in her room with illness.

I walked onto the terrace and spied Mariette running between the boxed gardens that lined the length of the driveway. Samuel was chasing her, and I could hear the bells of her laughter ring out far across the valley.

She waved gaily, a different picture from the one when she had arrived. She had adapted so quickly, accepted things, returning, I gathered, to the girl she was before. I waved back, willing her beside me yet knowing that Mother was right. I had no claim to Edgar's past. The best Mariette and I could be was friends. She had run from the kiss and was polite when she said good night. She had perhaps tried herself to tell me that such attentions weren't welcome. But in the back of my mind was that time in the house by the bay. She kissed me first that day. There had been something there: some willingness for something more. Surely I had not got it so wrong?

I spoke to Bert and offered him the afternoon off, which of course he refused. We took stock of the tasks we needed for maintenance, and I took a list of the items we would need to purchase to accomplish them. Bert was wondering if he could hire an apprentice, a young boy of fifteen years who had originally traveled up north from a workhouse but was soon to be let go from one of the farms. It was likely a silent plea from Bert also, a small surrender that he was looking for a way out for me more than for him, knowing that I'd had to do some of the labor to help him. I said I would get back to him, though in my head I had already been planning for this. Selling the bay property would provide funds to modernize the manor, better support the tenants, and hire more help for Bert until the economy righted itself. While Mother was still the trustee, I would take advantage of all the ways to improve and maintain the estate.

Back in the house, Mariette and Mother were already in the dining room, Peggy told me. I put my hand on the handle of the door to enter but stopped myself. It was best I leave some distance until I could get my head clear. I decided I would leave the two women alone this time. Several days hence, I would be back at work, and perhaps I would need to look for new accommodation since the lease of my current Manchester address was about to run out.

Peggy brought my dinner to the room and didn't ask why I requested this. I know she had long been my mother's confidante, and no doubt Mother had told her of her fears. I did not wish to give away anything else that might be taken back to Mother. I was in a vastly different state than the previous day.

There was a knock on my door after dinner. Presuming it was Peggy collecting my tray, I was surprised to see Mariette instead. She slipped into my room and shut the door behind her.

"I have just put Samuel to bed, and I thought we might spend a little time together. You seemed quite distant earlier."

I looked at her face, which seemed sincere, though all I could hear were my mother's words that had plagued and temporarily ruined all thoughts of Mariette for me.

"I am sorry, Mariette," I said. "I have things on my mind and some correspondence I need to attend to." It was true in part. Sorting out my feelings about Mariette, Mother's last words, and assessing what assets to sell.

"Is there something in particular you wish to talk to me about?" I asked.

"You seem in a dark place at the moment, and I don't like seeing you this way."

"I'm fine," I said stoically, though it sounded quite petulant, and anything but sincere.

She looked about her, then noticed the framed drawing of the manor on the wall above my bed and leaned forward to examine the signature at the bottom.

"You did that?"

"Yes."

"You are talented."

"It's just a bit of distraction."

"Then perhaps you should be more distracted," she said, throwing me a playful sideways look before moving to pick up a book from a shelf near my bed.

"I've actually come to talk to you about the . . ." She frowned and turned the cover of the book toward me so I could read it for her.

"Efficiency as a Basis for Operation and Wages," I finished for her. I had no idea what it was doing there. A book of Edgar's I had started curiously to read. I think it had been there for years.

"Yes, *Efficiency as a* . . . whatever you just said. Anyway, I think we should discuss it."

I couldn't help smiling.

"I don't think you do."

"Oh yes, I'm quite sure it would be fascinating."

She was attempting to lift my spirits.

I picked up the book and began reading to her.

"Stop, stop!" she said, humorously putting up her hands. "You win!"

It seemed that all my mother's words evaporated with the appearance of Mariette, and I felt determined that despite my misery, I would not take it out on her.

"That is much better. You are smiling." She stood up to go. "I shall see you tomorrow?"

"Yes," I said.

"Au revoir!" she said, and left a trail of the exotic scent of soap that she had arrived with.

CHAPTER 8

A cool breeze skimmed across the water toward me, ruffling my hair and cooling the dampness at my neck. The lake had captured the image of the downy hills on the other side, mirrored in the water's silvery-blue surface, and it beckoned to capture me, too. I couldn't wait a moment longer. The water was too inviting. I prized open the boat-shed doors that faced the lake, which had been jammed from the elements, then using the rusting lever, which had not been oiled in years, rolled the sailing boat on wheel tracks into the water.

The lake was another reminder of why I loved this place, and sailing had been something we had shared as a family, bonding us all briefly.

Mariette appeared at the edge of the lakeside terrace. She was holding on to Samuel, who was excited to see several other boats making the most of the sailing conditions. She wore her long black dress, and I assumed she was saving her new dresses for dinner.

She walked down the gentle slope toward me and took in my appearance as she approached. I had no shoes, and my trousers and sleeves were rolled up. Samuel spoke to her rapidly in French, and we both laughed at his enthusiasm.

"He wants to know if we can go on your sailing boat," she said. "He has been eagerly watching the boats from the window."

I remembered the thrill when my father took me out for the first time when I was very small. I could not deny Samuel such excitement, and I was finding it difficult to refuse Mariette anything.

I explained in English the safety of sailing. She would need to keep out of the boom's swinging path, and the peaceful breeze was deceptive when on land. It would be windy, the sailing fast. She translated for Samuel, who nodded, but he was so eager to climb on board that I doubt he listened to anything. The description, the way I made it sound risky, did not deter either of them.

"He is very excited," she said.

The bow of the boat parted the water slowly at first until the sail caught the full force of the wind. The lake glinted, and Samuel waved at the other sailors that passed by.

Mariette gripped the seat of the boat at the stern and held on to her hat with the other hand. She smiled back at me, facing the sun, squinting and beaming with exhilaration, and I felt so close to her then as we shared the same breeze. Something happened, I can't explain exactly, as I sat at the helm, looking down toward her, her face upward to me. In that moment I caught something, a sense, a knowing that things were about to change between us. I began to wonder if she thought of me in some other way. Her expression and pose were demure but beguiling, her smile secretive, if not seductive. Or was it all in my mind?

It was during this time, these moments that I wasn't very present in the boat, that we both failed to notice that Samuel was leaning too far over the side, and when the boat leaned slightly, he toppled off as easily as a ball from a tilted ledge.

I turned the sail so it was now swaying freely, the boat now stalled but rocking unsteadily. Mariette climbed across to the side where he had fallen, but I was worried about her also and told her to stay still. Edgar had always told me to never leave the boat for any circumstance, but the boy was yards away flapping wildly at the surface of the water.

"He can't swim!" shouted Mariette frantically. I dived in to reach him before he sank into darker waters, and then to drag him back to the boat, which had already moved several yards away. I lifted him up toward Mariette, who hoisted him from my arms to hold and comfort him. He had begun to howl from shock as I climbed aboard.

I was about to apologize for my failure to prevent his fall, but she did something odd then. She laughed, and the boy looked up at her curiously, the howling ceasing suddenly. Samuel laughed, too, his humiliation and the discomfort forgotten. And the guilt that I felt by not equipping the boy with a life jacket—that Father had never bothered with, either—eased in part.

"We should go back," I said, relieved, and not feeling the same level of joy shown by Mariette.

"Why?" she asked. "It is over now. We have all learned from that. I never make the same mistake twice. Do you want to stop, Samuel?"

"No," he said, his hair plastered across his eyes.

"Good. He will dry in the sun. We will be fine. Children are much more resilient than we think. They need to learn the hard lessons, and that life can change in an instant. Mistakes are the only way to learn."

She was strange and wild, I thought. She did not fuss about the wet clothes of the boy, something my mother and Peggy would have done. She held the boy a little longer, but he was suddenly eager to return to his place opposite Mariette.

As I finished fitting the boy with a life jacket, which had been in the boat all the time, she reached over to touch my hand. "This is wonderful!" she said, and I found that I could only look at the boy else give my heart away, not that I would avert my eyes from him again. I, too, would not make the same mistake twice.

We sailed for a time, and though I was soaked, it was strangely soothing to have the cold wind against my wet clothes, a way to slow my fast-beating heart. Mariette kept asking for longer each time I suggested we return, and by the time we disembarked, we were nearly dry.

in, Mother's turn, and the child now restless. It was important at least out of charity, as Peggy suggested, that Mariette and the child be shown some courtesy. Even though Mother was against it, I could not ask the newcomer to leave, as she had likely spent days traveling. She may have had little rest, assuming she had come from across the Channel. I could not set her and the child off into the darkening Lakelands to find accommodation.

I asked Mariette whether she and her son would care to sleep in one of the guest rooms since it was growing late. She let out a sigh of relief and nodded, but shook her head when I offered to carry her bag. She followed me toward the floor above, examining the wood-paneled stairway walls that held photographs of minor members of monarchy and well-known faces from London society, all of whom had attended manor events at the end of the previous century. Visitors these days were friends of Laurence, the last ones early in the summer: "vexing" men, according to Peggy, who left cigar ash on the rugs and wore their muddied riding boots across them without care. Poor Peggy had spent several days busily cleaning up after them.

I ignited the light above a large oak bed, and the lake-view guest room was revealed in lamp-lit shades of softened gold. Mariette's gaze fell across the books and prettily painted bowls on the shelf above the unlit fireplace opposite the bed, the green-and-peach floral wallpaper, the thick Moroccan rug, the ornate and elegant lamp bases, and the decorative, tapestried armchair in the corner. It was clear from the way she looked around in wonder, her eyes struggling to catch everything in the room, that she was overwhelmed by both the decadence and the size of the space. A writing desk overlooked the lake at the back, its hue now of blue deepened and shot with silver under the darkening sky. There was also a private bath area and a small separate room designed for visitors who once upon a time brought their personal maids.

The boy, introduced to me then as Samuel, was still solemn and keeping a close eye on me while he pulled uncomfortably at his fitted

Peggy took the boy by the hand as we approached the rear doorway and rushed him through to the warm kitchen as we followed, recounting the event. She *tut-tutted* me for allowing it, but she had seen many boyhood scrapes before. I went to my room to change, dizzy with visions of Mariette.

At dinner that night, Mother couldn't join us, and Peggy had set Mariette's place as the hostess in my mother's absence at the opposite end of the table. Mariette and I talked, seemingly uninhibited for the first time. She spoke something more of her time in France, each time a little piece of her past slipping through, of her father who had died, whom she had adored. Of their orchard and animals. It was one of the last places Edgar had seen, and in a strange sort of way, I was envious that he'd seen it. I wondered what he would make of my feelings toward his wife. I felt confused, conflicted, but even more certain that she was telling the truth.

Just as I was having those feelings, Mariette picked up her plate and walked to the head of the table to sit near me.

"I don't know why I have to sit so far away from you. It is a strange custom, don't you think?"

I laughed then, and she did, too. "Yes, I have to agree."

She reached across and put her hand over mine, and I thought how beautiful she was, how both loud and sweet was her laughter. And I wondered about her childhood, how much she must have been loved to have so much lightness in her heart.

"Has Mariette always been your name?"

She appeared caught off guard briefly before she slid her hand away, the back of my own still warm from where it had lain. I said it during a moment of incaution, remembering Roland's investigation, and feared now I had given something away.

"It is a strange question. Is that a question you ask everyone that you meet?"

"I-I-I'm sorry. I-I—" My stammering and difficulty to produce anything further seemed to highlight my guilt and crime. She relaxed suddenly, recognizing my struggle, and she moved again to cover my hand with hers. I focused hard on the exercises I'd been taught to slow my breathing and return my speech.

"It's all right, Rudy," she said warmly. "It is not a crime to be curious, and I realize under the circumstances you are right to query everything."

"I'm sorry if I sounded distrustful," I said, once more finding my voice. "It w-was not meant that way. It is such a beautiful name. I had not heard it before."

"I should go," she said, releasing my hand. "It has been a wonderful day."

She rose and left me with regret and reflecting on the insult I had perhaps caused. My question suggested that I still did not believe her. I was so consumed with want that I failed to contemplate the fact that she never answered the question. And I was angry with myself for drawing out the snake, which had been mostly asleep for some time now, to remind me that I was far from perfect, perhaps even unworthy of her attentions.

The next morning I left early and drove to town to check on the estate's bank accounts, deposit several checks, and withdraw some of my personal funds. Returning to the car, I passed a watchmaker and jeweler. In the window was a set of costume pink-and-black chandelier earrings; imitation stones had become much the fashion. Though relatively inexpensive, it was still a frivolous, fanciful spend, and a portion of my own savings. My mind, some might speculate, was no longer rational, and I wanted desperately to atone for the previous evening.

I returned to find that Mariette had taken Samuel for a walk in the woods and she had not yet returned. I took the opportunity to sneak into her room and leave the gift box on her pillow.

As I was leaving the room, I noticed the book that I had seen in Mariette's bag, sitting on the desk near the window. It looked exactly like the journals that Edgar always received at Christmas. I put my hand on top of the cover but was distracted by movement in the rear gardens. Mariette was collecting handfuls of flowers, soon to wither, and placing them carefully inside a basket that Samuel carried beside her. She had put color back into the darkened halls, with flowers and foliage already arranged in vases around the house. I looked once more at the book, with its dark-green cover and red binding that resembled Edgar's, with tattered edges and papers loosened. We were told that all his personal possessions were destroyed with him, so I had to assume the book cover was a likeness only. I looked up to see that Mariette was returning, and I quickly left the room.

That night at dinner she seemed unaffected by our previous conversation and appeared happy to see me. She wore the sleeveless pink dress with its deeply curved neckline, which exposed her long neck, arms, and back. The fabric molded to the top of her body before draping slightly at the waist and tightening again at her narrow hips. But more notably she wore the earrings that complemented both the dress and her eyes, and I could not contain my smile.

Mother joined us, and we made polite talk. But for some reason I found it difficult to talk, my mind on *her*. I think my mother could sense something also, and she became somewhat quiet and solemn. I then proceeded to try and engage Mother in conversation to no avail. She excused herself early with a headache.

Mariette and I shared a sherry, but it seemed the awkwardness of our first encounter had returned, and the tension between us was thick. There was wanting on both sides. She finally stood up to excuse herself, but as she made to go, I held her arm and turned her gently toward me.

"I'm sorry if I made you upset last night. And I'm sorry about this damned stutter—"

She laughed softly, interrupting the continuing speech I had prepared about my anxiety-fueled condition as well as my carelessness toward her. "You worry about things you shouldn't. You should not be ashamed of anything, Rudy."

She reached down then and cupped my face in her hands to kiss me. I was paralyzed with panic and wonder, unsure of what to do, what was expected, until finally she peeled away from me, her face flushed, and my fears then released too late.

That night I did everything I could not to go to her room to kiss her again, to tell her my feelings. *To hell with Mother!* I told myself. I tossed and turned. Could I do it? Was it right? Would Mariette think me common or bold? Was she waiting for me? I yearned and pined and prayed also. It was torture. It was love, I was sure of it. But despite the yearning, my head won the moment. I could not be so presumptuous nor put her in such a position. There was of course the boy to think of.

CHAPTER 9

Sweeping across the palatial foyer, visitors were greeted by two imposing doors, behind which an elegant hall extended two floors high. The floor was Italian terrazzo patterned in geometric shapes in shades of red, gold, and black. This was where my father had met my mother. It was my paternal grandmother's love of entertaining, with an invitation to my mother's family to spend a weekend here, that brought my parents together. Father had watched Mother from the viewing balcony on the first floor and knew immediately she would become his wife. Finding her fair and slim and light on her feet, he was smitten, and she was equally enamored with the handsome heir to a grand estate. Such stories I could see in the photographs. Though knowing my parents as I did, it was difficult to perceive the silent, fractious people as the charming debutante and handsome country gentleman whispering coy words of love at brief private rendezvous. Both prior to inheriting the estate and afterward, my father had shown little interest in farming matters and had relied heavily on Mother and the staff he employed to manage the property.

Half the top floor held a large suite that ran parallel to the lake. Edgar had claimed the space after inheriting the manor, and no one had rearranged the room since Edgar had left. Everything was preserved. Was it a little morbid? Perhaps, but it was the only thing linking us to him, and Peggy kept it as clean as the rest of the house, as if she were expecting him back. Mother used to visit the room often, but with her declining health, she more recently avoided the extra flight of stairs.

I ignited the lantern beside my bed and took it with me along the oak hallways. Up a set of stairs, I reached the top floor and turned toward Edgar's rooms. It wasn't the first time I had sneaked up here to watch the lake and imagine Edgar sitting there also. When I opened the door, I heard a sharp intake of breath. In the corner sat Mariette with a lantern of her own. She was dressed only in her sheer nightgown. She appeared visibly shocked and guilty that I had found her there.

"I'm sorry," she said, standing up.

"For what?"

"I shouldn't be here, but I had to see for myself where he lived, the room he had described. The striped gold wallpaper, the polished oak desk." She rubbed her hand over its surface. "Look, you can even see an indent from the last time someone wrote here. I was imagining it was left by him." She held up a piece of paper from a writing block, and I could see a faint etching. She studied my face as I did so.

"I'm sorry," she said. "This must be hard for you."

"And you especially," I said.

She nodded, pensively considering the objects around the room.

"I sense him here," she said.

"I'm afraid I don't know what you mean."

"He was connected to this room. It must have been a special place."

"Do you mean you can feel his spirit?" I asked.

"Not exactly. Just a shadow of him perhaps of how he was. I can see him sleeping in that bed, reading his books. My images of him are clearer here."

She ran her hand over a collection of books he had on the wall beside the window. She did not look sorrowful, rather curious and radiant in her ponderings.

"I imagine him everywhere at Lakeland," I said. "He was a big part of my life."

"I know," she said. "But I can tell you have been torturing yourself about his death. There is nothing you could have done to change it. You have to let him go."

"It isn't so easy."

She was watching me closely now, watching her.

She walked toward me then and placed her hand on my arm. I put my lantern down on the trunk at the base of Edgar's bed, and I took her in my arms, her head against my chest where my heart beat powerfully. I felt a strange mix of both passion and sorrow.

This talk of Edgar felt wrong alongside this intimacy, but when she turned her face upward toward me, I felt compelled to act. We kissed gently. After several moments she pulled away.

"Not here," she whispered, with no explanation necessary.

She collected her lantern, then clutched my hand with her other to lead me toward the annex nearby. I suspected that she had investigated Edgar's rooms previously. Once inside the annex she closed the door and placed her lantern on the floor. She removed her nightgown to let me see her briefly before stepping forward to reach her arms around my neck. We kissed slowly at first, my hands tenderly exploring until I could no longer contain my longing and I clung to her fiercely. Her hair, free and long around her shoulders, fell across my face as I pulled her gently down onto the single bed near the window.

I wasted no time to fuse our bodies, my arms around her narrow back, and she breathed my name several times, rising to meet me until our passions were spent and I collapsed to the side of her. When I raised my head to view her expression, our faces close, she smiled up at me, victorious in a way, before easing away from me and rising to sit at the edge of the narrow bed. From the window she gazed dreamily toward the lake and to the deep-blue hills beyond.

"This is paradise," she said. "No. This is heaven. There is nowhere on earth quite like it."

She was naked, and still, like a marble sculpture, one arm behind supporting her, the other resting on her lap, and her hair spilling down her back. I had moments to compare her to the same wanton pose I'd seen in museums before she stood up to leave. I reached for her wrist to pull her back down to me, but she resisted this time. She put on her nightgown and disappeared into the night without a word. And I wondered then what world she came from that she could slip in and out of my life and, with her gone, leave nothing but a gaping, empty wound.

I stood to dress before the rooster crowed and announced everyone to task. I went back to Edgar's room to see if there was any evidence of us. As I was leaving, I saw that a drawer was partially open. Inside, there were several papers left disorderly from whoever had searched through it.

I closed the drawer and wondered what they were searching for. And whether it was she. But only briefly, distracted as I was by blissful thoughts, and thoughts of purely her.

CHAPTER 10

The morning was dull, with a shower, and I wore the same clothes that smelled of Mariette. I yearned to find her. I had to see in her eyes whether last night had meant something or whether perhaps I was naive and amusing, or an object of pity. But in any case, I had to see her. A piece of me wanted to apologize, to tell her that it couldn't happen again until our relationship was officially sealed with an engagement. I was part ashamed and part excited, and I wasn't sure if, alone again with her, the first would override the other.

Samuel was in the kitchen and, Peggy reported, Mother and Mariette had already breakfasted and returned to their rooms. She said that Bert was visiting the farms today on the trap and said the boy could accompany him. He would be gone for hours, and she was making them lunch for the trip. Mariette had agreed that Samuel could go.

It was still quite early, and I hoped that the sunny days of autumn would not leave so quickly. The place, though beautiful when surrounded by snow and with wood fires burning inside, was limiting, and in years gone by, I would wait for months for the snow to melt, for the first new growth on the trees, so I was once again free.

I found excuses to idle around the kitchen a little longer until it became too obvious and Peggy was giving me knowing glances to suggest she saw through me. With breakfast passed, I decided to saddle Sheriff and ride out toward the fields and down the narrow track to the woods, where I let the horse roam in a grassy glade. Sheriff was rarely spooked, and trustworthy. There was no way I could sell him, and it was doubtful just how much I would get for him anyway. Chess, our youngest mare, would easily be sold for a fair price. But she had been Edgar's new foal only weeks before he left for France, and for this reason we could not part with her.

The sweet melodies of the starlings and the light breeze that rattled the leaves on the giant oaks brought some much-needed peace and composure to the exaltation and expectation I had woken to. I was determined to remain like this and not give myself away to Mother before she discovered the truth for herself, and to court Mariette in ways more befitting than with uncustomary nightly rendezvous. My resolution and the peace of the moment did not last long, broken by the sound of hoofbeats and the ground beneath trembling as another horse approached. At the edge of the small wood, Mariette brought Chess to an abrupt halt and threw herself off. Mariette wore a boy's riding pants, shirt, and boots that she had found in one of the trunks of clothes in storage. She rushed toward me, her hair free and framing her sweet face, as she wrapped her arms around my neck to kiss me.

She had a hunger, overwhelming and impossible to resist, that conflicted with her graceful feline appearance. While still panting from the fast ride and between her own breaths, she greedily consumed my own. She wanted me, and I could not contain myself any longer. She could have me.

She was dear to me and someone I must protect and respect, and these thoughts screamed at me to stop, to dignify her with chastity, to wait, but every inch of my body ached for her. Convention in that moment existed in some other time and place. She undid my shirt buttons and I hers, and I pulled her down into the dry leaves, our hearts beating against one another. She exposed a demanding and unapologetic ferocity that broke apart the confines of decorum; instead she seemed to extract from the wildness around us, as if she were an extension of it. We were unaware of sound or light, and in those most intimate euphoric moments, the world seemed to fade and recede respectfully.

Afterward we lay in the leaves, covered only by a blanketing beam of sunshine that had found its way through the clouds and the tops of the trees. She put her hand flat on my chest as I lay on my back. It was so fast, this relationship, yet her sudden appearance less than two weeks earlier seemed years away. "I think I love you," I said, barely able to catch my breath.

She rose up on one elbow, her chin cupped in the palm of her hand.

"Is that what you think, or is it that you are in love with how I made you feel?" she asked.

Her face was flushed and golden in the light, her hair so bright and wild around her face.

"It is love," I said too seriously. "And most certainly love for you. That you must know."

She sat up suddenly to climb into her shirt.

"Come!" she said. "Let's not waste any part of this day! Let's ride."

We dressed quickly, her enthusiasm infectious, then galloped through winding wooded pathways, across gently rolling pastures, and clattered dangerously over crags. She was an accomplished equestrian, and we rode without concept of time before stopping briefly on a heathery fell to glimpse the steely blue bay in the distance.

"I will race you there," she said, thundering Chess down the hillside.

"We should probably turn back soon," I called after her unconvincingly, but she chose not to listen. Sheriff sped after her, giddy, like me, from the excitement and spontaneity that trailed in her wake.

She touched the grassy slopes above the water moments before I did, but I caught her by the time we reached the shoreline, breathless and high from the chase. Our horses were frisky as their hooves pummeled and sprayed the sand, and Chess whickered at the salty air.

Mariette slid down to the sand and kissed and stroked the mare's face, and Chess returned with a nuzzling of her rider's shoulder. That moment captured in my heart forever, for it was beautiful, this love affair she had with horses. She had made it clear that she was a child of the outside, and I had vowed to know everything about her then, to understand what it was that made her different from any other woman.

"You are an accomplished rider," I said.

"My father taught me."

"And your mother?"

"I never knew her."

It was the first time she had presented me with something deeper about her past. Until that point, I knew only of her in the present, some of her time in war, and some of her time with Edgar. I felt certain then she had a past before Edgar that was thick with stories also, and I wanted to hear all of them.

"Did she die?"

"No, she left," she said. "But I don't want to talk about it. There really isn't much to say."

We sat on the sand, and I put my arm around her. From the hurt I was certain I heard between those words and the losses I knew about, I believed that she was in much need of nurture. That perhaps she was frailer than she portrayed. But I also had the sense that she could take care of herself when needed. I wanted to learn more of her time with Edgar, yet I feared that to raise his name might turn the conversation and undo what we'd begun together. I was so desperate to understand how she felt about us, and I wondered briefly if I was simply filling the void that had been left by Edgar. My self-doubt led me to also think that I was a poorer version of him in her eyes.

She had an uncanny ability to read my thoughts.

"I know that you are probably thinking about Edgar right now. That you are wondering if you are doing the right thing and why it is that I am with you and not still grieving. The point is, it has been some years, and I need to move on for the sake of myself and for Samuel. I do not want to grow bitter wondering what might have been, wishing for the past to come back so that I can finish it properly. I want to live, and I want to grow old with someone, and from the first moment I saw you enter the drawing room, I saw you not as his brother but as a man who is not like any other. I know a lot about you, Rudy. From everything Edgar told me, you are a good person, and he admired you."

I forced a laugh at that, though the words did not necessarily give me any security. The fact that she had said she wanted to grow old with "someone" still left me to wonder if it was really me she was referring to. The word felt disconnected from me somehow.

"I'm not sure that there is much to admire," I said to the sea.

"Well, he did. He said you were as honest as a man can be and you have only the best intentions for all. I know, Rudy, that you do not have the money to run the estate. I knew that before I came. But the boy must be with his family. That much I have always known. What I didn't know was how quickly I could fall for someone. That was never part of my plan."

She snuggled into me, and that "someone" that I was speculating about could only have been me. I felt better, and she pulled me down on the sand to lie beside her. We were alone here from the rest of the world, and under a faint shower of rain, we held tight to one another, fearful of our time here ending. I vowed then that I would marry her soon, and in that moment, it seemed unquestionable that it should be otherwise.

It was afternoon when we rode the horses back and took them to the stable. We were thirsty and hungry, and I knew that Mother would want us dressed and on time for dinner, if she turned up herself.

As we walked around from the stable, I saw a familiar car parked in front of the manor, and my heart sank. Laurence's shiny green convertible sat ominously like a spider waiting for its prey.

How to explain my brother leniently and without words like "selfish" and "vain" was difficult.

On the one hand Laurence was like my mother in his slightly cold and officious manner at times, but he did not have her head or heart when it came to other people's welfare. He also did not have her empathy, as selective as Mother's could be at times. Like my father he spent more than he owned, borrowed, then repaid late. But the difference was that where my father had no head for business, Laurence knew exactly what he was doing. He knew enough about law to know his rights, to delay creditors, and to find reasons not to pay; delaying tactics and cultivating relationships were the ways he always had the money to spend.

I am certain that Laurence had felt Edgar's popularity more than most. He had spent years trying to impress our parents but was unable to measure up to his older brother. Though this may have affected him, he was born affected also. He had never been sharing and would always find ways to upset the peace.

I walked a little more soberly with Mariette toward the front door. My brother's arrival had taken over the sweetness that had just occurred between us, that until then I had only imagined in dreams. She took my hand, squeezed it briefly, then let it go before we were seen. We looked a little disheveled: her hair, though hastily tied back, had several loose strands; her cheeks were flushed from our sojourn; and her linen riding shirt was badly crumpled. I imagined I appeared much the same. I hoped the redness in both our faces would be attributed to the wind against our journey homeward.

"Who is here?" she asked.

"My brother."

She looked at the house for a few moments and back at me. Her expression said nothing, though I knew she carried much information about him also.

"Edgar has told me about him. He is a little different from you, *non*? A little more concerned about himself?"

"Yes." She had summed him up well thanks to Edgar. Edgar and Laurence had had some terrible disagreements over the years. Laurence had also gone to war but had only seen a portion of battle before it was over. In some way I wondered if he felt a kind of victory that he had survived and not Edgar. I also wondered if our mother would have been just as upset if it were Edgar returned and not Laurence. A consideration that I think would have been in Laurence's mind also.

"Don't let him worry you, Mariette. He can be difficult, and you have my permission to leave the room if you do not feel comfortable."

She smiled. "Thank you, but I do not need someone's permission to leave a room."

Mother and Laurence were in the drawing room when we walked in. Mother wore an expression that I couldn't read, and she could do that well when required. But they weren't the only ones there. Laurence had brought two male friends with him and a girl as well. The men were dapper in dinner suits, and the girl dressed excessively shimmery for daylight hours. From the smell of alcohol about them, I suspected they had been celebrating long before their arrival.

Laurence's eyes were quick to discover Mariette, and I noticed that they stayed there purposefully, too long in fact, so I felt a pang of regret bringing her to meet him, and with such an audience.

"This must be Mariette," said Laurence, and he strode assuredly to greet her. He was impossibly handsome also. I felt weak.

"*Enchanté*, Mariette!" He picked up her hand, bent over, and kissed it. He left his lips there for too long also, and Mariette was first to draw away. I could see that Mother was still as a statue, but inside perhaps a tangle of nerves and concern about the unpredictability of Laurence and the fate of another pretty female guest he had brought with him to pursue.

We were introduced to his friends, who prattled on about nothing of interest, about some people they knew in London, and the group laughed amongst themselves at a private joke. The girl, I noticed, looked up and down at Mariette curiously. Mariette remained beautiful in her riding outfit: a fact I am certain no one missed. She made an excuse to leave, and Laurence said that he hoped she would return soon. Mariette did not respond but looked down coyly, a reaction I had only seen her have with me. The attention was obviously distracting, and if I could have plucked out Laurence's eyes without objection as he watched her leave the room, I would have done so. Mother used Mariette's departure as an excuse to disappear from the event also.

We talked a bit more as a group before the guests moved out to view the lake from the French doors in the great hall. Laurence then cornered me.

"So Mother has written and told me all about her. There is a boy here somewhere apparently," he said, eyes and brows raised toward the doorway behind me. "Mother seems to believe her. Do you? I mean seriously, Edgar knocking up some teenaged *Frenchie*. It does not seem believable. He avoided girls altogether from what I gathered."

"You are incorrect as usual, Laurence, always putting a slant on th-th—" The word did not emerge. Since I had grown and parted from Laurence, and with the exception of a slight awkwardness around Mariette earlier, occurrences of my impediment were rare; many months would go by without even a trace. I silently scolded myself, wishing that my brother did not affect me so. I saw the smirk before he corrected himself.

I repeated the sentence in my head, then said what I had originally intended. "A slant on things to make people anything other than what they actually are."

Laurence shrugged. He was a dreadful gossip; a purveyor of exaggerated information to make everyone else but him appear undesirable; selfish and thoughtless, too; and any similar descriptions I could produce. There weren't enough. He craved attention, and if he wasn't at the center of it, he would make damn sure that others weren't, either.

Laurence examined me. "It appears you have had a wild encounter this afternoon, Dear Brother," he said, dusting away some sand that had stuck to the side of my neck. "What sort of creature have you been fighting?"

I hoped I wasn't blushing. Though there was nothing to say I had been intimate with Mariette, my expressions often gave me away.

"I suppose you believe her?" he asked.

"If you had listened to all the truths from Mother then you would know that we feel somewhat certain."

"A piece of paper can be bought. And how do you know that it's her name on the marriage certificate she carries? That it's not someone else's? And whether the child is really Edgar's and not the fruit of some peasant?"

"That is detestable, what you say," I said, seething. "Do not smear her that way!"

"Oh dear! Have you lost your heart already, Little Brother? You were always soft."

"And you—you were always a sod!"

The girl, Elizabeth, had sauntered over to our conversation, and it gave me reason to disappear. She had been watching us as we talked, and I was certain there was or had been something between them. Laurence had casually discarded many women, though I could understand the initial attraction. He was tall, sandy-brown hair, forest-green eyes, perhaps too pretty, but men like Laurence seemed to be very fashionable at that time. What he did have in abundance was charm, and those in his sights were easily beguiled. He could draw one in effortlessly with words and his certain magnetism of looks and faux character. Though he could throw one out just as quickly if they did not meet his needs.

I felt sure that with Laurence as inheritor, I would be evicted from the manor quickly. I thought of the will that Mariette had shown me, the writing shaky but without a shadow of doubt Edgar's. Would it hold up in a court of law, and if I did use it against Laurence, how long would that particular war continue? Laurence was not a person who liked to lose. He would fight for as long as his vanity allowed. Just that thought alone made me feel as if the case were already lost.

From the kitchen, seeking solace and trying to calm down from Laurence's comments about Mariette, I watched my brother and his friends heading out to the lawn to play a game of croquet. I sought out Mother to plead for him to leave.

"I know you don't like him here," said Mother. "But he is my son also, as terrible a fop as he is sometimes. I want you to work harder to get along with him. When I am gone it is important. You will need each other."

I sighed. "Of course, Mother." Though the likelihood of friendship seemed to widen with every passing year.

Upstairs I looked in the mirror to see if I had given too much away. I did have a wild look about me. My hair was windswept and badly in need of a barber, my cheeks appeared to be blazing with color, and my skin was browned from working outdoors. I washed and changed for the evening while Mariette spent the remainder of the day in her room.

Tonight would be a full dining room, as all three of Laurence's friends were staying, Peggy informed me without expression. Bert was driving into town with her for more supplies.

"I'm sorry, Peggy."

"No need to worry about me, dear Rudy!" Though she treated us all equally, with rarely a bad word said about us, she also had felt the burden of Laurence throughout the years. Peggy had seen it all, and had kept her precious, pretty niece, Sally, well away from Laurence. Sally, two years older than Edgar, had worked here briefly after she turned fifteen but sought a life outside that of housekeeping.

Outside I saw Bert return with Samuel as they pulled up near the stable. As I walked toward them, a dog leaped from the trap. Samuel got out to follow the dog that was sniffing and examining the new surrounds.

"What have we here?"

"Missy!" shouted Samuel excitedly, rushing after the German shepherd.

"From one of the farmers' sons who left today for work in the city," said Bert. "Unfortunately, it is another mouth to fill that they can't afford. I thought it would be good for the boy. He seems used to dogs. But I will find another home if you'd prefer."

I looked at Samuel kneeling beside Missy, trying to get her attention with a wave of his hands. I could not refuse of course. It seemed everything was pointing to permanence for the boy. I should have been happy with events so far, but my mind was yet to lie at rest, and the picture I envisaged for the future still not complete. Not with Edgar in the past and Laurence here now to ruin things.

CHAPTER 11

I checked in on Peggy in the kitchen, lifting lids off steaming saucepans, the air thick with the smell of onions, fennel, and roasting chickens. In the days of my early childhood, Peggy would supervise the cook and a serving girl performing the kitchen work. My offers to help her were waved away, and I left for the dining room, entering the same time as Mother.

"Oh, Abigail, you look as bright as a sunny summer's morning!" gushed Laurence from the head of the table, addressing Mother chummily by her name, as he often did.

Mother lowered her head modestly, but I saw the way he affected her as usual, making her blush with secret delight.

There was much chatter while the group continued with their banter and reflections on their recent social engagements, gathering and gossiping of people Mother and I had never heard about before. They had already gorged on the appetizers of cheese pastries and pâté on thinly sliced toast and small dishes of seasoned mackerel that Peggy had magically conjured up quickly for them while they sipped on wine. Mother once would have enjoyed the dinner party, but I could tell from a tightening of the lips, ever so slight, that she felt a measure of disdain toward Laurence's choice of friends.

After twenty minutes there was no sign of Mariette. Just as I rose to inquire about her, Peggy entered carrying trays of food, followed by

Mariette doing the same. She wore an apron and looked flushed from the heated kitchen. Peggy apologized for the lateness.

Mother looked discomfited since she still demanded the appropriateness of stations for the sake of public functions. It was unheard of, one of the guests helping out in the kitchen, but I could see that Mother underneath it all was as impressed as I was. Was there nothing Mariette couldn't, wouldn't do?

"Mariette, please sit down," said Mother gently, though I recognized the terseness of it also.

"I tried to tell her," said Peggy, shaking her head, though I am certain it would have pleased her nonetheless.

Mariette left for a moment and returned apronless and breathtaking. She wore the pink dress and had pinned up part of her hair, leaving several long, thick tendrils spilling over the front of her shoulders. She also wore the earrings. I felt proud and possessive as she took her place next to me, and the appreciative eyes of the other men did not go unnoticed.

The more times I saw Mariette, the more times I wanted to be with her, and I found that she featured in my thoughts every single minute whether she was in or out of sight. That night she was arresting, and the doubts that lingered somewhere behind the euphoria of spending part of the day with her didn't rear their heads in those moments she was at my side. And whether any further truths about the past did in fact surprise me, I'm not sure I would have cared. She was now very much a part of my present.

"So tell me, Mariette," Laurence said, accentuating her name. "You and your son have traveled from . . . where was it again?"

"Northern France."

"Ah yes! Tragic mess! I was there, you know."

Mariette's interest was piqued, and she queried him on his service. He spoke of his time in France. He thankfully erased any combat detail that might shock Mother, while engaging everyone at the table with an episode of his heroic brilliance that his friends had likely heard already. Perhaps there appeared an element of jealousy on my part when Laurence spoke, but it was more annoyance that Laurence's descriptions of all events seemed only ever to feature him alone and not the other poor souls around him who undoubtedly contributed also. He turned again to question Mariette.

"Many people who left there are returning," Mariette said. "The place that I lived in was destroyed, taken over by Germans. I lived in a little farmhouse outside the town. Since then, and until his recent death, I lived with an uncle nearby in another village."

"And what did you farm?"

"It was an orchard. We grew apples and pears."

"How very charming!" said Elizabeth.

"And it was at the orchard where you fell in love with our brother?" asked Laurence, looking directly at me.

She smiled a little awkwardly.

"Yes, it was, Master Watts."

"Please, Laurence will do . . . You're my sister now. Isn't that right?"

One of the gentlemen with him smirked into his lap. Laurence had no doubt filled them in.

Mother stepped in before I had a chance. "Laurence, the boy is much like your brother in some of his mannerisms. You must meet him in the morning. Spend some time with him." I was surprised by Mother. She had until that moment still shown skepticism, but I wondered if this turn was merely to give Mariette a chance to survive the night.

"Of course," said Laurence, gazing thoughtfully at Mariette, and there was a flash of something ominous about the look that suggested there was much to come in the way of curiosity. More than anyone, Laurence was aware of the changes that might be afoot with a son of Edgar's: changes that would drastically alter his life. However, he was clever at disguising his concerns.

"I have a nephew, everyone. Please, let's drink to that."

They clinked glasses, but Mother was looking suddenly wan, her anxiety about to induce one of her headaches.

"Tell me about Edgar, Mariette. Did he talk about us much?"

"Hmm," she said thoughtfully. "I'm not sure, but I think that something about an ass was mentioned in the same sentence. No doubt he was talking about your horse."

Laurence looked at her, expressionless, and one of the other men laughed, provoking the rest of us to do the same. Laurence glanced around the room and back at Mariette, whose expression, haughty and winning in some way, had not faltered.

He laughed then as well, though he was accomplished at appearing genuine also. "To my sister and my nephew then! It seems you have a personality and wit to match your beauty, my dear."

He waited for Mariette to raise her glass. She made him wait, and then they clinked and made eye contact across the top of their glasses. I thought it was gracious of Laurence, congratulating her for the remark, perhaps admitting a minor defeat, but the connection they had made bothered me. The moment was so fleeting anyone else would have missed it, but I could tell that she was suddenly elevated to some higher standing in Laurence's eyes. I didn't like that they were now in a small way friends, and I felt excluded somehow.

Mother excused herself at the conclusion of the meal, and Laurence proceeded with the after-dinner drinks. We first took our sherry in the drawing room, and the others draped themselves across sofas. The men were mildly inebriated, and I took every opportunity to sit near Mariette. Perhaps it was protective or possessive, or maybe a touch of both. She was the focus of attention from Laurence's guests as she began talking about French customs and life on an orchard, with occasional anecdotes about the gossiping townsfolk. Laurence was watching her, hiding carefully behind his cigarette smoke, exhaling while inspecting every word for sincerity. It was part of the lawyer in him, but part of his own enjoyment to search for a weakness in someone. He was not so much enjoying what she was saying but learning from it. And suddenly, as he was so easily bored, he jumped up.

"Well, what say we get out of this place and have some fun? We'll take lanterns from the stable and go on a hunt."

"What sort of hunt?" asked Elizabeth with some apprehension, peering out the window at the night.

"Not exactly a hunt."

I knew the proposal was what we had often done as boys, to go searching across the meadows and clumps of trees for blackbird or skylark eggs or chicks. It was a competition, and the first to find any would receive an extra bun or toffee from Peggy. Though we were not to remove them from their ground nests.

Laurence explained the idea of it to the rest of them.

"Oh, that sounds like fun!" said Elizabeth with sudden enthusiasm.

"And what is the prize?" I asked dubiously, knowing the likelihood of finding any at this time of year was slim and hoping that there would be eventual and unanimous disagreement about the idea.

"The winners get half a case of champagne!"

Everyone but I clapped at this extravagant prize, and I wondered if Laurence was expecting to take this from our meager stash in the cellar. I made a note to remind Laurence to foot the bill for the alcohol already consumed by his friends and another note to keep what we had guarded.

I did not like the idea that as adults we would do this hunt in the night. If perhaps anyone else had suggested it, I might have been more receptive, but whenever Laurence suggested an activity, there was the potential for someone to be grossly disappointed. And in times gone by, it was often myself.

Laurence summoned Peggy to bring him and his guests each a lantern, then told everyone to bring with them their wineglasses, and he picked up a bottle of champagne to carry. As we headed through the hall and toward the rear terrace, I reached for Mariette's arm to pull her back from the group to talk privately.

"You can retire if you wish," I whispered. "He's sending us on a wild goose chase if you ask me. You don't have to do this."

She smiled at me, condescendingly I felt, as if I were a sulking child.

"But I want to!"

"And Samuel?"

"He is fast asleep, but of course you are right. I must check on him before we leave." She asked me to wait for her and squeezed my hand. She also gave me a look to remind me that what we had was not a figment of my imagination.

By then the rest of the group had left through the French doors to reach the lawn, chatting excitedly as they headed toward the copse of woolly trees that stretched beside the lake. Laurence stopped and called to me once he'd caught me waiting behind on the terrace.

"Come along, Rudy!"

"I'll wait for Mariette."

"I'm sure she'll find us all right without your chaperoning," he said with amusement in his tone. I ignored the comment, and he turned back to continue toward the lake.

"Is everything all right?" I asked when she appeared again, this time with her shawl.

"Yes, Samuel is fine."

Her eyes were wide with excitement. She reached for my hand as we followed the others into the darkness of the woods, following Laurence, who had assuredly taken the lead, seemingly relishing the position with his confident stride.

Mariette dropped my hand as we walked into the circle of lantern light by the group ahead of us. While Laurence organized the search parties, I scowled and clenched my teeth, watching Fred, Elizabeth's brother, throw back the remains of his champagne, then pitch the flute into the lake. I was paired with Elizabeth, Fred was paired with

Mariette, and Laurence was paired with the other guest, whose name I've forgotten. I did not like to lose sight of her in the dark with a strange man, but she appeared untroubled by the arrangement, if not delighted to participate in such an event. And then for the next half an hour, Elizabeth and I wandered aimlessly, occasionally tripping or stepping on each other, for I admit I had no interest in the game whatsoever. I spied the silhouettes of several clandestine birds that flew silently and teasingly low across the lake's silvered surface, wishing I still held Mariette's hand and could point these out; all the while Elizabeth talked somewhat vapidly, relaying London gossip and plying me for information about Laurence. She may have been pleasant company under other circumstances, but I was anxious about Mariette's whereabouts, and my sole thoughts were of returning to the house and somehow having some time alone with her later that night.

We bided our time, then returned to the meeting point empty-handed, each of us wishing for different company. Two other lanterns approached us, the light growing larger, and I hoped it was Mariette. But emerging from the dark were Fred and Laurence's colleague, announcing loudly that they had failed to find anything and were convinced there were no such eggs, that it was all a Laurence ruse and some kind of prank. I wondered why the pairs had changed and looked beyond them to the patches of woodland in the distance and saw no spots of yellow from a burning wick, just a barely visible mass of trees beneath distant deep-blue hills.

"I thought you were with Mariette," I said to Fred.

"Laurie met us, and we swapped. He felt certain that he would find what he was looking for and wanted to make sure the foreign girl would see."

I worried then, quietly panicked, and felt a sudden coldness slither up my spine. There was a silence across the shallow valley that unnerved me, and five minutes later, when I could wait no longer, I began the descent toward the clumps of trees.

"I'm sure they will return soon," said Elizabeth, calling after me, though I sensed some alarm in the strain of her voice. She did not like the idea of her potential suitor in the dark with a woman as lovely as Mariette.

I tripped once and cursed and kept walking through thick shrubbery, my eyes peeled for movement. A light appeared in the distance, an area much further than Laurence had first suggested, and I walked toward it.

Laurence and Mariette emerged gradually into view, and as I approached them, she seemed shocked to see me.

"Where did you go? Much further, it appears," I said to Laurence, his expression deceivingly innocent as always.

"I took our dear sister, as from past experience I was her best hope at finding them. Unfortunately, we're too late for them. What did you think we were doing, Little Brother?" I was so irritated by the term, the way he would always highlight me as younger and not with any affection.

"I thought something had happened," I said.

"Come on then," said Laurence. "You always cluck about nothing!" It was condescending and suggestive that I was regularly of such unnecessary fuss, and he departed us quickly to give me no chance to defend myself.

We merged again with the rest of the group, and Laurence suggested they were all worthy of more champagne anyway, though Mariette did not react with the same pleasure as the others. She said not a word as we returned to the house. As we entered the foyer, greeted by the softly chiming grandfather clock telling us it was midnight, she bade us good night.

"So soon?" queried Laurence, but she turned and left without explanation.

"We can continue the festivities," said Laurence, calling after her. "There is no reason to stop now!"

I left the group to their drinking and felt a little sorry for Elizabeth, who looked solemn, keen for the night to be over. I blamed it on my imagination at the time, but I felt a slight distance between Mariette and me during our return, not unlike the first days together in the house. I vowed that before the night was finished, I would find out if there was anything the matter.

I waited to hear the revelry die down, listening to the scrapings of furniture and the clunks and clatters of their shoes on the stairs, down the hallway, past my room. There were whisperings, perhaps too loud to call it such, as they parted ways. Finally the click and thud of heavy bedroom doors and the muted snoring of drunken slumber. I hoped Elizabeth had been catered for in a room of her choosing, and I felt some comfort that her brother was here hopefully to look out for her. My mother would be horrified to learn anything different.

The house now creaking from the stillness, I stepped quietly along the corridor to knock on Mariette's door. There was no answer at first, and thinking she was fast asleep, I turned to leave.

"Who is it?" came the whispered reply.

"Rudy," I said, my lips at the seam of the door and the wall.

She opened it to allow me in and was careful to close it again softly behind me.

"Did I wake you?"

"No, I've just been lying here. Samuel has a cough. I thought that I would stay awake to make certain he is all right."

"I just wanted to check to see if you were feeling all right."

"It has been a long day," she said, looking past me to the door. "I am dreadfully tired."

I had been hoping for some reassurance on her part that what had happened earlier that day was the beginning of something wondrous, but I sensed that she wished only for me to leave her.

"Very well," I said. "Sleep well."

She leaned forward to kiss me good night but pulled away when it became more ardent on my side.

As I commenced to turn the doorknob, she asked me a question that I did not give much consideration to at the time.

"If something happens to me, will you promise to take care of Samuel?"

I had already promised myself that regardless of what I uncovered about the past, both the boy and she were firmly in my heart and my life. But the timing and strangeness of the question would not be something I would think about again until several nights later.

"Of course."

"Thank you, Rudy, for everything."

I left feeling confused and slept poorly that night; then I woke late the following morning. In the kitchen Peggy and Mother were discussing some plans. They were taking the train to Manchester the following day to see Mother's medical specialist for her bimonthly checkup. They were also planning to make a day of it, seeing a show, lunching, and shopping. I had expected to see the others having breakfast on the terrace, but there was no sign of anyone.

Despite the fact that she was in her bed coat, Mother looked very well. I was beginning to believe that the child and Mariette had something to do with her improved health. Perhaps relying on the idea that she might have some living piece of Edgar installed in the house again. I knew in my heart she wanted to believe as much as I did that Samuel was Edgar's son.

"I am just going over the budget with Peggy. It seems that last night's dinner took some money."

"He should have let you know."

"Yes, I agree. But we must entertain, as dreary as it is. We must at least appear to have money for such events."

I understood. Mother came from an era, that still existed in certain circles, where just the whiff of a decline in fortune kept one out of society, and in that strange way she was looking out for her sons rather than herself.

"I will speak to Laurence," I said. "He needs to cover that expense. Where is everyone?"

"Laurence left for the station," said Peggy.

I was relieved. I wanted much time alone with Mariette.

I noticed that Bert was walking with the boy in the gardens, something that had become a morning ritual.

"Has Mariette eaten yet?"

"Yes, she has," said Mother. "She has also gone with Laurence for the drive to drop the others at the station."

My heart sank. Every bad childhood memory returned in those moments: Laurence always taking something from me, a new toy, undoing a compliment by whispering something of the reverse effect to me in my ear.

"When did they leave?"

"An hour ago."

I was frustrated and anxious, awaiting Mariette, and I searched for any occupation to distract me. I put Samuel on top of Sheriff and walked them around the paddock. The child was less nervous this time riding, holding the reins like he had seen me do. Then for the rest of the morning, I pottered about the house to keep busy, tightening hinges, nailing wonky chair legs, checking railings, anything, while all the time listening out for Laurence's car.

Mariette entered the drawing room where Mother was relaxing and I sat feigning interest in a book. Mariette wore the yellow dress and looked flushed from the drive, hair escaping a bun at the base of her neck. Laurence entered several moments after her, as if the pair arriving at separate times was less incriminating. He looked shiftily between Mother and me.

"Good morning," he said, his eyes bloodshot from the night before. "Don't mind me. I think I'll take a nap."

Mariette avoided my stare, and before he left, Laurence passed her the hat she had left in the car, too casually, as if there was now a certain familiarity between the pair. I didn't like it.

"Laurence took me on a tour to the villages around the lake," said Mariette, obviously aware that I was miserable. "We stopped for tea. I did knock on your door this morning, but you were fast asleep."

She seemed genuine. There seemed no reason to doubt her, and I felt some confidence returning.

Peggy entered to say that Samuel was calling for his mother, and Mariette left us quickly to remain in her room for the afternoon.

Laurence rose later that day to join me outside to check the horses, then sauntered around the property, pretending to be interested and supervising Bert on various improvements, even though I had never seen him lift a finger to the work himself. I asked him if he was returning that night, and he said that he would not be returning to London until Tuesday.

"And your work?"

"It can wait," he said dismissively.

The idea of him staying bothered me since he rarely stayed longer than one night. If Mother and Peggy were coming with me early tomorrow morning on the train as they had earlier proposed, then it would mean Laurence would be left alone with Mariette for the day.

I left him quickly to call on Mariette. She looked a little pale and less jovial than she had on previous days. She declined my offer of horse riding, with the excuse that Samuel was unwell, his stomach sore and still with a cough, and she should stay in her room for the rest of the day.

"I am returning to Manchester early in the morning."

"I know," she said, and looked down to avoid questions perhaps. "I don't know what I will do without you here."

"Then come with me," I said, suddenly not thinking of anything else.

"I have the child," she said. "I cannot bring him there. Where would we stay?"

"Then marry me and stay with me."

She smiled and touched the collar of her dress unsurely. She appeared indifferent, much altered from the girl I had lain with on the cold sand, clinging to me as if the day would disappear far earlier than she wanted.

"You have been so kind to me," she said. "But it won't fix anything."

"There is nothing to fix. I love you and you love me."

She looked at me for a moment, lips parted as if she would say something, before turning her attention to outside the window.

"I will see you at dinner then," I said.

She nodded, still unturned in my direction, and I reluctantly withdrew from her room to seek out Peggy to tell her the boy was feeling unwell. She was surprised, as she had seen him earlier and heard no cough.

In the drawing room I found Mother and Laurence. Laurence looked a shade of angry, a different sight from the day before.

"So, Little Brother, back to work tomorrow so we can all eat since this house is hopeless and is costing us more than it needs."

"You have said enough!" said Mother. "I take your point."

"What point?" I asked.

"Oh, you know your brother, Rudy! At every visit he talks about selling the property."

"But what will your fancy friends think?" I said. "Don't you want to show it off?"

"I prefer to have my own fancy place to show off."

I could sense that Laurence was worried about something that he had been discussing with Mother, and I suspected it had something to do with Samuel and the future of the estate. But this I will admit was not my primary concern at the time.

Neither Laurence nor Mother nor Mariette came to dinner that night for various reasons. Laurence didn't give his, Mother was tired, and Mariette was still concerned about Samuel's health. I did not feel hungry and left most of my meal, then cleaned the last of the plates in the kitchen to save Peggy from doing it since we had an early start.

I went to bed that night and thought frequently about visiting Mariette one last time, but the possibility of rejection prevented me from doing this.

I reflected on my bizarre marriage proposal in a desperate moment and ruminated on her confusing response. I was naive. With hindsight, I know that now.

CHAPTER 12

The next morning very early, I wrote a note for Mariette and left it under her door, telling her that I looked forward to seeing her in a week. I departed then with Mother and Peggy, with Bert driving us to the station. Without the chance to see Mariette again, I was feeling utterly glum. I kept dwelling on Laurence alone in that huge house with her. It must have shown on my face.

"Bert will keep an eye on things," Peggy whispered reassuringly as we climbed into the car.

Peggy had prepared meals for those remaining, even though we had learned by then that Mariette was capable of taking care of herself, and more worldly than anyone assumed. Mother and Peggy would get the afternoon train home again, and I would come back the following Friday night. Once we alighted from the train, I saw Mother and Peggy off in the direction of the medical suites before walking the several blocks to work. My boss seemed pleased to see me and briefed me on the projects I was required to complete urgently for the week ahead.

There was a letter arrived from Roland, and for tactful reasons he had preferred to send it here. Inside the envelope was a copy of "the missing" from certain pages of the book of recorded war casualties, now supposedly with the addition of Edgar.

I wondered if Edgar was perhaps watching me from afar, and feelings of guilt and loss arose. I had fallen in love with his wife, yet I had not found my peace with the loss of my brother. I questioned myself then and wondered what he would say if he arrived back now. I scanned down quickly to his name in print, then returned it to the envelope to examine at length later. I did not need any other distractions, certainly not until I finished my work.

I worked without a break, catching up on much of it before walking home while there was still daylight. I sat in the two-room second-floor apartment, which smelled stale from being closed for several weeks and was noisy from the factory machines in the buildings opposite. I would have to alert the landlord that there was water damage down the wall near the kitchenette. I boiled a saucepan of water and focused on the tasks I would need to commence the following morning, anything to distract me from thoughts of Laurence and Mariette. I paced with a cup in my hand before finding myself writing her a letter with some difficulty since I did not feel I could express myself quite as well in my limited written French. I screwed up the piece of paper and threw it away. I needed to talk to her face to face. I stood up anxiously and viewed the train tracks from my window, then made a decision to catch the same return train as Mother and Peggy, to spend the night at the manor and return by train again early in the morning. I was desperate to see Mariette. We'd hardly had a private conversation since the event at the beach, and I could not have gone through another week without the reassurance of seeing her. It was mad and desperate love.

Mother and Peggy were surprised to see me join them on the plat-form as the train pulled up, but I believe they both could read me. They each wore a new scarf, and Mother, though exhausted, seemed happier, having also spent much of the day at leisure.

Apparently the doctor's appointment had gone well. As usual they could not find anything specifically wrong with her, and I had to won-der how much of her condition was simply in her mind. She was pre-scribed further medication to help her relax. Again I thought the timing of my mother's improved condition had much to do with the arrival of Mariette and Samuel.

The train was busy, and Mother and Peggy talked the whole way, especially about the friends they had called on for lunch and the play they had seen, but Mariette was solely on my mind. Had she and Laurence spent the day together? Had they ridden to the beach? I shivered a little and fought to swallow back my fears.

The rest of the trip home is blurred in my memory, perhaps because everything after that seemed to happen so fast, and what started as a productive day turned into a chaotic search for answers.

The nightmare began when Bert met us at the station. He was flustered, the boy in the front of the vehicle with him.

"Something has happened," he said, and when I questioned him, he could not say exactly, only that he believed a fight had occurred between the other two adults. Bert had been away with Samuel visiting the neighboring farm on the trap. On the return, the boy had fallen asleep. As they arrived, he heard Laurence shouting out Mariette's name, and he put the boy asleep on the hay in the stable, with Missy beside him, while he went to investigate. He had then found the great hall in a state of disarray and Mariette gone from the house.

He was clearly concerned and eager to return home. The boy sat in the back now, sheltered by the two women protectively. Mother had one arm around the boy and her free hand against her chest anxiously. I sat in the front and willed the car to travel faster.

When we arrived at the property, it was well lit up, and Laurence's car was parked at the front as if in readiness to leave, the passenger door flung open.

I ran inside first to the drawing room and then to the hall. A Grecian statue that had been in the family for several generations was in pieces on the floor. Mother and Peggy had followed me, and I suggested that Mother go straight to her rooms, but she refused, wishing to investigate the situation herself.

Up a level, Mariette's room was empty, her bed made, and the two dresses that I had bought her hanging over a chair. Laurence's room down the hallway from her still had his things. Though his bed was unmade, and it looked as if he would return.

I heard Mother calling to me from the front entrance of the house. I ran down to see Laurence walking toward us up the gravel drive.

"What happened?" I asked, approaching him.

He did not answer, nor did he look at me; instead he pushed roughly past me.

I grabbed him by the shoulder and turned him toward me, finding strength I did not know I had, that perhaps I had never felt the need to use before.

"Where is Mariette?"

"She is gone. The whore is gone."

My response was reflexive. I lunged to punch him in the face, but he ducked fast and gripped my wrist to block me before pushing me so hard that I fell backward onto the ground. When I tried to right myself, he shoved me hard back down again.

"The girl, the one that you wish to marry, is gone," he barked above me. "She is not who she says she is. She is only after my money."

I was disappointed that he knew of my desire to marry her and wondered fleetingly why Mariette had released something so personal.

"Where did she go?" I shouted, righting myself.

"She left through the pastures," he said. "I offered to drive her, but she insisted on walking. Let her go!" When I ran for him again, he grabbed both my wrists. "You can't even fight, Little Brother. You did not even see the war."

It was a fact he constantly rubbed in my face. Not just that I had been too young to serve, but that I was not a fighter like he was. Perhaps he was right. Not until that moment had I ever had the urge to fight for anything. Perhaps I had never wanted anything or anyone as badly as I had wanted Mariette.

"Which way did she go?" I said, shaking myself free.

"Toward the station and lost in the hills for all I care. You will not find someone who doesn't want to be found. Let her go!"

I was seething with anger, but my desire to find Mariette was stronger, and I ran in the direction Laurence had come from, calling her name, calling her back, wondering why she would walk the tracks at night toward the train. It was dark; what remained of the moon was obscured by clouds.

With no response I returned to the house to retrieve a lantern. Mother was anxious, and Peggy stayed with her and Samuel, who had begun to whimper, while Bert and I both took lanterns to scour through undergrowth, along narrow paths and the paddocks and pastures in the direction of the town. I wondered why she did not take the more direct road to town. Was she running from Laurence? Was this her best chance of hiding? I assumed the worst: that it was some kind of escape.

We returned to the manor when the search along walking tracks seemed too slow and hopeless. Bert then drove to search the road, while I saddled Sheriff and rode across neighboring meadows and hills.

There was no sight of her as I rode all the way to the station. She was not there, and the station guard who was locking up for the night saw no woman who fit her description. The next train would not be until morning. She had disappeared. I wondered if she had continued walking southward, knowing that she would be waiting all night for the train. It did not make sense that she would leave the boy. Sheriff galloped me back to the house, where I believed she would return.

By the time I arrived back at the house, my mother and Laurence were in the great hall, standing by the French doors. Peggy had wrapped a shawl around Mother, who was distressed, and Samuel was asleep on a sofa.

"Laurence, what did you say to her to make her leave?" I asked.

"You were always naive. You couldn't see what I saw."

"You have done or said something, and you must admit what it is!"

Mother stood frozen, unable to look at anyone.

"Please," said Peggy. "Do not fight here in front of your mother. Rudy, let's hear his explanation."

"As I was explaining to Mother while you were gone," continued Laurence, "I questioned her about a few things, and I believe it was why she left. I asked about her family. I told her that I had ways to verify her story and call out her lies. That I had many contacts in France who could locate the truth. It seems that the very idea has spooked her, and she has left perhaps to hide the truth."

I reminded him about the wedding certificate and the photograph of them together.

"A marriage that is not registered, a photo that shows she met him, and an orphaned boy mean only that Mariette has attempted to think of everything."

"She has a will signed by Edgar, too," I said.

"What?" said Mother.

"It is legitimate. I know it is."

"Why didn't you tell me?" asked Mother.

"Where is it now?" asked Laurence.

"I don't have it. But I saw it."

"What you saw was obviously a forgery. She knew that too, else she would have shown it to Mother. She may have learned of this house, but there is no proof they are married nor that she is who she says she is. Who's to say that Edgar didn't marry someone called Mariette and she has stolen her identity, perhaps from that woman's corpse. And who's to say that when she learned of Edgar's death that she didn't do away with the supposed wife and steal a document? Who's to say that someone else didn't steal Edgar's name?"

"She would not leave the boy."

"She is a wandering fraudster, you fool! Isn't it obvious? She doesn't care about the boy. It is highly probable that he isn't even hers, stolen like the clothes she wears."

After Laurence stormed away, Mother began to weep, and I moved to comfort her. I was afraid from all this talk she would lose any belief she had in Mariette.

"Mother, don't listen to these lies," I said, my arm around her. "I believe her. You must believe her, too!"

Mother shook her head, unable to speak, and she put her hand toward Peggy to help her back to her room. I felt I had lost Mother's faith once more.

I moved to the sofa where Samuel was sleeping soundlessly and reached down to touch his face. I felt an immense sense of love, distraught that when he woke I may not have any answers to his questions. I carefully picked him up so as not to wake him and carried him up to the guest room to lay him on Mariette's bed. There was still the scent of her perfume in the room, and as I looked around for some evidence that would give me some clue to her whereabouts, I told myself that she would come back.

A search in the guest room turned up no note or clue as to her disappearance. I picked up the yellow dress and put my face to the fabric, where the sweet smell of her remained. I held it for several moments in despair. She could not have just disappeared. She would come back, I told myself before remembering the papers disturbed in the drawer of Edgar's desk and searching there, too. Surely she would have left the will at least, anything that would protect the boy. The will seemed his only chance now that she was not here to speak for him.

I heard a motorcar roar away down the front drive, and I rushed to the windows across the hallway to watch Laurence leave into the night. I carried such fury toward him that I callously wished he had never returned from war. A shout coming from the other side of the house distracted me from my dark thoughts, and I followed the disturbance toward Mother's room. She was in her nightgown already and Peggy beside her.

"My jewels are gone," she said, ashen-faced. "All of them!" Then she collapsed in Peggy's arms, sobbing.

"But it couldn't be, surely?" queried Peggy.

Surely not! The girl that I had come to love was not capable of deception and thievery. I could not reconcile this event with the girl I knew or in the days following, as the mystery surrounding her arrival and departure became thicker with conspiracies and confusion.

"We will get to the bottom of this," I said. "She will come back."

It took me near a full day before I went to the police, at the insistence of Mother and Roland. I needed to gather courage to believe she was not coming back, but I was incapable of relating her to the missing jewels. Until that point I was convinced that she had stormed off and would return when she was calm.

I sent a telegram to the newspaper to tell my supervisor I would not be returning to work. I did not ask for permission, nor did I think that the job would be there when I eventually returned to Manchester. It didn't matter. The future at that moment seemed to me very grim, and the only comfort was from Samuel, who needed more comfort than any of us. It would take a huge effort on both Peggy's and my part to appear unaffected so as to distract the boy from his misery also. Bert of course was his savior, and I saw him more than once lift the boy to hold him gently while he cried for his mother.

Mother had fallen ill again, and her headaches had returned. She had asked, the day following Mariette's disappearance, that the boy and she not cross paths until she was feeling better. I was disappointed she thought so ill of Mariette, believing that she had simply tried to gain money and jewels and land an innocent child on our family. I was not convinced that we had the full story yet. Laurence was good at lying, at skewing an outcome in his favor, but when I tried to speak to Mother about it, she refused to listen in those early days after the disappearance.

I had spent moments believing that Mariette's disappearance was far more sinister and wondering what lengths Laurence had gone to to frighten her away.

Bert one day brought a piece of torn lace that he had found in one of the garden beds that I felt certain matched the black dress of Mariette's. I kept it and examined it for days, believing it would offer a clue to her vanishing, before handing it over to the police, along with a banknote Bert had found scrunched and thrown from view. We were informed a few days later that these particular banknotes, long since withdrawn from circulation, had been used as illegal tender recently. The banknote, as suggested by Peggy, may well have been the property of one of Laurence's guests, but I could not rule out that it may also have belonged to Mariette, and speculated whether she was practiced in such fraud elsewhere.

There had been very somber moments when I had suspected a worse fate, then consoled myself that even Laurence did not cross certain lines. When asked by the police, Laurence had written a statement to say she had left of her own free will, which gave them very little option but to treat the case as a matter of theft by a foreign fraudster.

And as the week went by and there was no sign of Mariette, I started to accept the notion that she would never return. I searched often in the woodlands, even along the lake, expecting to see the worst. And then I had to ask myself if I ever really knew her, and I did in fact question myself whether she was really the boy's mother, Laurence's words ringing in my ears.

Just as suddenly as Mariette had entered my life, she was gone.

CHAPTER 13

By the following weekend I found it difficult to get out of bed to face the day. I was weary with nervous exhaustion and overthinking every second I had spent with Mariette. The only news I begged to hear was that of her whereabouts. I was done with Laurence. Mother of course wasn't. He was still her son, a living one and the one who would eventually take ownership of the estate. The boy—it was doubtful then without Mariette or solid evidence—would not be considered a threat to Laurence's inheritance.

Peggy sought me out one morning when I was drinking tea on the terrace, my head sore from too many whiskeys taken late the night before. I had not shaved for several days, and I stayed up late so often that it seemed unnecessary to change out of my crushed shirt and trousers. This new appearance was not by my design but merely due to the fact that my mind was often elsewhere, tortured with loss and self-pity, and in such a case as this, one's grooming is often the first to go.

"I would like you to see something," she said with a peculiar expression that I could not read.

I followed Peggy up to the top floor and into Edgar's annex room, which brought back fresh feelings of loss.

"I was cleaning here," said Peggy, "and opening the window to let in some fresh air when I noticed that something had been wedged between the bed and the wall."

She passed me the book I had seen with Mariette.

I touched the hard cover that had seen better times, the corners crushed and fraying, and the colors, green and maroon, mottled, as if they had been spotted by rain. Upon opening the cover and reading the first few lines, the discovery of its author gave me hope for potential further clues. I turned the pages one by one to see Edgar's writing. Deeper into it, the words became more illegible and haphazard, and sometimes in French.

"It looks like it was placed there deliberately," said Peggy. I remembered when I had first caught Mariette here. Maybe then she had first placed it in the desk drawer, the reason the papers there had been disturbed. And perhaps she later moved it to make sure it was safe.

The pieces of the puzzle about Edgar and his life seemed to be cruelly drip-fed by Mariette as if I couldn't cope with everything at once, and I felt a small resentment that she didn't show me this earlier. I had to wonder just what else she had kept from me.

I eagerly returned to my desk to examine thoroughly its contents, the pages appearing brilliantly gilded under the glowing afternoon light. As I began to read, I was transported back in time to some secret place in Edgar's mind. It wasn't a diary, that's not what Edgar used it for, but rather to note down his feelings, poetic and vague as they sometimes were.

I read Edgar's writings one by one, deciphering their meanings and searching for names and descriptions that might help me learn more about him and perhaps Mariette, too. The pages were soiled by hands stained with battle dust, smudges and fingerprints, and in places the ink bleeding and paper crumpled from water damage. The book, kept in a satchel I daresay for the most part, gave me some idea of what the soldiers had been exposed to, the elements and the conditions endured by both the book and the men on the battlefields.

He described the curious mélange of buoyancy, doggedness, and torment affecting the town residents near the front line. With little embellishment needed, he had captured the cold, the frailty of the human body, and the unforgiving, unrelenting sound of shelling in his words. I was there for a moment, sharing what he experienced, grippingly real, sensing the vibrations in the ground, seeing the ghostly shapes of an enemy emerging from fog, and feeling numb and despairing from the cold that permanently clung to his bones. I shared the fear of the unknown, of the future of mankind, of whether there would be another sunrise. Though half the book was empty, I felt that there was so much more he should have said, should have told me.

Dispersed between his stories were poems, sometimes just the first lines of something he intended to write, as if, waiting in the trenches, he was called up suddenly; as if disturbed by whistling sounds of incoming shells; or as if, by reliving the past, he had found it too painful, thus forcing him not to think. I believe I am mentioned in one of them, though not by name. *My brother sends his unburdened thoughts. / He is not to know. / He is innocent.*

Deeper into the book the thoughts and poems grew darker and more disturbed, with reimagined beginnings in a gloomy, bloody world where ghosts of soldiers wandered restlessly. Then it was summer 1917, and his writing suddenly changed. It was lighter, his soul given some temporary respite. *In a field of wilted blue, she is the peace amid the madness, an extra weight in my pack that I would joyfully bear to where the world is bluer still.* I wondered if he was referring to Mariette and felt stricken with guilt as large as grief. I lamented that I had disturbed a precious memory, had sullied something that he had found and lost and would not have again.

These strange notes, thoughts and poems, did not provide answers so much as give me more questions. Caught between the pages, I found a pressed blue flower also, alongside the last words in the book. *To the silence I must go.* Then the pages afterward were blank.

I could not yet give this book to Mother. It would torture her further in her current condition to speculate what these messages meant.

The words that weren't said, the detail omitted, still rose from the pages to be painted with one's own mind.

Turning to the last page of the book, I found the will that Mariette had shown me. I felt a surge of excitement, a connection to her, and mused on whether she had left this here for me to find or whether, perhaps in her haste, it was left inadvertently. Though unless circumstances did not allow it, I could not imagine Mariette as forgetful. The items were pieces of a giant puzzle, and I resolved that my life could not move forward without collecting all of them.

I searched once more through correspondence in the study until I found a letter sent from Edgar's friend, who had served also. Andrew was one of Edgar's close service friends who had returned from war, and using the address on the back of the envelope, I sent a telegram to check that he was still there and whether he would receive me. Andrew had attended school with Edgar, and Andy, as he was more commonly known, had stayed with us on a number of weekends. He had written this personal message to us after Edgar had been reported as missing, himself only serving for one battle and returning home to England badly injured.

Several days later, I made the excuse to Mother that I was returning to complete some tasks at the newspaper, resolving to get more answers before I spoke to her, then took the train to London. Arriving at Andy's house, I was ushered in by a housekeeper to a sitting room, and a few moments later, Andy entered in a wheelchair pushed by a young woman.

"I'm sorry I can't get up, but it's a pleasure to see an old face, or a young one as is the case with yours."

I shook Andy's hand, while the woman slipped away from the room. He reminisced about the wonderful summer holidays he had spent at Lakeland Manor. He was thinner than I remembered and heavily lined in the face for someone so young, and I thought that if war didn't take his life, it did at least take much of his youth.

"Thank you for your letter after the war," I said. "It meant a lot to us."

His mood changed then. He had learned of Edgar's death several months after it had happened. They had been together briefly at officers' training prior to the war and then entered the "French fields of fire," both as lieutenants. Edgar seemed destined to remain on the front lines.

"Many who knew him didn't want to put his brain in the firing line," said Andy. "He was promoted to captain, I heard, a year after I returned here, and then when officers were dropping like flies, another promotion was apparently bandied around. God knows he'd been there that long and deserved it. They needed strong leaders, but Edgar didn't have the ambition to rise higher. He didn't want to stand behind the men, but up front, and certainly had no desire to push a pen. He had done enough of that at school and university. From what I've heard since, he was encouraging and strong and an asset to the team. He was there when conditions grew worse. As soldier numbers decreased, many of the badly injured were simply patched and sent back out again."

"Can you tell me something of the village you were billeted near?"

"We were stationed in soldiers' quarters near Béthune. The whole village practically overrun with soldiers at the time. The school became the hospital. That's where I spent most of my time in France, I regret to say."

"Were you ever billeted with families there?"

"No," he said. "Why do you ask?"

I showed him the photograph and asked if he had seen the girl pictured or known of the place.

"Bailleul, the name on the back, is further north, but I was never there. Though I recognize one of the fellows," he said, pointing. "That's Roger Whitney. He was in our unit when we landed." He looked at me curiously then. "So tell me, what exactly are you looking for?"

There are some people one knows instinctively to trust, and I told him everything, bar my intimate relationship with Mariette.

"The whole thing seems highly suspect," said Andy. "I don't like the sound of it at all, and I'm not sure I can add anything that might help with your investigation, particularly about the girl. Your brother was quite taken with the French girls like we all were to start with, though war seemed to take some of the wanting out of liaisons, I have to admit. Praying for the future and returning to family became more desirable than the warmth of a woman. Though some sought the latter purely because it might be their last. I know that sounds crass, but it is the truth."

"I'm in no position to judge anyone," I said.

I realized he had not talked about himself, and I was aware the whole time that his legs were covered by a blanket. He must have seen my glance, and he pulled back the blanket to reveal a missing leg and a missing foot from the other one.

"I'm so sorry. You never said in your letters."

"I hated to be a wet blanket and send my thoughts of misery. They thought they could save the foot on my good leg, but I was sad to see that one go as well. That's how it is," he said, and looked out across the quiet street. "Time has healed me, though not in body and perhaps not completely in heart. In any case the lovely woman you saw before is my wife, Frances, and she was also my nurse at the Endell Street hospital. So there was a reason for all of this suffering. There has to be, don't you think, Rudy?"

I wished I could speak with better knowledge, having never endured such wretchedness and deprivations. I wanted to believe there was a reason for everything. I truly did, but not having Edgar here, I silently disagreed. I smiled and shrugged and muttered something about hope and wondered if it sounded sincere.

"Do you know where I can find Roger?" I asked.

"Last I heard, he'd been injured toward the end and returned from France to a hospital here. I don't know his home address, but I know someone who can probably find out."

He called out to Frances, and once our formal introductions were over with, Andy spoke briefly to her about the situation.

"I'm not supposed to give personal information away, but to hell with it," said Frances. "With so much tragedy I hardly think they will begrudge me an address."

She called the hospital from a phone in the hallway and came back with the information. I thanked them both, promised I would visit again, and caught the underground train across London, determined to make use of whatever light that was left of the day.

Roger's street was jammed with narrow terraced houses, and I stepped over several bags of strewn rubbish and potholes, counting down the houses until I reached the one I guessed to be his. There was no answer the first time I rang the doorbell. I tried again until the door was opened by a woman I assumed to be a relative of Roger's.

"Mrs. Whitney?"

She nodded, appearing weary and unwelcoming. I explained who I was, what had happened to Edgar, and that I had some questions I would like to ask Roger. She was courteous, commiserated in a few words about my loss, and then, with some detachment, told me her son wasn't home.

"Do you know when he will be back?"

"I can't really say," she said.

"I've been given this address—"

"As I said, I can't say." Her tone was so abrupt I wasn't sure how to progress.

"It's all right, Mother," came a voice from the room to the side. "Let him in!"

His mother looked toward the door where the voice was coming from, clearly torn about something.

"I won't take up much of your time!" I called out quickly.

The woman stepped back to allow me through and I nodded my thanks. Then as I proceeded toward another doorway, she pulled my arm to hurriedly whisper, "Don't talk about anything that might upset him. He's very ill."

She turned and left me. I found Roger sitting in an armchair by a front-street window. I sat opposite him in the cramped front parlor that overlooked a barren street. The air was stale inside the room, which was grim and dark and oppressive, and I felt sorry for him in such conditions even before I learned the full extent of his injury.

"You're Edgar's brother?"

"Sorry, have we met?"

"No, but you have the same eyes and look about you . . . Speculative, away someplace else," he said with a wheeze that rattled in his chest. "I thought I was seeing a ghost when I spied you from the window. I could tell anywhere. You'll have to excuse my mother. She's overcautious . . . Any visits only tire and worsen me, according to her."

"Thank you for agreeing to talk with me. I'm Rudy Watts," I said, moving forward to shake his hand before noticing the cylindrical mouthpiece he was holding. The article was connected by a rubber tube to an earthenware bottle on the table beside his chair and contained an inhalant of some kind, which I took to be the cause of a chemical smell I had also detected. "I'm sorry . . . If it's too much trouble, I can send a letter."

He waved me away, lifted the mouthpiece to inhale deeply through the tube before lowering it again. I looked around the room at the photograph of a young boy holding a trophy and another of Roger as a young man, at someone's wedding, a sister perhaps. But there were none in uniform.

"My doctor's had me experimenting with all sorts of treatment. This one's been the best relief so far."

It became obvious throughout the conversation why his mother did not want me disturbing him. His words were sometimes breathy and rushed, squeezing in as many as he could in a short window of time.

"The mustard gas apparently has had more of an effect than many first thought," said Roger. "It looked like I was improving briefly, but then my breathing has been getting steadily worse over the years, and I fear that by the time they have worked out a cure for whatever it is I have, as well as an appropriate pension, I will be dead."

He smiled wryly. "At least my mother will benefit. She has dedicated her life to me these past years."

I looked into his eyes and saw the extent of his misery. I also felt pity, but for his sake I was determined not to show it. Here was a man who had lost much and to whom the country owed a great deal.

"I suppose you're here to learn of Edgar's last movements."

"Yes," I said. "We know only of the date he went missing, and we are looking for some kind of end to . . . speculation. My mother has taken it badly, as you can imagine."

"Yes. I can," he said.

"But if you can tell me at least what you know, I would very much appreciate it."

He closed his eyes for several seconds and, after breathing through the tube again, held his breath longer this time, perhaps long enough to capture images from the past. "I saw your brother in a field of mustard gas, and we were then shipped elsewhere to field hospitals. They couldn't rip our bloody clothes off fast enough. You see, it gets through fabric and sinks into the skin. Your brother escaped the worst of it. That time anyway."

"Were you both in hospital for long?"

"I was. Ed went off to convalesce at a French hospice or something. I can't tell you, because I was shipped home pretty soon afterward when they realized that what I had might kill me or be permanent. He had various injuries earlier on. They repaired him, or rebuilt I like to say, then sent him back. I could tell from when I first met him he was determined to see it through . . . It was a bloody massacre the last battle he fought. I know that much."

"Could he have somehow survived?"

"No. If there were any survivors, they would have been picked up by Germans. The battle for Flanders was intense, like many others. When there are no remains, sometimes people talk. Some had said that he had run to the other side, believing they were going to win. But I can tell you that he was a good soldier. That it was good to have him at your back. He would not have been a traitor."

The very mention of the word caused me to flinch, the sound of it cruel and unforgiving.

"Though truth be told I feel sorry for the boy in Ed's unit . . . executed, I heard, for hiding, and I must admit I did not expect to learn of Edgar's reaction."

"Executed?" I'd heard nothing of this.

"Just turned eighteen, the boy. He'd lied about his age originally to join the war with hopes to see the world. Though he was not ready for the world as it was then. The boy had seen all his friends blown to bits and his best mate die in his arms, then he just up and ran. The war, the sights, the things no man, woman, or child should see. Blighty's soldiers found him, not the Germans. Though no good that did him. Found him at the back of a barn curled up asleep. Ed spoke up for him since none of his friends were there. All dead. Your brother could have been court martialed for it. From what I heard, the authorities decided then there'd be no further progression for Edgar in the ranks, not that he chased that sort of thing. Quite the opposite."

He must have seen something worrying in my face.

"I hope this doesn't upset you. I would have thought he would have written to you about this."

I shook my head. I wondered if Andy had known this, too, but had thought to spare me from any further truths.

"Anyway the boy killed wasn't the first or the last. There were others not fit for war. Still, I would have rather been shot by the Huns than my own. And you should know that Ed wrote to the boy's parents, telling them of his courage. Ed would have enclosed his own heart if it would have made it better for them."

"Is there any chance Edgar could have been captured? Taken elsewhere?" I had an irrational glimmer of hope. What if he had wandered behind enemy lines without realizing it in the chaos and been captured, and was somewhere still alive?

"I was never fond of false hope," continued Roger. "I know there was a lot of talk of soldiers switching sides. If you hear any of this, I want you to throw it out. Ed was a good man and one of the many who vanished without a trace. It is more torturous for the families of men who are missing. Being captured by the Germans was sometimes a death sentence as well. But in all honesty, I believe that he was going to die regardless."

"What do you mean by that?"

He coughed and cleared his throat. "It's hard for me to say, though I think you should know the whole truth. See, people think that if we sweep everything under the rug, then it didn't happen. Such illnesses are very real. I witnessed them myself. People called them malingerers, but there were only a handful of those in comparison."

I was still completely confused. "I'm sorry. I don't follow what you're saying."

"I guess I'm having trouble telling you . . . Ed had a death wish. He was considered suicidal for a period and a risk to the safety of other soldiers. They had to hide him away for a while. It happened not long after the kid was caught and executed."

"You mean Edgar was imprisoned?"

He looked at me strangely then. "You haven't heard. No. I can see that you know nothing of this at all. I thought at least someone would have written briefly. I'm so sorry you had to hear it like this. There were some who said he had Soldier's Heart. And God knows why they call it that, because it appears to have less to do with the heart than it does the head and a barrage of bloody shelling. In any case, it was Edgar's nerves that got him, you see. He had the shakes.

"He went to an institution briefly. Most now know your brother's actual condition as shell shock, a term that came about in war, if you haven't already read about it in the papers. The name speaks for itself. The shelling, day in, day out, shook the ground. The force of it went through your whole body and shook the teeth in your head."

This revelation added to the already layered issue of Edgar and his disappearance. I wondered why we were not told this. It seemed absurd now that we didn't know. There was a gap at the end of his writings and poems, the missing words, between the last one and the final months before he went missing. It was this space in time that I wondered about. I thought he might have been separated from the book itself for a period, however. Roger may well have revealed the reason.

"So if he was so ill, why did he go back in the field?"

"It is a question that many will ask you, but the answers won't thrill you. If you aren't bleeding and you're not missing any limbs, then you're qualified to fight and carry heavy weapons and face an enemy. And Ed was always secretive. He may have told doctors he was all right. The lad was good at playing his cards close to his chest. It was hard to read him. But what many of us don't see is that the fear on the battlefield follows you once you leave it."

He was calm and optimistic in the days before he left Lakeland. I would never have picked Edgar for suffering like this, and I wondered what else we didn't see about him.

"Open the window for me, would you?" said Roger.

I lifted up and latched the glass while Roger took another breath through the tube, then drew a lighter and a cigarette case he had hidden beneath his chair. Leaning close to the gap at the window, he lit and inhaled from a cigarette before blowing smoke outside. I noticed that his hand shook. "If my mother asks, tell her it was yours. She is always telling me off since she can't stand the smell, and it makes her cough. I usually say it's someone burning something down the street. I have to pay the newspaper boy to bring them to me secretly. Mumsy also thinks they're somehow bad for one's health, that they'll kill me quicker. But I don't think I would cope so well without them. I, too, have vivid memories, and sometimes in the night I think I'll go mad, I sleep so poorly. I expect I'll be back in hospital soon, and then I'll probably miss her fussing."

I smiled though I wasn't sure if I should. His fatalistic view of his future, on top of the devastating news about Edgar, saddened me.

"There is something on your mind. You have come here to learn something of your brother, but I can tell there is more you're searching for."

I told him then about Mariette and the child and showed him the photo.

"Yes, I know her," he said. "I know them all. Percy Davis, that fellow there, was blown up shortly after that photograph was taken. The other man, Jerome, owned an orchard where we were billeted, and the girl you're talking about was his daughter."

I straightened before leaning forward to hang on to his every word.

"Ed took over my billet after I was shipped out with Percy. And the next time I heard about him, he'd been transferred to a hospital for some respite."

"Do you have the billet address?"

"The orchard was about four miles outside of Bailleul."

I was excited by the news.

"I know the town took heavy bombings, and I've heard most are not yet in fit shape for visitors, but I can mark it on a map there if you wish. If you open the desk, you will find a map of France."

I passed him the map and a pen, and he left his cigarette in his mouth as he opened out the page and drew a small X on the place he guessed was "close enough."

"Did you know of a relationship?"

"He never said anything to me. He wasn't that sort of person. But from what you just said, he must have been keen on her."

He asked what Mariette's character was like, and I described her.

He nodded, examining the image. "That is certainly me and, yes, the girl . . . Flirtatious from what I remember. The soldiers loved her, and I can tell you that she loved the soldiers."

It must have shown on my face: a slight withdrawal from this information, from the sting of it.

"I'm sorry," he said, handing me back the photograph. "That was probably uncalled for. It's just that she was one of those French girls that you do in fact remember."

He looked sorrowful then, and it was his advice following that I would carry for longer and even to this very day.

"I can't say if what she says is true or otherwise, but there is a child now. And whether it's Ed's or not, he has come under your care. I think you should give him the benefit of the doubt and raise him as if he is your brother's. Though it is just my opinion of course. I don't know the whole truth of it."

I nodded.

"Anyway, to hell with the Kaiser, eh?" he said, inhaling an extra-long breath from the tube.

"Indeed. To hell with the Kaiser."

I was grateful for his frankness, and I wished him the very best. He shook my hand warmly, though his hand was cold, considering the autumn was still yet mild.

CHAPTER 14

On the train going back to Lakeland that night, I watched the darkened hills in the distance heading to meet me, amid a silent landscape that had seen no war in over a century. I thought how safe and wonderful it was here. The descriptions that both Andy and Roger had given me were frightening, and I tried to see the world through Edgar's eyes. I tried to visualize the horrors but found I couldn't. I wished I could. I wished I could endure some of it: if I had been older, if he had sent us a letter, a plea for help. Though there was nothing that I could have changed, I still carried regret that I had not been there to alter Edgar's fate.

I battled for some time with myself during the train journey over whether to tell Mother any of the things I had found: the diary, the stories from Andy and Roger. Perhaps it was better that she remembered him differently. The idea that her shining star had faded and suffered miserably before his end would affect her deeply. And then I had to think of Edgar, too. He had not written for a reason. He may not have wanted anyone to know, and I felt blessed in some way that the few who did were men who would not spread such stories around, for they would surely have done so by now. Edgar's secret had been kept hidden.

As I opened the briefcase to retrieve Edgar's diary again, I noticed the envelope from Roland that held the list of the missing, thrust between bylines and rough sketches of shopfronts that I was meant to complete. I opened the envelope cautiously at first, scanning down the list of the dead and trying to grasp the enormity of such a war and the fact that this was one page from many volumes. The page of names smelled freshly of ink, but the content, the message within was from another time. I stared at Edgar's name, a man with big plans and a world of opportunities, reduced to small black print. It seemed so wrong. His last moments that were trapped within the type—the date and the place he was killed—did not feel real to me, as if the information were about someone I didn't know.

As well from Roland was a small handwritten piece about the battles during this German offensive and the number of dead, injured, and captured. There was something about the date beside Edgar's that stood out, though I did not have to ponder, as Roland had already worked it out. *Have a look at the date. It seems the date of his official missing in service has changed from that in earlier vague correspondence from his regiment. I can only imagine it was chaotic during those final months. The confusion about the exact date may have been the reason someone inadvertently left his name out of the original published records. I think, though, this will not give you closure but the need for more investigation.*

Arriving back at the house, I examined all the evidence before me. Against the warm lamplight that spread across the pages, the words looked harsh, and the discrepancy was apparent. I stared at it dumbly. The date of his newly recorded death was less than a fortnight before his date of marriage.

I sat back and wondered several things. The first was whether there was an error in the recording of his death. Could the registry have got it wrong? But more importantly it triggered my mind to various places I wished it hadn't gone. Did he not die on the battlefield but elsewhere, perhaps a less honorable death? Or was the man on the certificate an imposter, Edgar's identity and handwriting stolen? My mind buzzed with possibilities, all leading to nowhere.

It would be another issue, I was certain, that would be contested if this information in the register were deemed accurate. If it came to it in a court of law to ascertain the authenticity of a marriage certificate, a document such as this would prevail: a record signed by a military officer. A dead man can't get married. I remembered the hesitation by Mariette before she handed it over, which I had assumed was for another reason. The inconsistency of dates would affect any inheritance for Samuel, whose chance of a legitimate endowment was narrowing. This new evidence from Roland also meant that Mother would never find a sense of closure. With Samuel, there was some part of Edgar's history that we could both hold on to. Without him Edgar was simply on a list of the dead and the mystery of his time away buried somewhere with him on foreign shores. I conceded I would need to talk to Mother about it and hoped that she did not involve Laurence until I had covered every avenue of inquiry. There was no doubt Mariette and Edgar were connected. The points in contention now were how and when.

And what to do about the child in the meantime? We had all grown so fond of Samuel. A part of me still clung unsurely to the belief he was my nephew, and part of me also believed he was brought here by Mariette for a reason, for a better fate than the one he'd had before. Of that I felt sure.

Mother was back to sleeping in late. It was after lunch the following day when I found her on the terrace of her room under the shade of a large sunhat. Peggy had encouraged her to seek fresh air, though from her restlessness I could tell she would not be there long. I asked if she would like to speak with Samuel, but she declined. It was the same mother after Edgar died. Mariette and Samuel had brought her out into the light again, and that light was quickly extinguished by a set of even more bizarre circumstances.

"Mother, there is something you need to read."

"Not now, Rudy."

She turned away from me, but I persisted.

"These are all items that Mariette left behind. Also, from Roland, a copy of Edgar's name on a list of those dead or presumed dead." Which until recent events had meant the same thing. I left the list on the tea table nearby along with the marriage certificate, the will, and the diary. One did not push Mother when she was in one of her dismissive moods, and owing to her current condition, I did not feel it was timely to mention the news of Edgar's illness, which would only add to her worries. Besides, I could not confirm such a condition to be true. Though I trusted the men I had spoken to, without an official account Mother might reject it as vicious speculation, which might also deter her from pursuing any further investigation that could reveal Edgar in a poor light. With the documents now in front of her, she would no doubt have the mind to compare the date of Edgar's death with the marriage certificate, which had only complicated the mystery and placed a more doubtful cloud above Samuel. "I'm not sure what you will make of it, but I think that these should now be in your care."

Laurence did not come back to the manor in the meantime, but he responded to my request for more details about Mariette's last night here with a rather hostile note to say that undoubtedly her purpose had been to manipulate Mother and me for money. Laurence himself had manipulated Mother for money in recent months, so his contribution to speculation meant little at this point.

But truth be known, I was also losing hope myself that there would ever be an answer. I feared the fate of the boy would ultimately lie in Laurence's hands, and I had to prevent that at all costs.

Mariette had taken her bag and earrings but left the dresses we bought her. Was that a message to me perhaps that the earrings meant something to her, some reminder of our time together? I didn't really believe it. In the back of my mind, I thought they were something she would likely sell. But what didn't make sense was the fact that Samuel was still here. I saw the way she was with him, possessive and caring. He had called her *Maman*. It did not seem possible that a child would do that if indeed the child had been stolen and used as Laurence suggested. The boy was undoubtedly foreign. He spoke mostly French, but understood a surprising amount of English also, which led me to suspect he may have been in England longer than we thought.

With his mother gone now for over a week, Samuel had grown more accepting of her absence, but his curiosity-driven enthusiasm had dimmed, and he preferred to spend more quiet moments lying with Missy. I vowed to devote more time to him and gave him a tour of the library on the top floor, which in times gone by had also been used as a formal room for entertaining special guests and had been off limits to children entirely. He was intrigued by the number of books and awed by the gold-framed paintings on the wall. Samuel looked at the marble fireplace and the silverware and ornaments on the top and, above these, pressed flowers put in small gold frames. There was so much to see, and his eyes were having trouble landing on anything.

I went over to a section of the library to search for books on farm animals to show Samuel. When I turned, he had walked to the end of the room and was staring at the wall. The wall had a selection of photographs of the family at various ages and some portraits as well: Mother in her wedding gown; us boys standing in various poses around the property; Father, in his better times, sitting at his desk, the photograph used by a newspaper when he was at the height of his career and dabbling in philanthropy, in this particular case donating funds for a new school in a rural village.

Samuel had found a picture on the wall of Edgar in uniform. The picture was taken on the station platform before he left. Mother had it placed in a large frame on its own in the center of all the others so you could never miss it. Mariette had seen these also. I remember her inspecting them carefully and wondered then why she didn't move to see them again.

I had presumed from the photograph kept by Mariette that Samuel had seen pictures of his father before.

"You know him, don't you?" I asked.

He nodded.

"Is that your father?" I asked, simply to start a conversation, but I was unprepared for the response.

He shook his head.

"He is the same man in the photograph that your mother carried. You've seen that one, haven't you?"

He looked a little confused before nodding.

I thought to be careful then. I had no idea what the boy had been told by Mariette.

He said something in his small voice in French then.

"Qu'est-ce que c'est?" I asked.

"That man is Uncle Fabien," he repeated.

I looked at the image again and back at Samuel. I stepped closer to point directly at Edgar in the photo.

"This man here? Is he your uncle?"

The boy nodded. I took the picture from the wall so he could look at it closely.

"Are you sure?"

He nodded again, confused by my sudden interest and without any idea about the information he had just unleashed. My mind raced. What had I missed? What was said? I thought of the conversations with Mariette, the uncle that she alluded to, the one she said had died. Mariette had said there were no relatives left in France.

"Did you see Uncle Fabien before you came here?"

"Before the boat. He came to say goodbye."

"The boat that brought you to England? To here?"

Samuel nodded. Mariette had said there were no relatives left alive, partly the reason for her departure from France and a likely explanation for her timing to bring Samuel here.

"Can you count, Samuel?"

"Yes! I can count to ten!"

"Very good! Can you count how many nights you spent in England before you arrived here at this house? How many nights from when you left the boat to when you first met me?"

He thought hard and shook his head.

"I can remember what we ate for supper before we came here!" he said proudly. "We had potatoes and, one time, beef."

"How many times did you have supper after you left the boat? Can you remember that?"

He shook his head.

"Can you try really hard for me? Can you think about all the times you stopped and where you slept?"

He counted slowly on his fingers, frowning and recounting, before settling on a number. "Four!"

I could not completely rely on this, of course, but it was encouraging. It meant if Uncle Fabien had seen Samuel off at the boat in France and Mariette and Samuel had only been in England days before arriving at Lakeland, then there was a strong chance the "uncle" that Mariette had mentioned—presuming she was referring to the same one—had not died after all.

Though the recognition of Edgar as Fabien might simply mean there was a confusing similarity between the two men as seen by a young child, I couldn't discount it. Why Edgar would change his name and what relationship he had with the boy only added to such a confusing tale.

But still my heart beat thunderously because what it told me was that if Uncle Fabien was my brother, then, according to the boy, Edgar had not only lived well beyond the war, he might also be alive today.

CHAPTER 15

Mother summoned me later that evening. She said that she still suspected the marriage certificate and will were fakes, though she sounded less than convincing. The will was scrawled and ragged, but I had seen an essence of Edgar there in the slant and weight of the strokes, and I believe Mother had seen this also. Laurence's talk of forgery had filled her with only thoughts of deceit. She tapped Edgar's diary that sat on her lap.

"How do you think she got this?"

"The same way she got the will. From Edgar."

Mother's expression gave very little away. She was keeping her thoughts well guarded.

"I would like to think she will collect her child eventually if indeed he is hers."

"And if she doesn't?" I asked.

"Then we will have to wait and see what happens."

I believe her attitude in that moment was simply armor against her true feelings about Samuel. She did not want to believe in something only to be disappointed to learn a different truth.

"Mother, what I am about to tell you might just help with your decision."

I did not want to give her false hope, but it was my wish that news of the mysterious Uncle Fabien would convince her there was enough truth to connect Samuel with Edgar. I did not yet wish to tell her what Roger Whitney had relayed. I still felt that such knowledge would keep her awake at night, wondering where she went wrong and taking Edgar's pain upon herself. I relayed what the boy had said about the uncle, and she sat there pensively at first while I awaited her response. Though I did not expect what came next, so accustomed to my mother's reserve.

She hugged the diary to her chest, then broke into heavy tears that shook her frail body. The crying was so wretched, her heart so broken, I thought my own would give out in that moment. I passed her my handkerchief, knelt beside her, and held her hand until she had calmed. Mother then gingerly handed me the notebook, almost reluctant to let it go.

"Find him!" she whispered.

I inquired of ferry times from Dover to Calais. From there I would take the train to Armentières, which was the next town from Bailleul, its station temporarily closed for more reconstruction.

The following day, after giving Bert a final hand with maintenance issues, I called into Mother's bedroom to say my farewell.

"Rudy," she said. "You and Edgar were always so close. Edgar was a good man, but you may even be a better one. You are able to look into people's hearts and see things that others can't. I also know that you fell in love with Mariette. It is easy to see why you did, and though I warned you against any relationship, I also trust your judgment. You have to know that."

I was touched by her words.

"Take this with you," she said, handing me Edgar's diary. "Maybe there is a clue there. So many of the lines I have gone over in my head, but I've come up with nothing so far. The marriage certificate is in the back of the book for you to verify if you get the chance, but I will hold on to the will. I believe it appears legitimate, but whether the boy is Edgar's still has to be proven. Whether the Mariette who was here is the same as the one on the certificate or an imposter is also in question. Regardless, Samuel will be taken care of. Of that you can be assured, since I know it is a question you have been burning to ask."

I smiled gratefully.

She closed her eyes, and I thought that was my cue to go.

"Rudy," she said, and sat up. "There is something I need to give you."

She opened her side drawer and pulled out a sprig of rosemary with a white ribbon.

"If the trip should give you a different truth, and should you come upon the last known place where Edgar fought, please place this there. I've had the vicar bless it, and hopefully it will give Edgar eternal rest."

"I will, Mother. I will do that for you."

"And this is also for you." She passed me an envelope.

I opened it, and inside was sixty pounds worth of banknotes.

"Mother, that is a lot of money. Where did you get it?"

"I sold some things when I was last in Manchester. Some silverware and several pieces of jewelry. I wish I'd taken the lot, now that most of it is gone anyway."

"Mother, you should not give me so much—"

"Nonsense! I was planning to use the money to put aside for Samuel's education, before all the terrible business of Mariette's disappearance, but I am not sure in any case it will be enough. I think for whatever you are planning, you will need the money, and I will send you more if need be." She paused. "I have to tell you, Rudy, I would be overjoyed to learn for certain that the boy is Edgar's son. If not, I do not think that our finances can stretch to the education our generations have been afforded. But I believe there is a solution somewhere that will suit him and one where he will not want for the necessities of life."

"Yes, Mother." She had made it clear. She was fond of the boy, but she still had reservations about Mariette and Samuel, regardless of her feelings. Economy for family would be applied differently than for those who weren't. Pragmatic she would always be, though ultimately I believed her heart would also guide her choices.

I leaned down and kissed her on the cheek before seeking out Samuel.

"Where are you going?" Samuel asked in the kitchen, looking at my hat and the soft leather travel bag I was carrying.

"I'm going to see the town where your mother and you lived."

"Will she be there?"

"I'm hoping."

"Will you bring her back?"

It was a question I had asked myself.

"If she is able."

"Are you coming back?"

"Of course, though I am not sure when exactly."

He looked about to cry.

I crouched down to hug him, and he threw his small arms around my neck. I knew he continued to feel the loss of his mother terribly, and for another person to leave him, albeit temporarily, his losses continued.

"Don't be sad," I said. "We'll have many more riding times ahead when I return."

I pulled him away to wipe his eyes. I had questioned him about his home earlier, as had Peggy, but we were unable to glean much, other than a brief description of the house, of fishing, of men that came sometimes to visit in the night, and of several dogs there that were his friends. These descriptions were at times confusing and seemingly overembellished.

I tapped him on the head and told him to look after Bert and Missy before he ran off to find them. Peggy held me tightly as if I were going to war or leaving for good, before Bert whisked me away.

At the station, Bert shook my hand firmly with both of his, like I'd seen him do with Edgar. It was as if I were following in my brother's footsteps, though there was a major point of difference. I was certain I would return.

"You're a fine young man, Rudy." Bert rarely called me just by my name, and I suddenly realized how very human we all were, how in many ways, despite class, we were much the same deep down. All just yearning to be known and at the very least remembered. Bert temporarily taking the hat of a proud father was testament to the barriers that had broken down between our stations.

I slept for most of the train journey from London to Dover, where I then caught the paddle steamer to Calais. After converting some banknotes to the local currency and spending the night at a hotel, I rose early to travel again by train, following the path where some of the fiercest battles were fought. In passing, I keenly viewed Bailleul from the window, the town showing signs of devastation, with a number of buildings still razed to the ground, but contrasted by a sense of hope from the people I spied and the emergence of new construction.

All along the journey there was evidence of war: shell craters overgrown with weeds and wildflowers; barren, abandoned crop fields; and the remnants of houses. One village so badly shelled only a ghostly footprint left to show for it. I passed no orchards, nor could I see remains of any from the train as I passed through to my final destination. The *X* on the map to the right of the town gave me little to work from.

In Armentières, the ravages of war were evident, too. I had learned from the ticket master that many people had returned quickly here after war, eager to rebuild their lives. On his recommendation, I found a newly renovated hotel. The woman behind the counter, pleasant enough but with limited English, explained the layout of the town and the service times for breakfast and dinner. I showed her the photograph of Edgar and the others, and she called her husband from a room where music was playing. The couple examined the images of Edgar and Mariette and shook their heads. They had also not heard of anyone named Edgar or Fabien nor an orchard owner by the name of Lavier.

I offered to carry my own bag, and the woman guided me to my room and pointed out the shared bathroom down the hall, which I had to myself, since I was the only guest.

My plan was to set out early the following morning, but with several hours of daylight ahead of me, I thought to walk around the town to explore and perhaps find someone to guide me the next day. I showed the proprietor, who served behind the bar, a picture of Edgar, and he shook his head and recommended I check the cemetery. The response was rather abrupt but not unusual. I had not found an overly welcoming face here, but one could hardly expect it as the country recovered from loss.

I decided to rest for a moment with a glass of ale and noticed a man watching me from another table. He raised his drink to me affably before coming to sit with me. He was small with dark hair and a long mustache, and he was somewhat overdressed in a black velvet jacket, too large for his bony frame, and a satin collared shirt beneath.

I told him I was looking for my brother, and he commiserated and said that he had lost several family members also.

"It is so unfair what war does," he said in broken English.

He introduced himself as Lester and told me briefly about the progress the towns had made. He said that he was injured in service and that now he helped his brother making business deliveries. Perhaps it was the beer, but I felt at ease and happy to have his company, especially because he was someone who lived here when the dust of battles had finally settled.

Lester said he could perhaps take me the next day to the places that Edgar might have stayed. He said he knew people in the area who had tracked down the last steps of their loved ones successfully. He also knew of several Englishmen who lived in a house nearby, who had been here during the war. He would take me to them first. He invited me to meet him at the edge of the town, where he would bring his trap the next day. The old orchard that I mentioned he knew of also.

I noticed throughout our conversation that the barman had been watching us carefully.

"I would be wary of those," volunteered the owner after Lester had left. He had overheard my conversation with the man, and any mistrust he had of me had broken down.

"Those?" I queried.

"He's not from around these parts, but he talks as if he is," he said in English.

The barman spoke briefly about some other relatives of foreign soldiers who had been through to pay their respects, and he hoped that I would find something to bring me peace. He had heard of orchards in the region, but since he had only come into the business after the war, he could not tell me much about the people here. From where I told him it was situated, he said it was unlikely it still existed.

I woke early at daybreak and shaved the two days of growth that had appeared patchy and unruly around my jawline. I then ordered a small food pack with bread and cheese and a flask of water for the journey ahead and proceeded to the edge of the town to meet Lester. The discussion and transaction had been so quick, and he had left before I had time to carefully consider it. I should have taken this as a sign, but in a foreign country, I was at the mercy of everyone and anyone.

Lester was not waiting at the meeting point, and I watched as the sun rose higher and time ticked by. People were on the move, and delivery carts swayed through the town. I looked at the map to the *X* and estimated roughly where I might find the orchard and farmstead that Roger spoke of. I waited in total an hour and a half before something told me that he wasn't coming. I tied a handkerchief around my neck to keep the sun off my pale skin and set off by foot.

The long, narrow road was bare, surrounded by pastures with grazing animals, scattered farmhouses, and wheat fields. I estimated it was an hour's walk northwest, the orchard halfway between the two towns, and hoped that I would reach it before the clouds opened up ahead of me.

I imagined Edgar here in the fields that were still churned and clumped with detritus now overgrown with tufts of grass and weeds. His diary showed some of his suffering through his poems and observations, and I wished that he had written more about the people here also. His letters became less frequent, wordy, and personal over the course of the war, and were mostly about the rations and the weather. I imagine he would not have wanted to tell Mother about the way he was feeling, about any injury and the terrible conditions.

Someone traveling by trap stopped to ask if I was lost. I inquired of the orchard, which he knew about. He pointed the way. He said most of the house was still standing but the owners had long since left. He could not tell me anything else about the previous owners since he had come to Bailleul to rebuild at the end of the war, after his northern village was wiped off the map.

The rain had just begun to fall, and I sprinted the last part of the journey. In the middle of a field was a small house and behind it the remains of a shed and those of a smaller building also. There was an arbor leading toward a field, and I could see where rows of fruit trees had once stood, some still growing wild. On foot the evidence of shelling was even clearer by the many grass-covered dips that made the ground uneven, including one larger crater that Mariette had spoken of.

The front door of the little house was swinging on one hinge, and I pulled it back gingerly to step inside. The house was mostly gutted of its contents except for the bones of a spring bed, an armchair that was leaking its stuffing, and a thick-legged table in the center that appeared to be kneeling with two of its legs removed. There were also signs of previous water damage and a cover of dust. I knew immediately that Mariette had not come directly from here, that she had long since gone. There was no trace to determine who lived here, no lingering smells of domesticity, just an earthy scent of dying grasses outside that blew in through several cracked windows. I walked to the small woodstove and peered inside at ashes that had turned cold and hard. The low house was small and square in structure, with a main living area at the front and two bedrooms and a bathing and laundry room situated at the rear. Across several windows hung curtains that were faded and torn, and there was nothing to suggest the owners might return.

A small navy-colored ribbon now layered in cobwebs and dust was swept to one corner. Above the bed in one of the rooms, I could see something scratched into the wall and leaned close to examine an *H* enclosed in a love heart, and I traced my finger around the grooved shape, feeling Mariette there and imagining it had once been under her touch. But it could have been anyone, and I brushed away the notion as childish nonsense, something desperate. Perhaps I was.

Opening the cellar door in the floor also opened up several years of stench that had been trapped. Stepping down the narrow stair and under the barest of light that filtered in through the doorway, I could make out empty barrels and crates but little else, and still no link to who lived here.

I left the house, feeling frustrated that I had reached a dead end, though I was still determined to find someone who knew of Jerome in the town of Bailleul, another hour from where I was. Someone had to have known them. I would not give up, I told my brother on the wind, knowing that Edgar would have done the same if our situations were reversed. Though I suspect he would have done this sooner.

I walked back out into the open and a waning midday sun. It struggled now to burst between clouds, and a spike in the air told me of the cooler night to come. Halfway toward the town, I saw tall ruins atop a hill, jagged against the bleak sky that loomed up behind them. Once I had passed the ruins, I heard someone calling and turned to look for the source along the road. They called again before I saw that there was someone waving to me from alongside the broken building.

I stepped cautiously upward in the caller's direction before recognizing the suited stranger from the tavern the night before. He had no cart. I was suddenly wary and walked no closer.

"Sorry, monsieur, I was so late, but in the meantime I made some inquiries about the family you spoke of," said Lester. "I told you about the Englishmen I knew, and one of them knew your brother and knew the family well."

I didn't feel right about this information, but I could not of course discount anything. There was something shifty about his manner, and I kept my distance.

"What are you doing here?" I asked, looking around me to see if he was alone.

"I was waiting for you and away from the road and out of the elements. If you wish, I can take you back and you can speak to the men directly."

"Can you give me the address of these men?"

The man frowned and squinted as if he didn't like what I had just asked. He did not like to be tested, and my instinct told me to turn and walk the ten yards back to the road.

"No, no!" he said. "They will not speak to you without me."

I realized immediately that this was completely wrong, that he was an opportunist, and I took a step back as he took a step forward. In my peripheral vision I saw someone else come around the side of the wall. The man, similar in appearance to the other, held a knife.

"You had better come with us," said the original scoundrel.

I turned then and commenced to run but felt someone close behind me before my world went black.

CHAPTER 16

I heard the sounds of a motorcar from afar. Something tapped my face, and liquid trickled into my nose and mouth. I opened my eyes to an overcast sky and took several seconds to realize that it was heavy raindrops that had woken me, the back of my head in a chalky brown puddle of water. The men, it appeared, had dragged me behind the ruins.

I tried to raise my head, but a sharp pain forced me gently back down again. I turned on my side, fluttered my eyes, and then eased myself upright. I blinked away the rain and the fogginess in my head and inspected the area around me. The contents of my bag, some food, and my identity card were scattered across the soaked ground, and inside my jacket my wallet was gone. They had not even bothered to pull me under the partial cover of a broken shed that sat behind the wall.

I reached for my things, shoved them in the carry bag, then dragged myself out of the rain and under the shelter, muddied and sodden and hidden from any passersby.

It was hard to estimate how long I had lost consciousness, but noting the purple-gray haze that was growing darker around me, I guessed it would soon be nightfall. I forced myself to stand somewhat shakily, the head injury still clouding my sense of judgment, and I proceeded toward the road in the direction of Armentières.

I do not know how long I'd walked, possibly not far, when someone in a motorcar stopped beside me and asked if I was all right. I told him briefly what had happened. He got out then, seeing that I was slightly disoriented, and helped me into the passenger seat before regaining his seat and heading back toward my hotel.

"You English, you are so gullible!" He did not say this unkindly. I heard only pity in the words, and declined his offer following to take me directly to a doctor. All I could think about was the soft mattress in my hotel room that should melt away the day.

I thanked the stranger after he dropped me in front of the hotel. With unsteady steps, a feeling of dizziness and nausea, and an aching shoulder as a result of the fall, I pushed open the door with some difficulty.

Cedric and Simone, the hotel owners, hurried toward me and found I was also bleeding from the wound at the back of my skull. They appeared shocked and flustered and led me to a chair in the restaurant. Simone rushed to bring me a damp cloth for my head and a drink of water.

They were very sympathetic with what I had been through and recommended I speak with the police. With my head throbbing the way it did, talking was the last thing I wished to do right then. It could wait until morning. If I had not thought to leave most of my money under the mattress in my room, my quest may well have ended that day. I felt both poorly and disappointed by my complacency toward my safety, so desperate I was for any information.

"Since the war we have had a problem with looters and some who prey on the vulnerable," said Cedric. "The ones who hurt you most likely travel from village to village so as not to be caught. The police are aware of these people, but there is little they can do. They can vanish into thin air when they need to. It was a problem before the war, and it is still a problem since."

He asked again about my brother, and they took longer this time to examine the photograph that had fortunately remained dry inside my jacket, though the couple still did not recognize those pictured.

"I can make inquiries of people who lived in Bailleul if you wish. I am certain someone will know something. There were several orchards in the region at the time, but we were not supplied by the one you have described."

I thanked them for their sincere concern. Simone brought up soup later on with some bread, but that is the last thing I clearly remember about that day. In the morning my headache had worsened, and I couldn't get out of bed.

Someone was knocking loudly on the door, and when I didn't stir, I heard a commotion on the stairs and the clinking of a key in the door.

"Are you all right, monsieur?" Simone asked, entering timidly.

My vision was blurred, and I did not feel well at all. She spoke fast in French and gave some hurried instructions to a maid who had walked up behind her.

"We will bring our doctor for you. He is retired now and only visits his old clients, but he will come if I ask. We will also report the incident to the police for you, and make sure they keep a lookout for the scoundrels."

I was only awake long enough to hear this before I fell into a restless sleep, dreaming of war and death and men chasing Samuel. I woke to Cedric lifting me up into a sitting position at the instruction of another man who was small and stout.

"Monsieur Watts, you must stay awake!" said the stranger. "You have sustained a bad concussion, and I will need to check that you are okay."

The man, then introduced as the doctor, checked my head wound and temperature; performed an eyesight test, moving a stick in front of my eyes; and listened to my heart through his stethoscope. As he was placing his instruments back in his bag, he said, "I saw the photo. Madame Bernard asked if I recognized anyone from it. Though the photograph is a little unclear, I think I know the people you are seeking, in particular the soldier I treated here. Simone described in more detail the girl you spoke of, red hair, very dark eyes, and I am fairly certain that I met her once, too."

I sat up a little straighter, the pain in my head momentarily eased by the news. The doctor gently pushed me back again. "Just relax. You have had quite a trauma. Before we discuss that, I want to check that you haven't damaged anything else. Do you feel pain elsewhere?"

He examined my shoulder that was stiff and sore, which must have also suffered in the fall.

"I think that you must take these painkillers I will leave you. You must not try to walk anywhere until the pain is gone."

I nodded, but I did not care about that. I only wanted to hear of my brother and Mariette.

"I don't know what became of her, but I remember treating the Englishman," said the doctor. "A man named Jerome Lavier was looking after him. The doctor who had treated him and his family in the past had cleared out of Bailleul during the chaos, which was why he approached me for my help. The Germans were searching houses, looking for those who might have harbored deserters. I remember thinking it was very brave. I lived in a village not far from here, but dangerously far for Jerome to travel to at the time. He did not say where the patient came from, but I suspected that he was on the run."

"What was his injury?"

"He had shrapnel in his thigh. It wasn't serious, but it could have been if there was an infection, as can often be the case."

"Do you remember the date?"

He thought for a moment and said that he could not remember exactly but that the Germans arrived for the second time in spring, so it was around then. Late April, several weeks after the evacuation, he said, though he chose to remain behind. It was the time also that Edgar was listed as missing in action, but I did not tell him that. I did not feel it necessary to state that my brother might be one of those deserters or the fact that he had an injury of the mind, which the doctor did not mention, presumably kept hidden.

"Their fruit orchard was decimated, I learned later. The girl you spoke of sometimes came to this town with her father. I knew Jerome briefly, and I recognized him also in the photo. He seemed like a good man, but he kept to himself. After the Germans left and the war was over, I was tired and went to stay in Paris with my son and his wife. My son was injured, too. I was keen to leave here and help them for a while. War nearly destroyed me, I have to say. So many people dead, dying, diseased, and broken. Then I came back to the region to semi-retire. This is my home. I can't live anywhere else. And people still need me here."

I tried to imagine what he must have gone through and read the sadness in his words.

"Do you know if Jerome had any other family?"

"He had a sister. I did not know him or his family very well. People tell me things if they wish me to know. But Jerome and his family kept to themselves for the most part. There were rumors before the war, though I am not partial to them of course. I think that Jerome would not have stood for any trouble. It was just people with too few things to concern themselves with. But you know how people talk. After the war started it was a different story of course. The town pulled together. Gossip at the time was more about the Germans and the fate of France."

"What sort of rumors?"

"Jerome's sister and the daughter, I believe, did not get on. Jerome's sister was unhappy with her behavior . . . A pretty girl amongst fertile youths, getting them flustered . . . Oh, I'm sorry. I see by your expression this affects you greatly. Don't mind such talk. I should not have even mentioned it. They seemed like people that kept out of the way. The girl, Mariette you say, was married to your brother, is that right?"

I nodded.

"Stories are exaggerated, and I can tell you that when war came they did their part. I know that firsthand. Jerome and his family, and others also, took in Allied soldiers, and it was much to ask since war went on for as long as it did and with food so hard to come by."

"And Jerome's sister," I asked, "is she still here somewhere?"

"No, I believe that she moved away."

This news was everything I wanted, that someone who had been here with Mariette was alive to tell me what had happened. I tried to sit up, but my head felt as if it had been anchored to the pillow with weights. The doctor saw me grimace.

"You need to rest; otherwise your next destination will be a hospital. I will find out the address in the meantime, but you need to spend the day in bed at least, and I will be back this afternoon to check on you."

I thanked him. I really did feel quite dizzy at the time and very tired.

"I will have Madame bring you up some food. You need to eat something."

I thanked him. I was very grateful for his help and especially for the news. Mariette was who she said she was. That much was very clear. I offered to pay the doctor, but he declined. He said he owed a great deal more for my brother Edgar's sacrifice, and that of all the other brave men who fought on French soil.

"You must rest!"

Over the course of the day, I felt better, though I drifted in and out of sleep, and the times I was dreaming, my head was swimming with faces of Edgar and my assailant, of finding dead bodies, one of them Edgar's. Whatever medicine the doctor had given me took over my imagination, and I woke up sweating profusely, and dazed, but at least my headache was gone. My appetite returned; Madame Bernard brought me some tea and some sweet rolls and a small casserole pot of meat and vegetables.

Dr. Durand came back to check on me as promised and reported that I was on the mend. He also came back with some information about Jerome's sister, Lenore Lavier.

"I managed to find her address from the post office. She lives in Rouen. I also took the opportunity to ask around, to see if I could find out any details about the family. It seems the fate of the girl is unknown, but I learned something sad and that is that Jerome volunteered to work near the front line in the final months of war and died. And there is something else, which I have only just learned, which may or may not be the news you want."

I held my breath.

"It seems that Jerome had a habit of taking in strays and feeding the homeless. The girl was not his, and Lenore did not approve of her living there. Mariette appeared out of thin air, it seems, when she was younger. I also learned that his own son from his marriage had died many years earlier. But I think, though, if you are to learn something other than gossip and guesswork, you had best seek out Madame Lavier."

I stood up to shake his hand, and this time my brain did not pound against the walls of my skull. "Thank you so very much. I must leave straightaway."

He did not push me back down this time but said it would be best to leave in the morning on the train. Without other travel options at that point, I agreed.

"One final thing I do remember also. Jerome and I did have a brief conversation when he was returning me home on his trap after I treated your brother. He was planning to leave the area very shortly. He saw no future there."

He spoke then about the region and gave me some history of the surrounding towns, about Rouen and the train times, and I told him about my home. He was warm, and I felt as if I had made another friend. I did not feel disappointed that Mariette was fostered, but the other hearsay about her distracting the men in the town perhaps affected me more than anything else. Regardless, I slept well that night, and in the morning after a breakfast of bacon, bread, and cheese, I thanked my hosts, paid them a little extra for all their help, and continued my quest for the truth.

CHAPTER 17

The train entered the station of Rouen, which was vastly different from the towns and villages I had passed. Here it was untouched by shelling, picturesque on the banks of the Seine River, and bustling with commerce and arts. I asked several people to direct me to the address Dr. Durand had given me and came upon a smaller, less ornate part of the city. I climbed the stairs to Lenore's apartment that sat above a bakery on a tired-looking street.

My first impression of Lenore was that she did not like visitors. It felt as if I had only seconds to explain myself, as the door she had first opened was closing again at the sight of a stranger. I quickly explained how I obtained her address and showed her the photo. I had her attention at least, and she curiously inspected the faces in the image before looking up at me. She was tall, thin, with gray hair, the skin on her face sagging from the weight of disappointment, though there was no doubt she was related to the man in the photo. She was a woman who was not used to smiling much, and I could tell immediately she did not view the world at large as anything to celebrate.

She asked for my name again, some of the suspicion fading.

"I hope you didn't give her any money!"

I pointed to Mariette. "Is this who you are speaking about?"

She nodded.

I tensed with anticipation, edging so close to the truth now. I had found someone who knew Mariette, who could offer more clues, but who perhaps knew some things that I did not want to hear.

"Do you know where she moved to?" I asked.

"I have not seen her," she said shortly, the gap in the door slowly narrowing.

"What about this man, your brother?" I said, pointing to Jerome in the photo.

She looked at me then, and I could tell she wanted to say something.

"Do you mind if I come in and talk to you about it?"

This woman was my only link. I could not let her go.

Perhaps it was my boyish face or the fineness of my clothes, I'm not sure, but I felt lucky that she let me in at all given the suspicion I was initially greeted with. She walked with a cane, which she used to point to the chair she wanted me seated in.

It was a small apartment, empty of those cherished items that people of a later age acquire through time. There was only a photograph on the shelf of her and a man, and a second one of her and another male from when she was much younger. When I asked about the pictures, she did not look my way. The subjects perhaps were the chink in her armor.

I then broached the subject gently because I could tell she was not someone who opened her heart to just anyone. I told her about my loss, my mother's grief, and the fact that we were searching for more information about Edgar's last days before his final battle. I did not suggest that there were things that led me to believe he might still be living.

She told me that she did not meet Edgar, though she heard through a friend that soldiers were living at her brother's house. After Lenore left Bailleul at the beginning of the war, she communicated very rarely with Jerome and did not wish to keep in contact with anyone else there. She had left for Rouen to get away from the shelling noises and the town, which had turned into a soldiers' fort. She did not like the foreign-speaking soldiers and their loud ways. She did not like the smell of fighting men, she said. She seemed cold and bitter, though I suspect that life had led her this way, and I tried to wade through the resentment to see the person beneath.

"My husband and my brother were friends as children. My husband was killed in the Franco-Prussian War. Only my brother came back, but he lost his own wife and young son to influenza a short time later. We had an orchard, which had been handed down from our parents, though I never really took to the work. I studied here in Rouen to be a teacher and then thought I would retire with Jerome to some years of peace, but Mariette came along, and that ended that. I supposed he needed help around the orchard, which I didn't give him. I have arthritis. It wasn't possible.

"I have to tell you, Monsieur Watts, that it is my belief that if not for Mariette, Jerome would have probably lived, perhaps the two of us here in Rouen, the orchard sold before the war came. His focus changed."

"What do you mean?" I was suddenly afraid of what she might tell me. Was Mariette a liar, a serial offender of such crimes as to enter people's lives to prey on them, to take advantage of their kindness?

"Before I tell you any more, why don't you tell me something about the girl yourself and how you came to be here, interrupting my afternoon rest."

She was a canny woman, I had discovered, her feelings cleverly masked. Perhaps my expressions had given something of my heart away at the mention of Mariette. Whatever it was, I had to give her more to receive more.

I told her then about the encounter with Mariette in some detail. I said that Mariette had become Edgar's wife and that they had a son, to which she raised her eyebrows. I left out the obvious details of my affections. I also wanted to know why there seemed to be so much secrecy surrounding Mariette's past.

"I do know Mariette, and she is not what she appears. I suppose she tried to pass herself off to you as my brother's daughter."

"She spoke of her father, Jerome Lavier."

"Yes, Jerome took them in, vagrants they were. He loved those girls despite what they were. But I didn't trust them."

"Them?"

"She and her sister Helene."

She studied me before getting up to sift through some papers in a drawer, digging something out from the bottom of the pile. She passed me the item.

It was a photograph of Mariette, several years younger, and beside her another girl just a fraction shorter than Mariette and darker skinned, dressed in trousers and a long-sleeved shirt rolled up to the elbows. The girl's hair was pulled back into a ponytail, and she had a slightly harder look than Mariette, with catlike eyes and wide, sharply angled cheekbones. I saw no resemblance between the pair.

"She didn't tell you about her sister. That's interesting," she said. "Perhaps they had been fighting over a man. Who knows? The gypsies are a crazy lot."

"Gypsies?"

Lenore viewed me carefully. "Oh, I see. You have absolutely no idea of her background. That makes sense she would not say anything. Now you know! She came from a band of thieves, and you might now see why I felt uncomfortable living with the girl. She had eyes that were always looking for trouble."

The organized and gentle interrogation I had been planning was lost as I was struggling to rearrange it with new questions.

"Mariette and Helene were thieves when we first met them, and I suspect they still are. I don't believe a person can change."

It was on the tip of my tongue to be as scathing of her as she was of Mariette, judging unfairly someone I had loved. It was hard to believe that the girl I met was the same girl Lenore was talking about, but at the back of my mind was the image of my mother's face at the discovery of her missing jewelry.

She told me how Jerome had brought them in as very small children even after they had attempted to steal food; though she did let slip during the course of the conversation that the girls were frightfully skinny, which explained why they would steal. Two homeless children who even Lenore admitted had been let down by the older gypsies in their wandering communities.

"Jerome dressed the girls in his dead wife's and son's clothing. I think it was this loss that made him act irrationally. He believed he could somehow replace his missing wife and son. But they were nothing like the quiet, sweet boy he had. They were wild, roaming around the streets, and Mariette was a troublemaker. Jerome was called in by teachers at the school several times to hear that Mariette was disruptive for fighting with others or jumping in the creek without her clothes on. Shameful really! I suppose old habits are hard to lose. I moved away quickly after that. First just to a town close by, and then after the Allied soldiers came, I left for Rouen. The older one was more stable, more a thinker. But still a gypsy, so I have to judge her much the same."

It was reluctant praise. Helene must have been a saint, for I did not think that Lenore handed out compliments generously.

"The girls worked with Jerome in the orchard, and he supported them. He did not listen to me anymore when I made suggestions. He listened to the girls."

I pictured the older man from the photographs running the orchard on his own. It must have been a godsend to finally have some help, which he had not been able to get from his sister. Though I did not voice these thoughts.

But she had not yet given me reason enough to think they were in some way bad.

"You said he would have lived if not for Mariette. What did you mean by that?"

She pinched her lips and blinked a few times. She was struggling with the answer, and I knew then that it was far more personal. I saw it all in the things she didn't say, the rushed glances that she gave me, that she was jealous of them. Jerome, who had returned from war to then lose his wife and son, who had lived alone with his sister on an orchard as the years passed him by. And then perhaps discovered a purpose again with the arrival of two small girls he could take care of.

"I believe that he would have sold the property and moved to Rouen long before the war arrived. But in the end he signed up to volunteer and got himself shelled to pieces. All I was left with were several photographs and a box of useless items he sent me before he left for the front."

"And what about the girls?"

"I heard from someone that they had left. I also heard there was trouble out there, some commotion, some trading of secrets with the Germans. And it didn't surprise me. Nothing about Mariette surprised me, and Helene was just as complicit. But I suspected that whatever bad came would have been Mariette's own doing. I did not hear of her other than that. Missing, perhaps killed, I even thought. I have little to tell you other than Mariette was wild always. Jerome brought them up and treated them as if they were his daughters, but I did not think it was right. They were not our kind. They were trouble."

It was vexing why the word "trouble" had come up several times. The shelling of the beautiful towns nearby and the fact that they were unwittingly living on the front line was the only scandal I could make sense of at that point. But my spirits were still dampened with each piece of news about Mariette. I had to believe she wasn't everything that Lenore described, that there was something more I wasn't told. I believed that to hear Jerome's word on it would have changed everything.

"Do you have any idea where the girls might have gone to? Were there any other family, contacts?"

"Gypsies. What does anyone really know about them? Even the girls couldn't tell Jerome anything when he questioned them about their past."

"They were very young, is that right?"

She shrugged and looked at me sideways, interpreting my question as combative, which of course it was. I had to wonder why, for someone reluctant to discuss Mariette and Helene in the first instance, she seemed keen to disclose every negative thought she had about the girls.

"It appears that they at least helped on the farm."

"They worked in the orchard. Helene was steady, and Mariette was a fast learner."

Finally, something positive about Mariette that she found dreadfully hard to say, though I could tell she felt guilty that perhaps she could not have been more help on the orchard herself.

We had reached the end of the conversation, and I struggled to find more questions. I looked around the room, saw the curtains that had not been changed for years, the cupboards wearing, the floorboards scratched and unpolished, and her aging body. Selling the orchard early might have given her some money, I realized, and felt some remorse for her situation.

I thanked her for the tea and was about to stand to leave, then wondered about the box she spoke of.

"Is there anything in the box of Jerome's that might give me some indication of Mariette's whereabouts?"

"I don't think so, Monsieur Watts."

"I can give you some money," I said, "for your trouble."

She frowned, though her expression was less aggrieved, her mouth not pulled so taut. She left the room, then returned with a small wooden box with a hinged lid and placed it on the table between us.

"I have taken what I wanted, portraits and letters that he wrote to his wife. There is nothing you can glean from them. They were written long before the girls arrived. But you can look at what's left."

I sorted through carefully, aware and sensitive that these were items that belonged to her dead brother.

There were various trinkets, a tiny pair of leather gloves, a box of bullets, a tortoiseshell snuffbox, a pipe: things that mean nothing but to the people who owned them. There were several other items, and then something caught my eye. I picked up the two small discs, one green and the other red. Inscribed on these were *E. S. Watts*, a service number, and the religion *C of E*. I took a moment longer to stare curiously at Edgar's identity tags, my head filled with images to suggest what this meant. When a body is found, the red disc is taken and the other one left with the soldier. It could be that, miraculously, these tags survived the battle that my brother did not. But with all the other evidence, especially with no body yet found, this was the clearest sign that he may have walked away from the battlefield.

"What is so interesting?" she asked.

"These belonged to my brother. May I take them?"

She hesitated, and I took several francs from my wallet and placed them between us.

"They are not mine," she said without looking at the money, though very much aware of how much I had left there, and more than she likely expected. "I don't see a need to keep them."

I thanked her, and she watched me walk away. I doubted I would see her again and felt much pity, as one does for someone who has lived their life in misery and is unable to see all the good around them. From her window, she watched me leave, and I wondered if she would notice I had taken the photograph of the two girls also. She had no need of that, either.

My last hope was to visit the priest in the small village, whose address Roland had given me.

CHAPTER 18

I found the chapel was a beautiful and dark medieval masterpiece in stone between tiers of barren poplars. Inside was a high arched ceiling and heavy crossbeams, which matched the rich ochre of the narrow pews, and fragranced with wood polish and incense. The elderly priest was at a desk in his office at the back of the church. He was a tall, thin, bespectacled man who was more receptive than the previous interviewee. I explained myself briefly, told him about Edgar, and he offered condolences. He said he had visited Bailleul and other places toward the end. He invited me to sit with him. I pulled out the certificate carefully folded in Edgar's book of thoughts.

He examined the certificate, his nose close to the page.

"Yes, that is certainly my signature," he said. "And this has something to do with the lawyer who contacted me?"

"Yes."

"I remember more clearly now that I see this and the names in front of me." He frowned a bit at this point and peered at the faces of Edgar, Mariette, and Jerome that I passed him. "Yes, yes, the girl I can remember something, but the man, the groom, he is a bit more vague."

"He had blue eyes and brown hair, something the photograph doesn't show."

He closed his eyes, frowning slightly. He was thinking very deeply.

"I don't remember specifically, and the picture does not show his face all that clearly. I vaguely recall . . . the groom's hands, I remember, were shaking. Nerves about the marriage perhaps." He smiled at me, lighthearted, before again peering close to the photo. "The father of the girl, however, I do remember very well from this photo, a very gentlemanly, quiet man with hands that worked hard. He did all the talking, and I presumed at the time because the groom did not speak any French. Owing to the terrible state of things and not knowing where our country was headed, I overlooked the fact that they had lost their identities in the bombings." Edgar in fact spoke the priest's language very well.

"I do remember that I liked the older man immediately," said the priest. "He was most gracious, though he was insistent that the marriage happen as quickly as possible, and he seemed a little downcast. There was no cause for banns of course. It was not the church I took guidance from here. There was the baby to think of."

I felt my heart quicken. "Was she pregnant?"

"No," he said gently, without any necessary explanation. That single word had confirmed what Dr. Macklin had suspected from the beginning.

"But the groom . . . ," he continued. "I'm sorry, I don't recognize him. It is difficult. There were several weddings and many since, I might add. He is familiar, but the girl I can tell is the same as I remember, if that helps you."

"Do you know where they might have gone from here?"

He thought hard.

"There was something . . . Yes, I think it was this couple. The father asked questions about shipping lines from the south . . . I imagine to get as far away from the north as possible."

"You mean a ship to England?"

He shrugged.

"Perhaps. I have never traveled abroad, but I had a brother who had left once from Le Havre."

"And you think that's where they were heading?"

He shook his head. "I can't say. I'm hoping I have remembered the right people at least, that I haven't just confused you further. And I wish I could tell you more that would bring some peace about your brother." He paused, then put his fingers to his chin reflectively. "But if I may be so bold, and in view of the fact that your brother is recorded as dying in action, the person on the certificate is someone perhaps with the same name."

I was beginning to feel a little disheartened, especially in light of what he had just said. Could the man the priest had married be an imposter to stage the ruse for Mariette to gain the certificate? Could Edgar have died after being seen by Dr. Durand? Could Mariette and Jerome have then stolen his name, having previously learned something of his past? But then what of Samuel's recognition? I said nothing further as I did not want to bother the priest with my clues and thoughts.

I had but one more avenue, which was to view the shipping records beginning at Le Havre before I returned north to Jerome's orchard to knock on doors in the broken town nearby. Though I was not feeling hopeful. If, according to the doctor, Jerome had left the house before the Germans were eventually chased from the city, it was unlikely due to the timing of this that I would learn much more about Edgar there.

On the train southward to Le Havre, I slowly turned the pages of Edgar's diary, attempting to interpret his thoughts once more. As vague as they were, I felt closest to him in these words. I wanted so desperately to understand, to relive his experiences, to know him better. *Tell me, Edgar. Tell me what you mean?*

Turning to his final writings, I caught the pressed blue flower as it slipped from the pages and read the last line again: *To the silence I must go.*

There was a memory here, I thought, reaching deeply to another time, to something Edgar had once read to me: *The silence is breathtaking, she said.*

I examined the flower, remembering an occasion he had received one such as this in a letter. Though I was sure the flower was connected to love he had found in France, there was another meaning also.

So many times that day, I had been filled with glimmers of hope, but right in that moment, my wildest hunch seemed the most obvious answer. I was seeing something that had been in front of me all this time.

MARIETTE

From 1906

CHAPTER 19

I cannot tell you much about my life before the age of seven. But I can reveal some memories in the years between that and the first real home I had in the year I turned ten. The memories are mostly of my sister Helene, since she was beside me all the way. Serious, always focused on finding the next life for us.

I have only one clear memory of my parents: *I can see the light filtering through the red-gold tips of my hair across my face, and I can see Helene standing nearby. She has her back to me. The tracks leading up a hill and away from us are worn and grooved, with slippery clay mud and puddles filled with red-brown water. We are standing under a large tree beside a sparkling river where we'd made our camp, and across the water are fields of purple-blue irises. I look over Helene's shoulder toward the backs of a man and a woman climbing the track upward. My memories are telling me that they are my parents. The pair doesn't turn around, but there are others with them who look back guiltily, I think now, though that might be merely wishful.*

Helene turns to me with tears streaming down her cheeks, and her pale-green eyes are glittering with the reflection of the river. She is holding our little sister, who is resting her head on my older sister's shoulder and staring at nothing. I am suddenly afraid, though I don't know what it is I am to fear. With her free hand Helene takes my hand, and we walk onto the track and into the darkening air. She puts her arm around me, and I can still hear her sniffles even long after dark. And we see lights ahead, and I am relieved because I am so tired and Helene is more so since she has been carrying our younger sister. There are faces, though I don't remember them exactly, but they are people walking in the street, looking at us strangely, and I see no pity or concern in their eyes. We walk until we find a small house that is raised off the ground, and we crawl under there to sleep. We are wrapped in a blanket that Helene has stolen from somewhere, and I am nestled into Helene's arms on the damp ground, and our sister is curled up in front of me, but everything is all right because Helene has her arms around both of us, and she has stopped crying.

So I believe that this is the only memory I have of my parents, just the backs of them. Helene, who was nine at the time, told it more coldly. Apparently there was much yelling that I don't remember, and my mother said she would find us one day but never did. The man our mother left with was neither my father nor hers but he was our parent at the end. Helene remembered the face of the man she thinks was my father, though she couldn't be sure because there were many men. For some time after, I believed that our mother was kidnapped, but Helene eventually put an end to speculation. We were abandoned, plain and simple. This was sometimes the case for children, especially when groups like us, wanderers, ran out of food and children could not be spared any. I was too young to be angry about the past, and now I am too old to be sad about it.

But apart from that one memory, I have little else of my childhood before my parents left; only the major events feature between that period and the time we met Jerome three years later. I cannot even tell you the name I was given after I was born, if there was one. I had been known simply as *jel'enedra* or "little sister," a name that was used so often it became permanent. Some time after we were abandoned, Helene thought to steal for me a proper name from the townspeople, who were not our kind, who walked freely in towns and had their own houses.

There were three of us to start with, which later became two. My younger sister is like a ghost now, whose featureless face and red hair appear inside my head from time to time. And perhaps because she was small, many townspeople felt sorry for her and gave us things, food mostly, a moth-eaten shawl they had buried in a cupboard somewhere, a worn-out pair of boots, and even some dried flowers that I thought was very generous until I grew up and realized that it meant nothing, that food would have been far better.

Though we relied on people giving us things, the nice people from the houses never invited us to stay. We were what I would learn about later, gypsies; a name that people used often to describe vagabonds, thieves, and troublemakers. Some of us were some of those things, but many of us weren't. Some of us even dreamed about having a life like theirs.

I don't remember how long we first wandered, perhaps only months when it was the three of us, but one day we found some of our own, a large group camped by the side of the road beside their horses and wagon, and Helene asked if we could join them, to which they agreed.

Our little sister, who was named Layla, had red hair like me. I believe from this that we shared the same father, unlike Helene. She remembered another man whom she called Papa, who was thrown out of the camp for reasons unknown to her, who also tried to take her with him and was beaten badly for it.

The last memory of Layla was that we stayed with this new group of wanderers for several days, and they fed us after they had eaten enough themselves. They paid special attention to Layla and me because of our hair but even more attention to Layla because she was so pale also. The men, women, and children from this group were burnt from the sun, as if they'd been traveling for weeks in their open wagon, and the event that followed is perhaps why my mind can never be free of the image of them. One day, one of the women said that Helene and I were to pick some wildflowers from the hills and the black-toothed woman, who appeared to be in charge, would say a special charm over them to bring us luck. We were very excited. We ran into the hills that overlooked a valley, and we could see for miles along a snaky river.

We stayed for an hour, rolling down the hills, and we laughed with the sun shining in our eyes. I remember the laughing, and sometimes I still hear it when it is quiet, as if the memory follows me, willing me not to forget. It is not only the sound that I remember but Helene's face on this day also, smiling back at me as if she had finally found a reason to be joyous. She was brown haired and dark skinned, but her eyes were light, which made her look different from any in our groups. She didn't match anyone I had or have since seen. She wasn't as pretty as some, I didn't think back then. Only later I realized that she was the most beautiful girl I knew; that I still think now.

We collected the pink and purple hyacinths, and I chased her back down the hill to the edge of the river. At first we thought we had reached the wrong place. The wagon was gone and also the people. Only the last smoky breaths from the fire spiraling up into the crystal-blue sky above the river and the sickly sweet lily scent of the women—used to mask other odors—still lingered.

"Are you sure this is the place?" I said over and over until Helene told me to be quiet, that she needed to think.

I saw the trees that they camped under, the same ones they tied their washing to. The remains of string were still around the trees and roughly shorn in haste.

Layla was gone. Helene sat at the edge of the river and swung her legs down, looking around her constantly, thinking they would come back. I sat beside her and waited for her to tell me what we would do. She broke a stick into tiny pieces and threw them harshly at the river as if to punish it. And all the time her expression didn't change. She could hide her anger from everyone but me. We waited until it was nearly dark, and then we headed along the road toward another village.

Helene asked a man if he had seen a group of people with a small child, and he just shook his head. Helene asked another woman, and she didn't wait for her to finish. She said, "Go away, gypsy," and that is how I first learned our name, knew what we were and that our journey would be continuous because there was no solid place for us, not here, not anywhere.

In the following days, I continued to ask about Layla, and Helene kept telling me that they had taken her and that we would meet up with them again. She believed that we had stayed out playing in the hills too long and they forgot all about us, though we have since thought otherwise. We didn't see them again, but after months of begging and stealing on our own, we found another group traveling, and we joined them. Herman, the leader of the wagon and the tent people, and his brother Adrian said we could only stay for a little while, but it ended up being longer, maybe a year, because we arrived and left when the trees were shedding their leaves. When we told them about the people who took Layla, Adrian laughed. He said he knew of them and that Layla would likely be sold.

Helene and I spoke about this and wondered who would buy a child and why, and for many years we could not think of any reasons. And today it continues to haunt me, and I wonder if she is still alive. If she married and had children of her own.

Herman had, I think, two, maybe three wives. I can't remember for certain, and neither can my sister, but there were several adults that slept in the small caravan with their five children, and at the end of the day, we were allowed the scraps from their dinner plates and the shelter of the wagon floor. And the first night, my sister had cried into her arms, and I put my face against her hair. I cried, too, but I didn't understand then that Layla was gone for good. And each night under the wagon, we would whisper to each other and hold our palms together to seal our togetherness, and sometimes if there was still light from the fire, we would sign to each other with our special hand messages. It was a language that we created ourselves. We adapted everywhere we went, changing ourselves to fit in, like shape-shifters.

Herman's caravan wasn't the only one we stayed in. There were others that he would meet up with occasionally. People would ask Herman why he bothered with two stray pups. Though by that time he had found a use for us. Helene was to be his new wife in the near future, and I was good with a needle and thread. We also did what we were told and were grateful for any food we were given.

The wives were able to sell their bodies for money occasionally, but mostly we begged and stole from markets. The idea of selling our bodies we understood from early on. We had not yet understood the physicality of it, but we knew that it involved things we did not find appealing and closeness with men who always stank of beer. And while the women were selling themselves, sometimes Helene and I would steal things, especially food. And sometimes we would return with goods for Herman, which was expected, and sometimes we ate some ourselves before we returned. At times it was the only way to keep our bellies full.

Though the picture I paint is bleak, we didn't notice because we had little else to compare it with, and the next memories that are clearer were of the children we would play with and the games late into the night and Herman telling stories around the fire: legends of men with two heads, giants that ate children, and curses that turned enemies to dust. Such tales would keep me awake at night sometimes, but still I wanted to hear more.

Since it was Helene's eleventh year, Herman said it was time to become his wife. Though now I realize that any year would have been "time." After Herman's announcement, the other women dressed Helene in well-used lace and lent her some colored beads, and Helene didn't like it. The women told Helene what Herman would do in more detail than we had occasionally witnessed ourselves, and when they saw our faces, they laughed, mouths open with rows of missing teeth. I did not like to picture what they said: Helene pressed onto the filthy straw bed and rolled out flat like dough.

Helene and I lay under the wagon, and we signed to one another. She said that we must run away, and I agreed because if Helene thought it was bad enough to leave, then it was. Helene was always right.

We ran then and stole a few things before we left: some fishing line and some pears. I was going to take a pair of earrings that one of the women had left on a table, but Helene told me that there was a difference between stealing to survive and stealing for greed. And we made our own track through the long grasses beside the river and into the next village.

It was just the two of us again for a time, and I liked that because we got to sing and dance whenever we wanted and there were no expectations and no plans of marriage. Sometimes we would pass fancy people in the street, but mostly we stayed out of sight because those people didn't want us here and they were less kind than Herman's women. We could tell from the way they looked at us and from the way they whispered. We needed to be with our own kind, though I think at that point I was starting to wonder about our kind. From what I had seen, they stole little children and slept with men in the villages for scraps.

One day we went into a church where people sang, and we liked the sound of it, and we hid under the last bench seat in lines called pews. The group of boys at the front of the church sang like angels, and I told Helene that if she was to marry anyone, it should be one of them, but she said she wouldn't ever get married. When the sermon was almost over, we crawled into a tiny room with a curtain. And when the murmurings of parishioners died away, we heard the steps of the priest walking toward us. As the curtains were drawn back, I moved to flee, but Helene grabbed my arm to stay. The priest told us not to be afraid. He turned to disappear through a back door of the church and returned a few minutes later with a loaf of bread, several apples, a bottle of milk, and thick slices of ham.

He told us that God was taking care of us, and I said that God didn't look after gypsies, and Helene elbowed me. The priest looked at us at first silently, and then he laughed softly into his chest. He said there were places that took in children, fed them, and gave them soft beds to sleep in, and he said he would take us there. We ate, and we drank, and I had never felt my belly hurt before from food.

We walked to a large house, and he introduced us to a woman, and she seemed pleased to have us. She led us into a big room with other children, and we had a bed just as he said. The lady told us we had to be quiet and say our prayers, and we copied the other children to learn them. The other children told us we spoke strangely, because our language was a mixture of mostly French and some of our mother's Romany, too, which in time we would forget.

The next day we ate a breakfast of porridge with milk, and then we were told we must scrub the floors, and we did, and so did the other children, and we told them stories from the gypsy camps, of how the souls of evil men will take them away if they sleep too long and that children can be sold as slaves or sacrificed for good weather. That night some of the children were crying and screaming, and a woman came in, a different one from the first, and when they told her why they were crying, she beat our legs with a stick.

When she left the dormitory, we learned from the other children, when they had calmed down, that people come and pick the children they want, but sometimes they don't take sisters together, and we might be separated, which was worse than any stick to the legs.

We climbed out the window and escaped, and the other children stayed and watched us from the window, shocked that we would run away from food and the chance of a real home. We had never had a real home, so we didn't know if that was good, but one thing was certain: we would never be separated, and we would rather be hungry than separated.

My recollections during this time are mostly defined by the wagons we joined, but there were also many months with just the two of us, sleeping behind sheds, in riverside weeds, anywhere we didn't think we could be found in our sleep. And when we grew cold and our beds of grass had hardened with frost, we would find barns filled with animals that we could sleep near for warmth. One group we found was better than most. Their camp was a small, flat space of land that was well hidden between trees and long grasses beside a river. There was only one family of five: one man, a wife, and three children.

We inched forward on our bellies through the long grass to spy on them. The woman had a blanket on the ground that was covered with tiny colored beads she was threading onto strings. The man had his back to us. It was late in the afternoon and getting cold, but they had a fire and a small wagon and a horse with a very shiny coat.

We could hear the crackle of the fire and smell the salty meat cooking that would warm our bellies. They sat beside the fire, and the man was smoking a pipe, and he never turned his head but called out to us.

"Come and show yourself."

I shook my head at Helene. *He is talking about someone else,* I said in sign language.

Helene and I stayed still, and he said it again.

Helene stood up. "No, he knows we are here. He has the sight."

Helene took my hand, and we walked near the fire, and the man didn't turn until we were right beside him. The woman and three small children eyed us, but the look was curious, not hostile. And the child on the ground gave a little cough while he watched us inquisitively.

"Where are you from?" he asked us.

"The village," I lied.

"No. That's a lie," said the man, and Helene elbowed me in the ribs. "Tell the truth. You won't be judged for it. Not the innocents."

"We come from nowhere," said Helene.

"I know no such place as nowhere," said the man. "There is always somewhere." I liked what he said, and later I would quote "from nowhere to somewhere" again and again until Helene grew sick of it, or perhaps in light of what happened, it made her sad, and she banned me from saying it at all, so that I could only mouth it to myself in the dark.

"Now that you are somewhere," said the man, "would you like something to eat?"

We had eaten early that morning when the baker in the village had thrown us a bone with the remains of gnawed meat—not the flour-dusted rolls we ogled in his window—and told us that his dog would now go hungry.

"You must first say your prayers," said the man, but we couldn't remember them from the orphanage, and he quickly realized this also. He said a prayer to God for us, thanking him for the meal, and even now I hear the words whenever I taste my first mouthful of food.

We tried hard not to gulp the food like hungry wolves. But we did, while the two oldest children watched us curiously and the smallest one, no more than one, coughed and whined.

"He needs the roots and leaves of dandelions," said Helene as we sat down close by but not so close that it might offend them.

"What does that do?" said the woman, who spoke like the people in the village.

"They heal. They healed my little sister when she had a cough," said Helene.

The mother looked at the father to see what he would say.

"It wouldn't hurt to try," he said. The mother agreed.

We ran off searching and digging in the dark ground, dirt embedded in the scratches on our skin and under our nails, and we took the roots as well, and we came back with armfuls.

Helene and I then crushed the leaves and ground up the roots, and we said to boil them and feed them to the sick child on a spoon and spread the remains of the paste on his chest. The wife looked at her husband curiously, and he nodded. After they did this, the child stopped coughing and became rested and fell asleep.

"And where are you girls heading to?"

Helene thought all questions were tricks, and she didn't answer, but I said that we were looking for Layla. They wanted to know who she was, and I told them about the others we had met and Layla being taken, and the wife put her hand to her mouth and looked at her own children and shook her head. She was odd and startled easily and looked about her nervously and seemed not like a gypsy at all.

Then she said, "You poor little rabbits. You can sleep here tonight. It is not too cold on the ground near the fire, and you can have one of our blankets."

And the man made us "earn" our food by helping his wife thread the rest of the beads, and she told us what color beads look best with others. There was a little shiny one made from tin, and I thought about putting it in my pocket and then thought that these people were too kind and I could never steal anything from them. We loved threading beads, and I imagined that this was what my life should be, with a husband, threading beads, and children, not sick, lying on the ground before me.

"We are going into the village tomorrow. You girls can come and sell the beads with us, and if you sell some, you can have a bigger helping of food."

When we lay down we faced each other beside the fire, and there was a sky full of stars, and Helene's face looked orange and beaming, and we held hands, and we sang a tune that we remembered from our mother's camp. The man said, "Shh! We are trying to sleep," but it wasn't said in anger. "You can sing it tomorrow for the people in the village!" We whispered, and then Helene made a whistling sound while she was trying to sing and whisper, and it sounded funny, and we felt happy with our new family, and we laughed into our hands and fell asleep like that, our hands over our faces and our heads together.

The mother woke us up and said we had to leave for the village, and she gave us a cloth and bowl of water to clean our faces, and the baby had begun coughing again. We stopped at the edge of a market with the wagon, and then the man tied the horses to a stake in the ground, and the mother laid out her wares on a blanket and suggested we sing our special song.

Several villagers bought some of the beaded necklaces and bangles, while Helene and I sang the song over and over, and the woman said that it was the best sale they'd had. But some people just walked past and whispered. A policeman came and said we had to leave, but by then we were ready to go. With the money, the father bought some bones of mutton, and we went back to the camp and played with the children all afternoon. I thought that we had found a permanent family, where we could be daughters and not wives to the same man.

Before it grew dark we went and found more of the plants to boil after a dinner of stew, scraping the meat off the bones with our teeth, and the man was true to his word. We had more to eat, and the woman stewed some apples, and we had that, too. The woman said that we were very thin, thinner than most children, but we didn't care, because we weren't hungry that night.

We found more of the plant for the woman to feed the child, who looked sicker, grayish, but was quieter and no longer coughed. The mother felt the child and said he was warmer than usual, but the father said he was fine, the child just needed rest after so many wakeful hours, and Helene and I went to sleep quickly that night by the fire.

In the morning we were woken up by the sounds of the mother, wailing as she rushed out of the wagon past us toward the stream. She was still wailing as she held her sick baby in the water, and the two other small children poked their heads out from the back of the wagon. The father stepped out pulling his braces over his shoulders. He walked to just near us and watched the woman.

"You should be going," he said without looking at us. And we jumped up and walked away without anything this time, no shawl, no food, and when we thought they could no longer see us, we ran until we could no longer hear the wailing.

Magic flowers didn't work, and we never suggested these again, because Helene said that the cure was cursed now. That maybe it was cursed because it had been used for Layla once and she was now stolen.

We were once again on our own.

CHAPTER 20

We came to a large town called Amiens. It was where a lot of children hid on the streets and came out at nighttime. We found some other children by themselves in a tent made from sheets of tin at the edge of the town. Towns were generally not friendly places. People did not like the sight of gypsy children at the entrances to their shops, and the general agreement was that we brought diseases and other things into the town.

According to Helene, I am an August baby and Helene is March, but the days of those months were lost well before my parents left. I had no birth certificate, and neither did Helene. There were no doctors. Babies were born, or died. The only help was from the women who knew things from before. There was no one to write our names down in a register, a church, or a hospital. No papers that said we were here. When I learned later at Jerome's that people were recorded, I thought that it was a strange thing people had to know, and in some way I still think it is better to be no one in particular at times.

We shared a tent with the other children. Some were only five, others were older teens who "worked," they said, but that was just code for stealing. For a period we were wild and free, with no adult to tell us what to do again, but Helene didn't like the idea of stealing any more.

"We have to find real work and pay for things with money instead of stealing," she said. When she would say this, the other children would laugh at her.

I loved Helene, but I was unsure whether she was right. Though the emptiness in my belly most nights told me that perhaps she was. Perhaps there was a better way.

She took seriously her role to protect me, and I'm not sure where I would have ended up without her. And I'm not sure where she got all her goodness from, either, because it wasn't from the people who raised us. Helene was just born good.

One of the older children, Babik, had his eye on me from the start. I was not quite ten, and although I liked attention, I did not wish it from him. He said he was fifteen, though we did not believe it since he sulked like a child. Once he tried to kiss me, and I roughly pushed him away. He got angry with this and told us that we could no longer sleep in the shelter, that I was a distraction, that I *do it* on purpose.

"Do what?" I asked.

"Do that!" he said, pointing at my bony body, and still I didn't know.

We had a very big argument, and we almost left that night.

"It is your fault," said Babik. "You try to be different. You think that you deserve better, that you deserve to be a Frenchwoman."

"I am a Frenchwoman."

"You are no such thing. You will always be Roma. It is the way it is, and nothing will change you."

"Gypsies don't have to be beggars all their lives, and you can't tell us what we are or what we might become. We will be whatever we want to be." Helene had challenged him, and I had never heard her talk like this, as if she knew for certain that things would change.

"We are Roma!" said Babik. "Our place is under the stars."

"And the rain and the wind and the snow! You tell the same lie that all gypsy adults tell us because they don't try to fit in anywhere." She was angry, and she pulled my arm to leave.

Suddenly Babik ran after us and said that he was sorry and we could come back. He said that he knew people who used to be gypsies who had a legitimate business and that Helene could get "real" work with them, though he was looking at me when he said this, and there was something odd about his stare. Most children would play with my hair and plait it and marvel at it. There were not many with my color. To have such color was both a blessing and a curse. Sometimes the attention it brought was from people I didn't wish it from, like Babik.

"Why don't you work for him yourself?"

"He likes girls. They are nicer," he said with a grin.

"Nicer?" queried Helene.

"Sweeter."

"Why didn't you tell us about this before?"

"Because he said that I could only come back if I brought some sweet girls with me."

I thought about the women who sold their bodies, who we didn't think were particularly nice or sweet, so this had to be different.

We walked back reluctantly but mostly because Babik and his young associates had stolen several loaves of bread and four onions and said we could share them. I was so hungry I did not care about Babik's gaze or Helene's anger.

It was cramped in the tent, and we slept on the ground bunched together, and in the night Babik put his arm across me. I was facing Helene in the dark, but I could see her eyes were open. She shook her head, telling me to be careful with him. I moved away, and Helene wrapped her arms around me protectively, and Babik turned over to face the other side with an angry bounce of his bottom.

But the next morning, Babik, true to his word, led us north of the town. It was a cloudy day, and the wind had picked up. We would need coats before winter, and the promise of work meant that we could buy them legitimately. In a shop in Amiens, I had seen a red coat with fur around the collar and matching gloves. Babik had seen me looking and said that I deserved it. If this man and woman liked me, I could afford it, he said. I grew very excited.

The place of business did not look legitimately anything. It was a small house, rundown and crushed between a noisy factory that made headstones, a tannery, a pig farm, and a butcher. The streets here were muddy and tired, and the houses weren't happy, either; they did not have windowsill planters full of flowers or pretty curtains. Babik knocked on the front door, and a plump woman answered. I was envious of her because she was well fed. This was a good sign at least, I thought.

"Hello, Babik," she said, slapping him across the top of the head with what appeared to be affection. "I have not seen you for ages."

"Hello," said Babik, who went bright pink. He was clearly enamored with her. She was attractive. She wore a tight blue satin bodice and a long black embroidered skirt. The bodice barely covered her acorn-colored breasts, and her hair hung around her shoulders, washed and curling.

We followed Babik in and sat at a table. Her name was Sybille, and she lived there with her husband. She gave us a hot cup of coffee and a piece of bread, and it took only two large mouthfuls to finish mine, while Helene nibbled at hers suspiciously. I do not know how Helene knew things, but she just did. There was a tale that some gypsies are born with an extra sense, and I've always believed that Helene had it. She could tell if someone's heart was filled with good blood or bad. She had already told me she didn't trust Babik, that he was simple and easily led, rather than malicious. She could tell when the weather would soon turn nasty and would lead us to places to find cover in advance. And just sometimes for no reason, we would be somewhere and she would say it was time to go. That she could feel or see things in the wind. I can tell you that one day in the years ahead, she had dreamed of fields of graves and whole towns on fire, but at that time she was yet to name it "war." If I told people today, they would think I was mad or that Helene was mad, but I lived with her, and I know that she had something that others didn't.

It was on such a day in Sybille's house that Helene had the feelings.

"My husband will be home soon," said Sybille. "And I think that he will be happy."

A girl around Helene's age came out of one of the rooms. She had a bruise on her cheek and dark circles around her eyes like a polecat.

Sybille laughed when she saw her. "Look what finally came back from the dead."

The girl said something I didn't understand, then walked past Sybille and helped herself to some of the coffee. She sat down opposite, and Sybille introduced us.

"They are the new girls Babik was talking about."

The girl laughed to show her missing front tooth. I was about to ask her about it, even though I knew Helene would not have wanted me to, when Aldo, Sybille's husband, walked in. He was a big man with a broad face and roaming eyes and a mouth that was fixed in a grin, which made it difficult to judge his mood.

"This is Helene and Mariette," said Babik. "The sisters who wish to work."

Aldo looked at Helene, who then looked down at her hands. I watched her and saw that she was unusually impolite, but when I turned to look at Aldo, he was staring at me. I had grown to be the same height as Helene even though I was two and a half years younger. I had gone from being too small for my age to finally reaching some kind of height, though I was not yet a woman like Helene, who at least had a figure, and small breasts appearing.

Aldo looked at Babik and nodded; then they left with Sybille through the back door, and we heard the three of them discussing something amongst themselves, but we could not make out the words. I peered out the window to see what they were doing. Sybille put a coin in Babik's hand and pulled his ear, though I could not tell if he was in trouble or if this was affection again, On the shelves around the kitchen, I could see jars of jam and spices and other foods. The food overtook any other thoughts.

The toothless girl who had been quiet got up and walked away.

"Pretty," she said, pulling my hair as she went past.

"We should go," said Helene. "There is something about this that doesn't feel right."

I looked at the stove and felt torn. Something was being cooked in a pot, something meaty and rich, and I felt sure that we would be given some.

I shook my head, and Helene just stared at me and stood up. "Now! We have to go now!"

I refused to budge. She pulled my arm, and I resisted, and that was when Aldo came back in.

"What is going on here? A fight between sisters!"

Helene looked at Aldo and back at me, and I saw Babik walk to the front door, blocking any exit that we might have made.

Sybille shut the back door and locked it, and I knew then that Helene's sense was right. I should never have doubted her. Not that I really did, but the pull of food was far stronger.

"You weren't thinking of leaving, were you?" Sybille asked.

Helene said nothing and stared at her lap, and I shook my head, my eyes not leaving Aldo's.

"You sure are a lovely one," Aldo said to me. "I think I can find you some work before your sister." He turned to his wife. "Sybille, go into the village. Tell Monsieur Devereux that we have a special package for him tonight."

"Package" was how they referred to the women we had met earlier who sold their bodies. My heart seemed to rise to the base of my throat, like it often did when I was nervous. I did not like the sound of their plans.

He sat opposite us and spoke to Helene in particular. "I think that your sister Mariette would be perfect for the job we have in mind. I am quite sure she is more to his specific liking."

Helene jumped in straightaway.

"We are leaving!" she said.

"You are the one who came looking for work, who walked in here freely. What else did you think you were going to do?" He turned his murky brown eyes onto me. "But it is you, Mariette, who will have the first job."

Helene stood up to stand in front of me. "You do not touch her!"

Aldo laughed then, mockingly and in such a way that left me feeling jumpy. "It's not me that will touch her, but someone willing to pay a fetching price for her."

It was only then I realized I would be the package.

"I will do whatever I want but not what you want me to do," I said. Sybille appeared beside me suddenly and slapped me hard across the face.

My sister lunged toward Sybille to return the slap and was pulled away by Aldo. Helene kicked out at him and yelled for me to run. I did so, only to find the front door was locked.

Aldo dragged Helene into a room, while I pulled at his sleeve to release her. He held me back with one arm and with his free hand turned the key to lock Helene away. I bit the arm that held me. So enraged, he picked me up and threw me on a narrow bed near the kitchen, my shoulder hitting the wall. The worry I had for my sister distracted me from any pain. Helene banged on the door from inside the other room.

"You can't damage her," boomed Sybille. She stood in front of Aldo, who loomed above me and looked as if he would hit me. She turned to me: "If you don't want to be hurt, or your sister, then you must behave."

Helene heard this and stopped banging, worried then they would harm me. I hated Sybille and Aldo and Babik. And I would not do as they wished, but I told them I would until I could think what else to do.

Aldo brought Helene out to sit next to me again.

"Girls!" said Sybille. "You will be rewarded if you behave."

Helene looked at her feet that had a layer of black dust on them from the street, her pale-pink toenails shining through the grime.

She then looked up and said, "It should be me, not my sister!"

Aldo turned to her, and I thought he might take her back to the room for being so outspoken.

"He will like your sister," said Babik to Helene, interrupting. "She is younger. We will send her first."

"Be quiet!" barked Aldo to Babik, whose expression turned surly.

"Mariette is scratchy and horrible and likely to hurt him and run away," continued Helene.

I saw dots of blood on Aldo's shirtsleeve and imagined he still felt my bite. Sybille whispered something in his ear.

"Are you a virgin?" Aldo asked.

Helene nodded.

"All right," he said. "Then we will save the other one for someone else."

"No!" said Babik. "You said I could have the red one after she was spoiled tonight. It should be her!"

"You will have to wait!" Aldo shouted. "Get outside and guard the house, you imbecile!" I saw Babik flinch. "They mustn't get away!"

Sybille was very sweet then, purring like a kitten, and she took Helene to have a bath. Helene did not make eye contact with me. They bathed her in a room at the back, and after she was cleaned, her skin smelled like jasmine and her hair like cinnamon. Then Sybille pulled out a dress that was red with armpits stained from years of use.

They fed us some broth, and suddenly the food wasn't important, and I felt sick with it in my stomach. Helene continued not to look at me, afraid perhaps I might see the fear in her eyes and attempt to hinder the task, which would then see us punished.

It was said that Aldo would take Helene on his trap; then he would wait outside to get the payment once the deed was finished. Though his terms were that he would always get half the money up front.

Helene left with Aldo, and Sybille said that if I behaved, I could earn some coins of my own one day. I had no intention to earn money that way. The other girl appeared from another room, wearing a similar dress to Helene's. Sybille fussed about her briefly, straightening her dress, sniffing her breath, and checking her nails, before unlocking the door to let her leave to perform her "work" elsewhere.

Helene had been gone a short time when I said that I wanted to go to bed. Sybille said I was not to get up to no good and that Babik would be waiting outside. She also said that if I ran away, Aldo would beat us both when they found us and ruin our faces. I should have been frightened because adults up till that point had made all the rules, but I wasn't, because the thought of Helene doing something she vowed not to do was a far greater hurt than being beaten.

Sybille locked the door to the room where she sent me. I looked out the window but could see no sign of Babik, who was supposedly guarding the place. I took out a packet of matches, which I had taken from the table when Sybille wasn't looking. I tore a large piece of cotton from the bottom of my dress and placed it in the space between the door and the floor. I lit one match, but it died out; then I lit another, and the cotton took slowly. The flames licked the wood of the door, and soon a small fire grew to a bigger one.

When the door was burning, I did become a little frightened, and smoke was filling the room. I called for help, and Sybille began to shriek from the other side of the door. From the window, I saw Babik then. At first I thought he would come in to help put out the fire, but he ran off into the darkness. I climbed out the window to make my escape.

As I ran fast toward the center of town, I thought no more of the burning door and the shouts from Sybille behind me but of reaching Helene before anything happened to her. It was after midnight, since Sybille and Aldo's work was the kind that happened long after dark, when the streets were silent.

It took me frantic minutes searching down several streets before I saw Aldo and his horse and trap, and I slid into the shadows before he saw me also. The house he guarded was large, with a front garden and decorative fence. There was light from a window upstairs, so I had to assume it was the right house, but I was surprised why a person with money would want the company of gypsy girls, and ones so young as we were. Aldo was leaning against the fence, counting some coins. I crept down low behind bushes on a neighboring property then over the side of the fence of the house. I'd spent most of my lifetime appearing invisible, and the skill of stealth was part of my grain. I continued down the side of the building to find a small street-level window open, and I climbed into a kitchen, where I grabbed a knife that lay on a butcher block. I had no idea what I would do from there. I had no plan but to find Helene.

I crept in the dark, expecting someone at every corner, but there was no one, only the muted sounds of a conversation from somewhere upstairs. I saw some ornate silver candlesticks and made a mental note that if I got the chance, I would shove them down my dress.

Some noises, the grumblings of a man, were coming from a room with its door partway open. Peeking through the gap in the doorway, I saw that Helene was under a sheet on the bed, the red dress discarded on the floor. The man, Monsieur Devereux, was standing in front of her in a shirt and no pants. There were two glasses, one half-filled with wine, on a table beside the bed.

The man, with his back to me, climbed over the bed toward Helene, and I walked toward him slowly. Helene saw me suddenly, and the man turned to follow her gaze just as I stabbed him in the buttocks. He cursed and grabbed at his bottom, and I then heard Sybille's shouts from the streets. She was yelling at the top of her lungs that the house was burning, that the "bitch has escaped!"

Helene then jumped up and kicked Monsieur Devereux hard between the legs, so hard he moaned in pain. He had one hand over his manhood while he used the other to pry the knife from his backside. We rushed down the stairs.

I heard the man yelling out to Aldo from the window. I grabbed a silver candlestick on the way, and this time Helene said nothing about my theft. We climbed out of the same window I had entered and then over a fence at the back. Then we ran like feral cats, weaving between buildings, leaping over fences, and charging through alleys toward the outer edge of town. We stopped only briefly so that Helene could pull on trousers and a shirt we stole from a washing line. Once we were on the road that led from the city, we vowed never to go back there.

When we were exhausted, gasping for breath, we sat against a tree. Helene reached to hug me, and then we examined the silver candlestick under the light from the moon and thought of the food it might buy us.

When I asked her what had happened in the room, she said not to speak of it. In her mind it hadn't happened. Helene believed that you must never dwell on bad things, because they will infect and blacken your brain like the plague. She said the only true way to heal was to forgive and forget and live a new day.

CHAPTER 21

We sold the silver candlestick to a peddler for a coin, which kept us from begging for only a day. In the following days, it grew colder, and Helene had stopped smiling at the sky, which meant that I could no longer smile at the sky, either. The world was gray, and I was sad, though I didn't really understand sad that well since we had been surrounded by sad often, so "happy" was when it didn't feel right. I had grown suspicious of happy.

We continued to steal, and Helene was too hungry and cold to feel remorse. I stole some leather shoes that were too big, and Helene stole a dress and some slippers and a horse's blanket, and she said sorry to the horse as she took it. And I stole a cardigan that had been left to catch a sliver of sun on someone's back lawn, and it was pretty and pale blue with matching buttons. The fine, soft wool felt feathery against my bare arms, and for days I imagined the life of the girl who owned it: where she went and the conversations she had with her mother, but mostly the food she ate and the warm bed she slept in.

Helene and I became efficient at stealing. We would watch someone's house, and when the man would leave for work, I would sneak to the back of the house while Helene knocked on the front door to ask for food. I would take something to eat: an apple, sometimes a whole pie, or a jar from the pantry. One time I took a jug of milk. If the person answering the door gave Helene something to eat or wear, we would leave some of the food at the front door as a kind of thank-you. If they didn't, then we would take the lot. We sometimes stole soap to wash ourselves in streams and lakes, and we would enjoy hours reveling in the soapy water. But the weather became too cold, as did the water, and we had to stop washing.

We roamed from village to village without a plan, without a future. We didn't expect charity.

Then one day, things changed.

We were at a new village down a long stretch of road far enough from a town not to be part of it, and the house was set well back from the road. In the fields behind were rows of fruit trees with pears plump and ready for their winter harvest. Though to get to the trees, we had to walk past the windows on either side of the little farmhouse, which billowed smoke from its chimney. Just the sight of smoke meant that it was most likely warm inside, but our intention was not to go in. We thought that we would come back later at night and pick the fruit but found we couldn't last all day. We were starving, and without exaggeration, Helene's ribs had risen out from her chest.

In a pen beside the house were chickens, and in another there were piglets. It was a pretty place, and for some strange reason, that day Helene said it felt wrong to steal from them. But I convinced her they would have lots of food with all that fruit. She looked me up and down, perhaps seeing how thin I had become also, and she finally agreed.

Helene went to the front door and asked the woman inside for food, and I heard the woman questioning her. I spied in through a side window and could see the woman, with her back to me, talking to Helene. I crept in through the back door to take a saucepan of warm oatmeal and half a loaf of bread, the bread placed under my arm so I was free to carry the saucepan that warmed my hands also. While I waited at the side of the house for the woman to shut the front door and for Helene to leave, I saw a man enter through the front gate. He hadn't seen me yet, but he passed by Helene on her way out. The man looked at her curiously and was about to question her when he spied me.

I ran then, attempting to dodge past him, but he was far nimbler than I had imagined for an old man. I squealed as he caught me around the waist, and the saucepan of warm oats slipped from my hand and onto his feet. He carried me on his hip, while I hung by my middle and pushed at him to release me. My attempts to free myself were useless. He was very strong.

"Gypsies!" said the woman, who had opened the door again after hearing the commotion. "They stole from us."

With the bread still squeezed tightly under my arm, the man put me down inside the house and told me to sit, while the woman shut the door behind us.

"You must tie her up and take her to the police!" said the woman.

The man stood in front of me with his hands on his hips. His face was very lined, and his hair was black and streaked with white, and he was nearly as tall as the door but skinny like a winter poplar. And he had a wide mouth but hardly any lips, and his face was neither angry nor happy, but it was just a face that appeared as if it had adjusted well to the way things were.

There was a faint knock at the door, and the man answered it to find Helene was standing there wrapped in her horse blanket. I remembered Aldo and Sybille and wondered if this new couple would have thoughts of selling our bodies.

The man said to Helene, "Are you looking for something?" in a big deep voice, and I thought for a minute we were doomed. And then he stepped aside to show Helene that I was sitting there.

"Off you go!" he said to me. "And take the bread with you."

"You can't just let them go!" said the woman. "They are criminals! You should take them to the police."

"They are children," said the man.

I thought it was a trap, but I stood up and walked, legs shaking, to the front door, and Helene and I left, and we kept looking over our shoulders as the man waved us goodbye. Then he shut the front door, and we began to run, then stopped again when I saw the saucepan on the ground. I picked it up and we scooped out the oats that had not fallen on the ground.

"I will take back the pan," I said. "I don't think the man is dangerous. And I want to thank him for the bread. We didn't say thank you."

Helene looked at me and pulled a strand of my hair and smiled and said that I was always a little strange in the head, just like Mama had said. But she agreed that they weren't dangerous.

I knocked on the door, and this time the man answered and looked down at us from a great height.

"Thank you for the bread," I said, and presented him with the empty saucepan. And he glanced in the pan that we had licked clean, and he appeared amused by something.

"Would you both like some milk?"

I looked back at Helene, and she made no sign, and the decision was left to me, and I said, "Yes," in a very frail voice, as I had grown more wary of kindness.

He turned and went inside and left the door open, and I waved Helene to follow, and once inside, the man shut the door again and told us to sit down at the table.

Around the room were photographs: a wedding portrait and pictures of the man and some others who weren't in the room. And the other woman wouldn't look at us but sat nearby folding washing, but I knew she was looking at us from her side-eye because I knew she didn't trust us, not like the man.

"Where are your families?"

We looked at each other, and Helene said it was "just us" and we were sisters, and we told him our names.

The man looked at both of us curiously and shrugged.

"My name is Jerome, and this is my sister, Lenore," he said.

"Is that all the family you have?" I asked. And the woman looked at me suddenly, as if offended, and I was expecting the elbow from Helene, but she was too far away to reach me.

The man laughed a little then.

"Yes," he said, "it seems we both have small families."

He cut us some cake with apple baked in the middle, and we ate that, too. He talked about his three horses, two of which he was planning to sell, and we told him about us, about our mother leaving us on the side of the river, and then Layla, and then how our medicine killed a baby. When I said the last one, Helene was closer and elbowed me in the ribs that time.

"I doubt it was the flower," he said. "That would have been no help or hinder. The baby was probably always to die. There are some conditions that can't be helped."

I felt better, but Helene didn't. She didn't believe him like I did. She thought it was still her fault. She always took things too hard, fell too hard, thought too hard, and one day she would die hard also. But that was years to come.

Then Lenore left the house to go toward a small building at the back, and the man turned to us and spoke quietly.

"My sister has aches in her hands, and she could use some help in the kitchen, and I could use some help with the orchard. I have to pick the pears and wash them, then take them to sell. For your help I can give you a bed to sleep on."

"And food?" I asked.

The man laughed up to his eyes. "Oh yes, food would come with it as well."

I liked him already. When Lenore came back inside, he told her that we were staying.

"There is no place for them here," she said, narrowing her eyes at all of us.

"They are staying," he said. "We can do with the help."

"They are thieves," said Lenore, but she did not look our way, as if she might catch a gypsy curse.

Jerome did not say anything else immediately, but after some thinking time, he asked us to wait outside.

Helene and I sat below the window, which was opened a fraction to let out the wood smoke, and we listened to the conversation happening inside.

Lenore said she didn't trust gypsies: "They could have family close by that might break in and rob us." And Jerome said that he believed what we said. And this went back and forth, and Lenore said that if he went against her wishes, she would leave, and he said she would never do that, and she went quiet for a moment. And then she said it was on his head if anything happened. And he said there was nothing that was going to happen. I made a vow then, to myself, that nothing was going to happen, because I knew us; I knew Helene and knew we didn't do anything bad apart from steal.

Jerome then called us in and said we could stay temporarily, and I said that we didn't have any family nearby who would steal and that our family didn't want us, and no other family wanted us, either, and he then just looked at me with watery eyes, waiting to see what else I might say. I made sure I was standing a safe distance away from Helene's elbow. Lenore sniffed and looked away, and she had gone red in the face.

Jerome said the first thing we had to do was to have a bath and we could boil some water from the stove and then use the bath that was at the back of the house in a small room attached. We sat in the bath and soaped each other and washed each other's hair until we were squeaky and shining and clean, and then cold.

We were shown around the property and told the jobs we would do, like brushing the horses and collecting eggs and cleaning out the animal pens and picking the fruit because Lenore's legs ached and Jerome couldn't bend and reach as well as he used to. Lenore slept in another room that was separate from the house, connected by a pathway.

Helene and I slept in a single bed, and it was the best bed we had ever had. It was soft, and we rolled down into the middle of it, but we didn't mind sleeping on top of each other. And I said to Helene, "Do you think he will make you marry him?" and I had said this too loud, and there was a knock on the wall, and Jerome called out, "Don't go talking such *merde*." Helene grimaced and told me to talk quieter, and then we laughed into our hands and talked in signs by the light through the window.

The next day Jerome opened a chest full of coats and dresses and trousers that had belonged to his wife and son. We learned that Lenore had lost her husband in a war and Jerome had lost his wife and son to influenza in the years after he returned from a war. He said we could wear what we wanted, and Lenore looked like someone who had just dug her own grave. Jerome asked if we could sew, and I told them how I could mend and sew and that women in wagons all knew how to sew. We remade the dresses that were too big so that they would fit us. Jerome said that Lenore might teach us to use her sewing machine, and I was very excited about this, though Lenore still hadn't said anything to us, pretending to be busy in the kitchen. All that week, we hand-sewed dresses and undergarments until we each had a dress and a skirt and a blouse.

Jerome was kind to everyone. One day, at the edge of town, I saw a group of gypsies who were cold and thin. I told Jerome about them, and he gave me a basket of fruit to take to them and a jug of warm milk. And that wasn't the only time. There were other wanderers over the years who were on the receiving end of Jerome's kind heart.

We made several trips to towns and villages, and Helene and I would take turns sitting on the front cart seat beside Jerome, since there was only room for two. People were polite in the town, but Helene felt uncomfortable with people looking at us and staring as if we had borrowed someone else's life. I didn't care if they stared. One day we were delivering fruit to a store in one of the villages, and the owner nodded toward Helene and me where we waited in the cart.

"You sure about those?" he said to Jerome. "They bring bad luck."

"That is a lot of superstitious *merde*," snapped Jerome, who walked away, climbed back onto the cart, and didn't look back. But I looked back and saw the owner shaking his head as if he knew better.

Then it was Christmas, and we had ham and potatoes with rosemary, and green beans, and then fruit pies with cream. We had never celebrated Christmas before, and Jerome told us stories from the Bible, and Helene would go through the pages with wonder when no one was looking, though she couldn't read the words.

Jerome made us another bed, and it was squeezed in next to the other one, and all of a sudden, Helene was fourteen and I would soon be twelve. I can't say Lenore was ever warm, but she had developed a level of tolerance toward us, though she liked Helene a lot more than she liked me. Helene was patient and helped Lenore in the kitchen some nights, whereas I hated chopping vegetables and I was impatient and clumsy. Eventually I was banned from kitchen tasks, but not Helene. I preferred cleaning out the chicken pen anyway and brushing and feeding the horses and sewing rather than helping in the kitchen. And so it was that we had our other chores when the fruit-picking seasons and deliveries were over. And when there were no tasks, Helene and I would spend hours riding the horses bareback, to exercise them, in the paddock beside the house or wandering over the hills behind us to explore the woods.

One day I asked Lenore why we weren't allowed to go near the town after dark, which had been the rule since we had arrived. She said that her brother was very old-fashioned and protective of young girls. I asked her if he had been protective of all the people he owned.

She pulled a face and made a blowing sound from her mouth. "No one owns you, you silly child! You're free to go whenever you want."

When I spoke to Helene about it, I was surprised that she agreed with Lenore and also said that I was silly. Till then I had always believed that you were the property of the owner of the house you shared, like it had been in the wagons.

Jerome said that he wouldn't have to sell his horses now that I was there to groom them. He gave us each a saddle, and Helene and I would gallop Carmello and Mira around in the paddock, and life was good and freer than ever. I named the young filly Hester since he'd never bothered to name her with plans to sell her, and she would soon be grown enough to ride.

Helene and I were only supposed to stay there for a month to help with the fruit picking and put meat on our bones, but then the month passed and we were not asked to leave. In the years to come, we would pick the pears in the autumn through to winter and the apples in late summer through to autumn, and we would fill the tray with fruit behind Mira the cart horse. And pies with fruit were plentiful.

CHAPTER 22

We had learned to read and write from Lenore, who had been a teacher, and both Helene and I wrote letters to each other to practice. Lenore would correct them, and I was just slightly better at words than Helene, who was slower, more careful, who sat and thought longer about things. But soon Lenore grew tired of teaching us, and one day insisted we go to school. We did not want to go, but Jerome agreed with Lenore and from then on took us each morning in his trap, and each day we would walk the long distance home.

It was hard at first because the children who had been schooled on gypsies by their parents seemed to know everything about us before we arrived. Their curious stares made even me feel uncomfortable. When adults did it, it was simply annoying, but now I was with peers, who were the harshest judges of all. It was quiet for a couple of days, and then came the relentless tormenting by other children, though I did not recognize it as unjust at the time. To me it was just life, a new battlefield that I must endure and survive, and for Helene it was about getting to the other end of the day without attention. But it was not to be. We were a curiosity.

One day I turned around to the bucktoothed girl behind me who had been throwing pieces of sticks at the back of my head, and I told her that as a gypsy I was allowed to grant a death wish on three people during my lifetime and that she was on my list and that day I would go home and burn a drawing of her and cast a spell. And she had screeched and bawled, and the teacher had sent me home for the day. But the toothy girl said nothing and let us join in her games, and after that we were part of "the group." However, I soon noticed that Helene and I weren't invited home with any of the other children and they were not allowed at ours. So while we could play their games, we knew that we would never be like the other children.

Although I loved the idea of fine gowns and dreamed of wearing them and marrying someone wealthy and debonair, there was a greater part of me that wanted to run free like the boys did. I would tie my skirt up, and sometimes after school Helene and I would part, and I would leave her so that I could run through the streets with the boys or swim with them in the creek in our underclothes. I was twelve then, and though tall I was still very thin and boyish looking. Sometimes I would stay out too long, and Lenore would scold me when I got home. Jerome would just sit there with a pipe and not watch me and not say anything, and the silence was even worse punishment than any scolding.

For the next three years, we went to school, and Helene was moved up a class and finished before me because she studied much harder. And by that time also she had lost interest in exploring the woods and running in the fields behind the orchard. Many in the town of Bailleul still referred to us as the "gypsy orphans," a title that was beginning to infuriate me, even when it was said harmlessly. Jerome would ignore everything that was said. Jerome had the ability to let most things slide off his shoulders.

"There is enough to carry in life without having to carry the worries of others," he said one day when I complained. "But you're not gypsy orphans anymore, and from now on I want you to stand up to people who say that. You have and always will have a home with me. You are the daughters of a Frenchman, and you don't need a piece of paper to tell you this."

I stood up to kiss the top of his head; then I had gone to my room to cry. Because he had reminded me that he had saved us from a future of cruelty and begging, which Layla and our mother might still have.

"We have to forget our mother," Helene said quite forcefully when I repeated what Jerome had said and explained why I was so upset. "Jerome is our real parent now. Our papa."

Though it didn't stop me from spying on the gypsy camps that appeared sometimes, to catch a glimpse of someone who I thought might be our mother, since I did not have any clear memory of her. And sometimes when we saw a little girl with red hair, even Helene would stop to examine her to see if she was Layla.

Then suddenly, according to Jerome and Helene, I had grown into a woman overnight, and another year had passed, and I was nearing fifteen, and boys went from pushing me over in jest to feeling awkward around me. And I have to admit I liked the attention. I must confess also that I liked their mothers' expressions of displeasure when they would see whom their sons were sneaking out to meet in the town square. And everyone except me seemed to think I was a problem. Helene accused me of teasing them, of getting them into trouble.

One day when I was grooming the horses, Jerome came and spoke to me.

"Ettie, you are a pretty girl. Trouble has a tendency to triple, and soon enough the problems are larger. Remember, the wrong choices you make can lead to more wrong choices until you can no longer contain them. Be careful, slow down some days, and take the time to look at yourself from the outside."

"If you are trying to tell me not to do anything with a boy, then why don't you come out and say it," I said in disgust. "Kissing them is one thing, but I am never going to sell my body for coin nor give it to someone for free unless I choose it!"

He looked shocked, then laughed. "You are certainly a different one!"

"Papa," I said, "I can make my own decisions. You don't have to worry so much."

And he had nodded and left.

I was angry that everyone was telling me what to do, as if they knew what was inside my head. So I went to the house of one of the boys, Felix—the son of the tavern owner, Gerard—who had sent me little notes of love in class, whom I had kissed beneath the bell tower. I knocked on his door, and he had answered, looking behind him fearfully.

"What are you doing here?"

"I missed you after school today."

"I couldn't come. Maman is angry with me." He looked down and guilty. "Because I'm spending time with you, but I told her it wasn't true. That you were different—"

He never got to finish what he was saying, because I walked away, and I would never kiss him again no matter how many times he asked. And later he would continue sending me notes that I would ignore. I realized that I would always be different, and perhaps it was my blood that would always make it so.

Helene had stopped going to school the previous year, and Jerome was now paying her a wage, and I told him then that I was not going back to school, that I had learned enough. And he agreed without argument. I knew who I was then: a girl who would make her own destiny. Though a few things would come along to get in the way of that.

Lenore moved to Armentières. She had said on many occasions that a rural life had never been for her. But I know in my heart that she never truly accepted us. Helene was then given the room behind the house, and I now had my own room. I made curtains and hung up pieces of fabric around the walls like from a picture I had seen of a palace in India. When Helene came in she joked that gypsy practices were hard to get rid of, and I had taken them all down again. I was becoming very self-conscious of who I was and who I wanted to be. But suddenly I wanted a name like everyone else: a surname that was mine, and legal, and to have a record that I existed.

Jerome was suffering from arthritis like Lenore, and we had taken to doing more of the picking, grooming, cleaning, manning of our fruit stall on market day in the town square, and helping with the delivery of orders. People got used to us. We were soon just known as "Jerome's girls," and just occasionally "Jerome's pretty gypsies," though by that time it wasn't said in a bad way, only because they were used to us and we were used to the name. Soon Helene stopped coming with us altogether, and it was just Jerome and I that went into town.

I wore a dress when we delivered things and did my hair up in case I should meet the man who would marry me. If I were to marry someone, they would need to be someone new to the town, an older male, and not one who had to answer to his parents.

I would parade in front of the tiny wall mirror now that I had the room to myself. I had no jewelry of my own, so sometimes I would sneak into Jerome's room and look at his wife's jewelry. She had a necklace of cream-colored pearls and a ring with an emerald-green stone.

Then one weekend Jerome decided to take us to Paris. From the train, we watched the fields disappear and the city buildings rise up spectacularly on the horizon. And once we'd arrived, there were lots of people, and color and noise and smells. Helene had told me that we had lived in Paris once, and though it was crowded, I looked to see if there were faces like ours.

From the train we walked several blocks with our cases, and we stayed in a little room in a tiny hotel, with two beds side by side and a shared bathroom at the end of the hall. We didn't mind, Helene and me, that we were back to sleeping together on this trip. It sometimes felt as if we were one person, with the one heart and head, as so often we would say the same things at the same time.

Jerome took us to a museum and then to a café, and we sipped coffee and ate cake and watched the pretty ladies in their dresses and the attentive men beside them. And then he took us to shops and bought us each a dress, and I wore mine straightaway, but Helene said she would save hers, and then we went to have our photograph taken. It was the best day of my life. No one at all suspected we were gypsies. Here I could be whoever I wanted.

And then it was time to go home to our orchard, and I made a vow that I would not live in the country, that I would have to marry one day and live in a city. I also knew that I could never marry any of the boys from the towns and villages we lived near, whether their parents allowed it or not. The place had suddenly grown too small for me.

One day Jerome came back from the town with news that we couldn't make sense of, and then our world changed. War had broken out, and we were standing in the firing line.

CHAPTER 23

From when we first learned the war was coming to our doorstep, it was the waiting that was killing us slowly, and the uncertainty ahead. Businesses kept going, but people were looking more carefully at things, at the sky and at the faces of passing people, as if the answers to what might happen were there. People stopped to discuss and grimly speculate. From the town and surrounding villages, young men—weavers, farmers, store workers, shoemakers, and more—who had been planning a different, peaceful future were being sent away to fight. Then the sky turned the color of gunpowder, and the ground moved beneath our feet.

German soldiers fired at the town of Bailleul, large heavy shelling that shook the fruit from the trees and killed many less fortunate than we were. It was autumn 1914. They had captured Armentières, and we hid in the cellar during the heaviest bombings heralding their arrival. When their boots finally made it to the streets of the town, many of our men had left and escaped behind the Allied lines. But Jerome made no plans to leave.

Though the occupation was only days long, the German soldiers for no apparent reason interrogated people on the street, thinking they were being spied upon. We were too afraid to leave the house. We had just enough time to hide our horses in an abandoned barn before several German hussars arrived to raid our fruit stocks and take our pigs and some of our chickens. There were stories of violent killings of farmers and the plundering of silver along the way as soldiers rumbled toward the town hall to set up headquarters in the hotel opposite. Then we hid once more inside the cellar while bullets and shells fired from both sides and the Germans were driven east again. Our house and orchard had thankfully been spared, and Bailleul was in the hands of the Allies.

When it was safe to come outdoors again, the mood had lightened because now the British ran the town, announcing their arrival by whistling their cheerful foreign tunes. Soldiers from across the world poured into Bailleul to then march back out again and into hellfire. As a show of thanks during their stay, residents baked them biscuits and cakes and delivered these to their initial camps close to the town. Young girls handed out their lace handkerchiefs to the soldiers who paraded in formation in the square, and I could flirt and say anything I wanted, and Helene and Jerome did not disapprove, because these were strange times, as if we were living outside our real lives. Without the constraints of feeling like an outsider, life, in an ironic sort of way, became freer for us. For a period anyway.

Life changed not just with the newcomers but with new attitudes also. Things that had driven us apart, petty gripes, grudges, and small crimes, were not the things to talk about. The talk for most was only about winning or losing the war, new factory work for the women, the threat of poison gas that could tear out our lungs and burn holes through our skin, and what to do with a town filled with soldiers. Helene and I would run to sit on a stone wall outside the church and watch them and listen to them speak, and they liked that we laughed and learned their stories in poorly told French and their humorous tunes that I would want to hear again and again.

A strange new reality planted itself in the town. Injured soldiers were being brought in to recuperate, and there was a constant change-over of billets. Hotels were full, and across the north people opened their doors with offers of help. The smell of engines and metal and men hung about the town, along with mashed earth and smoke that trickled in from the front line.

Though there was an urgency and vibrancy with soldiers and vehicles in and out of Bailleul, the war brought a change in economies. Our fruit trees continued to yield, with the battlefield smoke that blew across them, though not as plentifully. Much of what we had was offered in exchange for food from the Allied administrators and other traders in Armentières. We feared losing our three horses, Hester, Carmello, and Mira, to the British forces, but for the reasons we were too far out of town and our horses were needed for transport and deliveries, they were thankfully not requisitioned. We had only two hens that had somehow escaped German capture, but the things that we relied on to make money were diminishing, and we were forced to turn our sights elsewhere. We offered to clean, sew, and repair the uniforms of the men, and this became a steady income. Helene and I would collect the uniforms on the cart, take them home to clean them, sew up hems and shrapnel holes, and then return them.

Amid the casualties and carnage, the monotony of the shelling only several miles away, and the bleakness of recapture were stories of love to distract us. Madame Favot, a widow who owned a small hotel, had offered permanent accommodation to soldiers, and there was a rumor that she had found love with one of them who was younger than her own son. And there was another story of several daughters who had argued over their billeted soldier, only to lose him into the arms of the girl next door. There were also stories of midnight rendezvous and secret letters and promises of life after the war.

The first two years of battle were fierce, and a steady flow of wounded soldiers were carried from the battlefield. Many of those recuperating were brought by truck to convalesce at the asylum hospital in Bailleul. Until the war, the insane asylum had housed female patients, but the caretaking nuns offered part of the building to the British as a hospital and also allowed the use of their hydrotherapy and bathing facilities as respite for soldiers. In exchange, the nuns received coal, soap, disinfectant, bacon, butter, eggs, and other items that were becoming scarce as supply routes were either cut off or damaged, or factories were destroyed.

One summer morning we came to collect uniforms from the asylum hospital as usual, and Jerome sent us with a box of fruit for the sisters working there. Outside the building, a young man was discussing something with the mother superior. The man was tall, with brown hair and striking eyes of iris blue. He had a sweet face, a long jawline, and he was extremely handsome. The splattering of freckles across his face told me that he did not have the skin for the sun.

Several of the men beside him looked our way. One of them made a mock bow, and I pretended to be shy when he looked at me, though all I could think of was finding a way to speak with them. The one paying me attention had fair hair and a smiling, dimpled face. But my interest was in the handsome man who ignored us to focus on his discussion.

Helene and I slipped into the kitchen with our small delivery to gossip with the cook, who told us that many soldiers were using the baths for healing and respite. By the time we returned to the main entrance, our arms full of jackets and trousers, the men we had seen earlier had gone or progressed to somewhere else in the building. I was disappointed, naturally.

As we were leaving, two army trucks pulled up at the front entrance. Several of the men were piling out the back, some with bloody bandages around their heads, some on crutches, and others missing limbs. The nuns and nursing staff supplied by the Allies were directing them into the building.

Helene was very quiet on the way back, and I asked her what was wrong.

"Those men," she said. "They suffer for us, for our freedom."

It was rare for Helene to comment on things, for we had seen such sights before in the war years already passed, but in that year of 1917, these wounded men affected her.

When we got home again, there were two uniformed men in our house, talking to Jerome. He introduced them. An older officer, Jack, and the young yellow-haired man, Roger, whom we had seen at the hospital, were to be billeted there, and Jerome was fussing about with cups of tea and cake that Helene had made earlier.

The two soldiers would take over Helene's room, and my sister would move once more back into the tiny bedroom with me. In exchange for their billet, they brought meat in tins, tobacco for Jerome, bananas, and eggs. By that time Helene and I had learned many English words and sentences, and we were practicing conversations between ourselves and with the soldiers every chance we could.

Several mornings later we had to return to the hospital to deliver the uniforms. Roger was there with some other men, including the man with the startling blue eyes I had seen earlier. The man was shirtless, and his torso was marked with tiny shrapnel wounds. Roger introduced him as Edgar, and he spoke to us politely in French, but I could tell his mind was elsewhere. He excused himself, and I watched him disappear down the hospital corridors. Helene was the first to ask if Edgar was well, which was unlike her, to be so curious and forward.

"He lost a lot of men beside him and had to be carried from the field in shock," another man explained. "He is staying here a bit longer, and then he will be back in battle."

Roger had left for the front a few days later, and as we heard the terrible explosions, I prayed that all the men would survive.

I visited Lenore once in Armentières and took her some fruit and coal that we had been given by the English. She was appreciative, though still cold toward me. Lenore carried much misery. The death of her husband, Jerome had told us, had affected her badly. Only later I would learn that deep love and loss should never be paired.

"I'm moving," she said. "This place is too noisy for me. Too many soldiers."

It was just as well she did. In coming months poison gas would spread dangerously close to the town, causing civilians to be evacuated anyway.

One day there was a knock at our door, and Edgar stood on our threshold in his olive-green uniform beside Roger. Roger was being sent back to the field that day and had asked the garrison town's mayor, a British officer and close friend, for permission to pass his billet on to Edgar.

The house grew a little quieter, as we were nervous around the new-comer. We felt we should keep some distance, yet at the same time we were drawn to him like the insects to our lanterns. All drawn to want to know him, help him, and protect him. He was strong, big, dwarfing our little kitchen with his presence, but there was a strange vulnerability about him also. He was quiet, dignified, grateful, and considerate. Not that the others weren't appreciative. They had been a pleasure to be around. It was just that Edgar made us feel important. He complimented us on small tasks we considered unworthy of any praise, offered to wash our dinner plates along with his own, and graciously left us quickly after each meal, which at first I took a different way.

On the second night, after he returned to his room, we discussed him. "He doesn't like us!" I said.

"Oh, stop talking like that!" said Helene. "Everything is so dramatic with you." Even when she told me off, it didn't sound like it. But I got the message. "He is injured. He is missing home. He is stuck here with strangers. He has fought battles already and more to come. Do you really think he should be jumping around joyously? He is a hero. They are all heroes, and we need to treat them as such."

I felt ashamed for being so petty, though it wasn't Helene's intention to make me feel this way. She spoke about him with such passion, and it was not just to me but as if to everyone who wasn't there also, to the rest of France.

"He is a man with thoughts buried deep," said Jerome as he lit the sweet-smelling tobacco in his pipe and nodded. "We must give him space. He will be here for two weeks. He has been given longer to recuperate. He wears things inside that he does not wish to share, so we must make his stay here as welcoming and comforting as possible."

Jerome squeezed my shoulder as he stood up as if the message was more for me than anyone else.

For the next two days, the situation was the same. Edgar would come in for meals and then leave again to his room. One day, he asked if he could ride one of the horses, and Jerome suggested that Helene ride with him. But Helene declined, her shyness taking over. Jerome then asked me, and I agreed of course. It was an opportunity to have him all to myself.

We rode through the fields behind the orchard and stopped to rest under the shade of a tree. He seemed more relaxed on the horse, not so formal, and was always talking to and stroking Hester, which I had given him to ride. He praised my horse-riding skills. Several times he looked northeast toward the fighting, pondering over something, and I thought then how fearful it must be for him that he must soon take his gun again to fight. We let the horses graze while we sat and ate some dates that Lenore had sent us for Christmas, and I had also packed us a bottle of milk.

"Where do you and your sister come from?" he asked in perfect French.

"Pardon me?"

"Your sister and you . . . Did Jerome adopt you?"

"Yes," I said.

He nodded. How he knew, I don't know, but I guessed he'd heard from someone in the town. I told him how we were abandoned and about some of our journey.

"Did your sister attend school?"

"Yes, and I did, too." Though I didn't tell him I didn't complete it like Helene had done.

"She is very clever, your sister," he said, more to himself than anyone else. And I wondered how he knew this and remembered that she would add up the receipts and count them and write up bills for payment of goods.

"Do you think you could get her to come riding with me also?"

"Oh, but she is not as accomplished on a horse," I said, to which he laughed. I failed to understand at the time that he had seen right through my attempted diversion.

He was talkative that night at dinner, and he tested our English conversations and taught us more phrases. He told us about his brothers and mother. What he liked to do for leisure, his horses, and about his marvelous house in a quiet place that sounded like paradise compared to the turmoil we had grown used to. That night when I went to bed, I fantasized about going home with Edgar and being introduced to his family as his wife. In England I imagined we would ride together and have dinner in the dining room that he described.

Helene whispered in the dark because she saw I was tossing and turning and sighing a lot.

"Aren't you sleeping?"

"No, can't you?" I replied.

"No."

"Why not?"

There was a silence.

"Are you still thinking about the men on the battlefield?" I asked.

"Just one at the moment," she said. And I knew then that Helene, like I had been, was fantasizing about Edgar, and I had an ominous feeling that my own dreams might be over. I did not think at the time that she was also aware he was falling for her. What I did realize was that sometimes, when someone likes you, you just know. I wondered then if something had happened, some connection across the dinner table, some words spoken when I was not in earshot, something else that I had missed.

Even though I loved Helene, it did not stop me from feeling envious and competing with her. The next day I wore my Paris dress, and Edgar looked me up and down and told me I looked pretty, but his eyes rested mostly on Helene.

One day, after I returned from a ride, Mira and the cart were gone and Jerome was in the kitchen.

"Edgar and Helene have left with the deliveries. You have the morning off. You can go riding if you wish."

But I didn't want the morning off.

"She never wants to do the deliveries!" I said.

Jerome was shocked at my vexation, his mouth open, speechless, and I turned and slammed the back door as I left and ran out into the fields to sit and think and watch the road from the hills for their return.

Later, from behind the fruit trees, I watched them sit together on the cart, idling the horse along the track, not in any hurry to return. Edgar appeared talkative and expressive, and he looked at her often while she looked bashfully down. He seemed far more carefree than he had on previous days. Helene was smiling and laughing. It was such a rare thing to see that I was mesmerized by it. I went in through the back door and waited for them. I could hear them talking outside.

"I will see you at dinner then?" said Edgar.

"Where else would I be?"

There was silence, and I imagined Helene looking down shyly.

"Thank you for your company," he said.

There was a pause as Helene tried to think of a response, or perhaps they were looking at each other lovingly, or maybe there was a touch. I am not sure, but I think whatever happened in that moment had sealed their relationship. Edgar did not come inside but went around the side of the house toward his room at the back. Helene came into the house with a poppy tucked behind her ear.

It bothered me that Edgar had clearly chosen between us. And perhaps I was more bothered by the fact that I didn't see this coming. I was sour all evening, and Jerome caught me in the barn, brushing the horses, to inquire about my sullen mood. I did not respond, and he left frustrated with his arms in the air.

That evening Helene had replaced her trousers for a dress, which Jerome noticed also with a curious glance, and Edgar was in good spirits, asking me about the horses and Jerome about the town, about the customs and the fruit seasons. I realized how beautiful she was with her green eyes; her thick, dark lashes; and the dress exposing much of her brown shoulders. She was a flower in full bloom. I had never felt jealous of her before because I had always drawn the attention toward me, and Helene, being shy, had liked that also.

Helene gave Edgar a larger portion of mashed potatoes and less to herself, and Jerome looked at me with eyes that were smiling. But I felt no joy. I lasted only as long as dinner and returned to our room because I could not bear to look at them. Then Jerome went to bed, and later Helene and Edgar, I saw from the window, took a midnight stroll.

The next day Edgar was due to leave, and I decided that I did not want to say goodbye. I slipped into the fields in certain protest that I had been left out, my sister the victor of the soldier's affection. I was wishing that Helene would go away and leave and marry an old widower in the village and have seven babies. I had walked into town and sauntered past the other soldiers to encourage their admiration and flirtations. It did not make me feel any better, and suddenly I felt cruel, and I ran all the way home again, but by that time Edgar had left. A truck had picked him up and taken him to the front, and I felt miserable and confused. I cannot say why my head and my heart were all over the place, because part of me was happy for Helene and part of me feared for Edgar's safety. But perhaps the remaining piece of me was just conceited and irrational.

When Helene asked why I had left that morning, I just shrugged. She shook her head and said that it was time to show more respect like an adult if I wanted to be called one, and I went to my room and cried, feeling shallow and childish. Then thoughts of their togetherness frightened me even more. What if Helene and Edgar got married and moved away to England? What if I lost her? And suddenly my jealous feelings were replaced by the thought that I might lose the one person who had been with me from the beginning. My sister who had never hurt anyone, had loved me unconditionally through all my wildness and willfulness.

Wiping away my tears, I saw a piece of paper under her pillow, a corner jutting out from the edge. It seemed important somehow because of where it was placed, and I should have left it there, but I couldn't help myself. I opened it up, and inside was a message written in a neat but quivery hand. The note in French said, *Dear lovely Helene, you have made my time here the best it has been, and I sincerely hope that I see you again soon. Edgar*

It was very formal and not a love note, but his feelings were there in the spaces between the words. He had fallen hard for Helene, too, it seemed. The pieces fell into place just like her tidy bed. Helene's pillow was in its proper spot, and a little cross hung on the wall above her bed. Everything was where it should be. And love sat also in a tidy corner of that bedroom. Edgar and Helene had found each other in a situation that neither he nor even Helene had predicted, and they were now connected by love and promises. Suddenly I stopped wanting Edgar for myself, and in some strange way the letter freed me from my fantasies. I had grown up, and the lives of others were suddenly more important than my own.

I slipped the note back under the pillow.

When Helene came in a short time later, she sat on the edge of the bed and put her hand on my leg.

"I don't know what's got into you, but if it's something I've done, please tell me. I don't want to see you so upset. This isn't like you, and it scares me a little."

I said nothing.

"Is it because of Edgar and me?"

I nodded.

"I can't help falling in love, Mariette."

I realized before she had even finished that sentence that I didn't deserve her, and I threw my arms around her and cried into her neck.

"Will you go away?" I asked.

"Who knows? But I can tell you that wherever I go, it will not be without you."

I said I was sorry for being such a brat, and she knew that I was jealous also, though she would never say it. She would never humiliate me. The idea of finding a suitor was suddenly not as important as being with my sister.

"I hate seeing good men go to war," said Jerome at dinner. He didn't say it, but we all thought it: that Edgar may not come back.

"Are you sweet on him?" he asked Helene one evening when he was puffing on his pipe and Helene and I were playing a game of cards by the lantern on the table.

"Who?" said Helene innocently, though she was struggling to meet his gaze.

"I thought so," he said.

I laughed hard then; it had been a while since I had. Helene and Jerome joined me, and it was one of those moments that defined a change in the direction of our lives. It was acceptance that there was someone else now that had formed a part of our little family.

Helene grew a bit depressed as the days wore on, and her beautiful smile disappeared. She would not hear from Edgar for weeks. She had changed back into her trousers and shirts, and our cleaning, sewing, and darning tasks grew as more bullet holes appeared in the uniforms for repair. Though these ones had no owners to return them to.

More men were billeted in the room at the rear of the house. Jerome regularly went to the town hall to learn the news of soldiers we had met, in particular Edgar. He would also go to hospitals. One day he came back and said that one of the men who had been billeted here, Roger, had been badly injured with gas. Many others also, but Roger was one of the worst and had to be sent back to England. Dinner was a very solemn affair that night, and Helene had lost interest in our games of charades and cards.

Sometimes we would hear explosions, and we would rush outside to watch the fire from some distant battle, and always after these times, Helene did not wish to speak. I sometimes would catch her in the stable, crying, her face on the warm neck of Carmello.

"She has lost her heart to him," Jerome said once when we were collecting the last of the fruit.

"Will he come back, do you think?" I asked, knowing there was no real answer.

"If God wills it," he said.

The next day I found Helene stitching up the hem of a soldier's trousers, and I sat cross-legged opposite her to darn more socks. These times always reminded me of our childhood beside campfires when we only had each other. She smiled then as if she knew what I was thinking. And it had always been us. We rarely had to question each other on thoughts. We just knew, and she reached out and put up her hand, and I put up mine, palm to palm. I don't think we could have been any closer.

She said she didn't like the fact that people were dying "for us." It didn't feel right that we were here with a roof and warm food, while they were there in rain or sleet, burnt and blistering from the sun or their fingers and toes frozen, their bodies aching. She wished she could have gone, too, and we toyed with the idea of stealing uniforms and cutting our hair and pretending to be men. But we were just girls again, and it was idle talk, because we were young and full of good ideas that would never see light.

That night the soldiers who were billeted brought us big steaks of ham and coffee, and we added our potatoes and peas, and we had a feast. We left no plate with any food. Jerome brought out wine for the men and poured us two small glasses, too, and we toasted to success and we prayed that night to our God, because we knew only the one, not the spirits that the gypsies spoke of but the one that Jerome prayed to for our men to come home. We claimed the foreign soldiers currently in the town as our own, and everyone else who had come far to free us.

The next morning, early, there was a knock at the door, and it was Edgar. He was thin and haggard, with scratches on his face. Helene ran into his arms, and he picked her up, arms tightly around her, and I saw tears pouring out from his eyes, while Helene sobbed into his shoulder. And I knew then that it was real love, the kind that many of us dream about at some point.

CHAPTER 24

The soldier at our house was kind enough to swap billets with Edgar, and he had the place again, and Helene was smiling, and she wore her prettiest dress, and there was a spring in her step, and I loved to see her so happy. Even Jerome smiled more. And we weren't thinking about the future. We were rejoicing one day at a time. But Edgar's leave this time would only be short.

Helene and Edgar spent much time together, and their relationship was serious. I was awake when Helene sneaked out during the night and went to the room at the back. And the first night, I could smell pipe smoke and knew that Jerome was awake and probably knew about it, too. And the second night as she was leaving, I whispered a warning to Helene that she would get caught by Jerome, but she gave me a kiss and tucked me into bed like she was my mother because to me she always had been. I didn't know any other.

The morning following, the lovers were quiet, and they avoided eye contact, and I knew that something more had happened. Jerome said Helene could have the day off, and the pair took a basket of food and disappeared into the fields and trees behind the orchard, and when they came back, he had his arm around her and she was flushed, and there were grass stains on the back of her dress. But these weren't the only signs of their love. She was radiant and talkative. I had never seen her so free: so unlike the solemn, silent girl I had known my whole life.

I liked this new Helene, though I was also very wary. I was afraid of losing her to Edgar forever. Though if I had to lose her to anyone, it would be to him.

One day one of our customers from Bailleul visited. We rarely had visitors, so it was a little strange. He made light talk, asked Jerome about the fruit, and spoke about the war, a topic that was offered at every new meeting. Jerome had already suspected that the visit was a specific one and tilted his head in my direction to suggest I leave them. Helene and Edgar were out riding. I walked into my room and listened intently through the door.

"Thought you should know that they're singing about your girl down at the tavern."

"Mariette?"

"No. Your other one. They sing a song called 'The Gypsy and the Soldier,' which they have written themselves."

I laughed into my hand because it sounded wonderful, but I could hear from Jerome's forceful tone that he did not think it was funny at all.

"Who sings this?"

"The tavern owner, Gerard, and his wife, Aloise . . . It's rather lewd."

There was silence from Jerome.

"Anyway I thought you should know."

Jerome didn't thank the visitor but instead asked after his wife. Perhaps Jerome was too proud to admit or show that he was offended. But he was. And not just a little. After the visitor left, Jerome climbed straight onto the trap. I followed him a short way, and when he said he had some private business to do, I rushed to the other side and climbed up anyway. He was too angry to argue, I could tell. He had other things on his mind.

We rode into the town with the wind biting any exposed flesh, and Jerome said nothing but looked straight ahead. I read the sign not to speak to him. In the rare moments that Jerome was angry about something, we let him be, gave him time to sort it out in his head.

Jerome climbed off the trap, and this time he looked at me directly. "Don't follow!" he said.

His look was so serious I was forced to oblige. Well, in part. I stood close enough to the tavern windows to see and hear everything.

He went up to the counter and spoke directly to Gerard but loud enough that other people in the tavern heard also. He said that they should get their minds out of gossip. That while they were making fun of people, hundreds of soldiers were dying close by. He said to start thinking of them instead, start doing some good instead of trying to be hurtful. He didn't sound angry, just direct and forceful and disappointed. No one in the tavern there spoke. I think that they were too shocked and embarrassed to say anything. Then Jerome walked out, put on his hat, and climbed into the cart.

We didn't talk about it on the way home. Only when we had a view of the farmhouse did he tell me not to mention it to Helene. He did not want to see her hurt.

"And don't go finding out what was sung. It is best you not learn such things. And don't go telling Helene about it."

I was a little afraid for Helene all of a sudden, though I could not find a specific reason for this at the time. While Edgar wasn't around, I asked Helene if she intended on marrying him.

"No, of course not."

"Why not?"

"Because I don't have a birth date or even a last name. And you need them both."

I grabbed her arm and dragged her outside to Jerome, who was fixing a wheel on the trap. I explained the situation to him and asked him what we could do about it.

"Has he asked you to marry him?" he said.

"No," Helene said, embarrassed.

"No one will marry them because she does not exist," I said to Jerome.

"Stop talking about marriage!" Helene said, turning red in the face.

Jerome, ignoring her, said that he had already applied to adopt us but couldn't because the birth mother and father were probably alive. And it was also very complicated because legally we were adults, and he talked then of going to Paris and seeing what else he could do.

"Stop it!" said Helene, suddenly flustered by this talk. "There is no marriage."

No more discussions came of it, because Edgar was going back to battle the following afternoon. The pair stayed inside the back room that night and all the following morning. I kept going out to see if there was any movement, but the curtains were always still. They weren't eating or drinking, and it was just Jerome and I for lunch, and I asked if I should take them food.

"No," said Jerome calmly, drawing back on his pipe. And I could tell he was worried about a lot of things, but he didn't say. Grown-up things that made life more complicated. I'd heard stories of fathers chasing soldiers out of their daughters' bedrooms and wondered if Jerome was going to do the same, but he didn't. I couldn't help myself. I had to know what he thought.

"I thought you might chase Edgar off with a saucepan. Lucie's papa did that when she brought a soldier home."

"I guess I'm too old for chasing," he said, and I thought he would leave it there, but he continued in earnest, and I could tell he had done a lot of thinking about it. I knew he wasn't sleeping, and then I saw that his eyes were watery.

"Sometimes you only get a brief moment of love in war, and there's no telling where this will lead. I do know that if your sister, Helene, is sweet on a boy, it is the real thing. I thought that she would likely be a spinster since she never even turned her head toward one." I had to agree. Love had gone looking for Helene, not the other way around.

"And there is another thing that I know. Edgar is a good man, a soldier, a loving man, I can tell. He has his heart in the right place, and who am I to stop her. She is a grown woman."

"So what then if I'm sweet on a boy?"

His eyes crinkled as he laughed softly.

"You on the other hand, I would chase the boy out with a saucepan."

We laughed at the picture this drew, but it was sort of sad, happy laughing because we knew there was pain to come, and Helene would be without her lover soon, and there was, as Jerome said, no way of knowing what was to come.

They came out an hour before Edgar was due to leave, and he was polite and kind to Jerome, and Helene was red in the face like she had been crying.

"Are you in love, the pair of you?" said Jerome.

"Papa!" she said.

"Yes, sir," said Edgar. "I love your daughter. And it is my intention to marry her when this war is done."

Jerome nodded, then asked if his family would approve. Edgar said yes. Helene looked embarrassed and surprised at the same time. Jerome explained that there were some legal issues to be done in the meantime, and Edgar said he knew of those and appreciated what Jerome was planning to do. Edgar said that he would not let his family know until he was back from battle and the paperwork was settled.

We said goodbye. I hugged Edgar tightly because I believed he was family now, and I cried into his shoulder until Helene gently pulled me away. I saw the tears on his face and could tell he loved Helene but that he would also miss us all. Edgar shook hands with Jerome, who wished him well, and Helene took him on the trap to the town.

I felt my heart miss a beat because the thought of Helene married terrified me. Would she move to England? Would they move away, and would that mean I would have to live in England? She had promised we would be together, but I could not think of either of us leaving Jerome.

I asked Jerome if he thought they would move to England and, if they did, would he move, too.

"You don't need to worry about me. Young ones often move on. The old ones stay. That's just what happens."

I told him that I would never move while we had the orchard, and suddenly my fantasies about marriage and wealth and moving to England disappeared because my heart was still with Jerome. I would stay there till I died, and I would find my own soldier who would choose to live in France, which seemed easier said than done. It also seemed unlikely that love would happen soon. And I knew that when it did, it would be sudden. I just never figured it would be that way for Helene. I thought she would be there beside me till the end of time.

I had found no fault in Edgar, no annoying habit, no false words, no shiftiness. If he stood in the rain, I imagined water would bounce off his shoulders. All I could see was a man who was chivalrous, loving, kind, and brave. I was both envious and proud of Helene.

Jerome in the meantime had written to the civil administration in Paris to request that we be given his name, but he was yet to hear back. And if a reply did come some months ahead, we would never know about it.

What I had learned about lovers up till then was that love eventually dies and in most cases without reasons that make any sense. Love can leave suddenly, and you are left broken from the shock. Or it can just slowly edge away and leave you hanging and confused. Regardless of when it does leave, sadness always follows. Helene's case was sudden. In the first two months, with only miles between them, Edgar wrote often from the front line, and with words of love. Then one day all letters from him ceased, and she received no further replies.

Helene would go into Bailleul to inquire of the returned soldiers, but he wasn't amongst them. We continued to seek information from the mayor's office until one day we learned that Edgar was in a hospital in Saint Omer, recuperating from an injury. Jerome took Helene to see him, but with work to do, I stayed behind unwillingly. When they returned from their long trip they were both downhearted. There seemed no rational answer to my many questions, and Helene disappeared to the back room, where she didn't have to speak.

"What is so bad? Why won't you tell me?"

"Because it is difficult to explain."

"Is he wounded badly?"

"Nothing visible. Only that the doctor says he may have a bad concussion. He is unsure at this stage. They might have to send him elsewhere for treatment."

Helene traveled far to the hospital on her own early the next day but was turned away by nursing staff who had strict orders not to let in visitors. She was told to leave her address and they would send her a note if he expressed a desire or was well enough to see her.

Helene grew numb from the silence and then became silent herself. She appeared dazed, haunted, and hopeless, and I became frightened for her. When Jerome and I tried to talk to her about it, she chose not to speak.

She continued to send letters until one day when several were returned unopened. She withdrew completely and struggled to get out of bed. When Jerome and I returned from deliveries in the afternoon, she would often still be there. Then she became unwell and stopped eating. The trays of food I left beside her bed would be untouched when I came back for them later.

It soon became obvious why she was sick. It was the "woman's punishment," which is what some of the camp women used to say. Though from my early experiences, I had learned that there were other reasons than just sickness and painful births. Children sometimes drove the men away and left the women alone to find them food. Relationships were complicated, and babies made them more so.

Helene wept on me, and I wept for her. It was important that I spoke to Edgar now because he had to marry her with or without a record of her birth. Of all the people that this was to happen to, it must not be Helene, I thought. She had never done harm to anyone.

Jerome was very quiet when she announced to him that she was pregnant. Helene had finally come out of her room to sit with us at the dining table. She looked pale and fearful while Jerome took in her words with a draw back of his pipe.

"Are you angry with me, Papa?"

"I'm angry at the situation but not with you. Just disappointed for you."

She looked tragic. I could see her heart breaking before me.

One day on my own, very early in the morning, the frost crackling on the grass under my feet, I rode Hester to Saint Omer to visit Edgar.

Inside the building, I told an English nurse that I was the cousin of Edgar Watts and I'd been sent by family to inquire of his health. I told her that I must see him and report back his condition.

I watched her walk away to speak to one of the other nurses, who checked a clipboard with names that she carried, and then the second English nurse promptly returned to tell me in French that any visits weren't possible at that time due to certain restrictions she didn't elaborate on. She said that if there was anything further to report, family would be notified. I was angry that I was not allowed in, but I didn't show it. I pretended to leave, then sneaked back through the doorway to search through the wards. The nurses I passed viewed me curiously. I knew I had only a limited time to find him.

There were men bandaged, missing limbs and eyes, some in obvious pain, from their sounds. It was terrifying to see so much injury in one place. I entered a section where the men looked mostly whole but with gaunt, expressionless faces. Here I found Edgar sitting in his hospital gown on the edge of his bed near a window. He was staring not out through the window at the pretty trees but at the floor beside his bed.

I moved to sit by his bedside, aware that there were suspicious looks from the nurses now, as well as from the sick. There were no other visitors.

"Edgar," I said. He looked up at me, and it seemed to take him some time to gather his thoughts before he turned away to look out the window this time.

"You should not be here," he said.

"I'm sorry you are so unwell," I said. I could not see any damage apart from a bandage around his wrist, and his trembling hands. "Were you hurt badly?"

He didn't say anything.

"I have news of Helene."

"I do not want to hear anything of her," he said, and I felt such coldness from him, as if the man in front of me were not the man I had met before. "You must leave."

"Edgar, do you know who I am?" I was shocked at the response.

He dropped his head and drew a deep breath.

"Yes, I know who you are, Mariette," he said, looking directly at me this time. "I want you to go home and tell Helene that I can't come back there."

"But she is carrying your child."

He stared at me with glazed eyes before calling out suddenly for the nurse, who came over to tell me to leave. She ushered me out the ward door, and I looked back to see that Edgar was turned from me, staring once more at the floor, as if he'd already forgotten about me.

"Edgar!" I shouted. "What is wrong with you?"

He seemed not to hear me. With hindsight I might have done things differently, spoken with more care, if only I'd known. But all I could think about was Helene carrying his child and desperate for news.

"What is wrong with him?" I asked the nurse.

One of the nurses spoke in English that I did not understand. I shouted at her in frustration, shrugging away her hand at my wrist.

"You are a coward!" I shouted back to Edgar in French, before two orderlies appeared at my side to take each of my arms. I tried to shrug away from them also, but they held too tightly as they led me away.

The French-speaking nurse told me that I should not call him that; Edgar was unfit to receive any visitors; he was suffering from a nervous condition, after continued exposure to shellfire. Though such a diagnosis meant nothing to me then. We had all been suffering from that. I thought that Edgar was simply using perhaps any excuse not to return to Helene.

I cursed at the orderlies as they released me at the front door, and the nurse, only later I would recall, seemed genuinely concerned about me.

"Take care, my dear," she said, but I spat in her direction. It was spiteful, but I was too distraught to act rationally, feeling everyone there was against us, including Edgar. I had no idea what to feel about him and his dismissal of me, and as I neared the orchard, I wondered what I should tell Helene. She knew where I had been and had been watching for my return. She came to meet me behind the house as I dismounted to walk Hester to the stable.

"Did you see him?"

"No," I lied to spare her, then babbled. "But I have such news! Apparently he was moved elsewhere recently, which is why there was confusion about the letters. Which is why they sent them back to you. He has been unwell, the nurse told me, and they sent him to a resort for soldiers in the south until he is better. But the nurse remembered him well and said that he spoke of his beautiful Helene all the time. And that as soon as he is well enough he will write. Though the nurse told me also that it could be a while because he is planning first to go back to the battles."

She nodded her head as if it was the response she was expecting. I lied to protect her, but I also felt I had done something very wrong. To give her hope that might not come.

It was agreed that we would tell people she was now married, that she had married Edgar on a trip to Paris and he had left to fight again, since no one had seen her in the town for many months. Jerome, I discovered, was very good at lying, too, and one day he brought home several little marriage gifts for Helene, from people in Bailleul. Even Gerard offered Jerome a drink when he was passing one day, though Jerome declined.

With her growing belly Helene continued working until Jerome told her to stop. But it seemed the larger she grew, the more determined she was to keep busy, to keep her mind on her times ahead with Edgar.

She had moved back into the room with me to make space for more men to billet there. But she also did not want to be alone, either. She was growing fearful of the future, afraid of the world she was bringing the child into.

I sewed lots of baby clothes, and I fussed about Helene. I made her eat more even when she said she was too tired for food. Sometimes at night I would rub her back when she couldn't sleep, and sometimes I would hold her, like she had held me, when she grew sad with thoughts of Edgar. She no longer queried about where he might be but still waited with hope he would return.

Jerome would come home from the town with news of war. Sometimes there was good news, and sometimes there was not, and still we witnessed the distant sounds of gunfire and flashes on the horizon.

One night there was a loud explosion and the smell of fire. Outside, the separate room where Helene used to sleep was destroyed, smashed and smoldering. And part of the stable was also damaged.

I ran out to the stable and found that Carmello had been hit on his back, and he was on his side shrieking. Jerome told me to move out of the way. I wailed like a child when he shot him, even though there was nothing else we could have done.

Our lives had changed again, and for days the shelling contin-ued. The church was bombed, and the town clock lay in ruins. Several houses and businesses in the town had also been bombed. The British were evacuating Bailleul, and military trucks left with refugees, while most townspeople packed the roads west in their carts and others left on foot with their belongings strapped to their backs. Some soldiers came to ask if we wanted help, but Jerome said we would make our own way. There were also many townspeople who refused to leave, and others who remained in their houses in town and on farms on the outskirts, choosing to believe the north would not fall into enemy hands. Jerome and I began packing to move south to Rouen to join Lenore, but Helene experienced severe pains in the belly that left her doubled over, and this convinced us to delay our travel. We believed we still had days. Then, by the time she'd improved, we no longer had the choice to leave. The Germans arrived quickly this time, and they were battle worn and raging.

CHAPTER 25

The first thing the Germans did was to search the houses and farms for Allied soldiers and weapons, and the second thing was to take our food. They had expected the front line to be pushed well back into France by now, so their patience had run thin, and they were hungry, weary, and brash. They made their headquarters in a hotel near the town square, and the rest of the administration was installed at the damaged town hall. Bailleul residents and those on farms and villages nearby were ordered to remain, and would now be required to work for them. Any who protested were immediately killed, and some were taken to prisons in Germany. With so many Germans patrolling the roads, any evacuation at that point seemed impossible. We hoped that since we were some distance from the town, they would leave us alone. We were wrong.

Jerome was kind and courteous toward the group that searched our house on the first day, offering the fruit he had stored in the cellar. He did not want to give them any reason to harm us. We had only two horses left now, Hester and Mira, the cart horse. There were more whites in Jerome's hair, more yellow to his skin, and his stoop was more noticeable.

Some of the orchard had been wiped out in the shelling, and the earth that had been scorched was turned to mush from the rain. Helene had in previous weeks prepared fruit pies to store, jars full of fruit, and drying meat to put in casseroles. We had a sack of potatoes and wheat, which would last several weeks. We had hidden some of our stores, but they had taken most. However, it was the next visit that we were unprepared for.

"Ausweise!" said a soldier, who looked too old for warfare.

He barely examined our faces, hurriedly scanning Jerome's identity card before handing it back. But I noticed another officer standing behind him, looking over his shoulder, scrutinizing all of us while we stood with uncertainty. Several times the officer, a captain, made eye contact with me, and I suspected there was something menacing behind the gaze, and more than the pillage of food and a brief interrogation.

The older sergeant waved Helene forward to present an identity card that the British had issued each resident in the region as part of their security. Jerome had given our name as Lavier, which was not questioned at the time. The German soldier studied Helene's card briefly, without acknowledging her at all; then, as he moved to hand it back to her, the captain caught his arm to retrieve the card. The younger man introduced himself to us in well-versed French, though this formality was brusque rather than considerate. He was young, clean-shaven but for a small, narrow mustache. He did not look either tired or bored. I noticed that his eyes were very sharp, and he took check of everything in the room. He then eyed Helene, his gaze dropping to her belly before carefully examining the document that had her photograph and the name of Helene Lavier.

"You are married since?" asked Captain Lizt.

"Yes," said Helene.

"Can I see the certificate?"

I felt my knees go weak.

"Unfortunately, much of our papers were destroyed by your war machines," said Jerome. He pointed to the destruction at the back of the house, where some of the wreckage had been removed. The captain ignored him.

"You had some men staying here, I have been told."

"Yes, Captain," said Jerome, only this time his voice took a more severe tone. "We did our part as we were asked, though we had little choice. Unfortunately now because of the war, our accommodation is much smaller."

He was sending a message that there was no room for German soldiers here. We could already tell that the experience would be less amiable since our two countries were far from friends.

"And where is your husband?" the captain asked Helene.

"He is in Paris, working," Jerome replied for her.

"I wasn't speaking with you," said Lizt curtly, without looking his way, before continuing to direct his questioning to Helene. "Where does he work?"

I stepped forward also at this point, the top of my arm brushing hers for support.

"He works in a bank," said Helene.

The captain pressed his lips tightly together and stared at her for a moment.

"I have had word from someone that your husband is an officer in the English army."

I wondered at first who would have said this. Since Jerome had gone to speak to Gerard, the tavern owner, about his song, he had been polite toward us whenever we passed, but there was a touch of resentment perhaps from the humiliation. French people found it hard to hide their true feelings. But then it could be anyone protecting their families by diverting the attention from them. Helene stood still. She had never been a good liar, not like I was. It was just a matter of time before her silence would condemn her.

"The priest here says there was no wedding, and he has no record of it," said the captain.

"The marriage took place in Paris," said Jerome, interrupting again.

The captain paused for a moment, the corner of his mouth rising with a hint of cruel amusement.

"I believe that it is more likely that you carry an English bastard," he said.

"You are quite mistaken," said Jerome forcefully.

"There are some in the town who believe so, too."

"Then they are mistaken also," said Jerome.

"It remains to be seen what the truth turns up, but, Monsieur Lavier," he said, his words clipped and his manner cold, "your daughters are to come immediately to our headquarters to be questioned."

"But that sounds highly irregular—"

"Irregular how, Monsieur Lavier?"

"They are innocent women. They do not need interrogation," he said. "My grandmother was from Germany. This war is not personal. If it is provisions you need, I will gladly help you."

"Unfortunately, it is your civic duty to help us regardless of your generous words."

He spoke then in German to the sergeant, who stepped forward and grabbed both Helene and me by the arms.

"Stop that immediately!" said Jerome. "Mariette is just a girl. What could you possibly have to glean from her?"

The sergeant jostled us both toward the exit, with Jerome following too closely.

"You can take me instead," said Jerome.

Captain Lizt withdrew his pistol from his belt to point it at Jerome.

"Step away!" said the captain.

Jerome waited several seconds, and I sent him pleading looks to stop him from inciting them further. I would get us out of this. I had to.

"I will bring them peacefully in my cart," Jerome offered. "You can follow us."

The captain spoke again to the sergeant, who continued to lead us away.

"Let me at least follow you," said Jerome to the captain. "Helene is very close to giving birth. At least I am there if anything happens."

Lizt waved the tip of his gun at Jerome impatiently, indicating that he could follow.

"If you try to do anything, I can tell you that your daughters—a term that is not shared by everyone—may get hurt in any cross fire or altercation."

It was a not-so-subtle threat that he would likely aim at one of us.

Outside, the air was warm, the insects buzzing with new life. On a day like today, I would have taken Hester for a run, or Carmello if he were alive. The captain spoke to two others who had been waiting outside. Lizt and the sergeant climbed onto their horses, while the other soldiers put us in handcuffs and tied a rope between our shackles and their saddles. They, too, remounted, and we were led then like dogs, following them in the direction of town.

I saw Helene rub her belly and knew the baby was kicking ferociously. I had felt the baby a number of times, less than eight months grown. She looked at me with resignation. I knew Helene would be tired and wanting to sit down. She had not slept properly for days, a combination of the baby kicking and the fact that she was anxious with no word from Edgar. She wore a gold ring that had belonged to Jerome's wife, and as we held hands, I twisted it tenderly. At one point she gripped her belly.

I signed at her to see if she was all right.

She signed back that the baby was restless.

"Stop that," said the older sergeant, noting our communication.

There was no chance to speak with her to match our stories should we be interrogated separately. The walk took close to an hour, and when we reached the town, Helene was clearly exhausted. Several bystanders watched us curiously, and some turned in shock as they saw us. I saw Felix, Gerard's son, who was still not over his infatuation with me. He was about to step forward to ask what was happening, but I shook my head at him.

When we stopped outside the town hall, I saw Jerome not far behind in the trap. Something in my heart gave way, and I could sense his feeling of helplessness. He had done everything for us, but he could do nothing now. Several others from the town were grouped and watching curiously.

As the men dismounted, there were loud shouts from inside the building, and a German officer then marched a man out the front doors and down to the cobbled pavement. Everyone stopped to watch, even the soldiers who were leading us in.

The man, his wrists manacled behind him, was suddenly pushed away closer to where we stood. He stumbled and then stood up to face us. His shirt was torn, and his face was beaten until it was purple and so swollen it was hard to recognize the person beneath.

The officer who had pushed him forward then pointed his gun toward the legs of the prisoner before turning sideways to peruse the many who had stopped to watch. Some, however, had cautiously disappeared inside buildings by this stage.

"This man," the German officer called out in French, "has been caught trying to send his son away with a message about our weapons and our numbers here. I do not need to tell you residents of Bailleul that if anyone else is thinking about doing the same, this is what will happen."

He raised his arm and fired the gun suddenly at the head of the man. I jumped at the small explosion and started shaking, and I caught Helene just as she fainted. We had seen injustice in our lifetimes, but we had only yet heard of executions and never before witnessed such savagery.

"Please," I begged a soldier to help me lift Helene. He obliged, but another soldier pulled me away, and I watched Helene being carried unconscious toward a barred cell after we entered the town hall building.

"She needs water," I called out before being forced down some stairs and into another cell in the basement.

I was there for what seemed like hours, until it grew dark. The walls were thick around me, though occasionally I heard wailing from another room. Sometimes soldiers would walk past, and I would call to them to find out what was happening, but their ears were blocked to any pleas. I dozed, sitting against the wall, and was woken suddenly by the jangle of keys as a soldier unlocked the door. He ordered me to get up, then led me to an office upstairs, and I could see no sign of Helene along the way.

I was handed a glass of water and told to sit on a chair and wait. My throat was so dry, and my lips cracked. I drank the water greedily, hoping that Helene had been given some, too. Two soldiers stood by the door. They didn't speak directly to me, but occasionally they nodded in my direction and joked to one another in German.

Captain Lizt walked in a short time later. He sat on a chair opposite and began inspecting me with eyes that were scornful and intense, as if I was both insignificant and indispensable at the same time.

"What is your name?" he asked, while one of the soldiers was relegated to taking notes.

"Where is my sister?"

He slapped me suddenly across the face, so hard it forced my head to turn. I stayed like that for a moment, my hand against my bruised cheek, while my mind turned to thoughts of the man I'd seen shot, and the realization that I was no longer free to speak my mind. For years I had done as I wished, but my world had unjustly changed once more, and Captain Lizt now held my life in his hands. I sat up straight to look him in the eyes, my hands clenched in my lap. I was no longer dealing with people who were fair and reasonable and who treated women differently to men. I had grown so spoiled by Jerome and others that I had almost forgotten about the cruelty that existed elsewhere.

"My name is Mariette Lavier. I am sister to Helene Lavier—"

"That is a lie. She is Helene without a surname, just like you, and there was no marriage."

He had staring, shining eyes that refused to let go of my own. I didn't like the way he now looked at me, not just with suspicion but also with disgust.

"Where are you from?"

"Bailleul."

"That is a lie."

"I'm telling you the truth."

He threw his head back and laughed. The Germans had lost a lot of men, and we French were collectively inhospitable and without a lot of food to offer. If he'd had the manpower, munitions, and authority, he would have wiped our towns and villages off the map then and there instead of later on.

"It doesn't matter what you say. I was curious only. I have heard the truth from others."

I was quiet. There was nothing I could think of to say, and my thoughts were with Helene, wondering what she had said and what had been said to her and if she had revealed anything. If they had learned anything, I did not believe it was from her.

"You and your sister are gypsy runaways who cunningly wormed their way into a stranger's house, pretending now to be respectable."

"That is not true—"

He put up his hand to stop my talking, while both fury and fear hammered inside my chest.

"You can deny it all you want. But I have just been inquiring about you myself from several in the area. They have all cooperated. I am merely quoting some of the things that were said."

I hid my dismay.

"Where is my sister?" I asked.

"That is not your concern any longer. We know the truth about her. She is a spy for the British, and she carries an Englishman's baby. I believe she may have been sending secret messages after we arrived."

"That is not true. Whoever is feeding you this information is a liar."

"She will remain in prison until we decide what to do with her."

"But you can't!" I said, standing up. "She is no spy! What is there to tell? You bombed our villages and towns, raided them, and now you stomp around as if you own us, too!"

"Quiet!" he shouted, his small teeth clamped together viciously. "I will detain you both permanently, and you will be charged with being a spy also. Perhaps your false papa also."

He frightened me now because he spoke of Jerome. Poor Papa, who deserved no more suffering.

"Sit down!" he said in a quieter voice.

I did so because I was thinking of Jerome.

"In return for her information, your sister has asked that you be set free."

"What information?"

"She has told the truth about the baby's father, and this has been verified. I might say that there are several who don't like you much, who were eager to give up the information."

It seemed possible that those like Gerard, who had never really accepted Helene and me, were the likely culprits to give away our past.

"Can I see her?"

"No. If you attempt to return here, I will arrest you also."

I burst into tears and bowed my head, and I heard him *tch* his disgust as he left the room. One of the other soldiers picked me up by the arm and led me out to the front of the town hall. I looked at the first cell, where several people slept on the floor, and Helene was not amongst them.

I ran all the way home and found no one there, and I was frightened at first that Jerome was taken, too. Running back along the road a short way toward the town, I saw him riding toward me. He jumped out of the trap, and I rushed into his arms.

"I do not know where they have taken her!" I said.

I rambled everything out to him in one long sentence broken only by bursts of tears that choked my words.

"Your sister would do everything to protect you. But she also cares for the baby. Perhaps she has said and bargained for more than we know."

"They called her a spy, Papa! All because she carries Edgar's baby."

When I stepped away from him, I saw the split on his cheek.

He had tried to see her, and they had pulled him in and asked some questions. Jerome said that they considered Helene a traitor now.

"They also believe that Edgar will come back," he said.

Jerome said he would try again tomorrow to visit her, and he would offer Captain Lizt food or money for the privilege.

I saw then that he wasn't looking well. He appeared dazed, and I learned that he had temporarily lost consciousness after he was struck. I helped him back toward the house, both of us hobbling alongside Hester. I had never seen Jerome ill in his life, and he went then straight to bed.

I tossed, turned, and cried all night. Helene had been with me my whole life. To have her gone didn't make sense. She was innocent. Jerome was innocent. Edgar was in a hospital somewhere! He would not know of this perhaps for weeks or months. But what did it matter? He had abandoned us. It was disastrous for us all.

CHAPTER 26

I fell asleep just before dawn and woke up to the sounds of Jerome outside clipping Mira to the ropes of the trap. An omelet was waiting for me on the table, from the last of the eggs, which Jerome had kept hidden. We knew that it was only a matter of time before Hester and Mira were taken, and the thought made me suddenly rush to the barn to cry into Hester's neck. She smelled of good memories, so sweet and earthy, and she nuzzled me in response.

"I am going to try and see Helene," Jerome said back in the kitchen.

I ate without appetite, and we sipped tea silently across from each other, trying to formulate a plan from nothing.

Jerome got up from the table to reach for a jar on the top of the kitchen shelf. He took out some money and said that he would try and buy Helene out of prison. I said that I would go, too, though I didn't like his plan. He knew there was no point in telling me not to come but said that I had to remain out of sight when we got close to the town hall, now overrun with Germans.

We went first to the home of the deputy mayor to inquire about our rights. He had tried to leave the town but had been found in one of the villages by the Germans, and upon learning of his occupation, they had put him to use to supervise the remaining residents working now for the Germany army.

The mayor shook his head. He advised us that from the following day one member from each family was allowed to visit, but only to take food to their loved ones. They were not allowed to talk. The main cell was for people held for interrogation, but Helene and the rest of the prisoners, all incarcerated for various hearsay-only crimes of treason, were housed across two cells at the back of the building. The mayor also told Jerome his plan to offer money was futile.

"The Germans are more likely to imprison you, too, for attempted bribery," said the mayor to Jerome. We left for home again with little hope for an end to this madness.

Jerome was the only one who could visit since I was ordered by Captain Lizt to not see Helene. Each night I would listen to the shelling in the distance and hope that no bombs fell on the town hall, that Helene would survive another night. And each morning I would bake a small cake made from seeds and fruit, and we would take the trap into the town. I would wait down the street with the trap while Jerome made the remainder of the journey to the jail.

"She is doing well, considering," he told me on the journey home, and I wondered if perhaps he was lying to spare my feelings.

"I must go see her!" I said in frustration. Two nights had gone by, and still I could barely sleep without Helene. "I don't care if they arrest me."

"No," said Jerome. "You must trust me. This is for the best. Several soldiers from the prison had to be taken away with influenza, and some of the inmates were released to the hospital. I cannot let you in that place. Do not argue with me."

I saw that Jerome did not have the strength to argue, and I did not have the heart to defy him.

"And what good is it anyway if you are both imprisoned?"

Jerome decided to kill the last chicken so that we could take Helene some stew. And over the following week, we were sharing half the food we prepared between the two of us and taking the other half to Helene, knowing that she needed much strength for the baby. But we were starting to feel real hunger. Those in Bailleul and the villages surrounding who had chosen to stay felt the hunger also and were desperately searching for ways to now escape the town. I wondered if we would all die and prayed daily that the Allies would make fast steps to win the town back.

From Edith, a local woman whose son had also been imprisoned, I learned something about the conditions inside the cells, which Jerome had been keeping from me. Her boy had been accused of stealing guns and scouting for the Allies. He was only fifteen, and I felt for Edith, who was there visiting every morning also. Helene was looking very pale and thin in the face, and her dress had turned a dirty gray color, she told me, and Helene had been very kind to Edith's son. Several people had been released for no given reason, and there were half a dozen prisoners left. The cells were filthy, buckets of excrement left uncollected. Several townspeople were told to empty the buckets from the cells, but it did not stop the stench that remained behind.

I wondered how long the prisoners could go on like that. Surely something would happen and everything would return to normal, or whatever normal was before. Helene's only crime was to fall in love with an English soldier.

I waited for Jerome on a rainy day outside the prison, and he had an expression that was different. He had grown thinner and weaker since Helene had been taken. We had no more fruit, and our supplies in the cellar were diminishing.

"What is wrong?"

He shook his head.

"Everything is wrong," he said. I begged him to tell me what he had seen. He did not hold anything back this time. He said that the conditions were unlivable, and I saw that he had tears in his eyes.

"The young boy who was put in there for spying is dying. He will not see out the day. Helene cradles his head in her lap. He has not been able to sip water for many hours."

I put my hand over my mouth. It was so wrong for Edith to see her son, Jules, suffer. We climbed back onto the trap, and on the journey home, we were silent, and our hopes for any kind of reprieve were fading.

The following day on our visit, we learned that the boy had died in the night, and they had dumped his body on Edith's doorstep. She had awoken earlier than normal to take him food only to discover him lying in the street. She had lost her husband in war and now her son, and she had begun screaming at the sight of her son's body. Passersby carried her back inside and before soldiers had time to arrest her for the spectacle.

At Jules's burial the following day, Edith told Jerome and me that Helene had been so kind to her boy; she had torn her own skirts for cloths to cool down his body. We hugged, and she began weeping into my shoulder, her heart aching.

"I miss him," she said as I stroked her head.

"I know" was all I said, because there are no words to replace a lost child.

I looked at the new graves that had been dug recently. War wasn't right. Life was unfair. We were dying one by one, it seemed, until there was none. Several of the remaining residents had died from the influenza the Germans had brought with them also. People caught doing anything wrong were taken to the square and executed. A woman was imprisoned for attempting to send her young son with a message to his father in a neighboring town. The invaders took over households and treated the owners with contempt. The townspeople were at their bidding. Any couples that did not have a farm to run were called up to dig trenches, and their children were used elsewhere.

Children old enough to help had been captured and taken to pick the crops of farmers, carry supplies and ammunition to the front line, and run errands until late into the night. Even very small children were recruited to deliver messages between gunners on the front line and the servicemen in the town, often working long hours without water and food. One of the graves I stood beside held a girl less than ten killed by a bomb when she was delivering a message close to the officers at the front line.

Those who had fought back against the German invasion paid a price. One farmer destroyed all his own crops rather than see enemy soldiers take everything. For that he and his daughter were shot; the son, twelve, taken to work alongside the Germans, never to be seen again; and the wife left to bury half her family.

There seemed no escape from our wretchedness.

We could hear the Allies fighting to take back the town, but we feared also that the Germans were gaining a stronger foothold into France. We heard so little of what was happening elsewhere. During some of the bombings, more of the villagers escaped to the south. Jerome and I had a chance to flee also, but we could not leave Helene. Captain Lizt must have known this, too. He had not called us in to work, and we suspected he was leaving us here in the hope of luring and catching Helene's English officer. I went to bed each night listening to the sounds of firings in the distance, something that had become part of our lives.

Some nights after Jules's burial, there was a loud knocking at the door. Edith had run on foot along the dark country road to see us, risking her own life. She lived in a house close to the prison and came to tell us that she had seen Helene being carried toward the asylum. She said that Helene was holding her belly, her face in pain: it appeared that she was in labor, the baby early.

"The asylum is now used as a clearing station for German wounded," said Edith. "All the nurses and most of the nuns were evacuated with the British but a number of sisters stayed behind to take care of them."

Jerome, Edith, and I took the horse and cart to the edge of town. Edith had insisted on coming with us. She said that she had assisted with midwifery before and was certain she could help. She also had much to do with the sisters, as she worked sometimes in the asylum kitchen, and she offered to go ahead to see the nuns while we waited in the shadows of buildings, praying no soldiers would patrol. It seemed they had become a little sloppy with the loss of many men, and more so lately with their focus on the battlegrounds.

Edith returned after half an hour.

"The sisters have told us to stay away. That they are to let no one in."

"We must go in regardless," said Jerome.

"No, *you* can't, but I have another idea," said Edith.

She pushed some cloth toward me.

"What is it?"

"Some holy garments that I have not had permission to take, but I think in this case we will be forgiven."

I recognized her plan immediately.

"Yes," I said, and turned to Jerome. He looked at me with his sagging eyes and nodded. There was little other choice.

We donned the nuns' habits and veils, and both Edith and I furtively made our way back toward the asylum. As we drew closer, several muted lights revealed us, and we bowed our heads and held our breaths.

The side door to the kitchen was unlocked, and I followed Edith inside. She put her finger to her lips to signify that I was not to talk at all. "And keep your head down," she whispered.

We walked along the hallway, encountering no one at first, and then suddenly out of the corner of my eye, I saw a German soldier. Edith greeted him, but I did not look up, as promised. I thought that he paused slightly as we walked past, that he had recognized me, but it was my fear playing tricks on me.

I had no idea where I was going, but turning a corner, I was suddenly confronted by Sister Joan, the superintendent of the hospital. She recognized both of us, expressing surprise, but immediately understanding the urgency, she indicated to follow her into the laundry room.

"What are you doing? You will get killed!"

"I must see Helene," I said. "She has been brought here."

"Yes, I know. Sister Angela, our midwife, is with her at present, and one of our other nuns to assist. We have called for a doctor also, but the German doctors are busy at their field hospital. There are no others here."

At that there was a loud explosion close by, the force vibrating the ground beneath our feet and causing the walls to shudder. Joan looked around anxiously.

"I do not know how much longer we can stay here. Many have had to leave. I was just on my way to take some fresh linen. We are doing everything we can."

"Is she sick as well?" I said, alarmed.

Sister Joan paused before she continued. "She is weak but well enough, and the contractions are as normal."

"I must see her."

She looked at both of us, then reached for freshly laundered sheets and towels on the shelf.

"There is a soldier at the door, and I do not know if he will allow any more," said Joan. "They also might recognize you."

"We can replace the other sister with the midwife, with the two of us, so it is not as suspicious," said Edith. "You can say that she is needed elsewhere."

Joan thought about it, lines deepening on her forehead.

"Very well. But, Mariette, you must not draw attention to yourself. You need to tuck in that bright-colored hair of yours under the veil. I will do the talking."

"Thank you, Sister," I said.

I found that my whole body was trembling with anticipation as I longed to see Helene. We passed no soldiers in the hallways, but as we got to the ward at the end, I saw a soldier sitting outside with a gun. It was not a soldier that I recognized, thankfully.

Joan spoke to him, and he nodded quickly, much to my relief. It was clear he had some respect for Joan. We knew that many of our nurses had helped their injured soldiers.

As we entered the room, Helene was in too much pain to see the panic on my face. I could see immediately what else Jerome had been hiding from me. The change was too shocking.

Helene's face was the palest I had ever seen it. Her brown skin was waxen, with a yellowish tint, and her hair was plastered around her face with sweat. There was darkness below her sunken eyes, their normally green color appeared cloudy, and the whites around her irises were webbed with red. I had seen the effects of illness and lack of food in the faces in the street. Everyone had suffered in a small way, and we all felt the hunger, but Helene's was painfully obvious by her starved appearance.

The two nursing sisters who had been attending Helene seemed surprised to see Joan, who made a sign to be quiet. The other women had taken off their veils, and their sleeves were rolled up.

Helene had been gasping for breath during one of her contractions when she noticed me just inside the door. Her eyes closed briefly in relief as the pain ebbed temporarily, and I saw the hint of a smile as she reached out her arm in my direction. I rushed to her side. I had promised myself that I would not cry, but tears came, and I kissed the back of her hand several times, then left my lips to rest longer on her forehead. Her skin was hot to touch.

"I missed you," she whispered, and then she screwed up her face with another contraction. I squeezed her hand.

Sister Angela revealed that Helene's contractions had apparently begun hours before she had left prison and that the birth was close. The superintendent said she would be back to check on us but warned that a full evacuation might be necessary if the bombings came any closer. She wished us well, then led the other sister out of the small room so as not to draw suspicion with so many in attendance.

Edith and I were on either side of Helene, supporting her, and Edith held a cloth to her forehead, while the nursing sister watched for signs of the baby's head. Helene had been changed into a white hospital shift, and the sisters had been bathing and washing her. Though I could see she had not been kept well: there was much dirt under her fingernails, her feet covered in grime.

Within half an hour, Sister Angela reported that the baby was coming. And at the same time, another explosion sounded on the far side of the town.

Helene's body was bathed in her own sweat, and I helped her sip water from a glass.

"I'm so glad you're here," Helene said. "I've been worried about you. Jerome was not allowed to speak to me, just leave me the food. I've had to share it with others who have none."

My suspicion that Jerome had not been telling me about her deterioration seemed evident, and it was obvious why he had left the jail so pale the last time. Helene had not only lost weight, but she had a fever also.

The shelling outside shook the building again, and sounds of airplanes roaring through the skies were followed by rapid fire. Edith went to the window and reported that there was gunner fire on the horizon and the sky was littered with white and yellow flashes.

"Why are our soldiers bombing us?" Helene asked.

"They don't know we are here. They would have expected all towns-people to be gone by now."

"Do you think Edgar is out there?" Helene asked, her words sounding distant. "Do you think he is all right?" She was slightly delirious, I realized, and my heart ached so much for her. Despite her own pain, she was thinking of someone else.

The child came through at the sound of more distant gunfire, and Helene collapsed back on the bed. It was a boy, small but healthy, his tiny lungs strong enough to produce prolonged wails. He was dark pink in a white and greasy coating, but his small and wondrous face was clear. Sister Angela cut the cord and swaddled him in a soft blanket, then passed him to me.

I held the baby, who flexed his little hands and fell back to sleep, while Angela and Edith helped clean up Helene and change the bedsheets.

I showed Helene the baby, but she did not reach for him. She looked exhausted and frail. I touched his small fingers with wonder.

"I must go quickly to find a doctor," Angela said, touching my arm. Though her face was passive, I read the message in her touch. Helene was dangerously ill.

I heard Angela talking to the soldier outside, who was asking her many questions. He was hesitant about her suggestion, instead telling her only to bring back medicine. But the sister insisted that the patient would die if she did not see a doctor quickly. I could tell that she wasn't just saying this in the hope that the soldier would offer to go instead, perhaps for the benefit of us escaping, but that she meant it. I looked across to Helene, who had dozed and not heard the conversation. Finally the soldier agreed, but he was terse, and the shelling so close to the hospital had probably reached his nerves and propelled a hasty response.

Helene had her eyes closed, propped up against pillows on freshly changed linen. I leaned down, still with the baby in my arms, to kiss the top of her head.

"There is so much gunfire," Edith said at the window again. "I think the front line goes right through our town."

While Helene slept, I carried her sleeping baby around the room and wondered what his future would be. We were fatherless children for much of our lives, with strange men always around in the first years, and the thought that the child had no father also made me sad. I wished then that I could remember the face of my mother. There had been too many gypsy women in my past for me to feature one. It had always been Helene there at my side, the one I turned to. I looked at her at peace for now, temporarily oblivious to this dire situation. *What now? What must I do?*

Angela came back with some medicine but no doctor, reporting that he was not answering the door, no doubt part of the original evacuation. The sister woke Helene up and fed her some strong-smelling syrup that supposedly dulled her pain and helped reduce her temperature. She lifted Helene's wrist and checked her heart and then felt her neck and arms.

"She needs to be cooled very quickly," she said, and proceeded to bathe her with a cloth.

I looked across at Helene, then handed the baby to Edith. The shelling had stopped momentarily, and Helene now had her eyes open, watching me. She patted the soft bed beside her, and I rushed to sit with her and took both her hands in mine. She felt cold and clammy, and I felt the slight after-birth tremor within her body.

I told her that a doctor would come and then we would take her away.

"It is no good," she said. "There is no point."

"Don't talk that way!" I said as gently as possible without sounding like I was scolding her.

"Mariette," she said softly, her voice cracking with the effort, as if she had not used it for a long time. "I want you to take the baby and disappear from this place. It is too dangerous, and you must be safe. I want you to promise me that you will look after the baby and Edgar when he returns."

"I can't leave you. Ever!"

She gripped my wrist a little tighter, though there was so little strength in it.

"For the sake of my baby, you must take him away now. You and Jerome. I fear that things will get far worse than better. And they will never release me. You need to find Edgar. There is a reason the baby came early. He will help Edgar heal."

I had a sense that she knew I had lied about not seeing Edgar and that perhaps she had known all along about his illness.

"You must come, too," I said.

But I knew she couldn't. She was so weak she could barely raise her arms, and there was no way we could carry her from the building without being seen.

"The boy must know his family, and you must take care of both the baby and Edgar. He sacrificed for us, Mariette. He risked his life for *us*, for France!" She gripped my wrist tighter for a brief moment. I could feel the love and loyalty in those words, which she was transferring to me by touch. "Promise me!"

Machine guns sounded, and the smell of smoke permeated through the windows. I felt then that something big was about to occur and hoped the Allies would drive the Germans away. But she was right. She always was. It would be months yet before Bailleul would once again be in friendly hands, and then there would be little left for the townspeople to return to.

"I don't think . . . ," she whispered.

"Shh!" I sounded gently to hush her, tears leaking from the corners of my eyes. I knew what she was about to tell me: she wasn't going to make it.

She lifted her hands and signed, *Promise me. Protect them. Be brave. Promise me.*

I signed my reply.

I promise.

I held my palm up, and she placed hers against mine.

She seemed to lose interest in the people around her then. Much later I would speculate that not only was she too sick to care, but she was steeling herself not to feel anything, to let the baby go without attachment.

I fought to hold back the tears but lost. Suddenly I was sobbing into her chest, and she had her hand on the back of my head like when we were small. You see, in my heart I knew she was right. I knew that they would never let her go. And if the baby was left, who knew where they would put him, what would become of his little French life. He was the son of an enemy. A nuisance perhaps when there were already so many mouths to fill.

I raised my head and looked in her eyes, and she smiled back encouragingly. I knew that smile well. She had used it many times when I had been distressed or fearful. I would take her baby and wait hopefully for this madness to be over.

Sister Joan hastily entered the room.

"I have just had a message that the captain is on his way here with a number of wounded soldiers. You must go!"

I told Joan that I must take the baby out of here and hide him, and I whispered to her my fears about Helene's illness also. She nodded sadly but without much reflection, as if expecting both of the things I told her. Joan said that she would bring the other sister back, and Edith and I were to leave immediately. If the captain found us here, we would most certainly be imprisoned.

"It might be your only chance to leave," said Sister Joan, "while the shelling continues."

There were only seconds now to say our goodbyes.

I knelt by Helene's side and kissed her hand, leaving some tears behind.

Edith brought the baby over to Helene, who looked sheepishly away before finally resting her eyes on the baby's face. She reached for him to kiss his downy head. The sadness was unbearable to witness.

"Goodbye, my beautiful boy, Samuel," she said.

Sister Joan told us to hurry, and we followed her outside, and I felt sick leaving my sister behind. The soldier guarding the door stopped us to look at the baby. It might have been my imagination, but I saw the man's expression soften slightly at the sight of Samuel, followed by a sudden intake of breath. I wondered then if he had left his own wife and children at home for the senseless war and was now wondering why he was here and not with them.

"Where are you taking it?"

"The mother is very ill, and this baby is too small. It is doubtful he will survive the night here," said Joan. "There is a wet nurse in one of the villages."

"The baby should stay here until the captain comes to collect the prisoner."

Just then Samuel released a high-pitched cry.

"I will speak to the captain directly," said Sister Joan, "and we will discuss the child." And I thought then how brave she was. That she would likely be punished if this deed were uncovered. I could not see her giving away our location for anything. But I wondered how long it would be before the captain came to break down our door. He did not seem to be the type to give up on anyone.

The soldier briskly nodded and turned away from us, and we made our way back through the kitchen. Edith took some milk, and in our disguise we raced through the night, with Samuel held tightly to my chest while I prayed he wouldn't cry again. We did not at that moment have the sounds of war to drown him out.

We reached the orchard less than an hour later, and I could see through the window Jerome pacing the length of the small house. He rushed to meet us as we entered, discarding our habits. He had been distraught not knowing, and said he had stopped himself from loitering around the town, which might have aroused suspicion.

He looked tenderly at the baby now lying on a table in a fruit crate that I had just filled with bedding, and he touched Samuel's chest with his big hands.

Edith instructed us to dip some cloth in warm watery milk to soothe the baby until she returned with feeding bottles. I knew that the milk would not last and wondered how we were to come by more.

"Is it true what Sister Joan said about a wet nurse?"

"I don't think so, but there are people I trust who will help me with other things for the baby. Give me whatever you can, and I will barter for it." Jerome went to his bedroom and returned with the emerald ring that had belonged to his wife and a bag of tobacco.

"I know that tobacco is probably worth more than jewelry right now," he said.

"Papa . . . ," I said, and touched his arm, but he didn't look at me as he wrapped the items in Edith's hands with his own. He had some cash stored also, and I knew he would give that up as well should it come to it.

"Get as much as you can, anything that you can for the baby," he said.

"Be safe," I said to Edith, gripping her hands. I knew it wouldn't be easy under the noses of the guards in the town, and like me, she'd not had a proper meal in days. "And thank you. I can't tell you how much we owe you."

"You owe me nothing," she said. "I want to show my son, who is probably watching us from above, bless his soul, that these barbarians cannot take us all."

"His name is Samuel," I said to Jerome after Edith had left. We were sitting in the living room, gazing at Helene's tiny miracle. Samuel was sleeping and making strange shapes with his mouth, the innocence of this new life so startling that I could not pull myself away. I touched his tiny fingers and leaned down close to smell the newness and sweetness of his skin, to be close to Helene. I had seen many babies, but I don't remember ever wanting to hold one. Now with Samuel, I did not want to ever let him go.

I revealed Helene's condition and what she said about looking after Samuel. Jerome said nothing, and I watched him smoke the last of the tobacco that remained in his pipe.

Edith came back with the milk as promised but reported there was no wet nurse. From her pockets she also produced some turnips, honey, and bread, as well as a basket for the baby to sleep in, blankets, clothing, and bottles that she carried from her sister's. She instructed me to make a mixture of milk, water, and honey to feed Samuel until we could find him a better alternative elsewhere. We offered that she stay with us, but she thought it more helpful if she was in the town and reported anything she saw. Some people had secretly left the town during the chaos of the recent round of shelling. They had in plain sight walked past soldiers with loaded-up carts and traps. There were few left now in the town. Edith had also seen the captain busy reorganizing soldiers for battle to replace the ones killed.

"Perhaps it is too dangerous," said Jerome. "Maybe you should leave also."

"No," said Edith. "I cannot leave Jules behind. And there are other people here who need me also."

Jerome and I understood. It would be difficult to leave here without Helene if it came to it. Neither of us had discussed exactly when we would leave, both delaying the inevitable.

Before she returned to the town, Edith helped me cut up the nuns' robes to make some nappies and taught me some things about feeding babies, how tight to swaddle Samuel in a blanket, how to burp him, and how best to rock him to sleep. Jerome listened, too, though I suspect he knew much of this already.

That night we fed Samuel and listened to the sounds from the battleground. Jerome would often walk out to see what was happening on the horizon. Although people were leaving, I felt sure that the Allies would return to reclaim the town. Thoughts of Edgar, ever since my visit to him, had evaporated, or maybe I was simply willing him out of our memory and lives. Helene still believed in him, but I must admit my admiration for Edgar had waned, and the secret infatuation I'd had with him after our first meeting now seemed foolish. There were only feelings of anger when his name was mentioned.

CHAPTER 27

I was woken by the shaking of my bed, from another round of explosions. I jumped up quickly to check on Samuel in the basket beside me, but he had slept through it. Jerome ran outside and into the early morning, pulling his braces over his shoulders as he did so, and I followed in my nightgown. We could see smoke rising high above the town in the distance, and there was an eerie silence. After this several people came from that direction, carrying bundles of items under their arms, some of them covered in dust, others with faces streaked in blood.

I had a sense that things had changed that day. The landscape of Bailleul looked strangely misshapen. I hastily dressed then left Jerome with Samuel while I investigated, before he could offer to go himself. I was faster on my feet. Before I reached the town, I could see the rubble in the streets where bombs had landed and a cloud that hung above everything. Smoke and ash consumed me, and I had to hold my hand over my mouth so as not to breathe it in.

"Get out of here quickly while you can!" said one of the townspeople.

German soldiers, who normally gazed suspiciously at everyone, seemed not to notice anyone leaving. Soldiers hurried to vehicles and horses and called instructions to one other, some slapping their helmets on their heads to march for the manned machines south of the city. I think if not for the chaos, Samuel and I would most certainly have been searched for by the captain, but it was clear now that there were far more important things to occupy him at that point.

Down another street I stopped dead in my tracks. Edith's house was completely reduced to rubble, still smoldering. I stepped forward to query a soldier about the occupants, but he did not understand my French and swatted me away. Another man I barely recognized, his face dusted with powdery white ash, looked over at the building, shook his head, and walked away.

People ran through smoke, their faces smeared with ash and blood, and pavements flickered yellow, lit by buildings on fire. It was chaotic. The town hall had taken a major hit. I helped some people lift an elderly couple up from the street to carry them to a cellar where others had gathered. I did not stay, but returned to help others also injured to other places of refuge. When there were no more people to help, I looked toward the asylum hospital that appeared now as a jagged silhouette against an ashen sky. As I ran toward it, there was a loud and sudden crash nearby, the force of which shook the earth and sent me sprawling. Someone helped me up and told me to take cover. I ran home as fast as my legs could take me. Jerome met me at the door.

"Papa, Bailleul is being destroyed. We have to get Helene."

Jerome had a strange look on his face, like he hadn't heard me. In his hands he held a small dark-green book, which I recognized, and a string with colored tags that I had seen the Allied soldiers wear around their necks.

"Is that Edgar's?"

"Yes," he said.

"Is he dead?"

"No. He carried these down his shirt."

I was confused but only briefly, looking past him through the door to see Edgar sitting on the couch and holding the baby. Edgar was gaunt and covered in tiny cuts. His eyes were red, his face unshaven, and he wore ill-fitting trousers, a shirt streaked with mud, and no shoes.

I pushed past Jerome to take the baby from Edgar's arms, and Samuel began to wail.

"What are you doing here?" I said. "Why aren't you out there fighting?"

He looked at me with those intense blue eyes, but no words came out of his mouth, and his silence made me seethe.

The sounds of shelling were closer now, and our house rattled before Jerome grabbed milk for the baby, the basket, and food and water for us and urged us all to the cellar. Once underground, Jerome lit candles that were already there and spread out pillows for us to sit on. I sat as far from Edgar as I could. The hospital visit had left a scar. To me, Edgar was a different man from the one who had once stayed here with us and who had made my sister believe in a future that she might never have. I also resented the fact that Edgar was now here to take more of our food, our stocks nearly depleted. I wanted to tell him to go, that he had no right to be here, but I remembered my promise to Helene.

I got up to place Samuel in his bed while the floor above us continued to shake.

"It is because of you that Helene is ill, that she is in prison," I said finally to Edgar, who had been staring at the ground.

He did not look up at me but at his hands that were balled into fists.

"Hush!" Jerome said angrily to me.

"No, I will not," I said to Jerome, before turning my sights again on Edgar. "You still haven't said why you aren't out there fighting!"

"He is ill, Mariette. Silence now! The baby has just fallen asleep."

"Tell me!" I demanded, ignoring Jerome. "What are you doing here? Why now?"

But Edgar just sat there stunned, before then placing his arms over his head, as if protecting himself.

"He left the army," said Jerome. "In the middle of battle, men falling around him when he was left out there alone to die—"

"He looks perfectly fit."

"He is not fit for the army," Jerome whispered; however, I suspect in the small space Edgar could hear everything. "He ran, then kept running. He left so he could come back here and take us to safety. His mind is altered, Mariette. Surely you can see the change."

"What is your plan to save us then?" I said to Edgar. "Do you even have one?"

He looked up at me, and I saw something shattered, pieces of the man I had known before. His face was lined with anguish, the grooves in his forehead filled with dirt. His eyes, though, were still bright and clear behind the sun-darkened, freckled face. I was moved briefly, and then angry again that I had felt something for him.

"I had to reach you here—"

"To save your own neck, no doubt."

Samuel started crying, and Jerome picked up the baby and wrapped him tightly in the blankets that had belonged to Edith's son.

"I don't know what happened. I woke up in a field of bodies, and I ran," he said, his face contorted into one of misery before he dropped his head. When he raised his face to me again, there were tears in his eyes, though I remained hardened.

"I would rather see you fight on her behalf than hide behind civilians who appear braver than you." It was hurtful what I said, but it was, I see now, to cover my own feelings of hurt.

"Please," said Jerome to me. "Hear him out."

"I am not worthy to be a father. I am not worthy to ever be her husband. Jerome told me that Helene has been held a prisoner because of me. I feel so ashamed."

"So you should," I said, not looking at him, the candle flickering from another ground assault.

Edgar stood and looked up the short stairs to the floor above, then walked toward me. "I'm so sorry for Helene."

"Not sorry enough to write a letter."

He frowned, bereft, and I had a feeling that he was punishing himself more than my words could.

"She is in prison because she carried a British soldier's baby. *You* did this!" I shouted, pointing at him.

"You must stop, Mariette!" Jerome shouted. He had never raised his voice to me before, and it was enough to shock me into silence. Then his tone changed to one of pleading: "Please, Mariette . . . Stop torturing him. He's been through enough. We all have. He lost men and then almost his soul out there. He is not the man who left England."

Edgar stood there, a morose creature, not saying anything, looking at his hands. I saw his eyes rest on the baby in Jerome's arms, and I saw the confusion, the edge of derangement that I would be told about years later: that some men could only take so much.

I didn't look at either of them for the remainder of the time we were in the cellar. Once the shelling had stalled, we came out, and I put Samuel back into the basket. Edgar's limp was more noticeable, and Jerome asked to inspect the injury. He rolled up the leg of Edgar's trousers that had a patch of dried blood. A small piece of metal was wedged in his thigh, and the area was red and swollen.

"We must get a doctor!"

"No one can find the doctor, Papa. He has probably gone, taken his family to safety."

"Then I must look elsewhere. I know of one retired in one of the villages. He may still be there."

I noticed that Edgar was sweating and pale. He sat at the table with his head between his hands.

"But how will you get him there? He cannot be seen. If he is questioned, he is disturbed enough to give himself away."

"I will cover him in the back of the trap."

"But what if you are stopped? It is too dangerous. The doctor is more than likely gone. If you are caught with an Englishman, you will be shot." Even harboring Edgar at our house was dangerous enough, something also I resented now.

"Then I will bring the doctor here if I find him," said Jerome. "I will travel across the fields to avoid being seen." He did not wait for me to argue with him, and he left quickly. I tried not to think of him exposed to soldiers, guns, and bombs.

Edgar lay curled up on the lounge, but his eyes were open. He did not seem to have a desire to talk, to explain his actions any further. It was as if the fire that once shone within had burned out.

"Do you want some water?"

He shook his head.

As I stood up to check on Samuel, I heard the sound of horses trampling on the road between the two towns and coming from the direction of Bailleul. I raced to the window, and my chest tightened at the sight of Captain Lizt and two of his men.

"You have to hide back down in the cellar," I said. "Quickly!" I picked up the sleeping baby from inside the basket, praying he would not wake, and rushed down the cellar stairs, Edgar following.

I handed him the baby, and at first he seemed reluctant, looking at the child as if it were the first time he had seen him. Perhaps it was then I saw something more, something very wrong about him, and thought about his broken soul, and a small amount of compassion again crept in even during those fearful moments.

I looked around to see where they could hide. The cellar would be the first place they looked, but there was no closer place and no time to search for another. I turned a barrel on its side.

"Crawl in!" I instructed.

He crouched down and crawled into the space with Samuel enfolded into his arms. Once they were inside I pushed the barrel, open side first, against the wall, straining from the effort. I knew that sooner or later Samuel would wake up and cry for milk.

Someone banged twice loudly at the front door, and I jumped before rushing up the stairs and closing the cellar door. I rested a mop and cleaning rags inside the baby basket and placed it near the back door. The banging started again.

Captain Lizt stood casually as I opened the door, while he pulled at the fingers of his gloves to release them, gripped tightly in one hand.

"What is it?" I asked, forcing back my fear. "Is it Helene? Is she all right?" I clutched tightly to the front of my trousers so that he would not see my hands shaking and wondered if he was perceptive enough to see through my attempts to distract him with questions.

He looked around, his eyes roaming to scour everything his eyesight could reach. I was a bag of nerves but stood still, waiting, hoping he would not notice my breathing quicken.

"Someone said they saw a stranger on this road yesterday. An Englishman, they suspected."

I looked at him and bit down on the inside of my lip to stop it from trembling also.

He walked around the room and examined things. I wondered also why in all the chaos he was bothered to come here.

"Don't you have a war to fight?"

At the question a loud explosion sounded just south of Bailleul. He looked briefly out the window, and I could see that it rattled him, his mind on that also.

He turned back to walk around the room, and I spied the milk bottle in the kitchen sink.

"Why do you think he was English?" I said to distract him again, to turn his eyes on me and not toward the bottle.

He was smiling suddenly, but the smile did not stretch to his eyes, which were cold and cruel.

"Someone said they spoke to a man on the road a day or so ago. They said he looked disoriented. That he was rambling in English." He paused and watched me carefully, and I held on to the table between us.

"The penalty for harboring an Englishman is of course death. Just carrying an Englishman's child is an offense. But you know that already."

His tone was menacing. He was not looking for a missing baby, that much was clear, but it did not lessen the trembling. The captain wanted Edgar, and if he found him, he would take the baby, too.

"Well, there is no Englishman here."

"Where is Monsieur Lavier?" he asked.

My throat felt dry and my breathing fast, and it took every ounce of control to keep my voice steady. "He has gone to see about more food." I prayed that he wouldn't ask me where, that he would not head that way.

He looked at me, and I leveled at him steadily. He would not break me with his stare. He barked an order to one of the men to check the bathroom at the back and another to stand at the door, while he instructed me to open the cellar.

He commenced to descend the stairs when an explosion sounded closer, shaking hard the ground beneath our feet, which made him retreat and walk to the window. The soldier who had been at the back of the house ran inside and spoke hastily in German. The captain rushed to the front window. He then issued some orders before turning to me.

"Your sister had a baby, but I imagine you have already heard. Gossip travels and no place more than here. If you should come upon information about the stranger, please let me know. As a reward, she and her newborn will be free to go."

I drew a sharp intake of breath from his stare, and then I was freed from it. I waited till the horses were out of view from the window, then went down to the cellar and heaved the barrel as gently as I could. The baby was still curled asleep in the arms of Edgar, who was leaning over his son carefully, taking most of the discomfort for himself. He passed me the child, then crawled out silently, strangely asking nothing about the captain's arrival, and began to climb back up the stairs.

"You should stay down here," I said. I was unsure whether to trust him, whether he might undo us all. And I did not want to be alone with him.

He looked at me briefly, said nothing, then sat back down on the ground. It was as if I were talking to the dead. I left quickly and shut the cellar door, relieved to be away from him once more.

I thought of Helene on the bed in the hospital and knew pretty soon she would return to the jail. She was ill. If she remained incarcerated, I did not believe that she would live. At least for now, and possibly thanks to Joan, Captain Lizt was unaware that the baby had been taken elsewhere. He had obviously not been to see Helene the previous night, too busy with the Allied defensive and the wounded soldiers he was accompanying to the asylum.

But it was because of Edgar that Helene was imprisoned at all. I could not forget that.

———

It was almost two hours before Jerome came up the road with the doctor. I took Samuel and his basket into one of the rooms and closed the door. Jerome entered with the newcomer, whom I had seen in the town of Armentières once or twice.

"Where is—"

"The stranger is down in the cellar," I said, not letting him name the patient.

Jerome looked at me, and I saw that he was both curious and concerned about Edgar being kept in the suffocating room.

"Once he is fixed, I want him gone."

Jerome knew immediately why I had been so abrupt. I could not trust anyone, especially someone like the doctor whom we hardly knew, to think we had any special relationship with Edgar or were on a first-name basis. I had to assume that Jerome had revealed little. I would protect the baby at all costs.

Jerome helped Edgar up from the cellar and then to remove his trousers. The doctor worked quickly, extracting the shrapnel and sealing the flesh wound with stitches before applying an ointment. Edgar thanked him somewhat sheepishly, as if he deserved no one's help. Jerome walked Edgar into the bedroom where the baby was, and I hoped that neither would disturb the baby to wake.

"I wish you well," said the doctor, who seemed genuine enough, but since I believed that people in the town had betrayed Helene, everyone except for Joan and the nuns was not to be trusted. The doctor tipped his hat and left with Jerome, while I paced and prayed, watching the horizon glowing orange, until my father appeared home again late into the evening.

"It would have been good for the doctor to check the baby, but at least Edgar will heal," said Jerome.

"No one must know about the baby," I said.

I did not tell him about Captain Lizt's visit. I had been thinking about it the whole time he was gone again and imagining sweet Helene returned to us. Fortunately, Edgar also had said nothing about any visitors, not that he was saying much about anything. If Jerome knew what had been proposed by the captain, he would shut down any suggestion of it, and I could not burden him with my own plotting to set Helene free. I knew he would never trade the life of one for another, no matter what the relationship. It was not in his nature, so open and kind for the world to see. I felt guilty at the thought of it, but even so I could picture Helene pining for the baby that she might never see again.

I was tormented with indecision. I imagined Edgar and me not bound by the ties of my sister but rather us shackled together with heavy, rusting chains, and me with no way to forgive him. I wondered whether, in the best interests of the baby and his mother, my promise to Helene might be justifiably broken.

That same night when I could stand it no longer, I made an excuse to Jerome that I would ride back into town and see if I could find any more milk supplies for Samuel for the coming days. He did not like that I was going out alone, but he nodded and told me to hurry back while the guns and distant shelling remained silent. Both sides were taking the time to regroup, exhausted from their losses.

Many houses in the town had been destroyed, the place with only a scattering of pallid lights and near empty of life. I traveled first to the remains of Edith's to leave some flowers I had picked on the way. With the arrival of Edgar and the chaos, I felt she had been forgotten. I knelt at the site and prayed that she was now joined with her son.

Next, I went to the German headquarters to seek an urgent audience with Captain Lizt, expecting to find him resting this late after a day of heavy shelling, but was redirected to the tavern. Inside, the only patrons were German soldiers who were surprised by my appearance there. I hated being so close to Gerard, who did not acknowledge me. I had seen him often near the town hall and the German base, talking to the captain, and I wondered what sort of relationship they had. I wondered also if Aloise, his gossiping wife who worked behind the bar, really wanted to still be here, surrounded by so much destruction, with most of their friends missing or killed. She appeared tired and as miserable as her husband serving into the early hours of the morning.

Gerard appeared to always have food to serve, which had likely been traded for information. If anyone was a traitor to France, it would be Gerard. Felix, his son, however, once my friend, was working there also, collecting the dirty plates. He gave me a secretive wave as I came through the doorway. I did not reciprocate. I had assumed that since he was related to someone I despised, he was likely to be the same now, perhaps had even given evidence against us.

I asked the soldier near the door if I could have a private audience with Captain Lizt, who seemed to never sleep, maps covering the tables beside him. The soldier bent down to speak quietly in the ear of the captain, who appeared pleased to see me and obviously hungry for what I was about to tell him. I was brought forward and felt the eyes of the tavern upon me. I said a silent prayer and remembered Helene's request. *I want you to promise me that you will look after the baby and Edgar when he returns.* She had been so sure he would.

"I have seen the Englishman you asked about," I said. "He stopped at our house, and we kept him there for as long as we could."

Aloise had stopped washing glasses at the bar to listen carefully.

"Where is he now?" the captain asked.

"Heading south of Bailleul. I came as quickly as I could."

"Why should I believe you?"

"Because I trusted an Englishmen once, and I will not make the same mistake again," I said as convincingly as possible.

He watched me curiously for a moment before turning to one of the soldiers and pointing to the front door, and I heard the door open and close behind me. His attention back on me, he chewed his last mouthful fast before wiping his mouth with a napkin. I felt I was made to watch him, and I hated him more in that moment, the division between our positions made clear. Gerard came over to fill up the captain's glass with more wine.

Captain Lizt nodded, and one of the soldiers pulled at my arm to leave.

"Wait!" I said. "My sister . . . You said she could leave."

I detected the faint rise at the corners of his tightly pressed lips.

"You have not heard?"

"Heard what?"

"The asylum has been destroyed. Your sister is dead."

I paused, my heart pounding.

"And the baby?"

"We were told by the surviving nurses that the baby died in the arms of its mother."

I said nothing.

"But I am not so sure about the baby. You see, I've only just come from interviewing a soldier who had been on duty there, who said two nuns he had never seen before took the baby away someplace else. Would you know anything about it?"

I shook my head. I could not speak, afraid that my voice would fail me and my knees were about to give way. I kept my lips tightly together to hide any shock. I would not give him the satisfaction of seeing my pain.

"You should take comfort at least. Your sister was ill and not expected to live. It has reduced her suffering."

I wanted to rush at him, hit him. Instead I picked up the glass of wine and threw it in his face as Aloise gasped. One of the soldiers stepped toward me, but Captain Lizt put up his hand to stop him. He calmly wiped his face with the napkin, and I saw no humiliation but satisfaction despite what I'd done. I turned and left, the hurt of this news thundering through my heart and threatening to burst out from my chest.

Climbing onto Hester, I saw Felix coming out from the back of the tavern and rushing toward me. I turned away from him.

"Wait!" he said. "Whatever you think of my father, you have nothing to fear from me."

I turned back to see that he appeared genuine.

"Is it true?" I asked him. "Was the hospital bombed? Were people killed?"

"Some," he said. "I know that some got out before. I don't know for certain about Helene or who was killed. I can tell you that Captain Lizt lies to everyone."

I wanted to tell him then that I suspected his father was the reason Helene was imprisoned and how much I despised Gerard, but there seemed no point. I thought no ill of Felix. He held the reins of Hester and stroked her face. He had news he was holding on to, unsure whether to reveal it.

"What is it?" I asked.

"I believe that you and your father are not safe. I have overheard conversations . . . They are executing people over the smallest things. And now . . ."

The wine in the captain's face had made it worse for Papa and me.

"You should leave," Felix said. "And very soon."

"Thank you," I said.

He was looking up at me as if he wanted to say more, his brown eyes expressing much fondness.

"I'm sorry about what happened to your family," he said.

I nodded, grateful at least that there was still some humanity left inside this building. I thought to go first to the hospital, but the soldiers stationed nearby were watching me carefully. I rode back toward home and noticed that one of the soldiers was following me before the sounds of shelling started again to draw him back toward the town. I jumped from Hester and charged through the front door to tell Jerome what I had heard. I spoke loudly so that Edgar could hear me from the bedroom. I wanted him to know what he had done, how his arrival in our lives had caused Helene to die.

"I will go and find her if she is still alive," Edgar said, walking into the living room. "I will trade my life for hers. It is the least I can do to make amends."

"No," said Jerome. "You will get yourself killed."

But he was gone, and I heard Jerome calling after him helplessly from the front door. The way I had acted niggled me, but in those times, our characters weren't our own, changed into sometimes worse versions of ourselves. There was now shame interweaving with my anger, and I wondered if my shaming words toward him were about to cause his death.

Jerome was shaking his head and sat down, his head in his hands. I felt immense sadness and guilt. He was always trying to do the right thing for everyone. He had not judged Edgar as I had done. He had looked far deeper into his heart.

Why was there so much death to simply keep the life we had worked for? Why was it fair for others to think they could take something that wasn't theirs?

———

"We will wait another hour, and then we must go," said Jerome quietly.

"But where to?"

He had no answer.

I looked at Samuel. My heart said to stay, but my head reminded me of my promise to Helene to look after him. And we were no longer safe here.

We walked outside to see several other French running south. Jerome rushed over to speak to them, then returned, his head hanging.

"What is the matter?"

"The Allied soldiers have taken back some ground, but it will not be a short fight. It will get far worse. We must leave."

"We should first go to learn the truth about Helene ourselves," I said.

He shook his head, and he watched me carefully.

"What is it?" I asked.

"I've just been told that the German patients were evacuated before the bombing, but the French patients did not escape. The captain may have been telling the truth. But they won't let anyone near the hospital to see if there are survivors, perhaps trapped."

I handed him Samuel and turned toward the stable.

"Where are you going?"

"To get Helene."

"Do not go anywhere! It is not safe!" But his voice was drowned out in my heavy thoughts.

I threw myself onto Hester bareback and rode through the paddocks and turned toward the hospital. German soldiers who had grouped in makeshift hospital tents and areas of rest had seen me, but still I kept going, believing they would not shoot an unarmed girl on a horse. It was an impetuous part of my nature that I've fought hard to tame. They fired a warning shot in the air, but it just enraged me further, and I continued toward the hospital. I was possessed and unclear of my intentions, I can see now, as well as masking my grief with acts of rage.

I saw it firsthand, the ruins, smoldering and sending out their last surrendering breaths of pale-gray smoke. No one would have survived. I knew the truth then and reined Hester in, the madness of what I was attempting suddenly upon me. There was no one to save. I was in the thick of danger here, and as I turned Hester to return home, there was another shot, and she stumbled forward. I toppled over her head to land shoulder first onto the ground. A second shot fired at her again. I felt her warm body, kissed her one last time before turning and running back toward the farm, tears streaming.

Jerome was waiting for me. He did not look angry, but neither did he speak. He knew there was only one reason Hester hadn't returned with me. He could forgive me for Hester, but if I had been killed, then he would have lost two daughters. For so many years he had tried with his gentleness to calm the wildness I carried within me, that ran through my blood. I sobbed while I helped him load the trap with clothes and a few personal items. He tied Mira to the trap as I looked at the paddocks I had run across, scorched in places, and the orchard with its splintered, burning trees. I pined for Helene and our life before the war came and cruelly took it all away. But there was no time then to fully grieve for the past.

I took Samuel in my arms, my tears evaporating as I climbed up to sit beside Jerome. I think by that stage we had lost all other senses but the will to get Samuel and ourselves to safety. There was no certainty that we would even be able to leave without being stopped by Germans.

Jerome kept looking up the road expecting to see Edgar, but there was no telling where he might have gone, and if he was even alive.

We would head toward Hazebrouck, which others had said was safe, though at the time we had no way of knowing if it was still fortified by the Allies. Mira stumbled slightly as she commenced the journey, and Jerome climbed down to check her hooves while I surveyed the area, searching for Germans with guns and hoping for some magical sign to guide us to safety.

On the horizon the sun was rising to greet the carnage of the day. I turned to take one last look behind me at the house and orchard that had been my first real home, where Helene and I had discovered a life we had once dreamed about. It was hard to leave my sister behind and wonder if she would receive a burial. I felt I was abandoning her in some way. As Jerome climbed back atop the trap, I was distracted by a figure stumbling toward us. I pulled at Jerome's arm, and he peered in the direction I was pointing, suddenly recognizing the bundle of bloodied rags in the man's arms.

Jerome rushed forward, taking Helene from Edgar as he was about to fall, exhausted, covered in ash. Edgar sat down and put his face in his hands.

"He came back," Helene said through a weak smile as Jerome carried her to the trap. I placed Samuel in the basket in the back and helped Edgar up from the ground. I wanted to cry for joy, but the urgency of the situation allowed no time to rejoice or reminisce or discover how he found her.

Edgar climbed up onto the seat beside Jerome while I sat alongside Helene in the back, holding her hand, with Samuel between us, squinting at the day. The trap rattled over holes in the road overused by many vehicles as we headed toward the south. Our immediate plan was to find refuge and treatment for Helene. I kept looking at her and believing in miracles. But it was no miracle. We had Edgar to thank for her return.

Helene spoke to me, her eyes fluttering open and shut, but her words did not make sense. Her skin was like fire to touch, and she was bleeding heavily, the skirts of her garment soaked. I leaned in to hear what she was whispering.

"We are all together."

"Yes," I whispered back, and she fell into sleep despite the noise and the dips and bumps in the road.

Edgar turned often to look at her and the road behind us. He seemed more focused and present than I had seen him previously, and he directed Jerome along a route he knew of. We reached a village where many others had also camped in crude shelters and beds, to seek refuge briefly. Local people from the village handed out mugs of water and home-baked biscuits. I was given directions to find a doctor, and I walked through the town ankle deep in mud and under a sprinkling of rain that had just begun to fall.

I found the doctor frantically attending to others in a makeshift tent set up in a field behind a small church. I was shocked at the amount of wounded on the ground, waiting for treatment: women, children, soldiers, and the elderly. The work for one doctor was impossible. The nurse there said that there were army men on their way to help take survivors elsewhere, and they would also be bringing more food and nurses. I felt hopeful then. I told her about my sister. She said to bring Helene and the doctor would try his best to see her. She left me to continue her rounds to check the patients.

Jerome was watching anxiously for my return, and Edgar was now in the back of the trap, one arm cradling the baby and his other hand gripping Helene's.

When Edgar looked up I saw the tears that had cut a pathway through the mud that caked across his face. As he raised his hand to wipe them, Helene's hand fell away from his limply.

"What is it?" I said, pushing past Jerome.

Helene lay still, her eyes closed. I climbed into the trap and put my face to hers, but I could not feel her breath. Her skin was cold under my touch, and the raindrops that were falling heavily now pelted mercilessly at her face. I leaned over her protectively.

"We have to take her to the doctor now!"

"No," said Jerome, standing beside the trap and reaching in to gently encircle my wrist with his large hand. I wrenched my arm away to gather my thoughts, to take in what had happened.

I stared at my sister, who had been there since I was small, who had been my mother and my best friend. I refused to believe I had lost her. There had been too much loss already. My body trembled, and my heart ached like it had never done before. With her hand tightly in mine, I closed my eyes and prayed for her beautiful soul.

Edgar sat cross-legged and soaked with rain, tenderly cradling the child in his arms and protecting his tiny face from the rain. I now recognized his loss, his illness, and his sacrifice amongst this wreckage that had become our lives.

He passed Samuel to Jerome, who rocked the baby tenderly, and Edgar pulled me toward him. I sobbed into his chest. He was a victim like us, too. Not only had he lost the woman I believe he loved more than anyone, but pieces of his spirit had been left on the battlefields. I had no hate in my heart, only love then for the man who had loved my sister and who, I would come to learn, would never love another.

RUDY

1922

CHAPTER 28

It was Sally, Peggy's niece, writing to Edgar, describing her new home and the walking parties in Canada: *The silence is breathtaking!* Edgar had read out to me from her letter and held up a flower she had plucked during a tour. The connection to the words in his book I felt too strong to ignore, and the confirmation of my hunch, I felt, would be waiting at the port of Le Havre.

Sally, who had once had a brief romance with Edgar—who stole her attention away from Laurence, much to Peggy's relief—had caught the eye of a wealthy Canadian businessman who owned property in the Lakelands, France, and other regions across the Atlantic. She and her husband had made the decision to settle permanently in Canada a year before war broke out. Edgar and Sally had remained in contact.

Are there bears? A seemingly irrelevant and innocent question once posed by Samuel now held significance. Samuel's fear of bears came not from the books I read, but from his experiences, I know now.

At the port, I'll admit, it was dishonest to hand across Roland's business card and pass myself off as his clerk, but at this point I don't think anyone could blame me for such harmless fraud. My story was that I sought to distribute a large amount of money to someone who had emigrated, but I needed to locate their destination. The discovery of their names would be a monumental leap closer to the gold at the end of the rainbow and would of course affirm my suspicion. It would also alleviate some of the doubts I had on the train heading toward the coast that the clues—a child's words, a piece of poetry, and a pressed flower—were nothing more than rash hope.

The port officer at Le Havre went in search of the manifest dated the week after the marriage certificate, but after surveying several lists, he could find no passengers with the surname of Watts. I asked him to try searching in later weeks; but again this was to no avail. I was about to leave when I thought to ask if I could search the manifest myself. The man seemed wary at first, if not mildly offended at the implication he was not capable. It was irregular to do this, he said, except in a police investigation, but he reluctantly slid the large volume of names across the counter. I think that had I asked for anything else, he might well have called his supervisor, but I fortunately did not have to take up much more of his time.

It is difficult to put into words the excitement that ran through me as I ran my finger down the looped, tidy handwriting and recognized several names: Mariette and Jerome and Samuel Lavier on a ship bound for Southampton. The age of "Jerome," just as I suspected, was the same age as Edgar. I had found my pot of gold, or at the very least in what vicinity it was potentially located. Edgar had used Jerome's identity and somehow changed the age on the paper. Of course, a man thought to be dead could not suddenly appear alive, though it is doubtful that many of the missing soldiers would have been searched for at the port of Le Havre. Edgar had always been careful and meticulous, his workbooks so exact and painstakingly calligraphic. He would have been the same with providing falsified documents if need be.

"Is this the ship's only destination?" I asked the officer, who then checked his records.

He shook his head. "That one went all the way to Halifax, Canada."

Excited and motivated by my discovery, I booked a hotel nearby to wait for the next ship. During that time I sent a letter to my mother to say that I still had much work to do in my search, that the process was longer than I expected, though without noting any details. I did not want to give her any more worry or hope, but neither did I wish for Laurence to learn the particulars of my quest. I did not want to provoke him, nor did I trust him. His part in some of this was still in question. Another letter was posted also, marked confidential, to Roland to advise him on the direction of my pursuits in case I was not heard of again. At least someone would know what I had found so far, should something happen to me.

Aboard a ship days later, and with the salty breezes whipping my face, I followed Canada into an icy winter. During the weeklong journey from France, I'd had time to reflect on the mystery so far. From the clues provided, I believed there was a strong possibility that "Uncle Fabien" was alive. And from Samuel's recognition, he was Edgar. But was he really Samuel's father? There were other questions of a more self-doubting, personal nature. Had Edgar died and Mariette returned with the child in the hope of discovering a replacement only to find me a disappointment, a poor second to someone such as Edgar? I tried not to dwell too far from the quest at hand, to find them both, regardless of their feelings or mine, but the closer I had got to Canada's coastline, the more nervous and skeptical I had become, and I wondered if I was simply chasing ghosts.

From the train window onward, the great vastness of Canada threatened to swallow me up, with its stretches of remote wilderness between train stations and formidable mountain peaks that pierced through the clouds. If Edgar chose to be lost, here would be the place; the task of finding him seemed overwhelming at that point without knowing what still lay ahead of me. I clung to the thought of Sally, my starting point at least.

I'd heard stories of an untamed landscape, of bears roaming through streets, and of deadly winter storms and avalanches, but upon arriving in Calgary, I was surprised to find the most civilized of cities. I walked along its wide streets and tidy square buildings, and like most cities it bustled orderly with business and industry. There was the oily smell of new roads, the ringing of trams, and, persistently in the background, the distant hammerings and engines from construction. Despite the streets busy with motorcars, as they were in Manchester, the sky seemed broader here, and the scent in the air was also of new beginnings. There was a diversity of passersby in various colors, backgrounds, and apparel, including several mounted police, and I heard the collective tones of several accents and languages.

Upon inquiry the station attendant handed me a directory to look up Sally's address; then for less than a mile, I followed the route directed, as wind and sleet whipped around my legs and the sun attempted also to burn color onto my face. I knocked on the front door of the redbrick structure, and an older lady answered.

I gave her my name and waited just inside the entryway. It did not take long for the same woman to return to lead me into an elegantly furnished drawing room with a large window that overlooked the street. Everything was new and modern and airy, but there were elements of England everywhere: a painting of the English Lakelands, Royal Crown china, and a Union Jack that hung across the foyer wall.

I waited, and Sally sped into the room and into my arms.

"What on earth?" she said.

"I'm sorry; I meant to write." Though the real truth was that if my suspicion was right, I did not want the risk of Edgar, if indeed he did not want to be found, fleeing ahead of my arrival. I had to see her myself if I was to learn the full truth.

"You are lucky to find me home. I have many friends here to call on for various reasons. But alas, the weather might keep everyone indoors today."

After the usual greeting niceties about my mother, her aunt, and childhood memories, we took our tea and sandwiches in the drawing room. She had grown even more handsome than I remembered. She had a sweet oval face and a splattering of ginger freckles on the bridge of her nose. Her strawberry-gold hair was clasped on one side and hung thickly over one shoulder. She wore a fashionable dress, above the ankles but only slightly shorter than I'd seen her wear before as a young girl, and I noticed a hat and coat on the stand behind her that matched.

"Robert is currently in Europe on business. You must have passed him on the way."

She laughed at her own joke but seemed a little nervous also, and very talkative. She told me about her husband, about his brief stint in the navy before turning his head to commercial property development and the opportunities in Alberta that seemed limitless if one, like he, had money. Sally had grown up mostly remote from city life, and had not taken to London, but she had relished the idea of starting a new life in Canada, as well as learning her new task of bookkeeping.

For the whole time I was there, Sally talked constantly, in fact so much so I felt it strange that she had not yet asked why I had arrived.

"It is wonderful to see you, but I am not just here for a friendly visit," I said, interrupting her. "There is much more to it, I'm afraid."

She viewed me thoughtfully then, her mouth partly open, as she waited for something she knew was coming.

"I'm looking for my brother."

She frowned a little and gripped tightly her fingers in her lap.

"I'm not sure who you mean. Laurence was living in London last I heard. Edgar is missing in France. I was so sorry to learn that . . ."

Sally was always quite innocent, no more so than she was then, failing to sound convincing.

"Sally . . ."

She stood up suddenly and walked across the room toward the window, her back to me.

"I told him you would search. I told him that to leave people without answers is probably the worst thing, worse than the news of death, but he . . ."

My heart beat fast, and I felt a rush of blood to my head. I stood up, unable to sit still from the excitement I felt and a jumble of questions that threatened to burst out all at once. I walked close to her. Color had risen in her cheeks, and though teary, she also appeared relieved, her hands no longer gripping tensely, the weight of this knowledge now passed on to me.

I caught her gently by the shoulders and looked deeply into her tear-filled eyes before she dropped her head with shame.

"I'm sorry, but he made us promise, and when he explained his reasons . . . we couldn't."

I would come to learn those reasons, but the news alone that he had traveled here, that he was alive, was enough for that very moment.

I pulled her toward me, and she sobbed, and I wanted to yell and rejoice and scream across the Atlantic to let my mother know. I held her for a time, and then she pulled away and wiped her eyes with the handkerchief I produced, and we sat down again.

It was then she told me things, and I listened, absorbing every nuance, looking for pieces of the story that required scrutiny, examining her every word.

She said that Edgar arrived, just like I had, unannounced, with his wife, Mariette, and young baby. Sally's husband, Robert, was home at the time. Edgar had deserted the army; that description cut me deeply because it was at odds with the person I had grown up with. I had never seen Edgar fear or fail at anything, and it was a difficult scene to try and picture. Edgar, it seems, had let the army think he was dead, but according to Sally, he had also believed the war would never end.

"Why did he come to you?"

"He trusted me and needed my help. We were old friends, as you know. He wanted a reference for work, information, and they needed money, too, for a fresh start. And I can tell you that they paid every cent back. He sent money as soon as he was able.

"Robert was reluctant to help him at first. My husband wanted him to return, do the honorable thing, hand himself in to the military authorities, but after we had spent some time with him, we realized that he had suffered enough. Even Robert, big, opinionated Robert, if you remember him well, was quite full of pity."

She looked at me as if she wanted to say something else or expected a question at this point.

"They stayed here for a fortnight. I helped the young woman with the baby, even gave them an engraved silver spoon for Samuel. Such a sweet wee baby! Robert tried to find them a place to live and somewhere to work. Edgar was adamant that he did not want to be around people, and it became clear why."

"How so?"

"I will get to that in a moment. Robert was telling him that he knew of some government land grants being offered up north to immigrants. And then one night they just vanished."

Yet again, I felt a sense of loss, but more like abandonment this time, knowing that he had not died, that he had willingly left me behind.

Sally could see the shift in my mood.

"He is here somewhere. Of that I'm sure."

"When was the last time you saw him?"

"It was about a year ago, by accident. They never attempted to contact us again after they sent payment. And one day we saw him just outside the city. He was unloading pieces of timber that were being shipped by rail. Robert spoke to him, and he seemed to answer well. He said that he had found work northwest of here, in British Columbia, and then he made excuses to leave. Robert asked him if he wanted to visit us for tea, but he declined and seemed keen to hurry away."

"Was his wife with him?"

"No. Not then."

"Why did they leave the city in the first place? Why didn't they stay in contact?"

She bit her lip.

"There is something that you should know."

"I think I know what you are going to say. He is ill, is that it? His nerves? I'm aware that he was hospitalized for a time."

"Well then, if you come upon him, you should be prepared. He is harder, a man who doesn't see the world the same as he did before. He frightened me a little, yet there wasn't one particular thing he did to make me feel this way. It was just the way he looked at me, at Robert sometimes, as if he wanted to hurt us or didn't know us. It sounds silly, I know. But whatever has caused this is serious."

I felt I was running out of time. And I had to wonder whether he did in fact die recently, which might have forced Mariette to return with the child.

I told her then of Mariette and the boy's arrival.

She nodded. "Aunt Peggy wrote and told me they had come, though I have not had the mind or heart to write back, to continue with this lie. They begged me to keep their secret, and I promised that I would. I'm sorry, Rudy, that I did not write, but to see Edgar that way . . ."

"You thought to spare us," I said with a hint of bitterness. "To remember him as he was."

"Aunty told me how much the family grieved. I was heartbroken for all of you, for Edgar also. This new Edgar I met would not fit into your mother's world anymore, and that I believe would devastate her more. I—"

"It would have been good for us to make up our own minds." I did feel a measure of resentment that was in danger of spilling over into the conversation, but the idea that Edgar was still alive kept my anger in check. I might finally be close to learning the truth about these missing years.

"I'm so sorry, Rudy. Truly I am. Believe me when I tell you that for months after Edgar arrived I could think of nothing else but the situation I'd experienced, and my conscience was very clouded."

"Sally, I can move on from this if you can tell me everything about them, anything that might help me to find them."

She sat quietly for a moment before describing Edgar and his plans with as much detail as she could remember, eyes fixed to the window and some faraway thought.

"There was something wrong about their relationship. They did not strike me as close, though I suspect that Edgar and his aloofness made it so. She was wary and watchful and very protective of him. It may have been my imagination, but she never let us see him alone. I suspect it might also have been Mariette's idea to leave us here suddenly."

Sally frowned as she recounted an incident.

"Robert suggested that he could find some work for Edgar close by. That Edgar could once again return to some sort of normal life. That employment and routine might help him get over the traumas of war. Edgar looked straight through Robert as if he might strike him, before storming off to the guest room, where he remained for the rest of the evening and into the next day. Only Mariette appeared for breakfast and said that we must not discuss any future with Edgar, that Edgar must be somewhere where there are no people. When I asked if I might go to apologize to him for anything we might have said to upset him, she rejected the idea immediately, telling us to mind our ideas and informing us not to approach him until he was ready. Mariette was like a ferocious lioness protecting her cubs or . . ."

"Or what?"

"Or trying to protect us perhaps. It was odd. And something else, too. The baby was always with her. I did not see Edgar pick up the child once, which I thought was strange. In fact he barely looked at him. Though many times he would ask Mariette if the child was well, irrationally fearful there was something wrong with him. I thought perhaps the child had been very poorly previously.

"Mariette appeared to be a very independent woman, though she was not here long enough for me to form any solid opinion of her character, other than she was very formal and withdrawn, and not at all as you described her earlier."

Sally asked me to stay for several nights. She said it would be a good idea if I had plans to go north to search that I should at least speak to people who knew the area. It was vast and treacherous in parts, and easy to vanish in such places, especially in the winter. She would also buy and fit me with whatever I needed to make the journey.

I welcomed a soft bed. The temperatures were dropping, and so often I had gone to sleep chilled during my train journey to Calgary. I welcomed the fire in the rooms and the bed covers filled with down.

I went to bed mulling over our conversation, the effects of a second brandy leaving me feeling mellow, hopeful, and numb at various stages. I still believed that Edgar was alive. There was something in the intense way Mariette spoke of him, her words carefully arranged, as if he were always present in the room, telling her what to say. And of course then the words from the boy: he had said goodbye to his supposed uncle before he left for England. I would find Edgar, I thought. I would bring him home. It was the only plan I had.

CHAPTER 29

Loss, too, I believe, can be an illness. One day, while walking through the city, I spied a girl with dark-red hair and went from store to store to find her only to discover someone else, the event leaving me shaken. Mariette and Edgar never once strayed from my thoughts, so much so I started imagining them both close by. I felt possessed by the former and haunted by the latter. Finding one would uncover the truth about both. Though part of me did wonder if Mariette had in fact left England at all, or whether she had returned to France. And the question of the boy figured most. Why would a mother leave her child? Nothing made sense; in fact, as it came nearer the time to leave, I felt less certain about anything. It was clear that they did not want me, nor did they want to be found. This observation should have convinced me to turn back to England. But my purpose was only fueled by it.

In the following days, I spoke to several people throughout town, using the deception of seeking old friends from war who worked for a timber company to justify the several names I was querying. I did not want to reveal Edgar as my brother, which would only draw more questions about our lack of contact. No one knew of Edgar Lavier or Edgar Watts or anyone named Fabien, presuming he had used any of those.

Snow blanketed the city, and others who had come back from the north and the west said that the bad weather had come early. Passenger trains had stopped running, and to search thoroughly I would need alternate transport anyway. Sally feared that the journey wasn't safe for someone who didn't know the area, but she also knew it was pointless to attempt to talk me out of it. Instead, she assisted with my travel preparations, helping me purchase an old wagon, though it resembled more a trap with a cloth shelter roughly put together for some protection. She also provided me with blankets and extra woolen jumpers and snow boots that belonged to Robert, food supplies, and a bottle of whiskey to warm me along the way.

"You must not veer from the main route where there are no trails or tracks," she warned, while she pointed out the directions on a map.

"At least you are giving it everything, because to go back now would only torture you," she said as I departed the following day.

She was right of course. I hugged her and vowed I would return without regret. I could not bear a grudge against her. Promises were made for a reason, and she, too, had suffered with the secret.

I left on a day that scarcely cast a shadow, with the winter sun rising late and only briefly on my back, while the flecks of sleet pelted at the front of me. The journey would be slow.

I stayed at a hotel the first night and watched the snow pile higher beyond my window. The proprietors served me roast beef and fried potatoes and seemed bemused to hear of my journey. They also allowed me to put the horse in their barn and were eager to help answer many of my queries. There had been several Englishmen and Frenchmen passing through, and Edgar's face in the photograph was familiar, which gave me hope, but they could not say how long ago they had seen him. They did not remember any woman with him or a child but said that people in the northwestern townships were likely to know who lived and worked in the area.

I learned something about ice fishing and other helpful pieces of information about my trails. Not that I planned on any fishing. It was my best endeavor to get from town to town for a good meal, not catch my own. From the window of my hotel, I had a view of the train track and watched a freight train carrying timber bravely plough through the icy white terrain.

I would like to say that the journey was over quickly and in the comfort of inns, but after a second night in relative comfort, accommodation for the most part after that was scarce, and for several nights I slept minimally inside the trap cocooned in blankets, my limbs stiff and frozen by the time I woke. There were few other travelers mad enough to test this weather and shovel snow from their traps after stopping for a period, and there were no more passing trains. Throughout my journey, I'd made enquiries about Edgar, but no one had heard of or seen him. I stopped at a sawmill without success and was guided further west.

I was so weary by this point, clothes always damp, and the hardness of the wagon seat was something I did not look forward to each morning. Then there was the maintenance of the horse, the fear of encountering bears or cougars, and sometimes the cold, bitter winds slowed our pace down to a stroll. I veered northward, and after many hours I was fortunate to find more accommodation. This second-to-last room I stayed in was little bigger than a storeroom, though with the luxury of heating. On a piece of mirror above a wash tin, I was frightened by my reflection. Lines had appeared on my forehead, my hair was long and disheveled, and a stubbly, disorderly beard had grown. From my appearance, it seemed I was blending into the wilderness that surrounded me.

Further north, where the snow had turned to thick walls of white, I reached the oasis of a chalet late at night. Above the chalet door a sign offered "Boarding," and a light was on inside, but another sign on the front said "Closed." I could see nothing but white-coated trees and mountains around me, and this place appeared to be my only option. A woman answered the door and nodded reluctantly that she in fact had a room, perhaps feeling sorry for me, but she did not have the space anywhere for the horse.

"There is a house and barn down the road. You could see if they are still awake. They might put your horse up, but if not, it will have to stay out in the snow."

I patted the mare I'd named Sadie, regretting the challenges I'd brought into her life. I put my bags upstairs, and the woman, though terse, put some wild-duck stew, an apple, and some tea in my room. I almost inhaled the stew I was so hungry and then took the apple to Sadie before setting off down the road. I hoped they had more food for the horse, as the supplies I had brought for her had been rationed in the last two days.

There were a number of local men milling around some horse stalls, and they viewed me silently as I approached. I felt several sets of eyes scanning me suspiciously. I spoke to them about my plight, and they seemed very curious at first and laughed amongst themselves as they passed around the photograph of Edgar, amused that I might be chasing a dead brother. But they were sympathetic enough toward the horse and let me leave her there. We agreed on a price, and I paid them in advance.

Back at the chalet the bed was incredibly soft and warm, which made up for the not-so-warm reception I had received on arrival, and a small fire had been lit while I was gone. There was also a lantern on the wall, to brighten the room further, which I turned down to slip deeply into sleep.

Though hours had in fact passed, it seemed only minutes later that I was woken by a rapping on the door. I looked up suddenly to see that morning had arrived late in a yellow-and-purple haze stretching upward from the horizon, and the air in the room was a shade of pale gray. The fire in the room had died out to allow the chill to spread, and there was frost on the windows as I climbed into my trousers. In front of me, as I opened the door, was a man of native Indian appearance. He was broad shouldered, and was at least a head and a half taller than I was. He wore his long hair tied back with a string.

"Can I help you?"

"You are looking for a man, Fabien?" he said.

"Yes, yes, I am," I said eagerly.

I was suddenly very much awake and invited him in. He walked in and looked searchingly around the room.

"Do you know him?" I asked, suddenly a little fearful as I sensed that he was not here out of the goodness of his heart. There was something else driving him, just from the way he examined me and the things in the room and his long glances outside the window.

"They said he was your brother," he said.

"Yes. I'm told that he works in these parts." I heard the word "was." It did not fall away.

"Your brother Fabien is dead."

The news should have been more shocking, but I had been denying his death for so long now that I struggled to believe anything anymore.

"How do you know this?" I said, trying not to sound distrustful. His tone seemed so aggressive that I wondered if there was far more to it, if perhaps this was an old foe of my brother coming to exact revenge on a relative.

"He was crushed under logs."

It could not have come to this. *It cannot be,* I told myself.

"Did you see it happen?"

"Yes."

"Where was he buried? Where was his place of work?"

"North of here. He was buried without a name. I can't tell you where."

It seemed odd, the treatment of visitors in these parts, and he was clearly not receptive to my questions. Perhaps he thought that what little he told me would be enough. But it wasn't, of course.

"Can I speak to other people he was working with? They might know something more."

"They are gone for the winter. No use now."

I had come too far and felt quite angry then, and I struggled to suppress it in my tone.

"Well, I can't leave," I said, standing up and reaching for my jacket.

"The horse is out front, ready for you to go."

I was taken aback.

"Why?"

"There is nothing for you here. Strangers aren't welcome."

"This is a hotel for paying customers, is it not?"

He didn't respond. It made no sense why he wanted to get rid of me quickly, unless of course there was something to hide.

"I can't leave. Not until I know for certain. Not until I see a grave. I must speak to others. I must have some sort of proof."

He took a step toward me then, and I stepped back.

"Stop!" I said.

"You must go," he said, the tone laced with unpleasant consequences.

"Give me a minute then."

He paused and then walked outside the door, but I heard no steps descending the stairs. I sat for a moment and wondered about my next move. I even considered climbing out the window, which made no sense. I would probably kill myself in the process, and I was not particularly clever or fast at clandestine practices. I was not like Laurence, who had once scaled the walls of the manor to meet with friends in town for the night.

There was only one course of action, and that was to pretend to leave, then continue my journey by way of a different route and find other villagers more agreeable; though villages had become so infrequent at this point I had been lucky to stumble across this one. As it turned out it was both lucky and unlucky. I felt close to finding something despite the intimidating reception.

I buttoned up my thick coat and dragged a fur hat down over my ears before the hostile stranger greeted me at the top of the stairs to then follow me down.

"I don't need a chaperone," I muttered, to which he said nothing.

As I settled the bill with the proprietor, I caught a look between her and the man and wondered whether she knew something more and was in on this somehow. There was no time for a hearty breakfast or coffee to warm me up, even though I could smell something savory wafting from the room behind the service counter. Regardless, I could scarcely think of food at such a time, my nerves jittery.

I climbed on board the trap. The horse was brushed and had been given a fur blanket. I was grateful for that at least and offered the man some money, to which he shook his head.

I headed back in a southerly direction. When I looked behind me, the man was still watching, close enough for me to see the snowflakes in his hair. He wore a thin shirt and was clearly unbothered by the cold.

Once out of his sight, I stopped to pull out the map to find the next township that, according to my calculation, was several hours north. My plan was to bypass the village I had just visited, parallel to the road I'd just traveled, and continue through the forests.

Sadie was sluggish, trudging through the deep, powdery fall of snow, under a sheet of damp and falling whiteness that showed no signs of abating. Apart from a few trees and the white wind that swirled and whistled menacingly through them, the only sign of life was my mare as she continued on stoically. I felt alone, afraid even, my ears aching from the cold, but my purpose was still clear. I could not bring myself to turn around until I had evidence in some form that my brother had been here.

I had veered off the track for several hours and thought at some point I would have to head back toward a more obvious route. Returning to the map again, I studied the area of wilderness that I was ambling through. Our journey was slow and heading in what I thought was roughly the right direction. Some salvation came not half an hour later when I saw deep grooves in the snow that were not yet filled from the increasing fall, and I followed these with still a sense of optimism that

I was indeed amid civilization. I felt encouraged by what I perceived as a track that had been cleared for access, and I saw the remains of some logs; these signs giving me hope that there were buildings or a village close by, which perhaps had not yet been mapped.

I had already experienced how quickly day fell to night here, but that wasn't my problem, not at that point. The snow had increased heavily, and I was having trouble seeing in front of me as exhaustion began to consume me. I was running on a heightened state of awareness yet confused at the same time. I pictured dismally my compass, unused in the top drawer of my desk at the manor, never foreseeing that my journey to find my brother would take a detour into wilderness. I wrapped most of my face in my woolen scarf so my eyes could just see out of slits, though my eyelashes were caked with ice. Finally Sadie stopped. She'd had enough of trudging through thick snow. She was telling me this venture was hopeless.

I shivered. The fur that lined my jacket seemed not enough to block the chill, and my fingers, though gloved, ached to bend. I had been warned at an earlier stop about the cold, but I did not think much about it, my mind only on the prize. And one often has to experience something to fully understand. I had felt the icy English winters, but even they hadn't prepared me. Sally had warned me never to distance myself from roads, and here I was doing just that. And though I might add that circumstance had forced me, I scolded myself for being so ill prepared.

Above me the sky seemed to be descending, squeezing out the last of the light. I climbed off the seat to check Sadie's legs sunk in deep snow. I pulled her by the reins in front of her, stepping through the snow, and she reluctantly followed. But I understood the effort she was making, when I too grew very weary from weighty steps as my feet were saturated and the muscles in my legs grew stiff. Stopping, I looked about me and called out to see if anyone was someplace near.

There was no response. I felt completely alone in what appeared an eerie, alien world.

"Sorry, old girl," I whispered in Sadie's ear and climbed into the back of the trap, curling my body to fit. I pulled up the blankets over my head and body as before, hoping that the snowfall would pass and Sadie would feel energized to start again. This time, however, I was losing to the fierceness of the damp and cold, which had infiltrated the flimsy cloth walls. As I lay there with the wind whipping around us, rattling the rig, I thought of Mother and wondered then how she would handle things with two sons gone. I felt myself drifting, and more morbid thoughts crept in. I wondered if Mother would miss me as much as she missed Edgar and if I would still be here by spring, my body thawing. I thought all such things to do with my end.

I can't tell you how long I lay there, perhaps an hour, but at some point my teeth stopped chattering and I stopped feeling the cold. I felt in a strange way peaceful. This was broken by the sound of shouts and a dog barking. I was too stiff and tired to sit up, but I was able to raise the cloth wall slightly to observe wolf-like dogs appear from out of the misty clouds, ahead of a sled with two people wrapped up in fur and woolen masks.

One of them jumped off the sled and walked swiftly toward me, his face covered with a mask.

"Are you all right?" he asked.

I nodded, just.

"He's alive," the man said to another, who came to pull off the blanket and examine me.

"Can you walk?" said the second man gruffly.

I cannot remember answering as the two men lifted me out of the trap to carry me to the sled.

"I will bring the horse," said the same man.

I didn't question, nor did I care where I was being taken and by whom. And I did not understand what was happening to my body, my heart slowing down and my head giving up the fight. I was tucked warmly into some sort of tent structure that was lined with fur on the front of the sled. I heard the dogs barking and felt the sled lurch into action. In my delirium I was apparently thanking the dogs.

Eventually we stopped, though I had no idea of time or any clear memory of the journey. Someone called out ahead, and the man I was with responded. Several people lifted me and carried me up some stairs into a cabin.

I felt the warmth rush at my face, burning slightly, as they placed me on a low cot beside a blazing wood burner, and someone carefully pulled away my frozen mask to take a look at me. I was only vaguely aware of my shoes being removed and an examination of my feet. Then as several blankets were thrown over me and arranged, a large man bent down to put his face close to mine. His skin looked craggy, his hair cut badly, but his blue eyes shone.

I put my hand out to him, believing perhaps that I had died and that, if this was death, it wasn't so bad.

The man whose face was near reached for my hand.

"Rudy," said Edgar out of the haze. I felt his hand grip mine tightly.

EDGAR

From 1916

CHAPTER 30

It was awful, the war, but one knows that already because much has been written about it over the years. After months in a trench when our feet were swollen and we could no longer feel the tips of our fingers, our backs permanently damp from the rain and our minds no longer drifting to a future, I had grown a weary tolerance of fate. If I lived, that was good. If I died, it was good also. Both had their merits. Of course I did not voice these thoughts aloud. I was the one that people leaned on to bolster their spirits. The soldiers sought strength from me constantly, the pieces of me taken until there was nothing left to take.

There were many of us. I can picture most of their faces, but the ones that feature are the ones I saw beside me. Men I thought would be my allies through life as well, when we returned to dear old Blighty. Roger, Scott, Willy, Burke, Irish Ted, and the others were closer than any family. They are as clear as the raised veins in the back of my now-coarse hands. Roger was sent home with half a lung, Scott lost his toes by way of trench foot and Burke his brains, and Irish Ted was claimed by an infection from the shrapnel of an exploding bullet. And Willy was executed.

I received letters from Mother, who I knew waited on every small bit of information from me. The pressure of that alone seemed to add to the pressures in the trenches: the fact that I was so needed there as well. I was at least happy that Rudy was not involved in all this muck, that he had been too young. I imagined that he would have been good with army commands. He was quiet, tolerant, and did what was expected of him without complaint. He had been a lovable child, a sweet boy often overlooked because he was so quiet. People presumed that because he didn't ask for anything, he didn't need anything. But I saw early that he needed love like the rest of us, and I couldn't help but take him under my wing. And I promised to keep him there while I was in his life.

There is a mental picture I have of him that shows our differences. Rudy walking around picking up the dead bodies of birds that Laurence and I had shot, checking if they were badly injured or not, attempting to revive the ones he thought would make it, then burying the ones that were dead and marking the tiny graves with stones. He couldn't kill anything, so I'm glad he didn't have to join the rest of us in hell.

While Rudy was soft in the center when he was born, Laurence seemed to crawl out from under hell's rock, screaming and begging for attention. Blessed with good looks, he used them to get most places in life. Charm was something he could put on when necessary. Cruelty was something that came more naturally. He enjoyed saying things that would get under your skin, the mention of a girl you were keen on, bragging about a subject he did better in. To taunt and provoke was something that amused him: a laying of mines for someone to step on, waiting and watching for the reaction. He seemed to do as he pleased, his behavior unchecked. We weren't close, but God knows I had tried over the years to form a friendship.

I had heard late in the war that Laurence had shipped out, and I knew that he would survive. If I were a betting man, I would have bet my fortune on it. I suspected that he would not only survive the war, he would attempt to prosper from it as well. I, on the other hand, was born into expectation. The oldest, the leader, the one who would continue the family name and see the young siblings through adolescence as if having gone through it first alone made me an expert on all boys young. I was a model child, respected, allowed for, and I made good decisions. And though for the period before the war, I lived up to those expectations, it had been tiring and costly to my state of mind. I have to say that one's duty bore a greater responsibility than shown. I had to wear my disdain, my irritation, and my weariness on the inside. On the outside I had to be like Mother, accepting, tolerant, and not outspoken, but a leader nonetheless.

My sport was probably the only thing I lived for. I played rugby in the winters and rowed and sailed in the summers; and without sounding again like I'm boasting, I was always captain of something. In photographs I am there in glass cabinets along school hallways where also sits my name on plaques on trophies. My closest friends were spoiled toffs, but they were lovable spoiled toffs. We did not get up to all the roguish things that many of our peers did, but some of them. We once purposely sank one of the school rowing boats and another time climbed out of the dormitory windows to swim in the river. And that was about the extent of my misbehavior.

There was never any doubt about me signing up for the war. Duty above self had been ingrained in me by Mother, church, and school masters throughout my childhood. And of course there was another duty also, to take care of Mother, Rudy, and the estate. We assembled in Étaples at the start of the war, were given some information about the defense lines and the customs of the country, and were then sent to an area for our groupings. Then came talks by our commander advising us that only respectable fraternization with locals would be tolerated, though rules such as these were not possible for some, me included. I entered the war with the rank of lieutenant because of my class and the privilege of officers' training, which did not feel like a privilege most times. Being separated from others in the group by a title felt at first like I had been penalized and isolated. But solidarity won far above rank, and by the end of the war, titles meant nothing to many of us.

The first battle we fought revealed that nightmares are real. We stayed in trenches, and the shelling and the rain of dirt and ash, sometimes human, gave me an entrance into war that none of us were prepared for. Not that I hadn't been told about it, but partaking in it is something that words can only paint in watercolor, not blood, the retelling of our stories often muted so as not to shock the listener. We stepped out and faced the enemy, and bullets whizzed by me. I killed men sometimes with my bayonet and sometimes with hysterical anger that men will only experience in these moments. I can think of no other situation where one can charge like a beast and mutilate another human with a mixture built up from hate and lust for vengeance and then walk away and tell ourselves we are but human after all. It is these sorts of things that would encourage some journalists and civilians—who wrote and read about these accounts and published in cold, emotionless black print—to criticize such perceived depravity without understanding, without empathy. We simply had no choice.

Somehow miraculously I survived this and the boredom of hours, days, months, and years in the trenches, where to make fun of the dead in rare unfiltered and sleep-deprived moments had been the only source of entertainment, with the occasional letter from home to supposedly lift our spirits. Rudy's letters were the ones I waited for. He was truthful. If it was bad at home, if a horse was lame, he would tell me. Mother's letters would smell like roses as an accompaniment to the words, to supposedly keep me chipper. Her letters were also a little shallow and cold, though I knew that she loved me in her own way. She would describe the meals they had, unaware that food in the first months was something I dreamed about more than anything else, as well as lying in a soft, warm bed, listening to the drizzle of rain as it hit the lake outside my top-floor window.

But Rudy's letters I pined for. They told me that things would still be the same when I returned and the only change would be me. They were often beautiful, too, the descriptions so clear, about early morning sunshine and snow and the smell of the barn at Lakeland and the sound of Chess thundering across the greens and the clattering of delivery carts on the terrace pavers. And it was these that helped me, I believe. That got me through some of it.

So I begged him for more of his thoughts and observations and then wrote my own. When I first realized that my mind would often race to darker thoughts, thoughts I couldn't control, and these after my first battle in France, I began poetry as a way of coping. Though, these pieces I didn't send, not wishing anyone back home to read them. These told of the stench; the cold, damp socks; the moans of the wounded; the grotesque and fetid flesh wounds; the relentless shelling that could blow a man into hundreds of pieces; the way the earth exploded in front of you, jolting your body, sounding in one's mind hour after hour. The slosh and mud where we slipped again and again, wading through early morning mists toward an unseen enemy, helpless and strangely alone, hanging for my life on a rifle and bayonet in a large sea of dull army green and faceless tin hats. And during that first heated charge, one did not dare to turn toward the screams and shouts of the fallen.

The numbness of what follows after experiencing war is probably the biggest surprise of all, together with the feeling that we did nothing worthy or brave even though our commanders assured us differently, with pinned medals and congratulatory pats on the shoulder. At times, remote from the complexities of the whole war, the killings felt more personal. As if the battles we won would prove the better man.

My letters home became rare because I could not find anything to write about without Mother worrying. I could not describe the uniforms, which after days of wear felt scratchy and uncomfortable, or the rancid smell of trench foot when it was exposed by those beside me after weeks of rain, sunk in ten-foot-deep mud holes. I could no longer describe the tinned food that was indescribably tasteless, so much so that I would have to be reminded to eat it. Perhaps the loss of appetite was in fact the first sign that my mind was not equipped for war. I could not tell Mother that I lost three friends in one day, their parts left in sloshy fields that looked like the world had ended as the fog closed in to claim the remains. I sometimes prayed, too, something I had not ever felt the need to do before then.

So after weeks of battles, which we survived and won, we had our first leave, sent back to billet with families. I was first sent to a hospital in Armentières, released, and then to the baths of a woman's psychiatric hospital in Bailleul, where the nuns looked after us. I was still unaware of my disease, implanted in neurons and searching for ways to manifest.

The village was beautiful and starkly contrasted against the vestiges of others I had seen, now just shadows of structures, blights on the land-scape, and memorials in some abstract future. The shelling had ceased temporarily, though I could still hear it, feel the vibrations through my body. There was no sleep that night, tortured as I was with the tremors and the fear that I might not wake. I don't remember anyone from that first day, my mind at the time little more than a house for the noises that had followed me from the battlefield.

The following evening I was taken to a soiree organized for a num-ber of enlisted men, as a thank-you by the local community. Some of the women there were the prettiest I had seen, all eager to pay attention to us, in some way showing a certain gratitude I didn't feel I'd earned. That night, the beer swirling through my veins, there were no dreams of bodies and smoke. I had a sense of freedom that I hadn't felt in months.

The next morning I enjoyed once more the taste of food, the smell of coffee, and the sun that filled up the space in my tiny window, the memory of small pleasures returning. The steaming-hot baths were much-needed therapy, and the nurses and nuns there were some of the kindest people I had met so far.

My friend Roger introduced me to some girls. Mariette was very pretty. She caught my eye first, as well as the eyes of most of the men in the unit. She wore a fitted dress that accentuated a long, narrow waist, arms perhaps too thin, and a long nose that surprisingly suited her face. I remember now her features vividly: curious eyes of darkest brown and hair that had caught fire from the sun. She was beautiful, flirtatious, but her flighty mannerisms told me she was very young.

It was only when I turned to the woman next to her that my heart galloped faster. Helene was someone like me: someone who did not want the attention. She was pretty but withdrawn, with pale-green eyes, long dark hair, and satiny brown skin. She wore her hair tightly pulled back, an old work shirt, and a pair of oversized men's trousers that disguised her womanly shape, blending her into the heavy male landscape. I had a sudden yearning to know her, to hear about her life.

The girls looked nothing alike, and I am not at all certain that they were actually sisters of blood, but I would come to see that blood in this case didn't matter. They were closer than any family I had ever seen.

Roger was due to leave the next day. My respite was longer because the officers perhaps were a little unsure if I was ready. They had seen the shaking of my hands when I was first admitted into hospital. It was Roger who suggested I take up his billet at the orchard, promoting its friendly hosts, the perfect place to heal. There was no point, I concluded, in making friendships, but Roger in the end pressured me into moving in with the Laviers.

I stayed in a little room at the back of the house, separated by a patch of grass where several chickens were cooped and the occasional duck wandered freely. The main house was very small inside, the rooms at the back smaller.

I did not move there with any designs on Helene, and I can't say exactly why my thoughts about her changed from mere curiosity, to wonder, and then to love. She worked hard like Jerome, trimming branches from the trees and sorting bad fruit from the good. One day I watched her in the orchard alongside Jerome as they inspected the trees. She leaned in close to catch everything he was saying, her hand reaching up behind him to rest on his shoulder, such casual closeness only possible with those one trusts. The gesture, though minor, caused some of the stone that walled protectively around my battered heart to crumble and fall away. I suddenly wanted to know her, to be close to her, to feel her hand on my shoulder also.

Jerome was kind to me from the outset. Our conversations late into the night and our walks in the orchard showed that we shared many of the same thoughts. He had fought also, in the Franco-Prussian War, and I found myself opening up to him. He was a good listener and, what I was soon to learn, a kinder man than most. Because he understood, I could describe to him some of the horrors I'd seen, and he would rarely comment but tilt his head in my direction. It wasn't the polite nod of someone humoring me but someone who felt my pain and knew that death and soldiers stood shoulder to shoulder on the battlefield. That it was simply luck that sent you off on a stretcher, whether you walked yourself, whether you remained behind in the mud, or whether you became just a memory for the people who loved you.

Jerome cared for me, but the fact that he understood my position, even knew my thoughts at times, was the reason he felt torn about me pursuing Helene. He was protective of her, concerned that she could be hurt, either forced to endure the personal changes I might go through as a result of my experiences or scarred by my death as the relationship's possible conclusion.

Mariette was talkative and fun, and I enjoyed her company. She broke any awkward silences with her "discoveries," as I called them. Every day she had something new to tell us, about someone in the town, another story, information about another secret love affair that only she seemed to have access to. And I loved the way she would mimic people, hobble or dance or limp or stoop. She was entertaining, and clearly Helene was proud of her. Mariette thought she was more worldly than she was, something that frustrated Helene, though not enough to drive distance between them. More that Helene wanted to protect her from doing something impulsive or foolish. Mariette had captivated many men in my unit. Wild, beautiful, quick-witted, and what I would also come to see, incredibly loyal to those she loved.

Though I admired Mariette, it was Helene I sought to hold, who replaced my nightmares on the battlefields with dreams of her in my arms. I thought she could also be my cure. Often I would seek her out in the orchard to help her with her tasks, to feel the sunshine on my back, without the weight of a pack and rifle. It was exactly the prescription I needed for the ailment they were yet to medically name. Soldier's Heart had been talked about and terms like "shell shock," but the term "malingerer" had also been passed around, and I walked in its giant accusatory shadow.

Sometimes at night I would listen to the sounds of gunfire, and I would cover my ears and think of Helene. The townspeople had grown as used to the distant sounds of war as they were to the sound of bees or the rattle of wind in the trees. It was constant.

Helene avoided alone time with me at first. She did not trust herself, she admitted some time later. She did not trust a future with any man. She had watched men from an early age and learned that it was better to be out of a relationship than in one. Women get hurt, and get left to carry the fallout from any damage. I promised her I was not like other men, and I would not let her down. But I did, and I am ashamed for it. I became like the men she had known in her early childhood: a distant but ever-present void. And if I could have foreseen my weakness, I would have walked away from her without a backward glance before I broke her heart. Sweet Helene deserved the very best of people, which I was not. My mind was fragile, and one such as me cannot hold a relationship with any guarantees. Only with hindsight can I see that now.

I was shipped away to fight further battles, and my nightmares began again. Whether it was Helene who had temporarily healed me, I can't say, but I lasted the several months suffering only hypothermia, burns from mustard gas—though not as bad as Roger—a minor tremble to my hands, and a gash in my side that required extra time off. I was counting the days until I might return to the orchard.

By the time I came back to them, my French family, my trembling was still there but not as visible. In Helene's arms, the unexplainable crashing noises in my head lessened to some degree. I had read Helene my poems, and she had cried. She had loved me even knowing my fears, knowing that I wasn't brave. Though our togetherness did not mask all my fears. In my dreams I saw the finiteness of our time together. I saw a broken, barren future. I saw more death.

Helene began to trust me more. We would spend whole days together. In her free time we would walk the hills behind the town and sit amongst the wild and wilting irises and talk for hours. I told her things about my family. She never said how much she wanted to meet them. Helene would never say anything so presumptuous. But I wanted to take her home, present her like a prize, and show her the very best parts of me.

And one day she fell for the words I meant. I loved her. I kissed her, and she kissed me back, and it was a whole new world that had opened up to me. I had only ever expected a civil partnership in England, another landowner's daughter with whom I had already begun an affection. I was not one like Laurence to chase a girl; rather if it happened, then that would be the case, and for the sake of England and our name, I would endeavor to make a marriage work and a wife content.

Helene was like a warm sunrise, and she grew brighter and more colorful with each new minute I spent with her. I did not make any physical advances toward her beyond the first kiss, not at first. She was something rare and precious that I would wait an eternity for if it came to it. I recognized that she took much to heart and felt too deeply. In a little under a week, I suggested we marry and she should come with me to a town closer to my regiment once I was shipped out.

She was not so sure of course. The idea sounded grand, she said, but she could not leave Jerome. And knowing the man and what he did for these girls, I understood. So I said that after the war, I would live there. I would build a house on the land if Jerome allowed. Rudy could have Lakeland and run it indefinitely, to do with as he wished. It was impulsive, but at the time, I meant it. Perhaps being so close to death, one promises things they shouldn't. I wasn't the first, and that knowledge doesn't make me feel any better. When I heard from others boasting about their French conquests all in the name of their "last rites," I felt in some way that I was no different.

But I loved her in a way I hadn't loved any girl before. I had given all of me to the relationship at the time. Helene came to me one evening, and we spent the night together in the little room, and she left before the light tore open the truth. And I in that night had forgotten the war temporarily, forgotten even who I was, until I received a message several days later to say that it was my time to ship out.

The separation from all of them was unbearable. I had become family to each of them in a very short time, and their home was a place where I could be myself. Jerome never once looked at me as anything but an honorable man, even when he was counseling me over my relationship with Helene, telling me to not rush into anything. And then there was Mariette and her vivid, dark eyes. The disappointment in them was obvious when she realized I was in love with Helene, but then on my return our friendship grew stronger perhaps because of it. She no longer paraded herself in front of me like a debutante but spent time as a male friend would. We laughed, and she threw a bucket of water at me one day, and I would pull her hair when she wasn't looking. Little familiar things that told me I belonged. And we rode horses in the hours that Helene was otherwise occupied. Like a good friend, I loved her like the sister-in-law I hoped she would become.

She said that she would hate me, though, if I broke Helene's heart, and I naively assured her that I would not.

One night Helene lay under the window. She was clear in the dark, perhaps because I had already memorized every detail of her.

"You are changed from the last time," she said.

"What do you mean?"

"You are a little more distant, and you are thinner, and I can feel your heart beat rapidly. Your hands are unsteady. I think you need to speak to a doctor, perhaps spend some time at the hospital."

"I have never felt better," I said. I kissed her hard then, my hand reaching for her, a life raft, and a way to silence the truth of our situation. Our goodbye this time was long, and no longer timid: no more "I have enjoyed our time together" but an unquestioning "I love you." Though our thoughts of separation weren't totally without question.

"Will you promise me you'll come back?" she asked under the night-shine through the window, and I could hear the fear in her voice, seeing something ahead perhaps that I couldn't in that moment. It was a question I had hoped to avoid. There was no answer to it, and she knew this, too. One could not promise something decided by fate.

As I was preparing to leave the following day, Mariette hugged me tightly, frantically, which was her nature. Jerome could see the changes, too. I had spent but a total of two and a half weeks in their company, but it was like I was leaving my true family, the one in England now someone else's past. Not that I didn't love them; on the contrary Rudy was often on my mind; just that I was someone they might not recognize, someone who may no longer fit into their world.

As I headed off to the battlefields, it was as if I were suddenly torn from the womb, so secure I had felt in that brief time. Thrust into hellfire and the threat of death. But I was fighting then for different reasons. My battles were personal. I fought for Helene.

I felt guilty in a way that I had not written to my family in England, and I had no plans to go home. Some had returned to England for leave throughout the war, but I had chosen other places. Unintentionally cruel perhaps to Mother and Rudy, but I felt I couldn't face them. As if the killings would be read across my face. And I was afraid of questions that I might feel compelled to answer. And answers that would reveal I was afraid. Here at Jerome's orchard was where I found an existence that suited me. There were none of the expectations that I'd had before.

Our battles in Flanders felt like suicide as comrades vanished into dust beside me. Tanks firing relentlessly, ears numb, I ran over the sea of bodies, and I fell in the mud as shellfire hit the ground nearby to burst my eardrums.

But the most heartfelt loss was Willy, who was just a boy who reminded me of Rudy. A boy who lied about his age and then, when it all got to be too much, ran. He was considered a traitor to his country. In war perhaps. In civilian life, he was not, just a boy who wished only to return to his parents and his sisters, who had not foreseen the war as deadly but as an exotic adventure.

Wilbur was his name, and we called him Willy. He was fresh faced to start with like we all were. His smile was infectious. I could see he would have been all the time at home in trouble with his dear, frustrated mother. But he ran. That is all he will be remembered for in the years to come. When they took him away for execution, it felt as if it were my own. I think of all the things that brought me unstuck, and there were many; the one I think about, the one that comes up every time I close my eyes and ears, is the sound of him begging to go home as the soldiers led him away. I was the one to lead the others to the barn where he had fallen asleep after several days of mud and blood and smoke and noise.

I had tried to put young Wilbur out of my mind for months, but he loitered in my thoughts, ready to come again when I was at my weakest. And the thoughts and memories, the guilt and hurt, came to collect me finally at the next battle when we fell again. I was carried out of there and sent to a clearing hospital, wheeled into a hut for the ones they have no medical cause for, and then to a hospital away from the noise, the doctors said. I was in a giant bubble, unable to respond in a normal way to the world around me but intensely aware of the people near me, what they said to one another and the sounds. Noises made me cringe. Scraping noises, people calling out in pain. One night when I woke screeching, I was wheeled into a room of my own briefly.

They said they would write to my family. I begged them not to. How to explain what I was suffering from? I had scratches, bloodied knees, a bandage around my wrists, which was never explained to me, but that was all. There was nothing to show the internal damage. I looked whole, human, but my mind wasn't so at times, and the uncontrollable shaking could not be stemmed.

I could not let Helene see me like this. Her letters found me, and I had them sent back. I dreaded that she would come to visit.

Then came Mariette, and I don't remember the conversation, but I remember the face. She was my judge, and my sentence had been set before she left. A shunning that I deserved. I was then transferred to a place of respite while they decided what to do with me, where the shaking and the nightmares finally stopped. These weeks I have no clear memories of.

One day one of my superior officers came to speak with me. They were desperate. The war could be won with more men. They said I was needed back.

"Are you up to it?" he asked.

I paused. Of course I wasn't up to it, but I had been trained to respond differently.

"Some of those men in the hospital have lost legs, arms, half their faces. Be grateful that you are whole."

So I told myself I was whole, and I told myself to be grateful. Though I wasn't whole at all.

I was sent back out in the field, and my thoughts were then of my sweet family near Bailleul.

One of my colleagues grabbed me by the arm.

"Are you sure you can do this?" On the one hand he was concerned for my safety, but on the other he was concerned for his. He needed someone capable to watch his back, and although I had never let anyone down, I might.

I ran over the top of a slippery, trodden ridge, and we fought with weapons and rage, and I thought of my Helene. I had to do this for her. I tripped on the head of one of our soldiers dead and submerged in the mud, and I stayed where I fell, believing that this was where I should die. I could not fight another day. Exhausted, I fell asleep and woke to a strange calm. Under a cloud of smoke and darkening skies, I ran and hid like the coward that I am, stealing clothes, foraging in forests like some creature wild. I was a deserter.

In the chaos of shelling, I found Jerome with my son. The words he used, I can't remember, but I felt no connection with the child, not at that point. As if I were still crouched in potholed trenches, drenched and dreaming.

It was Jerome who woke me, who made me feel worthy, who stirred up feelings of who I was before. He passed Samuel into my arms as if to reward me. Jerome told me what had happened, and I felt the emotions as I once felt them as a whole man before: sad, thoughtful, curious, and angry.

But the look on Mariette's face when she saw me threw me once again into self-doubt. I had caused them all pain, and I could offer no reasons for it. I did not leave to find Helene to prove my worth; rather the urge was more instinctive. Something took over, perhaps the soldier deep within me, the carer, the son who shouldered high expectations. And I would not believe she was gone until I saw her for myself. I had found the woman I would spend my life with, and I knew, selfishly, the only one who could save my soul was Helene.

When Mariette repeated what the German captain had told her, I went carefully through the streets unnoticed. I had learned to keep my head down to watch for the enemy, and as I walked up toward the hospital, one of the sisters was rushing toward me. She paused when she saw me. She recognized my face and told me it was dangerous to be here.

I asked her about the hospital, if there was anyone still there. She said that some had got out before the bombs. If Helene had survived, she would have been taken elsewhere.

"And if not?"

She bowed her head and touched my hand. "Then she is still at the hospital." Behind her I could see the mutilated remains of the building. She then led me to a house that had been turned into a makeshift hospital, filled with the injured. Downstairs people lay bleeding and begging to be helped.

"Are you a doctor?" said someone attending to them as I entered, and I shook my head. Their hopeful expressions receded as they hurried back to their hopeless tasks.

I found Helene upstairs on a bed alone. At first I thought it was my mind playing tricks on me, because until that time I had imagined her caught beneath rubble, an image that clawed its way back each time I had tried to erase it.

I stepped toward the bed. Her head was turned sideways, her eyes closed, and I scanned the length of her. Her nightgown was bloodied, and I was yet to learn that it was not from fallen bricks but the after bleeding from the birth of our child.

She opened her eyes and saw me, and I caved then, tears falling.

She gripped my hand, and I knelt beside her while she stroked my hair.

"I knew you would come. I dreamed this."

I swallowed my remorse and tears that would in time unleash. We were caught between armies, and Germans walked beneath the window with guns, but we were together again and in love, and I vowed to her then that no one would draw us apart.

"I am taking you to a doctor in one of the Allied towns. Jerome and Mariette are leaving shortly."

She nodded, eyes half-closed. She was gravely ill, though her first thought had been for me. Did she know? I wondered since. Had she been told of my illness, or had she seen it in my eyes? I picked up early that Helene could read a person and understand things better than anyone.

I lifted her up gingerly, her head against my shoulder, then briskly walked down the narrow stairs to the streets. A German soldier saw Helene in my arms and said nothing. These were strange times that I was walking freely with the enemy. The soldier perhaps was too tired to question me, too aware that defeat was the difference between here and a mile away.

Mariette's face when she saw us was one of disbelief and then of wonder. We were all together, the four of us again—now five—and we made our way to a village, where Mariette left to find someone to help us.

"We have a son," Helene said, lying in the back of the cart. "Can I see him?" She did not have the strength at that point to turn her head to look at the child in Jerome's arms.

Jerome passed the little boy bundled in dampened blankets, and I held him before her. She smiled, but she didn't reach for him. She frowned a little, and I will never know if this was from the pain in her body or the ache of being unable to hold him. "He is beautiful. I remembered the name from a story you told me, one that you read as a child."

I nodded and put my finger to her lips that were blue and cold. She went very still.

"Stay with me," I whispered in her ear. But she didn't. She left us then. And Jerome reached for her wrist, then closed her eyes, and the pain of it, if not for the child in my arms, would have consumed me. If not for the child, if not for the task I was then given, I would have run toward the enemy, begged them to shoot me. But for Samuel then, I had to reach safety. Though there is still a question of purpose, whether I deserve to stand while Helene now lies deep in the earth in a graveyard behind a broken church.

Mariette returned, and there are no words to describe her loss, only that there were times hence when she did not live well without her sister. She had moments of darkness that I recognized, too.

It was Jerome who decided what we should do next, after discussing our possibilities beyond Bailleul, a future where there were no wars and no fear of capture from my own men. We reached a small church in a village that would later be destroyed. Jerome asked the priest to marry us, a way of protecting us all, telling him that our possessions and identities were destroyed but that we needed the blessing of the church without the necessity of marriage banns, for the sake of the child. A man of the cloth could deny that, might turn his back, but he did not. Though I think as the enemy threatened shortly to wipe out his village, he would not have turned away anyone.

Jerome took us to Le Havre and gave us what little money he had, along with his name, which would allow me to leave the shores of France without my tarnished name on record. Mariette begged him to follow, to find another passage when he could. But I could not see it. Not with his sister there, and his wife and son buried in Flemish soil. He was planning to volunteer at the front, to help support soldiers in any way they needed. It was personal then, his duty, to assist to drive the enemy out, to stop them from reaching Lenore. But we did not know his plans yet, not until we received a final letter from him, then heard no more. Not until Mariette had written to the registrar for deaths did she learn his fate a year later. He died from shellfire while delivering meals to a clearing hospital. Mariette was inconsolable for days, and I nearly lost her, the girl she was. But she is stronger than any of us. Of that I am certain.

And as for me, my struggles continue. Every day is different from the last. Not just that the sky or wind is changed, but within me fires burn and fires die, rage and fear run through my veins, and a purpose I am yet to find.

LAURENCE

1922

CHAPTER 31

Mariette's sharp movements and darting eyes reminded me of a restless filly eager to break from the herd to run free. Her seeming unrestraint was what drew me at first, followed closely by her belief that she was better than any of us, despite her peasant upbringing. She was refreshing, since most of the women and men I'd associated with had always known their place. But if I'm truly honest, what caused me to pause, to scheme, to plan for a battle, was that Rudy was lovesick. And the two of them together would spell my end. I had to put a stop to them first, and any notion of their future together. And if that meant breaking her in some way, so be it.

I saw something that I believe no one else had seen. I had always been more clearheaded and discerning, though one such gift in my family is not often extolled or appreciated. I had seen that the boy was most certainly Edgar's. Though the frame and colors were different, the way Samuel put his lips together thinly when he examined me took me back to when Edgar and I were boys. The times when Edgar would be judge and jury and executioner, and always just before I received the harshest punishment: I would be cut off from him, ignored, while he strutted around unchallenged by anyone, unseeing and unwilling to see that I was as good, if not better than he was at most things. Samuel's tilt of his head when he examined me—and the look in his eye of someone who is far away in some distant thought—was Edgar also. Edgar has seemed for most of my life cold and impenetrable. Not the quiet achiever everyone read him to be. Beneath the façade there were dark thoughts and insecurities, though, under general observations, they were too fleeting and subtle to knit them into something one could describe as an obvious flaw.

I learned my place from the moment I joined my father's dinner table. Edgar was the one who answered the questions, to whom, when speaking, everyone listened. Oh certainly, they would humor me, even enjoy the vitality and rhetoric I brought to the table, especially Mother, but they would *hear* Edgar. His voice was the clearest to all and the only one that mattered. So to draw attention, which I can admit to myself I did on more than one occasion unsuccessfully, would only ever end in more condemnation, more punishment. And each time, Edgar would shut me out further. I wanted to be seen as Edgar's equal, which never came. My mother, intelligent but insignificant in the scheme of things—since she had no control of the finances and was too worried about what everyone thought—doted on me, but it wasn't the same as respect. I had inherited her love of fine things and her skill of mistrusting everyone, though I was much better at covering it.

Edgar didn't always despise me. There were a few years, during our early days at school together, when he took me under his wing. I made friends quickly, excelled at subjects like Edgar, and the two of us played sport together on many occasions. We were both competitive by nature, and Edgar always respected a good competitor. I had grown tall quickly, though lankier and less muscled than Edgar. I was only just beneath his skill level in rowing and rugby. Edgar noticed this and appreciated me a little more than he had when we were small. We even talked about what we might do together when we graduated, entertaining the idea of starting a joint business.

If I have to pinpoint a time in history when our momentary solidarity fractured permanently, it was an afternoon when we were playing a game of rugby. It was a combination of my friends and Edgar's. Edgar and I were on the same team, and our side won because of my final goal. I was amiably jostled and patted by Edgar and company all the way back to the school clubhouse, where we made our plans to spend the rest of the day by the river. We were high on sporting adrenaline, shoving and pushing each other in the water and egging each other on to swing on a rope from a tree that hung over the river.

One of the boys from my year, and new to the group, was smaller than many of us and not very good at rugby. He should never have been included since he had nearly cost us the game by dropping the ball a number of times. I'm not sure why he was even there that afternoon, since he also chose not to swim. He was somewhat sickly, had taken many days off school. There had been a rumor that he lived with his grandparents and he had several younger brothers who would not be attending the same school, as they could not afford it.

Looking back, I don't see why Edgar thought "the event," as it became known for a short period, was such a big deal. It was an accident, but he made it appear far more sinister on my part. I told the boy, Nigel, to have a swing on the rope, but he refused, making some feeble excuse that he wasn't allowed to go in the water. So I grabbed him anyway around the waist and, with my other hand clutching the rope, swung out wildly over the creek. He shrieked as we swung back and forth, clinging on to me tightly. Most of the group stood on the edge of the embankment, waiting their turn on the rope, laughing and validating the prank, and it was perhaps this noise that drowned out the sharp rasps of Nigel's breathing. He begged me not to let go, but as I began to lose my grip, I instructed him to reach for the rope, which he did; then I released myself into the water, grabbing his shorts and pulling them down with me as I fell. I left Nigel pantless, hanging from the rope and whimpering for help. Nigel could not hold on and within seconds fell into the water and did not surface immediately.

The laughter from the embankment had died down a little. Some had stopped laughing, and the smiles of others were falling quickly away. And there was Edgar, who was not smiling at all. He was staring at Nigel, who had noisily resurfaced and flapped his arms wildly to stay afloat. Edgar's lips were pressed together thinly that day.

They say it was the coldness of the water that sparked the asthma attack. I didn't see it in the white wash of frantic splashing. We were close enough to the shallows, where he would have been able to stand, but he didn't, panicking, and I took the opportunity to push him and his noise back under the water. Moments later I didn't see the punch to the side of my head that knocked me sideways. When I turned to react to my assailant, Edgar was lifting Nigel up and carrying him to the grassy shore. I had gulped back so much water that I could not yell after him, which was probably for the best, once I'd realized the seriousness of the situation. The boys on the side were watching Edgar carrying the boy over the embankment toward them, their faces slightly aghast, which I took at first to be because of Edgar's violent act toward me, before they all turned to look at me. I climbed out of the water to witness Edgar turn Nigel onto his side. Nigel was wheezing, and his face had gone a bluish tone. Edgar then threw him over his large shoulder and walked swiftly toward the school, no doubt to the infirmary.

"He suffers from asthma," said one of the boys. "I thought you knew that."

I did. But I decided not to say so, nor add that I had little idea about such a condition, which would only make me appear stupid or cruel.

After that, Nigel left the school and didn't come back, though there was no word of the reasons, whether from health, humiliation, or finances. But it didn't matter. He died, we learned, months later from another episode. He was gone, and I was relieved that I would not have to see him again as a reminder of the moment that Edgar and I ceased to be friends and future business partners. Of course, it would be irrational to think that it was the only thing that had drawn us apart: an overexuberant brother and a sickly boy. There were other minor "events" before and since that have highlighted our differences and given Edgar some sort of perceived moralistic position of power over me. But it was not only one-sided. I never got over the punch to the head that left me dazed and bruised. He had humiliated me, and this I found hard to forgive. He never raised any discussion about what had occurred, but he no longer came to our rugby games and took more interest in other sports and books. When we went home he would find reasons to spend as little time with me as possible and while away the hours with Rudy or alone.

Once, several weeks after the event, I passed his dorm room and saw him sitting, reading.

"How did you fare in your exams?" I asked.

"Fine," he said, pleasantly enough, though he was looking back at his book, a touch dismissively, as if I'd interrupted.

I began to walk away but stopped and turned. "Look, Edgar," I said. "I had no idea Nigel was asthmatic."

He looked away at something over my shoulder, a habit that would grow to be annoying. It was as if I didn't exist for him at times.

"You should have known," he said. "He was your friend."

"Of course he was my friend."

"Well, let's hope your friends never have to rely on you on a battlefield."

He gave me his punishing blue-eyed stare that told me nothing I said would aid in my defense. I had made my peace with the episode at the river, but it seemed that Edgar had not.

"You show little empathy and don't know when to stop," he said. "I thought maybe you had grown out of it. Perhaps you never will."

I laughed then because he was ridiculous, and I stormed off. And on the battlefield years later, I would discover for certain that what he said was true. But it was a good thing to have in war: to not stop, to not become emotionally attached to those on either side, to keep fighting and killing until we ridded French fields of every last Hun. I had saved hundreds in my quest to *not stop*, to keep going until the end, regardless of those falling around me. And that weakness, which Edgar sought to highlight, proved to be my strength, for it would be I who returned a hero, not he. I would come home with medals, promotions, and bullet grazes alone. And not only would he not return a hero, he would not return to inherit the manor.

I never told Mother that when I was visiting some of my privates in the hospital, for I helped my battalion in the final months to victory, I had seen Edgar. I had heard he'd been admitted, though I had not gone out of my way earlier to visit. He was being treated in the wing where they sought to understand those unseen injuries that allowed men not to fight. I had seen him there shaking and trembling, and he had looked up as if he didn't recognize me. But he did. I am sure of it. Some might say the perceived contest I had made between us was petty. But as I stood at the side of his bed, above him, I felt like I had already conquered my enemy.

"Do you know him?" one of the nurses asked as she approached his bedside with a cup full of medicine, while Edgar stared me down.

"No," I said. What was the point? He had burned our bridge years ago, and I did not want it known that I shared the same blood as someone so ill equipped for war. Watching his suffering, I felt nothing and remembered only that he had despised me throughout our years together.

I had returned not to a hero's welcome at Lakeland, but to a wake for Edgar, missing in action. Lakeland, it seemed, didn't welcome heroes. My mother had been pleased to see me, but by that time, she was broken, and I could not claim victory, not in the way I'd expected. Rudy received me with suspicion and distance, as he had always done as a child, and his grief for Edgar was as clear as his regret that it was I who had returned, not he.

So I shed the uniform and went back to what I should have been doing, lording it up in London. Without the help of my father's poor record, and with only limited use of my future inheritance, I still carved out an existence of fellow acquaintances, and I took up from whence I'd left. Though, my life felt hollow, and the more I entertained, the hollower I felt until the only time it felt truly good was to be drinking, smoking, and frequenting illegal opium houses still operating in the filthy basement bowels of London, where it would help me to remember how successful I was. And each time I returned to the estate, Lakeland seemed to appear more monstrous, a reminder of a dull and lonely childhood that I did not deserve. I could not wait to be rid of it and place Mother somewhere else, to carve up the land and live in London. The estate was impressive for weekends, as it showed where I had come from, but that was all. It was not my future.

And the day that I received a letter from Mother telling me about Mariette's visit, I felt colder than I had since Edgar's dismissal at the river. Even the violence of war and the fear of death did not affect me near so much as those two moments. Was I flawed? Some would think so, but I like to think of myself instead as a survivor of a family that was flawed.

Mariette was restless but, as I learned quickly, not fickle, which I had not seen until we were alone in the dark looking for eggs. She was ravishing against the inky-blue night. I put my arm around her, and she didn't resist, not at first. Then when I drew her close to my cheek, to feel her warm breath against me, she pushed me hard away, forcing me to drop the lamp. I am honest when I say that I have never once been so brutally rejected. Women have pretended to be refined at such points, but never so blunt and cold.

"I am not interested in you," she whispered to me in the dark.

She turned to leave, and I felt humiliated, picking up the lamp again and running after her. I grabbed hold of her shoulder.

"What are you doing?" she asked, offended by my touch.

"Rudy will never give you the life you want here. If that's what you're thinking."

"You have no idea what I'm thinking."

"He will never love you. He loved Edgar too much. In the back of his mind, he will be thinking about Edgar every time he makes love to you."

She turned then but not before I caught some moment of doubt on her part.

"It is perhaps cruel what you do to him," I continued. "Keeping Edgar alive in his mind."

"It is perhaps not cruel if it is you I choose. Is that what you are saying?"

She had called out my hypocrisy, and at that moment Rudy's lamplight filtered through the trees to head toward us.

She'd had the last word, but I'd seen the effect of our conversation, more noticeable by her somewhat dismissive approach toward Rudy once we arrived back at the house.

The following morning, as fate would have it, Elizabeth was feeling unwell, and Mariette showed great concern for her. I suggested Mariette accompany us on the ride to the train station, to assist her.

"Oh, would you please!" pleaded Elizabeth, ever so sweetly so that Mariette could hardly refuse.

Once we'd dispatched everyone to the station, and Mariette and I waved our goodbyes, and we were alone, I had to atone for the night before to successfully enact my plan. I said that we should be friends, that whatever had been said about me, I had in fact attempted to change. I told her that I loved my brother and was genuinely concerned that she would hurt Rudy.

"I could never hurt Rudy."

"It is probably too late for that."

She wanted to say something, but she didn't, perhaps hoping that I would just be quiet as we commenced the drive back. She tried to dismiss me, but I could see that it got to her. I told her that I believed her about her son. She looked at me then, attempting to assess the truth. I told her that I had recognized Edgar in the child.

"I can help the boy's future better than anyone. If you are reasonable with me, then I will be reasonable with you. If you will hear me out, I will explain my intentions."

I had her attention. She perhaps imagined the potential of a bribe: a way of them both departing safely with some financial reward. I suggested we stop for refreshment at a teahouse to which she agreed after some hesitation, though I could see her eyes darting around, as if looking for an exit if she needed one.

We were seated near the window overlooking the street, and she examined the fine china we were given and the street with passersby. I told her briefly that the building was two hundred years old, and she analyzed the dark wooden table and intricate white lace with a mixture of awe and curiosity. I must admit her naivety and vulnerability were intoxicating. In the blink of an eye, she could go from someone strong and determined to someone that one might seek to own.

After some more light conversation about history and the merits of my company, she seemed to grow impatient, perhaps thinking of Rudy back at the manor.

"What is it that you can do for Samuel? And why should I trust you?"

It was interesting that she continued to assume she had the position of power here. But I feigned a certain amount of acquiescence. My final hand was yet to be played.

"Firstly," I said, "I must know. Are you here for you, or for recognition of Samuel?"

"Well, of course for Samuel! He needs to know his family."

"Is that what Edgar told you?"

"No, of course not. He was killed before he knew I carried his child. But I know it is what he would have wanted." I felt that a small part of what she said was genuine. As a lawyer I had been used to liars also. And this no doubt would be a contest as to how well she played a part versus how well I applied my craft.

"What we discuss here must not be spoken about to Rudy," I told her.

"Why not?"

"For various reasons, which I will get to, that you will understand shortly. But you are probably clever enough to realize that Rudy is incredibly gullible and too infatuated to search deeply for the truth. And as the older brother, I must protect him."

She smiled at this.

"You find it amusing."

"I do not believe your good intentions about your brother. The two of you are not close at all."

"Ah, but you must surely understand that no matter what, blood will always protect blood. Our history shows that we have killed to protect and preserve our family name, irrespective of sibling differences. I am not sure how close you were to your family, but I imagine you know exactly what I am saying."

Two small frown lines appeared between her brows. It was clear that I had reached deeper into her conscience.

"And Mother, though sweet to the boy, will protect her good name better than anyone. If it is not in the best interests of both Rudy and myself, she could look away from the truth even if it stood boldly in front of her. She has spent years to rectify the damage our father did to our standing."

Mariette was listening intently. There were no more casual glances outside.

"To obtain what you want, which I feel is recognition for Samuel, you need to tell me everything."

"There is little else that you need to know," she said.

"Oh, I don't know . . . I would have thought that Edgar's mental illness was important."

She opened her mouth to say something but found no words. I had pulled some of her assurance away.

"I was there, you seem to forget. Do you not think that a brother would inquire of his brother only battlefields apart? That I would not be notified if my brother was in hospital?"

She shook her head and stared at her hands.

"You can't mention . . . He couldn't . . ."

"He couldn't what? What couldn't he do?"

"The truth would destroy your mother and Rudy."

"Which is exactly why I've said nothing so far."

I witnessed genuine fear in her gaze as she waited and watched my lips that might deliver more of the truth she feared.

"If you know something else, you need to tell me," I said.

She shook her head. "He went back to fight, and then he went missing."

"Might he have deserted perhaps? Germans were not kind to deserters, even English ones, as you might be aware."

"Of course not!" she said.

"There was much talk about those with illnesses of the mind. He is not the only one to have gone missing, presumed dead. And many of those put others they fought alongside in danger."

"In my heart, I know he is dead."

"Poor Edgar!" I said. Though she did not buy my sympathy, for she narrowed her eyes slightly. She was planning to fight whatever else I might say. "Well, I must tell Mother the truth about his illness. I don't know why I didn't earlier," I said, feigning a slight naivety of the consequences of such an action.

"Edgar would not want that."

"Is that what he told you?"

"No."

"Then it shouldn't matter."

She was silent. She had been prepared to face the others, their questions. But not even my brother Edgar knew how I would react, what I would say.

"He's alive, isn't he?" I felt a pang of fear this might be true. And if she held the truth, then I had to get rid of the evidence. It was more important to me that the truth remained buried.

"No!" Though she could not look at me. Her normally olive skin had paled. "What a thing to say!"

"I think you are lying about Edgar."

"This talk is ridiculous!" She stood up. "Please take me back home immediately!"

"I know my brother well enough that he would never want his secret known. A secret he left in your care."

She looked down at her skirt.

"Sit down, please," I said in a paternal tone.

She eased back down in the chair. There were other truths behind her guardedness. I felt certain of it.

She raised her chin. "You obviously want something in return for you to stay silent about his illness. Is it me?"

I laughed at that, and she looked suddenly embarrassed. "Forgive me for that outburst. If you are talking about last night, it is quite in my nature to take an opportunity when and if one arises. But no, my dear, something temporary perhaps at the time, but the moment is gone."

She touched her throat.

"Not that you aren't desirable of course."

She turned away. I was playing with her. Sometimes such games got the better of me.

"I'm sorry for last night, and you are quite right. In return for my silence, I want you gone from here."

She sighed. She did not appear surprised.

"Rudy wishes to marry me."

"He will get over it in time." He had moved quicker than I thought, which made it all the more important to hurry this along. I imagined Rudy would be devastated no doubt. He was weak that way.

"I will think about it," she said.

This angered me slightly, that she was delaying a response. Though I had to remain calm.

"As you wish."

I finished my tea, then stood up and extended my hand. She stood and took it, and we walked to the car. Once both of us were inside, I sat there without starting the engine. I could not let her arrive home flustered, which might draw questions from Rudy.

"Mariette, I know that you are thinking about the boy. That is why you are here. And trust me, I believe you that Samuel is Edgar's son. But I'm not sure that either Mother or Rudy truly do or ever will. Rudy loves you and may keep the boy because of it, but in his heart he will always be wondering if you have been truthful."

She turned her head to look at me.

"The boy deserves to be here," she said.

"Of that I have no doubt." I paused.

I started the car, but I could tell she was thinking about my words all the way back to the house. I had put doubt in there. There were two things I felt were true, though neither could I prove: whether he was still alive, Edgar had lived at least beyond the end of the war and the boy was his. But Mariette's part in this I wasn't sure about, and it was the uncertainty about her and her designs on Rudy that were the reasons she couldn't stay.

She did not come out of her room that night to join us for dinner, much to Rudy's chagrin. I was glad at least that our conversation had had the desired effect.

In the morning, Rudy looked weary. He was clearly bereaved that he had not shared the last night with Mariette he'd been hoping for.

Mariette did not come out of her room for an early breakfast. I saw Rudy's fearful face as he departed, leaving me behind with the woman he had fallen in love with.

The child wandered into the kitchen, where I was preparing some tea late that morning, escaping the confines of his room. He seemed pleased to have company. I had no experience with children, though I knew enough about people that if you want the right answers, you have to ask the right questions.

"Do you want a piece of cake for breakfast?"

He nodded and eagerly climbed on top of the stool at the large preparation table.

I found the tin that held Peggy's cakes. She had not changed her hiding spot in twenty years. I cut him a piece, and he took it greedily, licking the jam glaze thickly spread between two sponge cakes.

"Do you miss France?"

He shook his head and frowned, slightly confused. Perhaps, I thought, geography was not his strong point.

"No?"

He bit his lip. "It isn't called France."

"Oh! What do you call it then?"

He shook his head. I could not tell if he didn't know or had been prepped for questions.

"I used to love it there," I said. "I left some very special people there whom I miss very dearly."

"I don't miss it at all."

"What a pity! Was it terrible?"

He nodded. "Sometimes there were bad men."

"Oh dear! Not anyone you know, I hope."

"Not my uncle but other men. My uncle told me they were bad men who might find him. My uncle took me across the sea when I was small."

"Is he expecting you back?"

He shrugged.

I went and retrieved a small service photograph of Edgar to show to Samuel.

"Is this your uncle?"

He looked carefully at the image and then looked me in the eyes and shrugged. "He doesn't wear those clothes."

I felt a sense of hatred. Hatred for Edgar for deceiving us, for being weak, and hatred for Rudy who had dismissed me, who had not looked up to me as he had done with Edgar. And Mother, too, for being too careless with her preferences. There is no doubt she loved me, but she had put us in a certain order within her heart. And in the moments after, I wondered whether Rudy had questioned the boy also. Though it was doubtful. Mother had said nothing, and they both were likely to dismiss the imaginative ramblings of a child if indeed they'd bothered to question him.

Bert came in moments later and said he was going to one of the farms to help with the last of the sowing and discussed the recent yield. Bert may have had a preference for Rudy, who loved to work alongside him, but he still had respect for those in charge and was honest at least to report that things were bad. Mariette appeared wan in the doorway and acknowledged us. She asked Samuel if he had eaten.

"I have made sure of it," I answered for him, and gave the child a wink. She looked at the empty plate on the table in front of him, licked clean of crumbs.

"Does the boy want to come with me?" Bert asked Mariette.

She didn't look at me as I translated Bert's words for the boy. Though the sudden eagerness in Samuel's expression suggested he partly understood.

"No, I don't think he should today," she said uneasily.

The boy looked solemn and crossed his arms, his chin on his chest.

"Oh, what a sad face!" I said to the boy, then turned to Mariette. "Surely it would be good for the boy in this sunshine. The sunshine won't last. It's better that he make the most of it."

Bert was watching Mariette carefully. Her tension was obvious.

"Please, *Maman*!" said Samuel, jumping off the seat, and bouncing up and down while grabbing her skirt. She bit her lip in thought.

"Very well," she said, and turned to Bert.

"Perhaps you would like to come also, miss?" said Bert, glancing briefly in my direction.

She paused before she answered. She was torn, though she knew as well as I that we had unfinished business.

"No, thank you. I will stay. How long will you be?"

"I'll be back just on nightfall, I expect," said Bert, perhaps to comfort her. "I've packed plenty of food and drinks, so he won't go hungry. And the farmers will no doubt spoil him silly."

They left, and Mariette watched them from the door, while I helped myself to a slice of pie that Peggy had made for us.

"Would you like some?"

"No, thank you," she said, and left me quickly before I had time to question her.

I ate in the kitchen. It was a cold, dreary place with a stale odor of burnt fat. I remembered the times as a small boy I'd sat in the kitchen with the help, wondering why I couldn't be at the table with Edgar and Mother and Father. It seemed like a punishment having to sit in there with Rudy.

On the top floor in the library, I stared at the photographs of us as boys. It brought no sense of nostalgia. The best times were when we were sailing. Or when I would go hunting with Father and Edgar. There were some good moments, though even back then I was planning something grander. Even back then I imagined being in charge of the manor. Though now it wasn't the building or the ownership but the money that it sat on that would bring me satisfaction.

I was becoming a little impatient and poured myself a whiskey in the drawing room. The longer I sat, the more I wanted Mariette gone.

And soon! I stood to find her when she entered the room. Her cheeks were pink, eyes swollen, it seemed, from crying.

"I will leave as you request, but I have left a letter to Rudy to at least put him at rest that nothing bad has happened to me." I agreed, knowing that I would likely have to destroy it.

"You have made the right decision for all."

"We will leave as soon as Samuel returns, if you would kindly drive us to the station."

"Us?" I queried.

She narrowed her eyes.

"I'm sorry if I wasn't clear," I said. "It is only you who must leave."

It was important to separate her from Rudy. Together they were a greater threat.

"Then you are as big an ass as Edgar described."

Perhaps it was the mention of Edgar, but something turned within me. She was wild and perhaps more difficult to predict than most. I would have to take a greater gamble.

"I know that Edgar is alive. And if he ever comes back here, he will be imprisoned or likely hanged."

"He is no deserter!"

"The boy identified him from a photograph," I said.

"He recognizes him only because he knows him from another one."

"He said that he saw him before he left. As 'Uncle Fabien.'"

"He is imaginative," she said. "He is only a boy, and it is more a wish that his father be alive."

I laughed. She was even craftier under pressure. She had no doubt been used to a different sort of life, the kind where one must fight hard to survive.

"Mariette! If you don't leave now, I can assure you things will become very uncomfortable for you here."

"You have no right to speak to me like that! You have no idea what you are talking about."

"I can tell you now that I will get to the bottom of it," I said. "You think you can turn up on our doorstep and turn our world upside down?"

"Edgar said you only look after yourself."

I could feel him close by, almost listening in. It gave me more reason to fight.

"Au contraire! I will look after the boy, make sure he is a ward of the estate and raise him as if he is my very own."

He remained a threat as long as she held on to him. Out of her control, his fate was up to me.

"I cannot leave him," she said.

"I can tell you that if you don't," I said in a tone that had turned threatening, "I will expose to the family that Edgar was mentally unfit to be a soldier, but also I will advise the authorities that Edgar was a deserter. Perhaps it might also be that Edgar has plans for you to marry Rudy, which is no doubt against the law if you are already married, with hopes that you will send him money. And you will be seen as the seductress of Edgar's brother to lay hands on the estate. Polygamy comes with some penalty. Or perhaps you are acting alone, and the boy is an imposter and actor also. Either way, it looks very bad for you. And with you in prison, the boy would have to be sent to an orphanage. I can tell you that Rudy might be thinking to champion you, but after I had explained my case, he would think to question the boy also, and once he does, and if he thought for one second that Edgar might be alive, he would drop you in a heartbeat. He is more loyal to Edgar than probably you are."

"Perhaps you are wrong about Rudy," she said, her words less confident, her hopes and plans fading.

"I have had years more to understand my brother. I understand him well enough. Regardless, Mariette, you can't fight the truth of the situation. You do not belong here."

Strangely, that seemed to reach her more than anything else I'd said. The look she had was that of someone who has come to some realization, which perhaps had been in front of them all the time.

"Is the boy yours?" I asked.

She hesitated before answering. "I can assure you that he is Edgar's, and I am the only mother he knows."

I let the question rest. She had answered it well enough. She had no cause to be here.

"I will give you money as well. It is in our mutual interest, Mariette," I said, resuming my former charm. "You obviously care about the boy, and no harm will come to him. The boy is most certainly Edgar's. He will be here in his rightful position, and you will return to yours. Wherever that may be."

She thought for a moment. She was trembling. She had been prepared for Rudy but not well enough for me.

"I can't just leave here without saying goodbye to Samuel or Rudy. You can't expect that Rudy will accept what you say. That I left. He will question everything."

"It is precisely for that reason you can't be here when he returns in a week. You will rewrite your letter to say that you wish to return to your life, that you do not love him, but that you wish to leave Edgar's boy. And I will take care of everything from there. And no one will know the dark secrets of my brother."

She bit her lip hard. I guessed to stop herself from crying.

"And you promise me that you will look after the boy."

"You have my word. Lakeland will always be his home."

Of course I had no intention of keeping the child.

"I will drive you to the station."

I looked at my watch, anxious that dusk was soon to fall, and Bert would return any moment.

"Let me go and collect my things," she said.

She took some time before she finally stepped into the foyer, wearing a black dress, carrying her travel bag and a little velvet money purse at her wrist. I knew we had only minutes before Bert appeared on the horizon.

I reached for my wallet and pulled out a ten-pound banknote, which she accepted without question. She then climbed into the passenger seat and placed her bag on her lap, and I shut her door and walked around to the driver's side. The plan was to take her to the station, but I'll admit I wanted to be rid of her forever, and thoughts and doubts entered my mind, wondering if the plan was permanent enough. And it was this that perhaps she picked up on.

"I believe you are not a good person, Master Watts," she said as I climbed in next to her. "And I like to do things my own way."

Suddenly she had unlatched the door to climb out, and I knew instinctively she was planning to run. I leaned across to grab her as she fled, but the cheap lace from the bottom of her skirt tore away in my hand. She ran then toward the house and into the foyer and through the doors of the great hall, turning at this point to see how far I was away, and as she did so, she bumped into a stand that held a statue, causing it to topple and smash to the floor. She had reached the French doors at the rear of the hall by the time I had entered, abandoning her travel bag behind her. I was about to follow her down toward the trees near the lake when I heard Bert at the front door.

I stood for a moment to watch Mariette run out of sight and into the darkness. I could explain this if she returned. I would say that she stole my money and was planning to flee but I caught her. I walked back into the house to face Bert. He asked if everything was all right, and I told him that Mariette had run off into the night and I needed to search for her. He looked concerned and had to tear himself away to fetch Mother from the station and made the decision to take Samuel with him. It was clear from this that he didn't trust me. But with both of them gone, it would give me time to find her.

I looked for her in the places we'd been the night before, the dark spaces under tree canopies, and called for her in neighboring fields. I came back to the house, found the letter she'd left for Rudy, and set fire to it. A con artist did not leave letters of apology. I even took Mother's jewels to make it look like she was there only for the money. I would sell them of course to pay for debts that were waiting for me back in London. Then I threw her bag far into the lake. As I came around the side of the house, I met everyone back from their day away and was surprised that Rudy was there, too. Of course he accused me of something devious and attacked me unsuccessfully. I had no time for any of them.

Mariette might resurface, but I would be ready for that fight when it came to it. I didn't have to worry, as fortune would have it. She had left of her own accord and had no one but Rudy to fight for Samuel's claims to the estate if it came to it. And certainly Rudy did not have the courage or resourcefulness.

But even then I couldn't rest. I couldn't be certain of anything. Back in London sleep did not come as easily as it had. The boy's recognition of Edgar and the question of whether my eldest brother was alive haunted me in the weeks ahead, with visions of Edgar back from the dead, or wherever else, to claim the house, alongside Mariette. The society parties, whiskey, and opium silenced these thoughts briefly; however, these came with a heavy cost. Mother's jewels were traded quickly for cash that dissolved into loans that exceeded their value. Soon my debts were mounting, creditors hounded my door, and friends were falling away. And while Samuel sat at the house at Mother's whim, Lakeland's debts were also growing.

I woke one night sweating from an opium-filled dream about Edgar rising up from a battlefield on fire, with fear that I had not done enough to protect my inheritance. I remembered the will that Rudy spoke of and wondered whether it might still be in the house. The thought of it terrified me. A scrap of paper that might ruin my future.

I left to do what I should have finished earlier.

RUDY

1922

CHAPTER 32

Edgar had spent all night at my side, occasionally helping me sip water, while I drifted in and out of sleep. I had been unwell, dehydrated, dazed, and exhausted, before eventually falling deeply into sleep. When I woke many hours later, with my condition much improved, there was no sign of my brother, but the man who had evicted me from the hotel sat nearby.

He nodded in my direction before moving to a pot on top of a wood burner and ladling some soup into a bowl to bring to me. I sat up stiffly. My fingers were red and swollen, and my face felt burnt. I took the bowl shakily.

The meaty broth reminded me that I'd had nothing to eat the previous day. I wolfed it down and was grateful to have it refilled.

"Where is he?" I asked halfway through my second helping, suddenly noticing the man was watching me carefully. Panic had also gripped me that Edgar might disappear from my life again.

"He'll be here soon."

"My name is Rudy," I said as he took the empty bowl away.

He laughed. "I know who you are," he said casually, and introduced himself as Joe.

My clothes had been removed, and I wrapped the blanket from the bed around my shoulders to stand up unsteadily. Joe moved to help me, but I put my hand up to decline his offer as I stepped toward the front window. His attitude of concern toward me was vastly different from that of earlier.

The cabin sat on a hill surrounded by spruce and fir trees, with sweeping views across a frozen lake framed by rolling hills and snow-covered trees. It was beautiful, and on a gold-and-gray-blue horizon, the sun was low and gliding sideways across its kingdom.

I was about to question Joe when Edgar stepped into the room, stamping his feet to shake the snow from his boots. He smiled in my direction, and my face gave my feelings away. I was a child again, and Edgar had come home for the holidays. It was those same feelings of relief and security, of knowing things will be all right. With sleep and warmth, I was returning to health. I went toward him, but he grabbed my shoulders firmly to lead me back to the cot.

"Sit down for a while. There is nothing to rush for."

Edgar went straight into a description about his logging business before I had any chance to explain or question. He had finished working elsewhere and recently started his own business with the help of his friends. He had been given a land grant and had sourced local men who had no land of their own, to work with him and equally share the profits. They would work in the winters when some businesses were closed. He'd seen an opportunity and had made a success of it. He strangely didn't ask what I was doing here, how I had found him, and he did not even ask after Mother, which at the time I did not see as odd, since I was just so happy to be there, to see him in the flesh.

"You gained a name here as 'the fisherman,'" he said, smiling.

"Why's that?"

"Rudy, you've asked after me since Calgary, fishing around. You've been spreading my name along the ranges. They thought you were from His Majesty's government, come to take me back. It was known by many that I would not be welcome back in England. I made the mistake of telling them what happens to deserters. They're a protective lot in these parts."

I did not remind him that he was classified as missing, and, more recently, dead, which I presumed he would assume, nor did I tell him that no one was looking for him. I was about to quiz him further on this when he stood up suddenly.

"I have to check on something, and then I'll return. There's an outhouse behind the cabin if you need it."

His casual acceptance of my arrival was unsettling. It was as if I had stopped by on the way to somewhere else. He left with Joe, and I sat there alone in the cabin to take in its snug, wooded surrounds: a small kitchen and storage area with a separate stove, a narrow bed in the far corner of the room, a wooden table with bench chairs, and stairs leading to another small bedroom. The other bed I sat on was close to the front door and placed near the wood burner, where water steamed from a pot above it.

There was still the question of Mariette. Some instinct had told me not to mention her yet, that it may be a sensitive topic, but I would build courage at the next opportunity. I entertained the notion that she had on purpose separated from Edgar and, no longer desiring the child, left Samuel at Lakeland. She may even have returned to France to continue her life as it was before the war.

With some difficulty from the stiffness to my back and fingers, I climbed into my trousers and shirt that hung across wooden stools to dry by the fire. The cabin felt too warm, and I was suddenly keen to find fresh air.

When I stepped outside onto a porch that faced the lake, the coldness hit me again, bringing back my near-death memories from the night before. But in stark contrast, the sky was clear.

I walked down the stairs and saw a large tray loaded with timber and a set of very small huts in the distance. Beyond that there was nothing but wilderness. It was a world of white surrounded by mountains of deep blue. The place was spectacularly beautiful. I was lucky to be alive, and my steaming breaths in front of me reminded me to be grateful. I found the outhouse before commencing an exploration of the area.

Down a track, I found several dogs chained beside the huts, and they greeted me excitedly. I had to meter out the pats and attention to be fair to each of them. Nearby I saw my trap, and Sadie wandering freely with other horses, and I was immensely grateful to the person who had brought her here. I was wondering where Edgar and the men had gone when I heard a voice in the distance and the sound of barking dogs. It was another sled, and I stood to watch the arrival. This person was covered in a fur coat and hat that blocked most of the face, but I saw it instantly against the white: a shock of red hair that spilled around her shoulders.

The sled jerked to a stop as she pulled back on the reins and called to the dogs, the arrival so smooth, as if it had been done a hundred times before. She turned to me briefly before jumping off the sled and taking away her face coverings.

My heart pounded with joy and relief. Even though it was everything I had hoped, to find both of them, her appearance was also bewildering. The sudden realization that she had abandoned Samuel to return to Edgar smothered the initial excitement I felt at the sight of her. I stood wordless and shocked as she approached the dogs nearby, but it was her reaction that confounded me further.

"Where is Edgar?" she asked, scarcely glancing my way as she gave a piece of food to each of the dogs.

"He has gone to check on business. But it should be me asking the questions." Her coldness was nearly as bad as the temperature I had experienced the day before, and she viewed me suspiciously.

"You shouldn't be here."

I followed her as she chained each of her sled dogs to their kennel.

"What do you mean?" I said. "Why did you leave me? Why did you keep such a secret from me?"

She closed her eyes briefly.

"You should not have followed me."

"It wasn't just you. It was for Edgar. Why didn't you tell me he was alive? You know how I felt about losing him. About you."

She stopped then, softened perhaps, knowing how close Edgar and I had been.

"How did you find him?" she asked as she crouched to scratch behind the ears of one of the dogs.

I told her a very condensed version, as it felt as though at any minute she would walk away, which in fact she did. But still I kept following her.

"You should have told me," I called to the back of her. She couldn't just walk away now. I rushed forward to grab her arm.

"You shouldn't have come," she said bitterly, elbowing my hand away.

"You think that you can leave and break my heart and steal my brother like you did, that you had the right to! That you can waltz into my life, then run out of it and let me believe the worst?"

She did something unexpected then. Yet when one knows her nature, one expects the unexpected. She rushed into my arms and sank her face into my neck. I could forgive her for everything and took pleasure in the moment of her in my arms. I loved her even then, without yet knowing the whole truth.

"You must be careful. He is not the same," she whispered in my ear. "Don't mention Samuel unless he raises him first."

"That looks like a very friendly greeting," said Edgar, appearing suddenly nearby.

She pulled away, leaving me with feelings of guilt and confusion at the sight of him. The situation was nothing if not bizarre.

"I see that you are well acquainted!" he said, brushing off our reunion. "Let's go inside and talk."

Mariette did not meet my eyes but picked up some bags that contained food supplies. Edgar took them from her and followed her into the house, and I followed them. I still had no idea why Mariette left, why Edgar didn't write, and of course no idea where the three of us were ultimately headed.

Mariette had moved to the kitchen. She pulled out cups of flour and mixed these with water to commence making flatbread, and there was silence for a period. I'm not sure that either Edgar or I wanted to be the first to start the conversation.

My brother and I stared at one another across the table. He sat on a bench seat, his back against the wall behind him, his expression wavering between amusement and fervor. I could examine him better now that I was feeling recovered. His hair had grown long and was tied back into a ponytail. He had growth around his jawline, and there were cuts to the backs of his hands and several scars and scratch marks on his face. The scars I would learn were not only from France but from the heavy work and tree felling he had performed since arriving in Canada. Most notably he looked well, stronger and larger than I remembered, his skin aged from the sun to give him a harder look than I recalled also. Yet the intense blue eyes, the broad shoulders, and the half smile that he always wore so that no one could read him unmistakably belonged to my brother.

"How did you find me?"

I told him everything about the journey then, about France and how a part of me believed he hadn't died, about the clue in his diary. I told him also that Mother had, since the telegram in the final stages of the war, been waiting for news of his recovered body, and about her more recent resurgence of hope with Mariette's arrival. He bowed his head solemnly, and I looked across at Mariette, who continued working, seemingly avoiding being included in the conversation. I left out the emotional turmoil and the years that Mother had confined herself to her rooms, and I wondered how much Mariette had revealed to him. In any case I did not want to focus on that yet. That would be another regrettable conversation later.

"You are cleverer than most."

"Then I must be the one to assure you I haven't made it. I write lines of advertising for a newspaper, and the pay is low and prospects limited, I feel. There are many more talented than me."

"You will succeed at it. I am certain. You would succeed at anything you do. You don't let the blinkered ideas of others steer your decisions."

He sounded so much like the encouraging older brother I had grown up with.

"And you, Ed, you were afraid to come back, but why did you not write?"

In my side vision, I saw Mariette pause before continuing with her task.

"You can't work that out?"

In my heart I knew the answer, but I needed to hear everything in his words.

"I deserted my post. I left the men. I failed."

"You can't look at it like that—"

He slammed down his fist.

"You weren't there!" he said angrily, in a sudden change of tone. "You will never know!"

"Edgar—" said Mariette, who never got time to finish.

Edgar stood up suddenly and stormed from the room, leaving the door open.

Mariette followed to shut the door after him. From the front window she watched him go, and I stood beside her to watch also.

"I'm not sure what it was I said."

"You have to be careful. He does not want to be reminded of certain things." She turned to look at me and sighed, taking my hands that were trembling from Edgar's sudden and dramatic change. "There is much I should have told you."

"Obviously."

"I presume you found the will."

I nodded.

"How is Samuel?"

"He is well enough, but he misses you terribly."

"And I miss him," she said, unable to disguise her sadness and a certain measure of guilt I detected also from the way she could scarcely meet my gaze when she said this. "It has been lonely here without him."

"Then you should be with him. You're his mother!"

"I have survived under harder circumstances. I knew he would survive, too."

"You must understand that I'm struggling with why you can't just return."

She shook her head. "Samuel is the son of Edgar and my sister, Helene. I lied to you."

I took a moment to digest the words, but my head was filled with too many questions yet to fit this into any context of recent events. And her words still had not answered my question.

"Why the secrets?"

"It is complicated. Edgar did not come back from the war a well man," she said.

"Do you love him?"

"Yes, but it is not like you think."

"What should I think?"

"My plan was always to return here to Edgar, though it grew harder the longer I stayed at Lakeland. I was to leave a lot sooner, but then I fell sick. I was torn between you and a promise to Helene to watch over Edgar. And then Laurence took the decision out of my hands."

"Did you take Mother's jewels?"

She looked shocked. "Of course not! I would not steal from you, Rudy."

She told me then about the events that happened on the night of the egg hunt and in the following days and the threats that were made.

None of it shocked me. Laurence had grown more unpredictable and even more distant from all of us since he had returned from war.

"I believed that Laurence was capable of harming everyone in some way if I didn't leave. The plan originally was to humor Laurence, leave with Samuel, then return when your brother eventually left the manor. But the situation became sinister when he suggested it was only me that he wanted gone, and everything seemed out of my control. I ran and hid and watched you all that night. When I saw you with Samuel through the glass doors, the way you looked at him, I knew that you loved him, that you would not let any harm befall him. If I stayed, I believe that Laurence would have carried out his threat to spread whispers of desertion. I thought, as Edgar wished, that it would be better if you all remembered him as the hero he truly was. With me gone, there was a chance at least for Samuel with Edgar's will."

"Why did you think that I would continue to believe you?"

"Because I saw the way you looked when you read the will. Because I saw your heart."

I paused for a moment to read anything else from those words.

"Without you there, we have no witness," I said. "It will be harder to prove the case for Samuel. It will be near impossible to win. You should have come to me. I would have fought Laurence. I would have been on your side. I still am."

"It is better this way, returning to Edgar to look after him, and Samuel to be safely with you where he belongs, and Abigail there as his guardian. You might perhaps get a better outcome that you would not have otherwise had. You have a better chance to remain at Lakeland."

"It could be better still. You and Edgar could be there. And I have every intention of presenting the will and the case for Samuel. But it means that Laurence may still announce to the world about Edgar's illness and his suspicion about the desertion."

"With me not there, I do not think so. It is only the will he needs to fight now with his plan to inherit the estate. And the boy will say his father is dead."

"Which means you and Edgar have been planning this for years."

"When we arrived here and I learned how deep his illness went, Edgar realized, too, that he could not be the father he wanted to be, and Samuel's health was not good here. It was a difficult but necessary decision to let Samuel think his father had died."

"Edgar must not have been expecting you to return here. He made you the custodian for the estate."

"Yes, he did, and I objected. All you need to know is that the wilderness is the only place for Edgar, but is no place for Samuel."

"The wilderness is no place for you, either."

She turned her head away from me so I could not read her.

"I promised my sister that I would watch over him and her child."

"But Samuel is no longer here. You are not looking after the child at all now, it seems. You are here with my brother only."

She touched her throat. It was not my intent to hurt her but merely to reach inside her mind and draw more out. To understand what it was that truly kept her here.

"Separating them hadn't been an option when I made that promise. You must know that my sister and I owe Edgar a great deal. Despite everything you have heard, he was very brave like all the men who served to protect us. The promise between my sister and me is not something I expect anyone to understand."

And I certainly didn't at that point.

"Your plan would not have worked," I said. "You must have imagined that the boy would give 'Fabien' away eventually when he recognized him from the photographs on the wall."

"As you can see Edgar is not just changed mentally. I did not think his young photographs would be so easily recognizable as the man he is today. But no, you are correct. I didn't think of everything. I underestimated how much a child can see. But I imagine with his age, it will be easy to explain that he might be confused."

"Edgar should be home in England," I said. "I struggle to make sense of that. You could be there looking out for both of them."

"He will be arrested. His service no longer honorable, but in tatters. And I can tell you he will not fit back in society, regardless of his reputation. His life will be prison and psychiatric wards."

"There could be other treatments. I can take care of him."

"It doesn't matter what you think. He can't go back, Rudy!"

The way she said my name, I realized I missed it, and I moved closer to hold her.

"Don't!" she said, widening the space between us.

"My brother let us believe he was dead, and then for you to disappear . . . It broke Mother, and it almost broke me, too."

"You are not the only ones broken."

I was thinking purely selfishly and was reminded that Mariette had lost much.

"In your civilized world, Edgar would no longer fit," she continued. "He carries so much rage. Memories darken his mood. Here especially, he is surrounded by space, not people who judge him. I wasn't sure at first whether to give you the diary. I thought it would only confuse you, make it harder, make you worry more. Maybe even give his condition away. But I had to leave something more of Edgar."

"This relationship that you returned to here . . . ," I said, looking around the cabin. "This life you choose here—"

"It is not what you think."

"Yes, you've said that already. What is it that I am supposed to think?"

"I can tell just from your tone that you are displeased. I am not the perfect person you wish me to be. I've made some harsh decisions. Some that in time I may regret. But I can't tear myself in two, either. I knew after meeting you that you and Peggy and even your mother would take care of Samuel once I was gone. I knew that night I saw him in your arms that he was safe. I knew also that you would always keep him that way."

"But I'm not there, either, am I? Who knows if he is even still at the manor?"

Her face darkened. It was cruel what I said. But in that moment I didn't care.

"It has been hard on everyone," she said.

"Do you love me?" I asked.

"It doesn't matter."

I reached for her, my hands gently holding her arms.

"Why doesn't it?" I said.

She looked down through the window.

"He is coming. You must not ask questions about the past."

"You planned to return here without Samuel. Did you change your mind about returning after we were together? Did you have doubts before Laurence gave you no choice? Or was I just something to pass the time until you left?"

She looked at me, and I found no answers in her expression.

"Mariette!" I begged for an answer.

"Yes, I had doubts."

It was what I desperately wanted to hear, though it seemed more likely her doubts were about leaving Samuel.

She freed herself and walked into the kitchen, and I walked to the front door to watch Edgar ascend the outside stairs.

"Little Brother," he said, sweeping through the doorway, his anger forgotten. "If you are feeling better, I can give you a tour of my business, show you what we do here."

He was a different person than the one who had left earlier.

"Yes, of course," I said, my words sounding uncertain. Though I was eager to learn about him and his new life, I was still a little shaken from his outburst and the conversation with Mariette.

He patted me on the shoulder. "Then let's go."

Edgar's manner, firm and gentle and the only side he'd ever shown to me as a boy, took away some of my anxiety about the situation. I was suddenly looking forward to connecting with him and talking privately.

We stood side by side on the sled, and our dogs yelped exuberantly across the frozen lake until we reached the opposite shore. Then through winding snow-covered hills, with the wind whipping my face and pine needles biting at me as we passed down well-used trails, we reached a thickly wooded valley. When I lost my balance at one sharp bend, Edgar caught me before I toppled. After all these years he was still coming to my aid.

We stopped at a patch of forest that was partially cleared. He showed me a cable machine he had saved for and purchased to drag the felled logs. His business had proved successful through his hard labor and determination. I marveled at his ability to carve out a life here in a foreign land.

"I couldn't do it without the other workers," he said. "We all look after each other out here."

I felt selfishly hurt and excluded. He had left the war, scarred and ill, and we his family had been left to make sense of life without him. I wanted badly to talk about his experiences and Samuel but sensed some distance still between us and heeded Mariette's warning. It felt as though I were getting to know someone I had once known casually, not someone I had idolized throughout a shared history.

"I missed you," I said.

"And I you," he said, seeming sincere, as we sat on felled logs, eating bread and strips of venison that Mariette had packed for us, our bodies growing cold but our hearts growing warm as we briefly reminisced about some early childhood moments together.

"In another life we could have been partners," he said.

The relationship between the three of us, Mariette and Edgar and me, was still confusing. I did not yet understand the connection between the two of them and how deep it was. Mariette had made a promise, but what exactly that promise included was still somewhere in the gray. I had seen that her bedroom was upstairs and his bed near the kitchen. But most of the time they were here alone, and I tried desperately not to let the thought consume me and weaken the bond I had begun again with Edgar.

As I looked across the valley and the dogs and the low sun, even the cold was beautiful that day. I saw what he saw, smelled what he smelled: the sweet scent of sawn timber, the rawness of the land, the chance to begin anew, and a lack of any societal expectations.

"Or you could just return with me?" I asked to test him.

He turned, his blue eyes bright against the tanned, scarred, and weathered face and the ice-blue air around us. He was rugged, but underneath was the handsome face I had grown to admire and the boy whom everyone had revered.

"I will never go back. This is home. This is where I should be."

We returned to a crowded cabin. I was introduced to several men and women from neighboring properties who were helping to prepare a feast to celebrate my arrival.

Outside, the group of men had built a large fire to roast the deer they had caught and killed earlier. I had noticed a central gathering place with logs around a firepit, and we sat outdoors, warmed by the tall flames. Several children chased one another nearby, and conversations ensued about railways, trees, bears, and fishing. The women eventually joined us, carrying dishes to set down on logs while the men cut strips of meat with their hunting knives.

Edgar sat away from me, and he and the other men were laughing raucously after Edgar roughly threw a log on the fire, which sent sparks in all directions and made the children squeal and flinch. He had always had a sense of fun and adventure, but his actions had always been deliberate. I don't ever remember seeing him appear so casual and unrestrained.

"It is good to see you, Rudy!" he said. "The only thing missing is a glass of whiskey to celebrate the reunion."

I remembered the bottle Sally had given me, which had warmed me several times throughout the trip here, and I revealed this suddenly. Though after the words were released, some inner voice told me to take them back.

"Then fetch it!" he said.

Mariette turned in our direction with a look of concern.

"Perhaps it is best saved for my return," I said. "I will no doubt need it if this weather keeps up."

"Nonsense, Rudy! We'll leave enough for the journey."

"No," said Mariette.

Edgar stared at her for a moment, perhaps absorbing some silent message that was passed between them.

"Just a small one," he said. "My brother has traveled all the way here. I have not seen him since I left England. There is reason to celebrate."

These words reminded me that Edgar had said nothing of his time in France. He had taken great pains to distract me with other things, to steer the conversation to only happy memories and very present ones.

Mariette returned with the bottle and two glasses, which were filled immediately by Edgar. He gulped his down quickly, and as the minutes passed, this seemed not to make a difference to his current affable temperament. He spoke humorously of me to the others of the quirky, shy boy I was as a child, disappearing into the hills to sketch pictures of animals, and yet made no reference to his inclusion in the household or of other family. It was as if he had destroyed those memories.

Most of the group got up to leave as the night grew colder and the children had run out of energy. Only a handful of us were left, and while Mariette was distracted discussing something with one of the other women, Edgar poured himself another drink and topped up mine. The liquid warmed me and dispelled any further inner warnings. Edgar seemed buoyed by the drink and food and conversation, and

I saw no harm in the second glass at that point. I was feeling much lighter myself.

There are triggers that force people to do things they didn't mean to do. I saw something, a look if I can name it, pass between Mariette and Edgar. It seemed not sisterly or brotherly but something old and familiar, from before she found me. And this was what moved me to act the way I did and ultimately cause effects I'd been warned about.

Mariette went inside, and Edgar was then in deep conversation with the remaining two men. I took the opportunity to go inside and speak to her.

She saw my intense look, and I saw caution in hers.

"Mariette, you have not yet said your exact relationship with my brother." The liquor had done this, given me the confidence to confront her, stupidly, I realized later.

She turned away, offended.

"I said I'd take care of him in place of Helene."

Something inside me snapped.

"Has that also included his bed?"

"Who do you think you are? You are not my keeper! You are acting childish! And you had best now hide the whiskey. He has not had a drink for years. And I am safe to assume that you don't need any more, either."

Her point made, she walked away upstairs, and I fought the urge to follow her, to apologize, upset with myself for the way I had acted. Back at the fireside, the remaining two men were making moves to leave. I saw the whiskey bottle near Edgar's feet, the level almost to the bottom. He had grown a little quiet, and still drawing confidence from the whiskey, I thought it was the right time to approach him with other questions. I had struggled to make sense of Edgar's abandonment of me and the years he had left us in the dark at Lakeland. I felt I deserved answers. Everything had been kept from me, and I felt punished for simply seeking it. This sense of entitlement was likely in my tone.

"Was it as bad as everything I've heard?" I asked him too casually, words coming out as freely as the insults and questions I'd posed to Mariette.

"What do *you* think?" he said.

"I saw the destruction, the remains of what happened. You need to talk about it, stop hiding from us, from your family in England. I have some idea—"

"You have no idea! You are a soft little boy who saw no war, who lived dreamily inside your head. I would not expect you to know it at all."

I was dismayed by this sour relationship that had formed between us. I wanted to tell him how sorry I was that I didn't understand, but he allowed no opportunity then.

"You think I was brave? I was scared like you are, Rudy, fearful of fighting. Forcing myself to run at the enemy, watching people shot down screaming. I see that every time I close my eyes. I live with the past every day."

"You need to see a doctor then."

"Doctors? They told me I was different. At first I was 'malingering,' and then it was just madness. They did nothing but pump me with morphine to ease my conscience. I am a fugitive, Rudy. A criminal who should be locked up! You think that by coming here you will have all the answers? Well, you are sadly mistaken and should turn around now."

Mariette must have heard the raised voices and had come down from the top floor to stand on the porch above us. The two men had also stopped in the middle of their task to listen, perhaps aware of certain signs that I had not yet had the experiences to recognize. I noticed that Edgar had begun sweating and was peeling off his clothes.

"Mother misses you dreadfully," I said, thinking that this might soften the conversation and turn it back to something we could both share. "She needs you back there."

He stood up and smashed his glass against a log and began to storm back toward the stairs to the porch. Mariette in the meantime had walked to the bottom to meet him.

Although his reaction startled me, a side of him that I hadn't seen, I stood up to follow him. I had to understand. I had to bring out what he felt, why he couldn't write.

"Mother was sick with grief," I said.

Mariette moved past him toward me. "No more."

He commenced the ascent, then stopped abruptly to turn and walk back toward me, stopping close. "Do you think I wanted that, Brother?"

He pushed me suddenly, and I fell backward onto the ground.

"Stop," said Mariette, moving to grab him, but he pushed her away also.

He then raised his voice: "Do you think that I wanted to see my friends die on the field? Do you think I had a choice?"

He stood over me. I witnessed the raw brutish power of him, the brother who had protected me, and whom I was now in fear of.

I could see that the other men had not yet moved, but Mariette hovered anxiously.

He leaned down. "Why aren't you at home, looking after my son?"

He punched me in the face, and the pain was blinding.

"Stop!" screamed Mariette. I felt dizzy but was still able to see the two men reach for Edgar. They drew him away, each man gripping an arm to force him backward as he called out to me.

"Rudy, you know nothing about life!"

He shook free of his human shackles and then turned to disappear into the night.

Blood poured from my nose. One of the other men helped me up and into the house, and Mariette brought me a damp cloth and a bucket of cold water. I took the cloth, put it to my bruised and bleeding mouth and nose, then turned away from her to face the wall. I felt ashamed.

Mariette discussed something privately with the other man, who left then, and I heard her bolt the front door.

She came and sat on the cot beside me, but I could not face her.

"You are not safe here," she said softly, and she put her hand on my leg.

"Then n-neither are you," I stuttered through swollen lips.

A tooth was loose, and blood filled my mouth. My nose was swollen and split. I leaned over to spit out blood in the bucket.

"Let me check you," she said.

I felt her hand on my arm and turned toward her pleading eyes. With another damp cloth she gently wiped my bruised and swollen face.

More than the physical pain I felt was the humiliation. I did indeed feel like a child. And I had failed to believe Mariette, to understand. Though there was no reproach in her expression.

"In case you are wondering, he would never harm me," she said.

"I'm not so sure of that."

And then an idea came to me.

"Did he harm the boy?"

"The boy grew up fearing his outbursts, and Edgar could see that it was not good for Samuel. Deep down Edgar is still the same good person. He cared for the boy, but his moods are unpredictable. He loves him so very much, you have to know that. He thought that no one but you could take care of him the way he wanted. And it is where you should be: with him. Not here. Samuel needs you, Rudy, more than me, more than Edgar. There is nothing you can do here."

"Edgar needs proper help, Mariette. I have heard about people who look after such illnesses and hospitals that specialize."

She scoffed. "They will keep him in a vegetative state, and he will die miserably condemned, imprisoned and drugged as a traitor to his country. Just as he told you. Here at least he can have a life. Surely you can see that?"

I could see that. I just didn't want to.

"Here he doesn't have to hide away. The men here don't judge him. He has no one reminding him of the past."

"I think that it's only a matter of time before he harms you, too."

She smiled sadly into her lap. I saw the care in her eyes toward us both, and my heart felt trapped and heavy.

"Perhaps. But regardless, if that is the way I go, then that is my fate. I can never leave him."

I did not like the answer.

"And the other men?"

"Has he hurt them, too, you're asking? He has been in many fights, Rudy, but everyone has accommodated the situation because they see the good also. They know the limits. The alcohol is the worst. You weren't to know of course. I think we all saw that coming, but now he knows again. Alcohol is not allowed here. It wakes the sleeping beast that lives within him.

"You must sleep now, and we will talk in the morning. It is doubtful he will come back tonight or even tomorrow. There is a small hut he goes to when he is like this. And in the morning his friends will visit him and talk him back."

She stood up, started to leave, then bent down to kiss the top of my head.

"You're a good man, Rudy. He will be regretting that he hurt you. He will regret that the most."

I didn't feel good. I felt quite the opposite, as if I had let them both down, and Samuel, too. I tossed and turned, expecting Edgar to turn up at any moment as well as attempting to find a comfortable position, but everything ached. I deserved it. I was young and unworldly and still living in the past. And when I did sleep, I dreamed of war, of Edgar dying at my feet.

The next morning when the sun rose late, I sat up gingerly and inspected my face. My nose was painful to touch. Edgar was right. I had lived a soft life, and these past two months along with my bruises, injuries, and assaults reminded me just how right he was.

The fire had been lit, and the cabin was unbearably warm. Mariette came toward me from the kitchen, bringing oatmeal. She sat next to me and began to spoon-feed me, but I took the utensil from her.

"I am still capable of feeding myself." The effort to smile was also painful. I imagined Edgar wounded in battle and each time having to return, patched and becoming more disillusioned. These thoughts fought off my own feelings of pain.

I blamed myself of course. There was something in me that said that I caused this, that I deserved it in a way, that I had pursued him when he didn't want to be found, and that I should have listened to Mariette. It had to be proven that he was not the same brother. I had caught glimpses of him, the Edgar I had grown up with. We had shared the same thoughts on things, had private jokes that belonged to no one but us, and had the ability to read between each other's words. The way he gripped my hand as we sat in the snow, like we had done as children. Those memories, feelings, senses were still there, gluing us together. Memories that would never fade, that would stay with me always.

But the air of unpredictability that enveloped him was stopping the person within, his heart unable to be freed. I felt that with proper care my brother could be fixed. But to fix someone they must first want that. And the previous evening had shown me that he didn't, that this life was his now and he wanted the past gone. Perhaps he even wanted me gone.

I sat on the snow-covered stairs with a blanket around me, looking at the sky growing gloomy to coincide with my thoughts, the light then barely squeezing through. Mariette came out and sat beside me.

"You must not feel bad about anything. I understand why you came, and Edgar will, too, when he calms down. It is a pattern that when he loses control of his senses and fights something inside his head, he will disappear for a period, perhaps avoiding the problem, distancing himself from it, but also out of guilt. He may not want to face you again."

I felt tears prick my eyes. I did not want to leave, but I knew I had to.

"When was he last like this?"

"Several months before I left here for England, but not since. He has really calmed. Everything from his past life seemed to be lifted away from him. And unfortunately you brought back all the guilt he carries, from abandoning you, from losing friends he believes he should have protected. I thought when he first spoke with you he might react, but only the love he had for you came through before all other memories. And that was strong enough."

"And it was only when I talked about *him* and expectations . . . always expectations . . . that he became like that."

She nodded.

"You must go, Rudy. You must forget about us here."

I turned to look at her, the vibrant colors of her stark against the white.

"How am I supposed to leave you?"

"You mustn't come back here," she said. "Your destiny isn't here. It is with the people who need you more."

She took both my hands and gripped them in her small ones, weathered from the harsh tasks she set herself here.

She said nothing but looked in my eyes, beseeching. I could see then that she was torn. That there was a small part of her that would have left with me, but she was a far stronger person than I had encountered before. And still I wondered if there was more to their relationship than I thought. Was she letting me down gently perhaps? Did she love Edgar more than just the promise? Regardless, I had to leave. I knew that then.

I took some writing paper from my bag and wrote a note to Edgar, telling him that I loved him and that I wished him well. I said nothing about the past and the future, only that I was pleased we met, that he had impressed me with the business and the success. I gave it to Mariette to read to ensure I had said nothing to provoke his dark thoughts.

I would stay one more night to repair, and then she would organize for someone to escort me to the closest town with my trap and to the main road that would be easier to navigate. She also reported that one of the men had returned with a message, that Edgar would be away working for several days with his crew to clean up the remaining timber.

We spent the day together. We spoke of France, of her family. She told me everything then about her childhood, about the love between Helene and Edgar, and about the changes in Edgar. How she'd returned here to learn that he'd not said a word after she left to take Samuel to England. How he had become ill from sitting outside for hours all day in the sun, and then all night in the cold. How guilty he had felt by wishing to part with his son. And how the women and men here nursed him through his fevers until she returned.

The snow fell heavily, encasing us inside the cabin. The fire roared, and the smell of the wood burning and meat frying made me feel soothed. I wished for an eternity with Mariette, but it was a matter of hours now, and I would be gone.

I had fallen asleep, and during the night she had crept downstairs. I had heard the cabin shift and the stairs creak, and she had climbed in next to me and kissed me softly. We had lain holding each other for hours, afraid of the minutes passing, and falling briefly asleep just before dawn. When I awoke she had left the cabin.

I watched her return from somewhere within the wood with one of the men. My image in the window glass was unrecognizable. The swelling in my face had gone down slightly, but the bruising had taken on an angry appearance.

"Edgar has sent back one of his work crew to make sure you don't lose your way," she said. "Arnaud said to get ready to leave."

I nodded, my heart in my throat, a pain in my chest and not from the bruising. I felt it was too soon to leave, and parting with Mariette and my brother again was difficult to contemplate.

She remained on the porch as I followed Arnaud in thick powdery snow toward my horse and trap nearby. As I commenced to climb onto the seat I turned to see Mariette watching me, unsurely, perhaps suppressing things she couldn't say, that would make the separation impossible. Her unspoken love and the same sense of loss as after I had learned that Edgar was never coming home punched hard at my chest until I could barely breathe. I felt wretched and drowning in sudden grief at the thought that I might never see either of them again.

I rushed up the stairs, and she stepped forward to reach for me. I felt her body mold to mine, shaking with the same feelings of loss, as she sobbed against my chest. I knew then that she loved me, that what we had shared was not imagined, that what she told me, all of it, was true. That the decisions she was forced to make were not impetuous and wrong, but selfless acts of honor. I pulled away quickly and strode back to the trap, my focus turning toward the small boy who awaited his future. I would tell him one day about the people who loved him, who sacrificed their own destinies to ensure his.

Arnaud rode his horse ahead, and I followed him along the winding forest track in silence. We parted at the road that would eventually lead me back to Sally. I had plenty of time on the return journey to relive the strange events of the past, which would also shape my life to come.

Sally greeted me along with her husband, who had recently arrived back.

"You look terrible!" she said, fussing.

Aghast at the bruising that still lingered on my face, Robert insisted on getting the doctor to check that there was no permanent damage.

"A fight with another traveler," I offered.

"Did you find Edgar?" she asked.

I thought about it for a second to put her out of her misery. "No," I said, and it seemed this endless supply of lies would continue.

"I don't believe you," she whispered.

"Am I so transparent?"

"Yes. Even as a little boy, you could not lie convincingly."

And we both smiled at this.

"But that's all right. I will tell whatever story you wish me to."

I trusted her, though I was tired of secrets.

The doctor came and checked me, and with his affable encouragement confirmed I would live another fifty years at least. For several days I rested there until Sally drove me to the train for the long journey back to England.

I watched the landscape disappear and the sea that separated me from the people I loved gradually widen. I could see the beauty in the shape of this distant but magnificent land, the expanse of sky and how this would have drawn Edgar. I hoped that he would take care of Mariette. I prayed for his torturous mind that he lived daily to control, and hoped that what she said was true, that the madness would cease with me gone. Whatever happened to both of them in the future, they deserved happiness. They had both been through much in their lives.

There was a cruel irony in loving two people but being unable to love either of them as I wanted.

For the second time, I read the letter from Edgar that Arnaud had given me as we parted. Attached to the letter was a torn photograph of Helene, her name written in Edgar's hand behind it. It was the missing piece of the photograph that Mariette had first given me.

Letter to Rudy from Edgar, dated 17 December 1922

Dear Rudy,

Where to start . . . Just writing now seems in some way
indulgent to explain my feelings, but firstly, I must ask
that you do not write to me, nor think that we can begin
anew. That you just remember us as we were. I think if
not for the war, I would probably have made a damn fine
accountant, or perhaps a poet. One or the other. Maybe
both. Mariette told me she left you my diary from the
war since I have no use for it, nor had I opened it in the
years since I left France. There are things I don't wish to
remember. And this is perhaps the longest piece of writing
I will attempt.

My head is not clear like yours, dear Brother.
Sometimes I wake, and with absolute clarity I see the day
ahead, and I look forward to it. The past is somewhere
buried deep at these moments, and I am at peace with
the world, connected to it in a small way. Joe, Arnaud,
and the rest of my brothers here have taught me to respect

the space around me, to not fill it with things that in the end I can't take with me. It is probably this that heals me.

But many days I wake up with a cloud in my head that shifts and breaks and never fully dissipates, and I struggle through the fog to see purpose. I am just a man by instinct doing what I must. It is this that I fear the most, that I cannot chance. And there are those, like you, who remember me as before, who love me unconditionally. Who believe in redemption, rehabilitation. But, Rudy, I am a traitor, I am ill, and if I should return that way, it would be my end. Know that it is safer for everyone if I am here, but know, most of all, it is where I wish to be.

I was in love with dear, sweet Helene. She is there inside the envelope, and the other end of the photograph you have of me, Mariette, Jerome, Roger, and Percy. I kept it because with Samuel gone it was the only thing I had of her. But now her son should know her and treasure this image. Sometimes I dream of the life we might have had together if the world had not been so full of smoke and sadness.

I loved Helene in between the war damage. It was a desperate love, an untidy love if I can call it that. It did not fit into any category. Even the soldiers who married their French sweethearts and took them back home cannot be compared. Ours was hurried but beautiful and then over before it should have been. And Samuel is the result.

I cannot swear you to secrecy. I know that to keep a secret from Mother will feel like a crime, so, Brother, you have my permission to tell about me. On several conditions: that she does not come here, that she tells no one, that she sends no one. That she must remember me as I was.

I saw with my own eyes the look you had for Mariette, and though she covers it well, I suspect there is something there also. I regret deeply that she is here, that she cannot continue a full life. I have told her on many occasions that it is no fit place for her, but she is here all the time taking care of me, as if she must in her sister's stead. Though I will selfishly admit she brings me joy, and I'm not sure I could live without her. You should know, little B, that there is no intimacy in our relationship. But even if I could send her back, she would not go. I sent her with Samuel half hoping that she would fall in love with you and never return, because I offer so little. But I must admit when she returned I felt a balance again in the world, and not only is she a soldier herself, perhaps selfishly she is also my link to Helene.

I know that Samuel's best hope is with you. I hope that you know I love him in my own way and that I did not give him away lightly. But as you have seen, this is no life for him. If I were a different man, I would raise him otherwise. I cannot offer him what he needs. And though it is a big ask, I know that you will take this seriously.

I am not the man who left for France. I sometimes offer no humor, as you have seen, something that should not infect a childhood. Sometimes I have no conscience, and that worries me also. Sometimes I forget who I am. These were the reasons I sent him to you. I did not trust myself.

I have learned to heal since, and Mariette has helped me through the worst of it, I believe, but I must never come home.

Raise my son, Samuel, like I would have done had war not taken my soul. Take this to prove to Roland, and tell Mother, that Samuel is my son and therefore bequeathed Lakeland Manor and the estate. It is my dearest wish that you and Mother act as joint guardians of Samuel and, as per the original terms of the estate, for Mother to continue running the estate in my absence. This letter is to be presented as my final binding will. (Tell my brother from me that if he considers contesting, it is worth my while to return home and risk prison. It is the only thing that will bring me home, but tell him also that I will be paying him a visit first.)

It is my wish that Lakeland Manor always be your home. That you find peace also with everything that has happened. I know that a greater life awaits, if you're game enough to find it, Brother. If you take a chance, if you have no fear.

Your loving brother,
In spirit always,
Edgar S. Watts

CHAPTER 33

I arrived in central London, the hub of the world it felt like: noisy, crowded, and metallic, something that should exist far in the future. The contrast to where I had come from was jarring and seemingly less approachable and colder than the mountains of ice I had walked through.

I felt a relative calm on the final leg of my journey. I held the other piece of the photograph that had once included Helene. I stared at the faces of Mariette and Edgar, resigned to put them in a place in my heart now, remember them well, and remember Mariette in my arms on the last night and Edgar like he was before, things I would carry with me forever.

As I strode defiantly over the final crest toward my home, with the secure knowledge that it would remain so, I stopped suddenly to take in a chilling new reality. The glass windows of the house were shattered, and the ghostly black shadows of fire crept over the sills and across the stonework outside. I ran the final distance, passing the flowerbeds that had been trodden by heavy boots, into the cavity that was once the grand entrance. The house was strangely hollowed in places, yet walls still stood in others. The stairs and the shining oak floors were missing or blackened. There was an acrid smell of burnt things, and the floor was littered with rubble and piles of dampened ash. Part of the roof had sunk, but the shell for the most part had defiantly stood its ground, though deemed irreparable in coming months. The memories here reduced to remnants of things that I barely recognized. Lakeland was gone.

"It's in a bad state, Master Rudy."

I turned to find Bert behind me. My mind was so numb I had not heard him pull up in the car. I was relieved also to see him before panic quickly followed.

"Where are the others?"

"Everyone escaped the fire. Do not fear. Both Peggy and Mother are in hospital, though it is mostly their spirits that are broken. They are recovering from the shock."

I breathed out in relief.

"I'm sorry you found it like this. I was on the O'Learys' farm. I saw you walking from there. The firemen did all they could."

"When?"

"The day before yesterday it happened. Roland came to see your mother when he heard about it and passed on that you had left France to travel to Sally in Canada. I sent a telegram there, but you were obviously already at sea. I'm sorry you had to find it this way. Though you should not investigate any further. It is dangerous; more of the roof could fall at any minute."

I followed Bert outside.

"The horses are all fine. It did not reach the stable, as you can see, but I've taken them elsewhere for now."

"And Samuel is with you then?"

Bert hesitated before answering.

"Laurence has taken Samuel with him. I can't tell you everything. But Laurence was here when the fire started."

His final sentence put me instantly on edge; the words unsaid here spoke of other things more sinister. A sense of urgency replaced my feelings of loss toward the house. I dropped Bert off at his temporary lodgings and drove first to the hospital.

Mother cried when she saw me. By her bedside Peggy sat faithfully with her arm in a bandage. She had a burn from when she went to rescue my mother, who had tried to pour water on the fire before realizing that any attempt was useless. It was not the time to tell Mother about Edgar, and she did not yet ask, still overcome from the tragedy of losing the manor. But that wasn't all Mother was distressed about.

"Rudy," she said, her hands to her chest and her face heavily lined from worry. "You have to go see Laurence and collect Samuel. There was nowhere else for him to go with us in hospital. I'm sure the boy is fine, but it would be better he be with you."

There was something desperate about both her request and assurance. I knew she had the same fears as I did, yet as a mother she could not believe them also. The doctor came in at that point and, seeing that Mother was agitated, reminded her to stay calm.

"I will take Rudy outside and explain the rest," said Peggy, warmly gripping my mother's hand. Mother closed her eyes, a little more at peace, her trust in Peggy absolute.

Outside the hospital room, Peggy explained in more detail.

"Laurence came looking for a fight. He told your mother she must sell the property. He was quite unreasonable and would not listen to your mother explain that the house was and could still be left to the boy. She reminded him of the handwritten will she had witnessed, and this it seemed sent him mad.

"Laurence demanded she give him the will, but Abigail lied and said she did not know where it was kept. He didn't believe her and searched her room and everywhere in the house then, and your mother was quite overcome with the trauma of it. I told Laurence he had to leave, that his mother was ill, but he continued searching. He went upstairs, tore open drawers in Edgar's room, and then went through yours. He was not himself.

"I left to find Bert, but as we returned to the house, Laurence had left and the top floors were burning and smoke was pouring out of the window. We had to get your mother out."

Peggy was weeping then that they had no time to attend to Samuel, but the urgency of my mother inside a burning building diverted them.

"He took the boy," she said apologetically, and seemed to feel in some way to blame. "The police went to speak to Laurence about the fire and to check on the boy as requested by your mother, but he wasn't home."

"I will find Laurence and bring Samuel home." Though where home was now, I couldn't say. "Laurence is selfish, though I do not believe that he would harm a child," I said to reassure her.

I returned to Mother to console her that I would look after everything. She was a little more rested but filled with melancholy, blaming herself for not foreseeing the trouble with Laurence. I could have told her then that he dazzled her with words and that her love made her turn a blind eye to his indiscretions.

"And what has happened to you? What news of Edgar?" she said now that she was calmer.

"I will tell you everything when I return," I said. "Rest assured it is something you will want to hear. Though we must leave it at that for now."

I saw the look on my mother's face. I saw some color restore to it and knew that I had made the right decision telling her something at least.

"You must go," she said. "You must hurry!"

I left the hospital and drove for hours to London, first to Laurence's office. I bounded up the stairs of the opulent office building with its lead-glass doors, gilded decor, and marble floors.

The door to his office was open, and inside were a frenzy of papers scattered across the floor and pieces of furniture missing.

Someone walked in behind me.

"May I help you?" he asked.

"The lawyer who worked here," I said, "do you know where I can find him?" I did not of course wish to divulge anything more.

"You mean the *shyster* who used to work here?"

"I don't understand."

"I am the manager of this building, and he owes lots of money. He's had heavies come to visit wanting credits paid and customers sending demand letters. I can tell you that he does not come in bright-eyed and bushy-tailed, that's for certain. Do you know him?"

"Yes," I said, but had no time to explain.

"I've tried him at home, but no answer there. If you are looking to get paid, I would try the clubs and bars, anywhere there's whiskey . . . and let me know if you find him."

I thanked the manager and walked solemnly downstairs. At Laurence's apartment, I had the same absent reception. I asked a neighbor if he had seen him.

"There are always comings and goings, so for it to be quiet is unusual," he said. "He has not been home in days."

I then went to his favorite club, where I was not a member. At the door I asked if a message could be passed and waited in the stately hall of the Victory Club. The doorman returned to say that there was no one there by that name. I was unsure about what to do when I recognized Fred leaving the club: the friend of Laurence's who had been to our house. When he saw me he turned sheepishly away.

"Fred!" I called. He could not ignore me.

"I'm sorry, Rudy, I cannot tell you anything. Laurence doesn't want to see you."

"Did you ask why?"

"Apparently you are trying to weasel him out of his inheritance with a child from a sham marriage."

"Fred, it's not true. And whatever else he told you is a lie."

I could see that Fred was not completely unknowing. He had probably experienced Laurence long enough now to understand the underside of his personality, but the old establishment and keeping mum were hard to fracture.

"He's in there," he said quietly, guiltily. "But don't tell him I said anything." He was gone quickly then.

I grew angry. If he was at the club, then where was Samuel? I could not wait another moment and barged past the doorman, who failed to grip on to my shoulder as I passed. I walked through the tables until I found him at the back. He was amongst new faces that I hadn't seen before.

He stood up unsteadily as I approached and pointed a finger at me. "You need to leave!"

"Where is the boy?"

One of his friends stood up and asked me to remove myself, but I did not budge. The man from the door had called another to deal with me and escort me from the room. I had only one card to play.

"This man here," I shouted to room, "has burned down his own home!"

It was intense, but I got the reaction I was hoping for.

One of the group told Laurence to go somewhere with his brother to deal with his family issues in private.

"I will leave quietly," I told the heavyweight gripping me, "if you let go of my arm." He did so, and I followed Laurence storming toward a small private wood-paneled room.

As I entered the room, he grabbed me and threw me against a wall. He was strong and with alcohol perhaps stronger. He had also learned to fight, and if it came to it, he was the sort of chap who, although vain and shamelessly worried about his appearance, would fight to the death to prove he was the best.

"What are you going to do? Beat your own brother to a pulp? I think the club would likely rescind your membership!"

I could smell the abuse of alcohol on his breath, and he looked like he hadn't slept in days.

"Tell me where Samuel is, and I will go."

He released me, then straightened his suit and ran his fingers through his hair, then pointed his finger at me.

"You had no right to allow him in that house, to fool Mother like that. That house is mine!"

I smiled. "If it means so much, then why did you set fire to it?"

He recoiled slightly. He could not stand to be known as an arsonist; even a whiff of it in circles would oust him once and for all from London society.

"You always think the worst of me."

"I don't th-th—" The stuttering had returned, and always at the wrong moment.

He laughed sharply. "Oh, Rudy, you are pathetic! And now you are pinning the fire on me. Do you think anyone would really believe that?"

"The insurance assessors will s-s—" I would not let the damned speech-stealing snake beat me this time. "You took Mother's jewels to sell, didn't you? It wasn't Mariette."

"A vicious lie!" he said, pointing at my face.

"I went to your office, too. Things aren't looking good for you right now."

"You should not be prying into my affairs," he said.

I wondered then if others knew and how long he hadn't been working, perhaps weeks, pretending, borrowing, sleeping on couches.

"You set fire to the house to ensure the transfer of inheritance to pay your debts."

He knew that he was cornered, though I did not believe at any point he would back down. Usually any provocation made him worse.

"So I am a thief and an arsonist now?"

"Whether you are or not, right now I don't give a damn. Just tell me where Samuel is."

"Oh yes, the boy," he said too casually. "The note from Edgar you think he wrote—"

"The will I know he wrote. The will you wished to be rid of. I have more evidence now that cannot be questioned."

"Forgeries are good these days, and you were suckered by the girl. She hooked you from the start. You were never very clever, Rudy. It has something to do with the slowness, the stutter."

"Where is he?" I felt fury building, and I tried to suppress it. He wanted to see me riled, and I would not give him such a gift, and I would not give in to the snake.

"He is with others of his kind. Bastards without parentage."

"You mean you placed him in an orphanage?"

"That is where he must be," he said. "A nobody like the woman he came with."

"I will find him and return him to his rightful place with our mother."

"I wouldn't do that if I were you."

"He is Edgar's son, and I will find him."

"The money is ours, Rudy. When the insurance money for the manor comes through, I will give you some of it. When the lands are sold also. I will see to it."

He admitted his guilt in these words, in his fake sincerity. I would not be fooled this time. He was lying as he had done his whole life. I remembered the nights on the hills when he would leave me to find my way home, the dark cupboards he would lock me in. The constant forgiving on my part. And then the repeat of the same crimes. I could not forgive this time.

"You have nothing to give me, Laurence."

"It is you who has nothing, Rudy. You will be a failure your whole life, but at least with me you will have some money. Edgar had every-thing. Got all the privileges. Everything was laid out for him. As if he were king. The girl was another one to take away our share. Yours and mine."

"Since when did you care about my share?"

"I didn't hate you, you know," he said, a little quieter. "You just didn't even care if I was there."

I saw something then the alcohol couldn't conceal, something I had never seen before. He was frailer than all of us. I saw his insecurity, even felt some pity that I did not understand him.

"If you and Mariette were together, then you would take everything from me," he continued. "I couldn't let that happen."

"Is that what you're worried about . . . that I would win somehow?"

It wasn't only that he couldn't bear the thought of losing money. But me taking something he couldn't have. Mariette.

I looked at him there, red in the face, grinning to cover the fear. He had lost his job, his apartment. He had nothing. The life one chooses determines one's punishments. And I believed Laurence's punishments would come, without anything else I might have done to him that day.

"Just so you know, I gave her money to leave, and she took it."

"You mean the worthless ten-pound banknote we found? She left it behind. She didn't want our money . . ."

He appeared both skeptical and confused. Though I saw some hint of defeat and weakness there also.

"Where is Samuel?"

"I cannot tell you that. It's best you let him go. It is best for you."

I turned and walked toward the door.

"You should know that I offered to drive her, but she ran off into the night. It is the gypsy blood, you know!" he shouted after me. "You can't help them. You can't trust them or keep them."

I ignored him, opened the door, and kept walking.

"Rudy!" he said, following me partway. "We will always be brothers."

I felt it was too late to make amends. He had hurt too many, and I couldn't let him do that anymore. He had lost, and I felt no glory in this reveal, and also oddly no more anger.

I hoped that Laurence was telling the truth. I traveled to the closest church orphanage to find Samuel wasn't there, but I was given a list of other houses by the vicar in charge.

I tried two other places with a knot of fear in my stomach of losing him, of never seeing him again. I walked to another house on the list: a large rectangular gray-brick building that resembled a prison. At the end of a long hallway, leading to an outdoor area, I followed the sounds of children laughing.

On a bench he was sitting, watching the other children in the playground area. He was concentrating on them, perhaps not caring to be a part of what they were doing. He did not appear anxious or wistful, only curious, as if wondering where he fitted in. Though his eyes were puffy from crying.

I walked nearer, pondering his golden skin, his pointed chin. Like Helene, I imagined. But when he turned in my direction, I saw the half smile and love in his gaze. I saw Edgar then.

Samuel stood up and ran to me, and I held the three of them in my arms.

CHAPTER 34

Missy bounded ahead along the shoreline and barked playfully at the gulls as I strolled to watch the mist slowly rolling in across the water. The sea was unforgiving and dangerous yet beautiful at this time of day. Spots of rain hit me, and it reminded me of another time when I brought Mariette here.

It had been three years since Laurence had started the fire. The insurer did pay a sum. But nothing close to its value, even though the firemen's initial report suggested the fire was started from a lit cigarette. There were too many questions, and our lawyer, Roland, persisted with the paperwork until we received at least some funds.

Mother, Peggy, Samuel, and I had moved to the bay house. We had sold off most of the land belonging to the estate and paid out money to the farmers so they could begin new jobs or trades elsewhere, and we had dealt with Laurence through Roland. With the letter I had from Edgar and instructions by Mother, Roland had altered the inheritance.

Samuel's money was to be held in trust until he turned twenty-one, and we would take care of the boy until then. He gradually spoke more English than French, though occasionally, and with the same sense of humor as his father, he would mischievously revert to French words.

Our new home was large enough for us, and we had adequate land where Mother, with her share of the money, was in the process of building separate living quarters. She had improved considerably. There were no more migraines or afternoon naps. She had taken to things with gusto, even helping Peggy with various tasks. It was easy to imagine this lively woman with whom my father fell in love, and whom many before him vied for.

Bert moved to another village nearby to live with his brother and nieces and nephews. He was happy to retire, and we had been to visit him.

Several times my mother had taken the train to meet Laurence for lunch, though she chose not to update me on his fate. I suspected that she was still giving him money occasionally. I cannot judge her. She knows it was Laurence who took the jewelry, and the fire still hangs above us all, and yet as a mother, she has forgiven him. Perhaps he did her a favor in a near-disastrous sort of way. The estate, though beautiful, had become a burden, which had added to her poor health, the unpaid rents, and the constant worrying about the upkeep. She had not aged a day since the time we moved.

Mother told Laurence about Edgar's letter to me, and he did not challenge it nor mention any desertion. I think there was some negotiation during her private conversations with Laurence that Mother had not told me about, such as the fact that she decided against pressing any charges of arson, even though the insurance assessment made clear the blame. There were even greater things that may have prevented Laurence pursuing claims to the estate: the fear that he might have to face Edgar if he did anything to upset the beneficiary transfer to Samuel.

But Mother did not abandon Laurence in any way. He was her son after all. She had no doubt sweetened the deal by offering to pay off all his debts using money from the sale of her own assets. Though with hindsight, I believe that Laurence's earlier threat to Mariette to reveal Edgar's desertion was hollow. I believe that vanity would have prevailed to prevent his name ever being linked with such an act.

Roland had found a keen buyer for the Lakeland plot, someone who would live there and rebuild. Mother and others from the area were worried that the Lakelands would turn into a hodgepodge of hotels and lots of little properties, taking away from the delightful openness; she had joined a committee to ensure that property would not be sold to people who would overdevelop for commercial reasons.

I kept Sheriff with several other horses in the paddock behind our new residence. Samuel was taught to ride Chess, and we would often ride along the beach together. In the years since his arrival, his confidence and strength had grown, and I saw so much of my brother there, which made us even closer. Samuel in time accepted that Mariette had had to move away to take care of "the uncle," and letters were exchanged between them, Mariette collecting the mail from the closest town, I imagined, secretly so as not to upset Edgar, whose clear separation from the boy ensured less pain and a restful mind. Samuel learned about Helene, but he still referred to Mariette as his mother.

Although I would have happily lived on my portion of inheritance, I continued to work as an illustrator for various publications as well as some advertising companies where demand for my services was growing. I now took the train to Manchester once a week and occasionally to London, which meant I could live and work mostly from the bay property. I had finally succumbed to the new mode of transport and now drove in a car to the train station.

The advertising work wasn't the only reason for my occasional long train journeys, but to visit the hospices and homes of men who had served in the war and sketch their faces. The pictures would then be offered to them as gifts when I had finished. Soon families of the missing, who had read about my work in the newspaper, were contacting me, sending photographs of their sons, brothers, fathers, and uncles, asking politely if I would do the same for them. Though there were offers of money, I never accepted it. They had paid enough in blood. There were other subjects also, links to the past—sailing boats, charming French chateaus, and fields filled with flowers—and these I did show and sell, donating all the money back to the hospitals. At first these activities were a way of distracting me from the loss of Edgar and Mariette, but soon it became a passion and a purpose also.

As you might have guessed, Mother heard the story I told of Edgar. She had been anticipating the account of my adventure since the last time I indicated I had some news about him. Though the news she was expecting was only that of Edgar's final resting place.

She was unemotional at first, the shock of such news too great to make sense of.

I told her the story, and all the while she gripped my hand, her hands trembling as she slowly absorbed the truth of it.

"My poor boy," she said, finally breaking down and sobbing into my chest. "How he suffered."

"He is someplace where he wants to be," I consoled her. "And I believe not only that he is there for himself, but that he is there to protect us also." Edgar, even in his illness, must have known the grief he would cause if he were to return. Not only by the punishment from authorities that his family would undoubtedly be drawn into, but his moods and irrational ways that might harm us.

Mother's grief was no longer about her own loss but about Edgar's losses. She had to come to terms with an illness she knew nothing about and to resolve why Edgar would want to live so far away. I thought she would continue to be upset about his terms of contact and be desperate to go to him, but she was quickly accepting. She became strangely alive, awakened, for want of a better word, and eager to leave the hospital to make a new home at the bay.

In the weeks following, she had transformed, abandoned her need for solitude, her health improving, and one day I caught her smiling at the sea. She threw herself into caring for Samuel: disciplining, caring for, and instructing the young boy. She had never been overly affectionate, and Samuel did not change her in this regard. But she loved the boy in a way that was far more giving than I expected, and without expectation. She no longer separated herself from the worries of children that had come with her station, but she embraced and enjoyed the role of grandmother actively, involved in every aspect of Samuel's life. He would wake every morning and seek her out in her bedroom to share a pot of tea and discuss the day: a habit that continued into later years.

I thought often of Edgar and fought the urge to write to him. He had asked me not to, but he had never said anything of Mother writing. He replied to her letter eventually, thanking her for her understanding. Though he only wrote the once. And that was the final reassurance Mother needed. Just knowing he was out there had inspired her further in her various local endeavors.

And as you can imagine, I dreamed about *her* often. I did not receive any letters personally from Mariette, though I understood that for the separation to work, there should be no words, as they would only make it all the more painful. How could someone I only knew such a short time leave such an effect? That of course makes it love. What else could it be? I'd had no desire to court someone else and try to love again.

The fog crept inward across the shoreline this day, and my thin cotton shirt failed to block the chill from a light northeasterly wind that brought with it spots of rain. Gulls squawked around me, expecting me to offer something from the pockets of my coat as my footsteps crunched across the cool sand.

A figure in white stood on the bluff to watch the sea below. Her bright-red-colored hair was piled high above her head, strands escaping with the wind.

It wasn't her. Nor was it the only time since I'd left Canada that my mind had played such tricks.

Though barely a day would pass that I didn't think about Mariette and Edgar, I had found a place in my mind to rest them both. I had over the past years made sense of everything and found my peace with our estrangement.

Missy barked behind me, and I turned to see the cause.

Samuel was running along the beach toward us. He called out something that was lost in the wind, waving his arms wildly in the air. As he was drawing closer, I saw that he clasped a piece of oatmeal-colored paper, his face was pink with exertion, and he was grinning.

"What is it?" I called, always so pleased to have his company. He had grown to be a sweet and gentle boy who affected us all in ways for the better. It was difficult to imagine our lives without him now.

"It's *Maman*," he shouted excitedly before he had quite reached me. "She's coming."

It took only a moment to realize what that meant, my heart surging with a mixture of emotions: elation and trepidation of course, to be followed shortly by sorrow.

Revelstoke Herald, Dated 15 March 1925

A lumberman was killed in a felling accident in the Albreda region. Fabien Brown was approximately twenty-eight, according to those he worked alongside. A large contingency of Native Canadian Indians was in attendance at the burial. The deceased has no wife or known heirs; however, distant relatives from England were said to be planning a headstone.

EPILOGUE

Manchester News, July 1945

Rudolph Leon Watts was posthumously awarded the Victoria Cross for his WWII service in the battle to liberate France in 1944. Major Watts, a renowned artist, led an intense battle that waged for forty-six days and was shot and killed in the final days of the campaign. Major Watts was the son of Stuart (deceased) and Abigail Watts from Lancashire. Abigail Watts is a well-known Lakeland conservationist and active campaigner for better postwar treatment for soldiers. Following WWI, "Rudy," as Major Watts was known, had donated earnings from his paintings to fund support services for soldiers with shell shock, a condition that affects a large number of returned servicemen.

Abigail outlived all her children: the first son also died a hero, in WWI, and the second son, Laurence, was killed in a fiery automobile accident in 1927. She said the loss of her last son has been difficult to accept, but she has been greatly comforted by her daughter-in-law and grandchildren.

Rudy Watts is survived by his wife, Mariette, and their four children, Samuel, Helene, Edith, and Layla.

At the service, Mariette, who is French by birth and saw firsthand the devastation from the Great War, thanked all the men who served alongside her husband. She especially paid tribute to Rudy's service as a husband and father and said that it is not only a loss for her and their children, but a loss for those he counted as friends. Mariette also revealed that Rudy had followed his conscripted son, Samuel, into the army in 1942.

A private service was held at Bardsea.

ACKNOWLEDGMENTS

I want to take the opportunity to thank the Lake Union team for their incredible editing, art, marketing, and production. The quality of work behind the scenes has made this experience seamless once again.

There were countless sources for background information to assist me with the completion of this book, but I would like to give particular credit to the Cercle d'histoire et d'archéologie de Bailleul, the Sir John Monash Centre, and the Franco-Australian Museum of Villers-Bretonneux. Invaluable to my understanding and the storytelling were the firsthand war accounts by my grandfather, Alan Lindsay, who served at Gallipoli, and the archived diaries and letters of servicemen, which allowed me a very personal perspective of the relentless shelling and unimaginable conditions that soldiers were subjected to. Also helpful were the letters home from my great-uncles who established a lumber company in British Columbia in the early twentieth century.

In April 1918, Bailleul and the surrounding villages were evacuated, and the Allies were once again forced into fierce battles to take back the region. I was fortunate to visit there, one hundred years later, to absorb the enormity of those sacrifices made on the western front.

Most people in the region of Bailleul and the villages surrounding were evacuated prior to the second invasion by the German army. Some who didn't leave were captured and taken to German prisons. But for the period of occupation in April 1918 in my book, I've taken some fictional license to imagine the conditions and setting for my characters at the end of their war experiences.

ABOUT THE AUTHOR

Gemma Liviero is the author of the historical novels *The Road Beyond Ruin*, *Broken Angels*, and *Pastel Orphans*, which was a finalist in the 2015 Next Generation Indie Book Awards. In addition to novel writing, her professional career includes copywriting, corporate writing, writing feature articles and editorials, and editing. She holds an advanced diploma of arts (writing) and has continued her studies in arts and other humanities. Gemma lives with her family in Queensland, Australia. For more information, visit www.gemmaliviero.com.